THE VINYL DETECTIVE

WRITTEN IN DEAD WAX

Also by Andrew Cartmel and Available from Titan Books

Written in Dead Wax
The Run-Out Groove
Victory Disc (May 2018)

THE VINYL DETECTIVE

WRITTEN IN DEAD WAX

ANDREW CARTMEL

TITAN BOOKS

The Vinyl Detective: Written in Dead Wax
Mass-market edition ISBN: 9781785655975

Published by Titan Books
A division of Titan Publishing Group Ltd
144 Southwark Street, London SE1 0UP

First edition: March 2018
10 9 8 7 6 5 4 3 2 1

A CIP catalogue record for this title is available from the British Library.

Printed in the USA.

For my brother, James Cartmel,
the coolest cat of all.

SIDE ONE

1. THE DEATH OF THE DRAGON

The heating on our estate had originally been provided by a huge central boiler, which resided under the car park in a vast sealed concrete chamber. I used to imagine it curled there like a sleeping dragon, and when I eventually got a look at it, I found I wasn't far wrong. It was like being in the engine room of a submarine: long gleaming steel cylinders receding into the shadows with a subdued hum of power.

I just walked in one day down the steps and through the door marked BOILER ROOM, which had been left ajar, and wandered around in the shadows until I found the guy who looked after it, an affable fat Geordie in blue overalls. His official title was Estate Environmental Domestic Heating Manager, but I didn't hold that against him.

He let me look around because my cat had managed to get himself lost and I thought he might have wandered in here. But no feline fugitive. The boiler guy seemed to genuinely share my disappointment. I guess he could see how worried I was. As I left he wished me luck finding the cat.

I walked back up the steps from the boiler room into the daylight, blinking. As it turned out, luck was the one thing

I didn't have, eventually locating a small black and white corpse on the grass verge at the entrance to Abbey Avenue.

I took what was left of him home and buried him in the garden. It's surprising how much comfort you can derive from knowing some bones are close by. Shortly afterwards, as if in a token of respect, the boiler on the estate also died. I blamed that on the succession of lowest-bid knuckleheads employed by the council who had failed to maintain it over the decades.

My dead cat I blamed on the clientele of the Abbey. Dizzy had evidently fallen foul of one of the luxury cars driven by the assorted Premier League football fatuities or ferally sculpted supermodels who sped along the road en route to London's leading detox centre.

Once a genuine working abbey with its own bake house, stables and mill, the Abbey was an elegant old white structure, which I could see looming beyond my garden whenever I looked out the sitting room of what I called my bungalow—I actually lived in the lower half of a former two-storey house. It was now converted into separate dwellings and I had the ground floor rooms and the garden. The wall of my garden backed right onto the Abbey's grounds.

Which is why I had occasion to meet one of the inmates.

It was a bright morning in an unseasonably warm September. The man had somehow managed to get into my garden and he was standing there, in a royal blue dressing gown with a gold monogram 'A' on the pocket and blue flip-flops.

He was staring at me as I drew back the curtain. I had been listening to music in the darkness, which is what I tend to do in the mornings while drinking coffee until my consciousness surfaces sufficiently to face the day. The man yelled something and I opened the back door and went to see what he was raving about.

"Max Roach," he said. It took me a moment to register this. And by that time he'd also said, "Red Mitchell on bass. George Wallington on piano."

"It's the Gil Mellé Sextet," I told him. I stepped out the back door and joined him in the garden. It was a little chilly. "Recorded in 1952."

"On Blue Note, right?" The man frowned at me. He was deeply suntanned, completely bald, but heavily bearded. Which gave a mild impression that his head was upside down. He started searching the pocket of his blue dressing gown for something.

"That's right," I said. It was clear that the trespasser at least had a working knowledge of some rather esoteric jazz.

"It's vinyl, of course," he said, rummaging in his pocket.

"Of course."

"Original Lexington Blue Note?"

"No, sadly. It's a Japanese reissue."

The man took his hand out of his pocket for a moment and made a curt, dismissive gesture. He shook his head with satisfaction. "I didn't think it sounded like the original."

I thought this was pretty rich considering he was standing in the garden. "I've got an original Blue Note pressing of this," he announced. "With the Lexington Avenue address on the label."

"Deep groove?" I said.

"Oh yes." He reached into his pocket and triumphantly drew out an expensive-looking cigar. The cigar had the effect of making him look less like an escaped madman in a bathrobe and more like the denizen of an exclusive resort hotel who happened to have wandered away from poolside.

Which effectively he was.

"It's a flat-edge pressing, my copy. You know what that is?" I had been trying to identify his accent, which was very faint but discernible. Something about the decisively didactic sound of the last sentence made me think Scandinavian.

"Yes," I said.

"Those are electrostatic speakers you're using?" he asked. I nodded. He took out a box of matches, struck one, let it burn for a moment, presumably to allow the sulphur to disperse, then ignited his cigar.

"You can always tell." He exhaled a mouthful of smoke, shook the match out and threw it into my flowerbeds, which didn't exactly endear him to me. Then he reached into his pocket again and took out the mangled butt of a previous cigar. Why was he carrying that around? Probably because he wasn't allowed to smoke them in the Abbey and the discarded butt would have been a clue.

But he felt free to discard it here, in my garden. He chucked it into the pond.

That really was the last straw.

I said, "You have a flat-edge copy of this record?"

"That's right." He grinned. "All of my Lexington Avenue first pressings are flat edge."

I had him right where I wanted him. I looked at the cigar butt floating in my pond and said, "You do adjust the vertical tracking angle, of course."

"What?"

"When you play one of your flat-edge LPs. You adjust the tracking angle of the cartridge?"

He stared at me. "What do you mean?"

I tried not to overdo my look of wide-eyed innocence. "Well, your tone arm and cartridge will be set up to play standard records. And the geometry required for tracking properly on a flat record is completely different. But you know that, of course."

He stared at me in silence. I said, feigning surprise, "You mean you don't adjust the system every time? That means you're getting distortion and groove wear. Your vertical tracking angle is way off. And that's before we even start talking about the azimuth."

That shut the fucker up.

He took his leave presently, loping back to the Abbey in his dressing gown.

I never expected to see him again. But I did. When his face turned up on the front page of the free local newspaper.

It had been jammed through my letterbox along with an assortment of pizza leaflets and taxi cards. I opened the newspaper and saw a headline that read ARCHITECT DIES IN FALL. Underneath was a photograph of the man, Tomas Helmer. He wasn't wearing a bathrobe now, but a rather snazzy suit. Apparently he lived—or had lived—in Richmond, in a large house where he'd been having trouble with his guttering.

Fed up with the situation, he'd climbed onto the roof to do something about it—and had slipped to his doom.

The poor bastard. I switched on the valve amps and put the Gil Mellé Sextet on the turntable in his honour.

It sounded great. I picked up the newspaper again. The main thrust of the brief story was how ironic it was that, being a multi-millionaire and all, Helmer had proved too cheap to employ properly trained professionals to repair his guttering and had consequently paid the ultimate price.

Nevertheless, I was sorry for the poor guy. It was a shame he was gone.

But I must admit my very first reaction was to wonder what had happened to his record collection.

Soon I had other things to worry about, though.

When the boiler died, the tenants on the estate were offered the choice of a new heating system provided by the council or installing their own. Both options cost money and, given the current state of my finances, I couldn't afford either.

So I decided to just brace myself and tough it out that winter.

It was worse than I could possibly have imagined. For a start, I hadn't realised that a large hot water pipe from the boiler had run under my house, heating in passing the slab of concrete on which the house rested. When the boiler was decommissioned this pipe abruptly ceased its regular cycles of cheery warmth and the concrete slab around it rapidly grew cold as a crypt. And my bungalow stood on it.

It now acted like a giant refrigerating unit, chilling the whole place. The floors were soon stingingly freezing and my little house as cold and damp as a cave. Sinister black mould took hold above the windows in the spare room.

My cats looked at me with matching appalled expressions, wanting to know what the hell I'd done.

After Dizzy had been run over, I'd ended up with two kittens, sisters, called Fanny and Turk. Now a year old, they had manifested very different personalities. But they looked at me with identical expressions of betrayal as the floor gradually transformed into a freezing slab of stone.

Turk took to spending all night outdoors, perhaps on the theory that it wasn't any colder out than in. Meantime, Fanny took to climbing inside my duvet at night, a refugee from the cold. I mean right inside. She crept in through the slit in the duvet cover and curled up, a warm bundle at my feet as I slept.

Every morning as soon as I finished breakfast I went out for the day—there was no point staying in the freezing house. The cats followed me out through the door and took up their stations among the frost-struck stalks in my front garden.

I then spent the entire day outside, and so did they.

My one extravagance was a London Transport travel card, which allowed me—for an extortionate fee—unlimited use of buses and trains. I'd owned a car for a few years, but the novelty of sitting unmoving in traffic jams had rapidly worn off. So these days when it was too cold to stay at home, I took my trusty travel card and set out.

To hunt for records. This is what I did.

I went west then south, towards Twickenham. I spent the rest of the day working my way back home, seeking out every charity shop, junk shop or antique shop that might have a crate of old vinyl lurking somewhere.

I was wearing my crate-digging shoes, which were cut low and were therefore comfortable when I was crouching on the floor, as I so often was, going through a musty box of records. It's largely a discouraging business—in the crates I'd find the usual mix of unconvincing rock and pop, leavened by the occasional brass band or church choir. Now and then you'd discover a dozen identical albums by some singer or group you'd never heard of, and realise they'd been donated by the artists themselves. You'd stumbled on the heartbreaking marker of a failed career.

Just as the low winter sun was sinking in the sky, in a little shop near the bridge in Richmond, I struck gold. An original Elvis RCA red label. It was in beautiful shape. My first impression was that someone had really looked after it. Or, better yet, never played it. I wondered what domestic upheaval—death, house move, existential crisis—had led to it being discarded here. When you thought about the series of coincidences that were required for this object to be right here and right now, in my hot little hands, it was dizzying.

The cover was immaculate. But what was the record going to be like? My hands trembled as I took a look. The LP crackled as it came out of the sleeve, the static electricity causing the hairs on my arms to stir. The black vinyl gleamed. Pristine, virginal and perfect. I could see my reflection in it, grinning foolishly.

I paid the pittance they wanted for it and headed out into the winter night with the carefully wrapped record tucked safely under my arm.

The best part was I could sell it without a qualm.

I recognise the virtues of Elvis. Like Sinatra, he has an enormously relaxed voice, which is consequently relaxing and pleasurable for the listener. Listening to these guys is like sitting in the most comfortable armchair in the world. But Elvis also had a glutinous and saccharine way with ballads, which, I felt, lumbered him with the same Achilles' heel as Stevie Wonder. No more sappy slow numbers, guys.

Anyway, I already had the complete Leiber-Stoller recordings and that was enough Elvis for me.

I set off homewards, changing buses on the winter roads. Heading back to my icy house I felt like a trapper returning to his frozen cabin with a prime pelt.

Except, in this case, no animals had been harmed.

When I got home I would resume the usual winter routine, which consisted of making supper before retiring to my glacial bed, warmed only by a hot water bottle and, with any luck, an opportunistic cat. With the difference that, tonight, I'd first go online and flip the Elvis LP, scoring enough money for us to live on for a few more weeks.

When I got home I immediately knew something was wrong. Fanny was outside the front door, shivering, and she darted in after me. There was music coming from the living room. I hurried in there and froze in the doorway.

Sitting on my sofa was Stuart "Stinky" Stanmer, listening to my hi-fi. Turk cautiously emerged from hiding behind a speaker as I came in with her sister.

"I let myself in, sorry," said Stinky. "I had to. The neighbours would have spotted me otherwise. You know, my fans." I had known Stinky since university. Like me he had been an aspiring DJ, working his way up through college radio. But unlike me he had prospered, to such an extent that he had recently acquired his own radio show and even subjected the nation to an occasional appearance on television.

"Actually, Stinky," I said, "my neighbours are quite blasé about the presence of stars around here. Because of the Abbey and all that."

He looked out the window at the white shape of the Abbey against the dark winter sky. There were discreet floodlights that made it look moonlit, even on a night with no moon. "I suppose they would be," he said wistfully. Painful as it was to accept, there were people more famous than he.

"To what do I owe this pleasure?"

"I was just in the neighbourhood and thought I'd drop by if you were at home."

"And even if I wasn't," I said. The record he'd been so presumptuously playing had reached the end of the side. The cartridge was now riding noisily in the run-out groove. I went and rescued it, taking the LP off the turntable. It was a Japanese *Godzilla* soundtrack. I returned it to its sleeve. While I did so, Stinky leaned back on the sofa. Fanny, walking across the room, gave him a wide berth.

"So what are you up to?"

"Oh, this and that," I said, filing the album away on the shelf. I was sure he knew damned well anything I might be up to. I suspected that, under a variety of pseudonyms, Stinky was one of the most avid followers of my blog, Facebook page and Twitter stream. He poked at the piles of CDs on my coffee table.

"Playing a lot of CDs, I notice."

"I have to listen to something while I'm changing records."

"Or while you're turning them over—eh?" Stinky chortled. Now that he'd created a variation on the joke, he allowed himself to laugh at it. I noticed that he'd been looking through the stack of records I'd left on the armchair. They were in a different sequence to the way I'd left them. The armchair is where I'm in the habit of keeping the records I'm currently listening to. My top picks.

No doubt he'd been making notes.

Since Stinky had a radio show he also had a constant voracious need for new material. And because he had a virtually infallible tin ear himself, he needed to get ideas from people like me.

After some desultory conversation and much bragging—both professional and sexual—from Stinky, I finally managed to get rid of him, shutting the door behind him with a small moan of relief. He had let himself in by using the key I kept under the plant pot. I decided I would have to hide the key somewhere else. But if I did that, would I remember where I put it? I stood there, holding it in my hand, then I sighed and returned the key to its traditional place.

I got on the computer and listed the Elvis LP on my website. It sold within the hour and for slightly more than I'd hoped. I decided I would go out and celebrate. It so happened it was half-price burger night at Albert's, my local gastropub. So I went there and had a meal and a glass of wine. It was a very good burger—they filled the beef patty with butter and herbs—but rather spoiled by Albert insisting on switching on the radio behind the bar. No one else in the pub seemed to mind, but I felt someone had to speak out against noise pollution.

"Can't we have a bit of hush?" I said.

"Just want to catch this one programme," said Albert.

"I thought there was a no-music rule in here."

"This is the exception that proves the rule." He tuned in the radio and as he did so three cute Eastern European au pairs, all with matching blonde hair, hipster jeans and discreet tattoos, drifted towards the bar to listen. A treacly, insinuating voice came on and I realised with a sinking feeling of inevitability that it was Stinky.

Of course. The Stinky Stanmer show.

"That was a CD," said Stinky. "After all, I have to listen to something while I'm changing records. And turning them

over, eh? Now here on vinyl is a little something I found."
The music started and, thankfully, he stopped talking. I
recognised the music. *Godzilla versus Anguirus* by Akira
Ifukube. It sounded great. It was, of course, the LP I'd had on
my turntable when he'd come around. He must have raced
out and bought a copy as soon as he'd left my place. Or,
more likely, had one of his minions do so.

I reflected philosophically that at least he'd had the good
sense to choose the best track on the record. Then I realised it
was the *first* track on the record.

He probably hadn't got any further.

All three au pairs were swaying their hips to the music.
It sounded like Sonny Blount commissioned to score a
sixties spy movie. As the au pairs began to bop around,
Albert gazed worshipfully at the radio like Nipper in an old
HMV advertisement and shook his head in admiration.

"Where does he find this stuff?"

I got very drunk.

The next morning I woke to a hammering hangover and the
ringing of the doorbell. I jumped out of bed, displacing a
scandalised Fanny, and pulled on my ratty old dressing gown.
I shuffled to the door and opened it, blinking in the daylight.

A young woman was standing there. She was wearing
jeans, a camelhair coat and black polo neck sweater. Her jet-
black hair was cut short in the manner of the silent movie
star Louise Brooks. She looked at me. Her implausible,
almost laughable, physical perfection suggested she was a
model or actress. I knew at once why she was here.

"I'm not the gatekeeper," I said.

She brushed her hair out of her eyes. "Well, that sounds rather alarming."

"This isn't the gatehouse."

"Just as well, since you aren't the gatekeeper."

"You want the Abbey. It's the large white building behind my house. But this isn't the gatehouse and I'm not the gatekeeper."

"Well, maybe you should be. I'm sure it's a nice job. There's probably a uniform." She gazed at me in my dressing gown. "And it might involve epaulettes. I like epaulettes. In fact, I just like the word." She looked at me. "Epaulettes." Her eyes were a disconcerting clear cornflower blue. I studied them for signs of blatant drug abuse, but could find none.

"To get to the Abbey," I told her, "you need to go back onto the main road, drive about fifty metres and turn right."

"Who said I was driving?"

"How else did you get here?"

"Perhaps a friend dropped me off."

"Well, you can walk from here. It's only two minutes. A minute and a half. The Abbey."

"I don't want the Abbey," she said. "I want you."

Despite the evidence of her clear blue eyes I decided she must be off her rocker on something. I said, "Me? Really? Why?" She took out a card and handed it to me. It was a cheap and rather gaudy business card and it was very familiar.

Because it was one of mine.

Underneath my name and address I'd printed the words VINYL DETECTIVE.

2. FIREBIRD

"Where did you get this?" I'd handed out a bunch of the cards, at record shops and gigs, pubs and clubs. But that had been years ago.

She looked at me and then at the card in my hand. "Is this you?"

"This is me."

She took back my card and handed me one of her own. I felt like I was in a novel by Trollope. Her card read:

N. Warren
CONSULTANT | INTERNATIONAL INDUSTRIES GMBH

Unlike my card, it was printed on heavy cream paper stock and beautifully embossed. I gave it back to her. "The thing is, if you're trying to sell me something…"

"I am not trying to sell you something," she said, somewhat impatiently. She glanced over my shoulder. "Look, could we talk indoors?"

"Of course. But I have to tell you I really don't have any money to invest in any… schemes."

She turned in the narrow hallway to watch me as I closed the door behind us. "I told you, I am not selling you anything. I am not trying to get you to invest in anything. I don't have any *schemes*." She gazed at me.

I became suddenly very conscious of how scruffy I must look, wearing my ratty old black cotton bathrobe, my bony knees and hairy toes on display. Meanwhile there she was, poised, chic and flawless. Compared to her I was basically a Basil Wolverton cartoon.

She said, "I am here to offer you a job." At least her mouth moved and words came out that sounded like that.

I clutched my dressing gown a little closer around me. "A job?"

"Yes. You are capable of doing what you claim here?"

"What do I claim?" I said. I'd printed up the cards in an airport once when I was between flights and very bored. Possibly also very drunk.

She sighed and handed me the card. It had my name and address and some nonsense about how I could find any record for anyone. For a fee. It was boastful trash—but perhaps not sufficiently boastful or trashy because it had failed to ensnare a single client.

Until now.

My heart began to beat a little faster. Maybe I *was* about to get a job. I told myself not to get too excited. Obviously this would turn out to be some kind of hilarious misunderstanding.

"You know what," I said. "If you're looking for a record, really the best thing to do is search on the Internet."

"The Internet will be of no help in this situation."

"I see." I didn't.

She tapped the card on her thumbnail. "What we need is

someone who can do what you say you can do. Well, can you?"

"Can I do what I say I can do?"

"Yes." Her impatient blue eyes were steady on mine. A cold draught was blowing up under my dressing gown, probing my nether regions with icy tendrils.

"Yes," I said. "Look, let's go into the kitchen where it's warm. Can I make you a coffee?"

"I don't know. Can you?"

Stung by her remark, I got out the good coffee beans and commenced the whole elaborate ritual of making it properly. While the kettle was gasping and sputtering in its battle with its no doubt horrendously calcified heating element, I managed to dart into my bedroom and put some clothes on. I might also have sparingly applied some expensive aftershave. I got back just before the water boiled and switched the kettle off.

If you're making tea you want the water boiling, but if you're making *coffee* you want the water just short of boiling. It's an article of faith.

My guest was sitting in the orange plastic Robin Day chair which resided in my kitchen, chiefly so I could hang the tea towel on the back of it to dry. She seemed quite relaxed. At home, almost. Which was galling because at the moment even *I* didn't feel at home, and it *was* my home.

When I commenced grinding the beans she put her iPod on. I didn't entirely blame her. The unearthly scream of the coffee grinder always caused my cats to flee and hide, only to emerge and give me scandalised looks after I'd safely silenced the evil thing and put it away again. When I finished grinding the beans I had a nasty moment, remembering I didn't have any filters. Then I recalled there were some stored with my German record cleaner. I took down the box from its appointed place, lurking above the kitchen cupboard. She switched off her iPod and looked up.

"What in god's name is that?" she said.

"A record cleaner." I unpacked the box and took out every component: the record bath, the drying rack and drip tray, the bottle of cleaning solution, the funnel, the label protector and spindle and finally the coffee filters that were lurking at the bottom. "I use it for cleaning records."

"I see. That would follow. And it comes complete with coffee filters?"

"No, I substituted the coffee filters, which in my humble opinion work just as well but are considerably cheaper than the paper filters specifically designed for use with it. The record cleaner, that is."

"How thrifty of you."

I fixed the filter above the coffee pot and poured in the dark brown, fragrant grounds. At last. We were almost there. "In fact, they work slightly better. What are you listening to on your iPod?"

"'Gloria'."

"By Van Morrison?"

"By Vivaldi."

I shut up at that point and got on with making the coffee. It was soon smelling so good I began to feel glad I'd embarked on the whole marathon. The cats didn't quite see it that way. Turk was only now emerging from her hiding place behind one of the big Quad speakers.

As I started clattering through cupboards, looking for

the good cups, N. Warren rose from her chair. She said, "Do you mind if I snoop?" She didn't wait for an answer. My bungalow is mostly open plan, so you wander straight from the kitchen into a large sitting room and dining area. From the sitting room further doors lead off to the bedroom, bathroom, a spare bedroom and a small area which had once contained the hot water tank but now housed shelves filled with, perhaps not entirely unexpectedly, records.

I poured her coffee and followed her into the sitting room. She was staring at the records. She glanced at me. "Maybe you *are* the right man for the job," she allowed. "How many vinyls do you have here?"

I put her cup down on the table by the sofa. "We don't say *vinyls*, plural."

"What do we say?"

"LPs or albums. Records, if you like."

"Well, how many do you have here?"

"In this room? I don't know. A few hundred. Those are just the ones I'm currently listening to. There's plenty more scattered around the house."

"Currently listening to," she said. She gave me a look and then went and sat down on the sofa and picked up her coffee. She was evidently entirely unaware of the cat's presence nearby as she sat there, warming her hands with the cup.

Turk silently stole up and jumped onto the back of the sofa behind her, landing lightly and without a sound. I'd once had a female visitor who reacted rather badly when a cat unexpectedly hopped into her lap. She had jumped out of her skin and commenced screaming in a manner that had rather raised my stock with the neighbours.

Now, as my new guest sat leaning forward, sniffing her

coffee with suspicion, Turk took the opportunity to stride silently behind her back. Then she eased down, one slow paw at a time, onto a cushion beside our guest, who still showed no sign of having registered her presence.

I was beginning to think I should issue a warning, to prevent a terrible accident involving hot coffee, when she reached out absent-mindedly with one hand and began stroking Turk.

"Who's beautiful then, who's lovely then, who wants to be rubbed under the chin then? Do you? Do you? Under the chin? Oh yes, oh yes. That's right, you do, you do, you do, don't you? Who's lovely then? Who's lovely then? Who likes having his chin rubbed then?"

"Her," I said.

She paused and looked at me. "Sorry?"

"Her chin. She's a girl."

She resumed rubbing Turk's chin while Turk exalted. "What's her name?"

"Turk."

"Funny name for a girl."

"Short for Turquoise."

"Because of her eyes." She got it immediately. "They're gorgeous eyes. Who's got gorgeous eyes? Gorgeous-gorgeous turquoise eyes?" She stroked Turk's head, gently pinning the cat's ears back then releasing them. "It is you? Yes, I think it is you. It is. It is you, isn't it?"

"That's her sister." I pointed at Fanny who'd emerged from under a chair at the sight of Turk getting all the attention.

"Oh, I didn't realise there were two of them."

I felt it was time to get down to business. "So you want to hire me to find a record?"

"My employer wants to hire you."

"Can I ask who your employer is?"

"No."

"No?"

"If he wanted to get acquainted with you he wouldn't have sent an emissary. To wit, me." She sipped her coffee. "Besides, he's very busy."

"So you're not going to tell me who I'm working for?"

She looked up. "For all intents and purposes, you are working for me."

"And you're not going to tell me who *you* are working for?"

"A businessman."

"A very busy businessman?"

She sighed. "The senior head of a very large corporation. Who wishes to remain anonymous. However I can tell you that he, like you, is a vinyl devotee." She looked at the shelves of records. "And he has the money to indulge his pastime."

It's more than a pastime, I thought. But I didn't say anything. She looked at me. "And he is willing to pay you to find a particular record for him."

I sat down in the only one of the armchairs that wasn't covered in records. It was a modernist black leather chair that matched the sofa. I'd bought leather furniture because I thought it would prove cat-proof. One of many fondly held theories that had fallen by the wayside over the years. As if to demonstrate this point, Fanny stood up on her hind legs and began to diligently scratch the leather with her front claws, scoring and gouging it.

I said, "Okay. What's the record you're after?"

She set her coffee aside and took out an iPhone. Studying the screen, she said, "Have you heard of Everest?"

"The record label?"

"No. The mountain. Yes, of course the record label."

I smiled happily. She could be as sarcastic as she liked; I was on my home ground here. I said, "I know it quite well. Everest was founded in the late 1950s by Harry Belock, an American who'd spent the Cold War running a company that manufactured precision components for intercontinental missiles. He decided that instead of dreaming up better ways to blow up the world, his talents would be more happily employed finding better ways of recording music. Which he proceeded to do. One of his innovations was to record onto 35mm film."

I could see that, despite herself, I'd got her attention. "Why on earth would he do that?"

"More bandwidth."

"But it's film. Surely it's for recording pictures, not sound?"

"It's all information," I said complacently. This was my specialist subject.

"And it sounded good, did it, this 35mm film?"

"It sounded great. Belock knew what he was doing. He spent a fortune on making custom-built recording decks that could handle the film and he hired a terrific engineer, Bert Whyte, who used them to record music with a classic three-microphone configuration."

"Ah, yes," she said. "The classic three-microphone configuration."

"They recorded good repertoire using top orchestras and conductors in acoustically ideal locations like Walthamstow Town Hall."

"Of course. Good old Walthamstow Town Hall." She consulted the screen of her iPhone. "Well, my employer is looking for a recording of Stravinsky's *Firebird Suite* on the Everest label, conducted by Eugene Goossens with the London Symphony Orchestra." She gave me the catalogue number.

"Have you got the matrix number?" I said.

"What's a matrix number?"

"It's written in the dead wax," I said.

For the first time I saw a trace of hesitancy in her. "No."

"Doesn't matter," I said and wrote down the information she'd given me on the back of an envelope. Fanny came over and attacked the pen as it moved in my hand. When I finished writing I gave her the pen to play with. "All right," I said, looking up at my visitor. I tried to keep my voice normal. "Now, about money…"

"There's a thousand-pound finder's fee."

I tried not to let the happy astonishment show on my face. With a thousand pounds I could install underfloor heating and finally build shelves for the records I'd had lying around in crates ever since I'd bought them from an unhinged clergyman who lived in Barnes.

I forced myself to speak. "I'll need a daily fee as well."

"What? A daily fee? Why?"

"I'll be spending all day looking for records."

"I see. And what would you normally be spending all day doing?"

She had me there. "But I may not be able to find your record."

She gave me a lopsided smile. "You're not exactly selling yourself as the best possible man for the job here."

"Still, the fact remains that I may not be able to find it. And if I'm not getting some kind of payment for looking I'm wasting my time."

"Well, we wouldn't want you to waste your valuable time." She looked around my little house, making it very obvious just how valuable she thought my time was.

"A *per diem* of fifty pounds would do."

"*Per diem.* A bit of Latin. Nice. But sorry, no." She smiled.

"But I'll need travelling expenses," I persisted. I didn't, of course, because I already had my travel card.

She said, "That might be possible."

I shook my head and spoke in what I hoped was a firm and confident manner. "It's non-negotiable."

"How much do you want?"

"Thirty pounds."

"Sorry, no."

"Twenty-five."

"You can have twenty."

"Done," I said. With my travel card, the twenty quid every day would be pure profit, put straight into my pocket. Or, more likely, converted into cat biscuits.

She smiled broadly. "What do you know, it turned out to be negotiable after all." Putting down her iPhone, she reached into her pocket and took out a large bank roll and peeled off a twenty-pound note. She put it on the table with her business card, gave Turk one last caress, then stood up. "Well, happy hunting. When you have some news, get in touch. You have my details on the card." She started for the door.

"Wait a minute," I said. "What do I call you?"

She paused by the door. "You've got my card."

"Miss N. Warren?"

"Yes." She opened the door.

"All right, N. Warren."

"Miss," she said, and went out, closing the door behind her.

* * *

The first thing I did was get online and search the Internet. Like I'd told her, this was usually the best and simplest way of finding a record. If she chose to ignore my advice and I happened to find a copy lurking somewhere in cyberspace for five quid and resold it to her at an enormous profit, that would serve her right.

But I didn't find a copy. Not for five pounds or five hundred. There were some images of the record—it had the usual wacky Everest cover art—but no copies for sale. And no information about copies having ever been sold, anywhere, in recent memory. It was obviously a very scarce item. There were various mentions of it on vinyl chat rooms; sundry losers talking about how they'd love to find a copy, and speculations about how much money it might change hands for.

But no hard facts.

So I put my coat on, told the cats to expect me back in a couple of hours and went out. I tramped across the common through the long wet grass and caught a train to Waterloo and then got the Tube, the Northern Line, to Goodge Street. Between Goodge Street and Charlotte Street there is a warren of narrow back alleys, although the word "alleys" doesn't really conjure up the scrubbed and gleaming affluence of the neighbourhood.

The area is a mixture of upmarket shops and narrow terraced residential buildings. I walked down some whitewashed stairs to what looked like the gleaming red front door of somebody's basement flat until you read the brass plate on it, which read STYLI in a discreet typeface.

There was an illuminated doorbell on the left but I pushed

through the door and walked straight in. A short hallway led to a staircase on the left and a door on the right. I went through the door. It led into a small lounge, carpeted and full of handsome but mismatched armchairs with green shaded reading lamps.

The walls were shelved from floor to ceiling and lined with records, CDs, and a few DVDs.

On the wall there were small, framed pictures of conductors and opera stars whom I couldn't have named if my life depended on it.

The room was empty at the moment except for Jerry, who was sitting in his favourite chair near the window reading a book about Bernard Herrmann. "Hello there," he said, putting a pencil in the book to mark his place and setting it aside. "I haven't seen you for a while."

"Cash flow problems." I sat down in the chair nearest to him.

He shook his head. "That should never be a problem," he said. "You know your credit's good here. If there are things you want, just take them home. Pay me later, or whenever." He smiled. Jerry Muscutt was a small, contented man with enquiring grey eyes. Despite his considerable age he had an unlined face and sleek red hair and a pointed beard. The hair and beard at least were the products of artifice. Some wag had once left a package of Tints of Nature red hair dye in the kitchen unit to tease him. It hadn't bothered Jerry in the least and the hair dye packet had remained proudly on display for months, on a high shelf beside a boxed set of Gounod.

"We've just bought a large collection, including a lot of jazz," he said. "Haven't got it sorted yet. I'm still going through it at home. But when we bring it into the shop I'll let you know. You can have a sneak preview. I think there will be some items to interest you."

"Thank you."

"In the meantime you want to pop upstairs." Upstairs is where they kept the jazz. "We've got some Spanish Fresh Sound reissues on vinyl that you'll want to see. Tell Kempton I put them behind the counter for you."

"Thanks, Jerry. That's great. But actually today it's the classical department I wanted to explore."

He looked at me shrewdly. "Classical music? That's not like you."

"I'm on commission," I said. "Looking for a record."

"Well, if it's classical, I'm your man."

"It's an original Everest pressing."

He smiled. "The turquoise and silver label, then."

"I imagine so. It's the Goossens *Firebird Suite*, recorded here in London."

His smiled widened. "Ah, really?" he said. "Why don't you make us both a cup of tea—coffee for you, of course—and I'll tell you all about that record. Fascinating story."

She was waiting for me in the café behind Denmark Street where I'd arranged for us to meet. It was a cramped place with chipped green linoleum floor and scuffed metal tables. She'd chosen a seat at the back, as far as possible from the bellowing hiss of the coffee machine. She had a notebook and pen on the table in front of her and looked in a bad mood.

"What is this place?" she demanded, as I sat down. "Couldn't you have found somewhere a little more squalid?"

"Wait until you try the coffee."

I went and bought two cappuccinos and took them back

to the table. She sniffed cautiously at her cup, took a sip, and nodded as if confirming a long-held theory. No more complaints about the venue, though. She took a few more sips then she set her cup down and squared her little red notebook and pen on the table. She opened the notebook, all business.

"Now, about finding this record."

"We won't be."

"What? We won't be what?"

"Finding this record."

She closed the notebook and looked at me. "Why not?"

"Because it doesn't exist."

She looked at me for a long time. "What makes you say that?"

"I asked a man who knows about such things."

"And you trust him? You trust his judgment?"

"Yes. Because he knows about such things."

She put the pen and notebook away very slowly, as if to give herself time to think. To fill the silence I said, "The record was scheduled and it was announced. The musicians and the hall were booked. They even printed copies of the sleeve, which is why you can see pictures of it online. But there was never a recording. It all fell through, due to some kind of contractual dispute."

She nodded thoughtfully and said, "Well, that was incredibly honest of you."

"What was?"

"Telling me, instead of just stringing me along endlessly and collecting your twenty pounds a day from now until god knows when. Your *per diem*."

"Travelling expenses, actually." I tried to conceal my delight at the implied praise.

She looked at me shrewdly and said, "Actually it's probably more likely that you just couldn't resist smugly showing off the knowledge you've just acquired."

"I prefer the incredibly honest theory," I said.

She laughed and then reached in her pocket and put a neatly folded twenty-pound note on the table. "Well, I suppose this is goodbye, then." She gave me a polite smile and took out her phone. I had been dismissed. I got up and considered leaving the twenty there. I felt hurt and insulted and wanted to return the hurt and insult. But the brutal fact was I couldn't afford the gesture. I took the money and left.

I was halfway out the door of the café when she called. "Wait." I turned and looked at her. "Come back and sit down," she said. I went back inside and sat down opposite her. "Well done," she said.

"For what?"

"You passed the test."

"I see," I said, not entirely truthfully.

"We knew the record didn't exist."

"Did you?"

She nodded. "We just wanted to find out if you knew your stuff."

"So you're saying you *do* have a job for me?"

"Yes, my employer would like you to work with me."

"Because we've built up such a foundation of mutual trust."

She laughed. "That's right, yes."

3. SNOWFALL

"So who is this chick, then?" said Tinkler.

"She works for the head of some big corporation. In Germany, I think." I handed him her business card.

He sniffed it. "Hmm. N. Warren. She smells nice. What does the N stand for?"

"I don't know, but I intend to make it my life's work to find out."

He handed the card back to me. "Sounds like you should make it your life's work to find this record of hers first. What was it again? *Disraeli Gears*?"

Disraeli Gears is a classic album by Cream. My friend Tinkler was more of a rock specialist, though he did know a bit about jazz.

"No, you deaf idiot," I said. "Easy Geary."

"Oh yes," Tinkler nodded, his hair swaying across his face. In the glow of the lava lamp his plump face was that of a depraved Sistine cherub. We were in the upstairs room of his narrow little Victorian house in Putney, in the spare bedroom he had converted into a listening room. It was a small cosy room stuffed with records and hi-fi equipment.

In pride of place on the wall was a framed Valerian album cover, the gatefold with the naked young woman and all the cats on it.

Tinkler said, "The Beatnik poet of the tenor saxophone."

"He was a pianist, actually," I said.

Tinkler snapped his fingers, anxious to regain lost ground. "That's right, I remember, a pianist. Easy Geary. Mid 1950s, West Coast. Sounds a lot like Monk."

"A lot more like Elmo Hope," I said.

"He was interesting."

He was more than interesting. A considerable composer as well as a pianist, Easy Geary had died the traditional tragically premature jazz death, long before he had revealed the full flower of his true potential. His music was raw, primitive, abstract and urgent, always hinting at a profound underlying complexity, as if he knew much more than he was letting on.

Tinkler was nodding and smiling. "His arrangements were something else. So what's this record?"

"It's called *Easy Come, Easy Go*."

"Cute. Never heard of it."

"There's a good reason for that. It was released on an obscure little label called Hathor. They were a West Coast outfit like Nocturne or Mode or Tampa. Except Hathor went under in their first year of operation."

"Gee, why am I not surprised?" said Tinkler. "Nocturne and Mode and Tampa are all great names for a record label. And Hathor is a fucking terrible name."

"It was an ill-omened one, anyway. When they went bust the owner killed himself. They only ever issued fourteen LPs and this was the last one. They produced records in steadily decreasing print runs as the company slowly failed. By the time they got to *Easy Come, Easy Go*, they were only pressing tiny quantities."

"So that's why it's so rare. How much will they pay you if you find it?"

"They're offering me at least a five-figure finder's fee."

"A five figure… I can't even *say* it." He went over to the mantelpiece and took down a small yellow enamelled box. It had a colourful swirling design of dragons on it.

I said, "When the drug squad busts this place that will definitely be the last place they look for your stash."

"Don't be snippy. Listen, if you find this record what's to stop you just selling it yourself?"

"What do you mean?"

He sank back on the sofa and opened the dragon box. "If you find it, they're offering to pay you a percentage of the market price, correct?"

"Yes, I guess so."

"So why not sell it yourself and keep everything? The whole market price."

"Because that's not what I agreed to do."

Tinkler chuckled as he started to roll his joint. "So the Vinyl Detective has a code of honour?"

"Well, if you're going to be sarcastic…"

"Down these mean crates a man must dig," he said. "Sorry, that *was* a little sarcastic. It's all highly theoretical anyway, though, isn't it? I mean, if this record is as rare as you say it is, you're never going to find a copy."

I thought carefully for a moment about how much I should tell him. But Tinkler's my friend and I knew I could trust him. "They've got some information," I said.

He paused in the process of licking the cigarette papers.

"What sort of information?"

"They have reason to believe someone has recently got rid of a copy. Put it on the second-hand market."

"Where?"

"Somewhere in London."

"Oh well, best of British luck."

"Somewhere in south London."

"Like I say, best of luck."

"Southwest London."

He paused in assembling the joint and scrutinised me. "You know, that might actually be doable." He grinned. "Have you heard this record?"

"Never on vinyl. Just CDs. And never the whole thing. The CD reissues always omit one track."

"That's kind of mysterious. Not to mention annoying. Why do they do that? Copyright problems?"

"No, the master tape is missing."

"That's a major bummer. What was the track?"

"A vocal number. Just for this one track Geary was joined by a singer called Rita Mae Pollini."

"Rita Mae who?"

"Pollini. For my money the greatest jazz singer who ever lived."

"Never heard of her."

I shrugged. "A lot of people have never heard of June Christy or Betty Carter or Lucy Ann Polk."

"I've got some Betty Carter here, somewhere," said Tinkler. He rose from the sofa and went over and checked the amp, which was warming up. Tinkler's hi-fi system consisted of a vintage Thorens TD 124 turntable, some mammoth Tannoy horn-loaded speakers, only slightly smaller than prehistoric elephants, installed on either side of the chimney breast, and an amplifier using valves from obsolete television cameras that looked like the control panel of a flying saucer in a 1953 movie.

It all sounded pretty good, though.

While he was checking the bias and DC offset on each output valve—a finicky business but necessary if he didn't want his speakers bursting into flame—I went over and looked at the fitted shelves that filled an entire wall except for a narrow strip where the Valerian picture hung.

The shelves were mostly crammed with records, of course, but there was also a narrow section devoted to books about music. I reached up and took down Wilson's *Singers of America*. I'd sat back down and found the page I was looking for before Tinkler finished fiddling with the valves.

When he finally concluded his task he came over and frowned at the book. "What's that?"

I showed him the picture I'd found of Rita Mae Pollini. Taken in 1958 it showed a stunning beauty with dark hair and wide dark eyes. It was hard to tell in the black and white photo, but her skin seemed to be a beguiling olive shade. A Mediterranean beauty who might have gazed out of a Renaissance painting.

Tinkler stared at the book. "Good Christ, my underpants are exploding. Why have I never heard of this woman?"

"Well, she only recorded a handful of albums before vanishing into obscurity. It seems she married a dentist, did her last—and best—recordings, and then retired to raise a kid."

"Yes, that will do it every time. Particularly marrying a dentist." He offered me the joint.

"No thanks. I've got an early start tomorrow." Coffee

was the only drug I really approved of.

"Yes, the first day of your quest." He parked the joint in a blue crystal ashtray on the coffee table. "I'll be back in a minute."

"Where are you going?"

"To get some provisions from the kitchen." He went out the door.

I called after him. "Got the munchies already?" There was no reply, just the familiar sound of Tinkler falling down the stairs.

I went out to take a look. "Are you all right?" I stood at the banister, peering down. His pale face smiled tentatively up at me from the shadows below.

"Fine. Just took a little spill. One of the stair rod screws is a bit loose."

"One of *your* screws is a bit loose," I said.

He came back a few minutes later with a big white ceramic bowl full of Kettle Chips and placed it on the coffee table. While I helped myself, he went over and rummaged through his records. "You know what I found the other day, at a record fair? A copy of *Beggars' Banquet*. Red label. Original unboxed Decca mono."

"Nice," I said. Although I primarily listened to jazz, I shared Tinkler's fondness for the Rolling Stones.

"Yes, and it was in great nick. Near mint. I paid for it with trembling hands, got it home and went to put it on the shelf, and you know what?"

"You found you already had a near-mint mono Decca copy of it with unboxed red labels?"

"I already had five of them," said Tinkler.

* * *

I had been looking for an excuse to avoid smoking dope with Tinkler, but I hadn't been lying—I really did have an early start the following day. I got up as soon as the cats woke me, fed them, had a quick shower and then caught a train into town. Styli wasn't yet open when I arrived, but I knocked on the window and Jerry let me in. "Put the kettle on while I finish opening up." I made myself a coffee and a tea for Jerry and then went back into the front room and sat down opposite him. Jerry had a pile of *The Absolute Sound* magazines beside his chair. "A little light reading," he said.

"How's that new collection you bought?"

He nodded happily. "Very nice. Some very fine stuff."

"And you say there's some jazz?"

"Some rather excellent items, as it happens. I think you'll definitely be interested. But I haven't finished sorting them yet. The whole collection is still sitting at my house and it will be a few days before we can take the van around and bring the records back here."

"That's all right. No hurry. I actually didn't come here to talk about that. I want some information about an obscure record label. It's called Hathor."

He nodded immediately. "A jazz label, of course—since it's you that's asking. Small West Coast firm. Mid 1950s. Named after the Egyptian goddess of music and beauty." Well, that explained the stupid name. Come to think of it, there was an Egyptian look to the design of the label.

"It was run by a fellow called Bobby Schoolcraft," said Jerry.

"Who committed suicide," I said.

"That's right."

"Because the label went bust."

43

Jerry shook his head. "Not quite. There was more to the story than that. I seem to remember reading something…" He frowned thoughtfully. "I'll look it up when I go home tonight." He had an extensive library of music-related books and journals in his house in Primrose Hill. I had never seen the place but I'd heard it was huge. It had to be, to house his record collection.

"But Hathor went bust because their records didn't sell?"

"Oh no. On the contrary, their records sold very well indeed, at least initially, and for a while it looked like they were going to turn into a major jazz label." Jerry sipped his tea.

I said, "They're definitely an intriguing outfit. Danny DePriest was their engineer, wasn't he?"

He nodded. "Ron Longmire was his mentor and the senior engineer. And I think Bones Howe might have worked there too." Bones Howe was another great sound engineer of jazz in the fifties. He had gone on to fame in the rock era and memorably produced some classic Tom Waits albums. "I'll check on all that when I get home," he said.

I tried my coffee. It was instant but I could drink it. I said, "So if their records were selling so well, why did they go broke?"

Jerry set his teacup aside. "Legal problems. Rather nasty legal problems. They were being sued by some very heavy people."

"Heavy in what way?"

"People who owned a major piece of the American entertainment industry. Have you ever heard of the Davenports?" I shook my head. "They were teenage impresarios. Second-generation show-business exploiters. Very unpleasant."

"And they sued Bobby Schoolcraft."

"It was a protracted and nasty—and costly—business

and apparently the pressure got too much for poor old Schoolcraft. He put an end to himself and, along with him, one of the most promising record labels in America."

I got back to my house mid-morning, just in time to make a sandwich and be greeted by the cats before my rendezvous with Miss N. Warren. It had turned cold and wet and she arrived wearing a dove-grey raincoat and white knit hat with a large red strawberry embroidered on it. On anyone else it might have looked ridiculous. On her it looked elegant and fetching.

I came out of the house and joined her. "How did you get here," I said. "Taxi?"

She shook her head. "No, I got a lift with a friend. Well, I say *friend*. He's actually this barrister I'm sleeping with." I felt like I'd been stabbed in the heart. I turned away from her and locked the door. The cats came out through the cat flap to watch us leave. She waved goodbye to them.

"We shall catch a taxi now, though," she said. We walked to the main road and flagged one down. There was always a black London cab cruising in the area thanks to the proximity of the Abbey. This one was driven by a striking young mixed-race woman with a shaved head. I gave directions.

"So, where are we going?" said N. Warren.

"Every charity shop between here and Chelsea," I said.

"God, I don't think I've ever been to a charity shop. I'm not sure I want to. Do they smell funny?"

She followed me into the first charity shop contentedly enough and waited patiently while I looked through about half the records in the first crate. But then she said, "Are you going to look at every single one?"

I was crouching over the box of records, squatting comfortably on my heels in my crate-digging shoes. I smiled up at her. "I don't know any other way of doing it."

She tapped her foot. "Can't we go to another shop?"

"Not until we finish in this one."

"You really are going to scrutinise every record?"

I looked up at her. "I could stop right now and we could leave the shop. And the very next record I was about to look at might be it, the one we're looking for. And we'd have missed it."

That shut her up. She turned away and began taking a pointed interest in the rest of the shop's wares. She started going through a railing of women's clothes. I could still feel her impatience weighing on me, though, as I looked through the records. I'd found a nice old Philips pressing of *Anatomy of a Murder* by Duke Ellington, but that was about it. Behind me I heard the impatient squeaking of coat hangers on a rail as she went through the clothes.

The squeaking gradually slowed down and then stopped. After a pause she came over to me and whispered excitedly, "There's a Nicole Farhi linen biker jacket there and it's exactly my size and it's only twelve quid!"

"So, why are you telling me?" I said. "Do you want me to lend you the money?"

"Very funny. But it is exactly my size." She gazed wistfully at the clothes rail. "And my colour."

"So, go and buy it."

She hesitated. "Do you think there will be a problem with insects?"

"Insects?"

"You know, vermin."

I felt like informing her that the underclasses had got a lot cleaner since indoor plumbing had become the norm, but instead I just said, "I think they steam clean the clothes."

She turned back to the clothes rack with a glint of determination in her eye. "Do you suppose they take credit cards?"

"I'm sure they do. You really haven't ever been in a charity shop before, have you?"

"Why would I have wanted to?"

Now things were reversed. I would finish searching through the crates of vinyl in a shop and have to wait impatiently around while she combed through the clothes. She rapidly acquired a cluster of bags of purchases and soon had me carrying them. By the time we'd exhausted the charity shops, working our way back from the King's Road, the light was fading.

"I suppose we should call it a day," she said. She took out her phone and a business card.

"What's that?" I said.

"It's from our driver this morning. Was she or was she not the coolest taxi driver in London? I got her business card." The woman was obsessed with business cards. "She can be our official driver."

"I'm sure the two of you will be very happy together."

"Ha ha, very funny." She called the number and we waited in a coffee shop until the taxi came and picked us up. We sat in the back, headed home, tired after a long day of failing to find the Easy Geary album. We were surrounded by the bags containing our purchases—well, *her* purchases. We had just turned off the North End Road when she suddenly announced, "We are being followed."

I had been going through the few records I'd found, trying to study their covers in the glow of the passing streetlights. She was sitting opposite me in the dark back of the cab, perched on the fold-down seat and peering intently out the rear window, watching London go past in the night.

"Oh, come on," I said.

But she turned to the driver. "Excuse me, but I think that car is following us." This was greeted with silence. She added, "Can you take some evasive manoeuvres, please?" More silence. "I'll make it worth your while." A disgusted sigh, then the clicking of the indicator as we took a sharp turn, then another turn, then another.

Then our driver said, "You're right. We're being followed."

I felt a cold irrational chill on the back of my neck. We were streaking along dark streets through Fulham Broadway. The brightly lit shop windows looked inappropriately cheery.

"What do you want me to do?" said our driver. In the back we looked at each other. We were rolling towards Putney Bridge.

Miss N. Warren said, "We can't lead them back to your place. Where shall we go?"

I said, "I have an idea."

I had phoned ahead, so I wasn't entirely surprised to discover that Tinkler had his hair neatly drawn back in a ponytail. He was also wearing a clean shirt, his face looked freshly scrubbed and there was a suspicious odour of aftershave in evidence. He held the door open for us and said, "Miss

Warren. I'm so pleased to meet you. I've heard so much about you."

"This is Jordon Tinkler," I said. They shook hands.

She said, "Jordan like the glamour model and the breakfast cereal?"

"No," he said, "it isn't spelled with an 'a'. It's spelled with an 'o'."

She chuckled. "How unusual."

"It isn't that unusual," said Tinkler, a little stung. "There was a very good midfielder who played for Birmingham called Jordon Mutch."

"Oh, the Birmingham midfield, of course."

I had to admire the way she'd managed to put him on the defensive within about three seconds of stepping through the door. Tinkler ushered us upstairs. "Thank you for letting us take refuge here," she said. "We won't bother you for long."

"Oh, no bother," said Tinkler, opening the door of his listening room. A waft of warm air flowed out to greet us. The amp was on.

Miss N. Warren went in and sat down on the sofa, glancing at me as I joined her. "He has more light bulbs on his system than you do."

"They're not light bulbs," I said. "They're valves. Thermionic valves."

"In America they call them tubes," added Tinkler. "Vacuum tubes."

"Well, they certainly warm the room up nicely," she said.

"It's because my amp is OTL. Output transformerless."

"What does that mean?"

I said, "It means it delivers a very pure sound, but if you get a spike in the DC your loudspeakers explode."

Tinkler snorted. "Like that's ever happened." But I noticed that he began to double-check the output valves. Meanwhile, N. Warren was searching through her shopping bags. She handed one to me.

"Here you are," she said.

"What is it?" I opened the bag and took out a dark blue jacket lined with silk printed in a winter camouflage pattern.

"It's a Paul Smith jacket. Try it on." I did as I was told. It was perhaps a little long in the sleeves, but otherwise a perfect fit. In fact it was very nice. She watched, nodding with grave approval as I walked around in it. Tinkler caught my eye and gave me a look.

She noticed the look and said, "If I'm going to accompany him on crate-diving expeditions, then he's going to have to look presentable."

"Crate-diving," said Tinkler. "I like it. Now how about I fetch us all some snacks?"

She said, "Only if you can provide something containing a great deal of salt or sugar, and fat of course, and which has no nutritional value whatsoever."

"I may have just the thing."

He left the room and she turned to me to say something. But I held up my hand for silence and listened. There was a thunderous noise. "My god," she said. "What's that? It sounded like the house falling down."

"No, just Tinkler falling down the stairs."

"Christ, is he all right?"

"I'm all right," called Tinkler.

She looked at me. "Does he often fall down the stairs?"

"Only when he's been smoking dope. But that's all the time."

She leaned back on the sofa, then glanced at me again. Despite the heat in the room, I was still wearing the jacket. I was quite taken with it. She said, "It's Nevada, by the way."

"What is?"

"My name."

I stared at her. "The N in N. Warren?"

"Yes."

"So you're Nevada Warren."

She gave a mild sigh of exasperation. "Yes."

"Was it where you were conceived?"

She spun around on the sofa and glared at me. "No it was not where I was fucking conceived. Why do people always say that? It's a word. It means 'snowfall'. It happens to be Spanish, but it's one of the most beautiful words in any language."

She sat fuming silently. Obviously people had floated the conception theory in her presence one time too often. I didn't break the silence. Instead, I got up and went over to Tinkler's record collection. I selected an LP and put it on the turntable. Music swelled from the big Tannoys, filling the room. After listening a while she said, grudgingly, "This is nice. What is it?"

"The Claude Thornhill orchestra," I said.

"What's the tune called?"

"'Snowfall'."

She looked at me bleakly then gradually cracked a smile. Her head was moving, just ever so slightly, to the music.

I said, "One of the most beautiful words in any language."

"Oh, fuck off," she said.

But she was still smiling.

* * *

I was anxious to hear what Jerry Muscutt's research on the Hathor label had revealed, so I went to Styli first thing the next day. But as soon as I got there, it was clear something was wrong. The downstairs room of the shop was crowded with regular customers and members of staff, all looking downcast. Jerry was nowhere in sight. I went over to Kempton, who worked upstairs in jazz, and said, "What's going on?"

He looked at me glumly. "It's Jerry."

"What's happened?"

Glenallen Brown, who also worked in the shop, came over and joined us. He was the opera specialist. He said, "I knew it would happen. He always went cruising for dangerous types."

"What?" I said. I looked at them.

Kempton shook his head. "Why did they have to kill him?"

"Kill him?" I said.

Kempton kept shaking his head. Tears gleamed in his eyes. "They didn't have to kill him."

I turned to Glenallen. He nodded. "Battered him to death."

"Oh Jesus," I said. "Jerry?"

"Yes."

"Who did it?"

"We don't know. Some piece of rough trade. Kempton went over there first thing this morning with the van. He was supposed to pick up some records. We'd just bought a big collection. He found Jerry lying there and called the police. The whole place was a mess, apparently. A bombsite. And Jerry kept it so tidy. Kempton said the entire place was torn apart. There were records everywhere. All over the floor. You couldn't move for them. They'd been pulled off the shelves and strewn everywhere."

I said, "Almost as if someone was looking for something."

4. THE UNKNOWN JAZZ FAN

We held an improvised wake for Jerry at the shop. There couldn't be a funeral yet because the police hadn't released his body, but we felt we had to do something, to mark the occasion, so to speak. Jerry had always made a point of drinking decent single malts and someone went out and bought a couple of pricey bottles of Islay in his memory.

It felt wrong to be drinking whisky at ten in the morning, but that wasn't the only thing that felt wrong.

I got home to find Miss Warren—Nevada—waiting for me on my doorstep. She was fuming. "Where have you been?" she said. Then I brushed past her and she smelled the whisky. "Have you been drinking?"

"Shouldn't you be waving a rolling pin?" I said. "And have curlers in your hair?" I took out my keys and tried to open the front door.

"You're drunk," she hissed.

"Nonsense." I fumbled with the lock. Actually, I *was* feeling a little light-headed after the morning's boozing.

Fanny and Turk sprang out of the dense plot of vegetation that occupied the centre of the square outside my bungalow.

It was like a giant concrete planter raised to waist height and protected by a low fence of blue enamelled steel railings. The cats loved it because it was a miniature jungle and they could play hide and seek in it. They jumped up onto the fence and dashed to join us. They had heard me jingling the keys.

"Oh, look who's here," cried Nevada. The cats swirled around her ankles and she bent down to pat them as I struggled with the front door. "Who's a darling?" she said. "Who's a honey darling, who's sweet? Yes, you are, and you are too. Yes, both of you, yes, yes, yes." And then instantly and without transition she resumed her tirade against me. "It isn't even lunchtime and you are supposed to be meeting me and spending the day working and instead you are late and you are deeply unprofessional and you are drunk."

"I am not drunk." I got the door open and the cats sped in, followed by Nevada. I was the last through, wrestling the keys out of the lock and clumsily closing the door behind me. "I had a few drinks. All right?"

"Why in god's name were you having a few drinks at this time of the morning?"

"A friend died," I said. "We held an impromptu wake."

"Oh," she said. "I'm sorry."

"It's all right. I mean, you didn't know him." I took my coat off and wondered if I had the moral fibre to make us some real coffee. While I was making up my mind I poured out some biscuits for the cats. Turk crunched away at them enthusiastically and immediately. Fanny played hard to get for a while, wandering to her bowl, then wandering away again, but she finally deigned to start eating.

"Who was it?" said Nevada.

"Just a friend. A guy I knew. He worked in a record shop.

Actually I mentioned him to you. He was the one who told me that the Stravinsky on Everest was bogus. Your little ruse."

"It wasn't a ruse," she said. "It was your job qualification exam. How did he die?"

"He went cruising for a playmate and he took the wrong bloke home."

"My god."

"He got beaten to death."

"My god."

I belched whisky fumes. I decided I couldn't face grinding the coffee beans. I was dreading the noise of the grinder as much as the cats. I could already feel the distant painful promise of my looming hangover, like a storm cloud approaching on a summer's day. I got out the jar of instant and put the kettle on. "I didn't even know he was gay," I said. I spooned the freeze-dried granules into the mugs. "I suppose the fifteen thousand albums of show tunes he owned might have been a clue."

"Fifteen thousand?"

"Something like that."

"Good lord."

"Maybe it was only five thousand."

"Still, good lord."

The kettle was just approaching the boil. I switched it off. "And that was just a small part of his collection."

Nevada shrugged her coat off and sat down. "Any jazz?" she said. And I knew what she was getting at.

"If he'd had a copy of *Easy Come, Easy Go*, I think he would have told me."

"Are you sure?"

"Sure. And if he'd owned an original he wouldn't have

had to run a record shop. He could have sold it and retired on the proceeds. However…"

She peered at me. "However what?"

I poured the hot water over the instant coffee. "Jerry had just recently bought a big collection of records. There was a lot of jazz in it, he said. He hadn't finished sorting through it yet, so who knows what it might contain?"

"Well then, for god's sake, let's go and have a look at this collection."

I sighed. "That's not going to happen."

"Why not?"

"Jerry was killed in his house. The records are in his house. It's a crime scene. The police are crawling all over it and they won't let anyone in for at least a week."

She said, "Well, as soon as we can get in there, we must."

"Yes," I said, "that should definitely be my first order of business, now that my friend is dead. Rifling through his record collection."

"Are you going to stir that?" she said.

"Oh, sorry." I finished stirring the coffee and handed her a mug.

She blew on it and took a sip. "Still, it's a pity. Not being able to check if the record is there."

I shrugged. "Actually the real pity is not having access to Jerry's reference books. He definitely had some information about the Hathor record label. He was going to go home and look it up for me."

She set her coffee aside. "What did you say his name was again?"

"Jerry Muscutt."

She nodded, as if it meant something to her.

In the back of the cab she sat as far away from me as possible. "You stink of whisky," she said.

"You don't have to come."

"What do you mean?"

"I could look for the record on my own. I'm a big boy."

"Oh no," she said. "I couldn't do that."

"Why not?" I remembered what Tinkler had said. "Because you don't trust me? Because you think I'll find the record and keep it for myself?"

"No," she said. She shot a nervous glance at our driver. She'd made good on her promise to hire the young woman with the shaved head. But the driver, sealed away on the other side of the glass, seemed appropriately oblivious to our conversation. "Of course not. Of course I don't think that."

But she didn't convince either of us. I said, "Why don't you just look for it yourself?"

"You're not making any sense. Look, you're just despondent about your friend, and that's understandable. Plus it doesn't help that you've had a skinful. But we have a job here and we have to do it."

"We." I sighed. I was coming down from the whisky and everything looked bleak. We were driving through Strawberry Hill, along the narrow curving Waldegrave Road. The entrance to St Mary's University flashed by on our left. Our driver, whom I'd begun to think of as Clean Head, was making good time.

Nevada said, "Besides, without you, where would I start? I mean, I'd never think of going to exotic places like

Surbiton to seek out fascinating institutions like this, what did you call it? This record fair."

"Don't get your hopes up," I said.

The record fair was a monthly fixture, held at a church hall near the tall, elegant white art-deco railway station, which to my mind was the best thing about Surbiton. Well, that and the charity shops. The record fair was in a small building in the courtyard of an old redbrick church, situated opposite a pleasant little park.

I got the taxi driver to drop us on the far side of the park so we could stroll across it in a leisurely fashion and appreciate the greenery. However, I don't think my power-walking companion even noticed it, as she strode implacably forward, focused intently on the grey rectangular building ahead. There was a poster on a sandwich board outside which said RECORD FAIR, THIS WAY!

"Why did you tell me not to get my hopes up?"

"It's a record fair," I said.

"And?"

"And everything that ends up here has already been picked over by dealers." I held the swinging door for her and we entered. "It would be a miracle if we found something really special." It was chilly in the hall despite a battered ancient chrome electric heater which was standing in the centre of the room with its power cord taped to the floor to prevent excited record lovers tripping over it as they rushed blindly to seek out treasures.

I noted with approval that the device, bars glowing a cheery orange, had been placed as far as humanly possible from any of the records. Vinyl and heat: not a good combination.

"Then why are we bothering at all?" said Nevada.

I looked around. It was a long narrow room with dusty wooden floors. There were folding tables set up along three of the walls, in a U-shape around the heater. The dealers, all men except for one formidable-looking middle-aged lady with a hooded orange sweatshirt and Brillo pad hair, were still setting up. On the tables were boxes and crates of records, some yet to be opened.

Despite myself, I felt the familiar pang of excitement. Who knew what I might find? I said, "Because not all of these guys are on the ball, because most of them aren't jazz specialists, and because miracles happen."

I started going through the crates and Nevada became bored almost immediately. It didn't help that the heater was kicking in and the smell of large and largely unwashed men hauling in heavy crates of records to beat a deadline pervaded the place. "Listen," she said, "why don't I go out and get us some coffee? I suspect they have coffee in Surbiton."

"That's a good idea. And see if you can—"

"Yes, yes, I'll search out some gourmet connoisseur blend of the kind that you won't turn your nose up at." She waved her hand, more in a gesture of dismissal than farewell, and headed for the door.

I didn't blame her for fleeing a place that smelled at worst of sweaty trainspotter and at best of budget deodorant. Plus, to be honest, it was a relief not to have her constantly tapping her toe impatiently while I gave all of the boxes of records a thorough inspection, including the ones lurking under the tables. It was the usual overpriced junk with the occasional item apparently price-stickered by somebody on a grandiose and florid LSD trip. Ten pounds for a Culture Club album of no discernible scarcity, anyone? But there was also the occasional nice, or at least intriguing, record.

I found a Prince bootleg I'd been searching for for years. It was the one where he jammed with Miles Davis. Unfortunately it was in poor condition, crazily expensive and turned out to only feature Miles on a single track. Three strikes and you're out. I put it back in the box, to my regret and obviously also that of the avaricious clown behind the table who had optimistically saddled it with its stratospheric price tag.

"Found something?" It was an all-too-familiar voice. I turned to see Stinky Stanmer standing there. I suppose it wasn't so surprising. I had introduced him to this place, years ago. He bent down and checked the box I'd just been searching through. He found the Prince/Miles Davis record right away and glanced at me. "You aren't buying this?"

"Too expensive."

He chortled and took out his wallet. It was bulging with banknotes. He paid the dealer, who had perked up considerably. He put the record in a bag and Stinky tucked it under his arm.

"So," he said, looking around. "Found anything else?" For a moment it was the good old sincere, ingratiating Stinky whom I remembered from university. "Found anything really choice?"

I shook my head. I said, "It's hardly likely, is it?" I looked around at the dealers, their overwhelming shared attributes being obsession, a poor sense of personal hygiene, passion and greed. I said, "It would be like finding a virgin at a pimp convention."

He gave a loud bark of laughter and people stared at

us. I was appalled to notice that some of the dealers and customers had recognised him, and doubly appalled to realise that in their eyes my status had been elevated through being in his company.

It was at this moment that Nevada returned with two cardboard cups of coffee. She saw us and paused. There was a faint buzzing, like a wasp trapped in a jam jar, and Stinky started digging into his pockets, apparently in search of his phone. He took it out. "Probably my agent," he said.

"Well, don't let me keep you," I said.

He scrutinised the screen. "No, it's just this model I met. She keeps pestering me." He shook his head and switched the phone off. I smiled at him. Knowing Stinky it was just as likely the call had been some spam from his phone provider. He said, "You haven't been writing much on your blog lately."

This was a surprising observation from someone who pretended not to read it. "No," I said. "I've been doing other things."

"Well, you have to keep the content refreshed, or you won't get any hits." He noticed Nevada, who was hanging back, politely waiting for him to finish talking to me. He turned to her and smiled. "Hi. Do you want my autograph?"

Nevada gave him a look. It was the same look she might give to something unpleasant that had attached itself to her shoe. "Christ, no," she said. "Why would I?" This was enough to give even Stinky pause, and the smile froze on his face.

But he rallied with surprising speed. "Are you *sure* you wouldn't like my autograph?"

Nevada turned to me and nodded at Stinky.

"Do you know him?" she said. "Or has he escaped from the local asylum?"

I felt all warm inside, like I'd been drinking rum punch. I said, "Unfortunately, I do know him."

"I'm Stinky," he said.

"Well, you're certainly in the right place," said Nevada.

"Stinky Stanmer."

"Give it up, Stinky," I said. "She hasn't heard of you." I looked at Nevada. "Stinky and I went to university together."

"Well, these things happen."

"Is one of those coffees for me?" I said.

"Ah, yes. This one." She handed me one of the paper cups. It was hot and it smelled good. "I've been assured it's made of the finest coffee beans which have passed through a monkey's rectum."

I sipped the coffee. It was great. "A civet, actually. And I doubt you managed to source any authentic *kopi luwak* around here."

"Perhaps I exaggerate a trifle," said Nevada. "Are you finished here yet?"

"Just about."

"Pretty thin pickings," said Stinky, who was unfortunately still standing with us. "But that's hardly surprising. Finding a choice piece of vinyl here is about as likely as finding a virgin at a pimp convention."

If Nevada had found this plagiarised remark irresistibly charming I would have had to kill Stinky at this point, but luckily she treated his whole attempt to talk to her with the *froideur* it so richly deserved. "Ready to go then?" she said. I nodded and we headed for the door together.

"See you, Stinky," I said.

But he was already rooting through a box of records.

* * *

We hit the charity shops. I found a nice French reissue of a Verve album by Gerry Mulligan and a few Illinois Jacquet air-shots, which is to say recordings of radio broadcasts. Fortunately, Nevada had the designer clothes rail to rifle in each shop and eventually she got lucky and found a Prada merkin or something, so she didn't feel the outing had been an entire waste. Plus it kept her from nagging me about buying records that weren't the one we were after, as if I should pass them up for that reason.

I flipped through my LPs, gloating, in the taxi on the way back. Nevada was sitting opposite me, looking at something on her phone and giggling. Our driver, now officially designated Clean Head in my mind, and only partly as a tribute to the noted alto sax player Eddie "Clean Head" Vinson, was getting us home at an impressive clip. Eddie Vinson had been bald as a billiard ball, as the result of a hair-straightening calamity. For our driver it was clearly a fashion statement rather than a terrible chemical accident.

In any case, thanks to her skills behind the wheel, we were already passing Kingston Hospital and I suspected she was heading for Richmond Park to take a shortcut.

Inspecting my records, I was just thinking they'd probably come from the collection of the Unknown Jazz Fan when Nevada looked up from her phone and said, "Who is this Unknown Jazz Fan?"

In response to the look of blank astonishment on my face—had she read my mind?—she said, "I've just been reading your blog. I heard you talking to your, ah, friend Stinky about it and I thought I'd take a look."

"Of course, I blogged about him. The Unknown Jazz Fan, I mean. Not Stinky."

"Of course not."

"So, wait a minute," I said. "Does that mean that when you were giggling a moment ago you were giggling at my blog?"

"I wasn't giggling."

"Yes you were."

"I'm not the giggling sort. Anyway, what about this Unknown Jazz person?"

"I blogged about him. You've got the blog there. You can read it."

She put her phone away and gave me her big eyes, all soft and attentive. "No," she said. "You tell me."

I sighed. "Okay. It's just some guy who's getting rid of his record collection, in instalments. It's a hell of a collection and I don't know why he's getting rid of it. Divorce? Moving home? A massive collapse in taste? Perhaps he's like the vicar in Barnes."

"What vicar in Barnes?"

"He had a crisis of faith. By which I mean he foolishly renounced LPs in favour of CDs and got rid of all his vinyl. And it was a hell of a collection. Perhaps the Unknown Jazz Fan is like that. Or perhaps the poor sap has copied all his LPs digitally and is even now listening to music files on a computer." I glanced at the records in my lap. "In other words, he had sent them across the digital Rubicon. Actually, the river to the underworld more like."

"The river Styx."

"Exactly."

"You've really got it in for poor old digital recording, haven't you?"

"Anyway," I said, "I keep finding batches of records he's got rid of. Here and there. In charity shops, at jumble sales."

"We haven't been to a jumble sale yet," she said. "In our supposedly exhaustively thorough search for this record."

"I've got us booked for one tomorrow night."

"How dizzyingly stimulating. Tell me, this Unknown Jazz Fan. How do you know the records belonged to him? Does he write his name on the cover?"

"Christ no."

"Then how do you know it's him? For that matter, how do you know such a person even exists?"

"I cover that."

"What do you mean?"

"In my blog. I cover it."

"I see. You expect me to read it." She took out her phone and scrolled down the screen. "Oh yes. Here we go. 'Does he even exist? Maybe it isn't a person at all. Maybe it is just a statistical cluster, an analytical artefact, a certain population, a given age group, a shared taste, a demographic bubble…' My god, you do go on a bit, don't you? 'A cultural profile, a sociology paper…'" She looked at me. "So, to cut a long story short, the Unknown Jazz Fan may not even exist?"

"That's right. But that doesn't mean he's not out there somewhere."

She smiled at me. "It's like something out of Borges," she said. "Or do I mean Cortázar?"

"Don't strain yourself."

The cats were waiting outside when we got home. They milled around impatiently with an equally impatient Nevada while I opened the door. There was actually a cat flap installed in it, but Turk and Fanny disdained the use of this whenever they could have someone actually open the door for them. They were the first through, followed by Nevada. And, as was rapidly becoming traditional, I brought up the rear.

I stepped over the door mat. The post had come and there was a jumble of letters lying there; even at this most casual glance obviously mostly bills, and laughably unpayable ones at that. I picked up the pile of mail and began to go through it when suddenly a man's voice shouted from inside.

"Easy, easy, easy!"

I ran into the sitting room. Nevada was standing there—a study in dynamic tension, arm extended rigidly, holding my largest and sharpest kitchen knife.

She was aiming it at Stinky who was standing by the sofa, his face pale and his composure fled for once. "Easy," he said.

"Christ," hissed Nevada. She lowered the knife and looked at me. "What is he doing here?"

"I have no idea," I said.

"I just walked in and saw someone was here and I grabbed this." She waved the knife. "He scared the shit out of me."

The colour was starting to return to Stinky's face. "Likewise," he said, "I'm sure."

"You shut up for a minute," said Nevada. She turned to me. "You had no idea he'd be here?"

"Of course not," I said.

"How did he get in?"

"I, um, let myself in," said Stinky. He held up the keys.

Nevada set the knife down on the dining table and went and snatched the keys from him. "How did he get hold of these?" She waved them at me accusingly.

"I leave them outside."

"Outside?"

"Under the plant pot."

"The plant pot?" she demanded.

"Yes, that's right, the plant pot," said Stinky.

"You shut up," she said.

"In case I lock myself out," I explained. The cats, who had wisely made themselves scarce during the armed confrontation, began to emerge from hiding. Turk jumped up onto the sofa and Fanny went to her favourite chair. Business as usual. Nevada watched them for a moment, then looked at Stinky.

"Why didn't you wait outside with the cats?"

I said, "If he'd waited outside, they would have waited *inside*." One of the things that endeared the little monsters to me was that they couldn't stand Stinky.

"I couldn't wait outside," said Stinky. "My fans would have recognised me."

"Your fans?" said Nevada, managing to combine contempt and incomprehension in about equal measure.

"I have a radio show."

Nevada made a snorting sound that couldn't quite be described as laughter. "And they'd recognise you from that? They'd recognise your face from the radio?"

"Stinky has also been on television," I added reluctantly.

"And I'm also very active on the Internet."

"I'm sure you are," said Nevada. It was impressive how she didn't actually add the words "No doubt surfing for porn, you pathetic loser," yet we all clearly understood that's what she meant. Stinky returned to the sofa from which he'd so recently risen in fear for his life. Nevada glanced at my hi-fi. "Your thermionic valves are on," she said.

I nodded. "So they are."

"I've been listening to CDs," said Stinky. He casually sat down on the sofa, ignoring Turk, who snarled at him and jumped down. "There's nothing quite like dropping the needle," continued Stinky, addressing Nevada and ignoring me, "but you have to listen to something while you're changing records." Had he actually forgotten he'd stolen that line from me?

"Well, I hate to be rude," said Nevada. "But we have business to discuss."

"Business?" said Stinky, looking from her to me. I went to the CD player and took out the disc. He'd been listening to *Bullitt* by Lalo Schifrin.

"Yes," said Nevada. I found the CD case for *Bullitt* and opened it to find that it contained *The Taking of Pelham 123* by David Shire. I sighed and looked for the CD case for that, opened it and, logically enough, found that it contained *The Organization* by Gil Mellé.

"What sort of business?" said Stinky. I found the Mellé case, which was empty, duly put the correct disc back in there, then restored the Shire and Schifrin CDs to their rightful cases. The old CD switcharoo. One of Stinky's many annoying habits. Useful for anyone who wanted to do a forensic analysis of his listening habits, but otherwise just plain annoying.

Stinky repeated, "What sort of business?"

"None of your damned," said Nevada.

"What? Oh, very clever," said Stinky, catching up. "So how do you guys know each other?" It was obviously this question that had impelled him to make today's latest uninvited visit. He couldn't imagine what someone like Nevada was doing with someone like me. And in some sense his universe was threatened. So he just wasn't going to let it go.

He was smiling at Nevada politely, or with what passed for politeness in Stinkyland. He made a vague hand gesture, waggling a finger back and forth between us, "You know each other, how?"

"We met at Lord Rudolph's fifteenth annual zeppelin race," said Nevada.

"Okay," said Stinky. He evidently decided he wasn't going to get anything else out of her. "Well, I'll be shoving along then." He picked up his coat.

"Would you?" said Nevada. We accompanied Stinky to the door and saw him off the premises. The cats didn't stir. As soon as he was gone Nevada turned to me and I was startled to realise she was boiling with anger. "How could you?" she said.

"What?"

"Leave your key outside, unprotected."

"It's hidden."

"Hidden. It's under a plant pot! Show me this plant pot." I took her outside and showed her. She was still furious. "How could you? Just anyone could walk in off the street. And be waiting for you."

"Hard to believe they could be worse than Stinky."

She ignored the joke and stood glaring at me. "Are you simple-minded?" she said.

"Look, I have to have a spare set of keys. In case I lock myself out."

"They don't have to be under your plant pot." We went back inside and shut the door.

"They have to be where I can get at them," I said.

"I'll look after them," she said.

"What?"

"I'll look after your keys." She put them in her handbag.

"Are you sure?" I didn't argue with her. In fact, to be candid, I found the notion strangely appealing.

She nodded. "If you need them, if you lock yourself out, you've got my number. Just ring me and I'll bring them round." She paused thoughtfully. "Oh, one more thing to do." She took out her little red notebook and a pen and went back outside. I followed her. She opened her notebook and wrote in large, bold letters, FUCK OFF STINKY. She tore the page out of her notebook, folded it up and put it under the plant pot where the key used to reside.

"There," she said happily. "That's that."

"Of course, what she's going to do," said Tinkler, "is let herself into your house, sneaking in one night while you're asleep, glide through the darkness, shedding her clothes, stub her toe on a crate of records that should have been properly shelved years ago and then, cursing, hop under the duvet with you and bang your brains out."

"You're saying that as though it could never happen."

"Yes," said Tinkler. "What other possible reason could there be for her wanting to hold onto your keys?" He shook his head despairingly. "You always go for the gorgeous ones and you always get kicked in the teeth. When are you going to learn?"

"Learn what?"

"That they don't go for insolvent, failed DJs who are record-collecting nuts." He added politely, "Not that I'm saying I'm any better off. They don't go for solvent database managers who are record-collecting nuts, either. Would you like something to eat?"

"I'll fetch it," I said. "I don't want you falling down the stairs." I brought a selection of snack foods back and found that—surprise—Tinkler was building a joint. He looked up at me happily.

"I got a new shipment from Hughie."

Hughie Mackinaw, known affectionately to us as the Scottish Welshman, had a business manufacturing and restoring turntables in his own factory near Llandrindod Wells in rural Wales. He had rebuilt Tinkler's Thorens TD 124 and done a nice job. Hughie's work was pretty good, and his own turntables had their admirers. He also made a state-of-the-art record-cleaning machine. But he didn't sell quite enough of any of these to make a living, hence his sideline in "shipments" to people like Tinkler.

Concealed behind his rambling, antiquated factory overlooking leafy Rock Park, Hughie had a yard where he'd erected a network of poly tunnels in which, screened by tomato plants, he grew an impressive cannabis crop. He shipped his wares to customers all over the mainland UK in boxes purporting to contain hi-fi equipment. I noticed that there was one of these on the floor now, labelled PRECISION AUDIO COMPONENT, HANDLE WITH CARE.

Tinkler had handled it with anything but care when he'd opened it. It looked like a wolverine had torn the box apart. I guess he'd been impatient to get at the goodies inside. He showed me the dope. "Here, have a sniff of this."

He held open the glassine bag. The rich green foliage inside resembled tiny cabbages, perhaps miniaturised by the experimental ray of a mad scientist. You could see pale crystals of THC on the buds, like minuscule flakes of cake icing. He said, "It's as if somebody gene spliced Bob Marley and Pepé Le Pew." The smell was indeed raw, rank and complex. Intoxicating. I looked up at Tinkler. "Go on," he said. "Try some."

"No thanks. At some point tonight I'm going to need to remember where my house is."

Tinkler shrugged and ignited the joint. "Your loss."

I said, "I found some more stuff from the Unknown Jazz Fan today."

Tinkler slowly breathed out smoke and examined it as it hung in the air. I was getting a buzz just from being in the same room with the stuff. Hughie evidently knew what he was doing when it came to more things than turntables. Tinkler stared at the far wall of the room, the wall that was almost solid LPs. "Do you know what I think?" he said. "I think that when a record collection reaches a certain complexity it becomes a kind of vortex of possibility, summoning new records in out of the void."

"You mean like a magnet?"

"Yes, a magnet that attracts the records you're looking for."

"Now, *that* is like something out of Borges," I said.

His eyes slowly focused on me again. "Did you say you'd found some more records from the Unknown Jazz Fan?"

"Yes. Welcome back."

"Any British rock or R&B?"

"Well, there was an original copy of John Mayall and the Bluesbreakers on Deram with the 'Beano' cover. It was in mint condition, but they wanted three quid for it, so I left it there."

"What? You did what? Are you out of your mind?" Tinkler's eyes were agreeably a-bulge with outrage. Then he realised I'd got him.

"You bastard," he said.

I did manage to remember where my house was, but it was well after midnight by the time I got there. As soon as she heard my keys Fanny came out to meet me, emerging from the house through the cat flap, and Turk joined us, bounding in from the outer darkness of the estate and giving a little yelp of triumph as she surmounted the final fence.

We went inside. I turned on the lights and saw the pile of mail, exactly where I'd left it during this afternoon's drama with Stinky at knifepoint. One envelope jutted out from the pile. It was handwritten, the envelope addressed in a neat italic script, apparently written with a fountain pen. I opened it carefully. Inside were several folded handwritten pages.

I started reading the letter. My stomach did a funny little flip.

It was from Jerry.

5. JERRY'S LETTER

It felt very strange to get a letter from a dead man.

Underneath his address and the usual salutations it began:

Forgive me for writing to you in this old-fashioned way, but I find that putting pen to paper helps me to organise my thoughts.

When I got home tonight I realised that if I'm ever going to sort out this behemoth of a record collection that we so recklessly purchased, it's going to require some concerted effort on my part.

So I'll be taking a few days off work to stay at home and go through it until it's finished. I've already started and I'll get the chaps to bring the van around tomorrow to convey the first batch to the shop. (Don't worry, I'll see that you get first sniff at the jazz!)

But I know you're eager to hear the story on Hathor Records. So here we go. I've had a good look through my library and I've been able to piece together the following.

It was a highly regarded but very short-lived West Coast jazz label that was born and died in the same year, 1955, in Los Angeles. In the space of a few months Hathor released a total of fourteen LPs (catalogue numbers Hathor HL-001 to 014) by the following artists, in order of release: Easy Geary (first of two albums), Marty Paich, Richie Kamuca, Johnny Richards, Jerry Fielding, Russ Garcia, Cy Coleman, Howard Roberts, Rita Mae Pollini (two consecutive albums, 009 and 010), Manny Albam, Pepper Adams, Conte Candoli and of course Easy Geary, second of two albums, with *Easy Come, Easy Go* (HL-014).

You'll know better than I that there is some top-shelf West Coast jazz in this list (and some from the top drawer of the East, viz New York).

Rita Mae also sings on one track, as you know, on *Easy Come, Easy Go*, and there are other crossovers in terms of personnel too numerous to mention. I'll photocopy you a complete session discography if you're interested.

I felt my eyes sting. For a moment the words were too blurred to make out. Jerry wouldn't be photocopying anything for me, or anyone else. I wiped my eyes and continued to read.

As you can see, Easy Geary bookends Hathor's history. Which is appropriate, since he determined their fate.

Because, despite their impressive list of talent and strong early sales, Hathor was plagued with bad luck.

Bobby Schoolcraft, the label owner, died a few days after recording HL-013, ominously enough.

And Easy Geary vanished shortly after recording Hathor 14.

As you no doubt know, his disappearance is shrouded in mystery. Some maintain Easy was shot dead in an altercation over a woman, rather in the manner of that famous jazz trumpeter. A genius cut short. Others insist that he didn't really die at all. Like Elvis.

He meant Lee Morgan. The jazz trumpeter genius whose life was cut short. Fanny was nudging my elbow, so I moved over and allowed her to sit in my lap. She seemed quite content for me to rest the letter on her head, so I did that and went on reading.

Bobby Schoolcraft, as we discussed, was nominally a suicide. But all my sources are in agreement that he was actually hounded to death by a man called Ox.

This is a nickname for a Los Angeles cop called Oliver Xavier. A murderous knucklehead of Irish extraction, Ox was notorious for preying on those elements of society who didn't abide by his rigid moral criteria, which is to say just about everyone except other Irish-American cops.

He was in the pay of the music companies, who used him as their "hammer man", or enforcer. If one of their recording artists got out of line or tried to free themselves from an onerous contract, Ox was used to put the fear of god into them.

There was a sudden unearthly screeching outside in the night. Fanny jumped off my lap, alarmed, and stood tensely on the floor. The ghoulish, tortured shrieking came again. It was unmistakably the barking of a fox. This is what we'd have to make do with in London until someone managed to successfully import the jackal.

While Fanny paced nervously back and forth, I went back to the letter.

Easy Geary had the misfortune of awakening the wrath of these people, and of Ox, when he put out his first album for Hathor. Fatefully, it was entitled *Easy Geary Plays Burns Hobartt*.

Jerry then went off on a tangent about the Davenport cousins. "Nasty pieces of work", he called them. It was a virtual tirade. It was touching to see how angry they made him. They'd evidently been a couple of young hustlers, a man and a woman with a peculiar relationship that, it was rumoured, veered into the incestuous, or whatever you'd call sex between cousins. And they managed to get their hooks into some of the great jazz composers.

And, as was all too often the custom in those days, they got their names on the compositions by these jazz men. It was reminiscent of what had happened with Irving Mills and Duke Ellington. The Duke was a musical genius. Mills was just his business manager. But Mills ended up being credited as co-composer on many of Ellington's masterpieces, even though he didn't write a note of the music.

This meant of course that he also ended up with a permanent share of the revenues.

The Davenport cousins, also referred to in Jerry's letter as "those young parasites", had performed a similar scam with the music written by another jazz great, Burns Hobartt. They had taken—or if you prefer, stolen—a credit on everything he wrote, for the privilege of publishing his music.

Which meant that whenever anyone recorded a Burns Hobartt composition, it was supposed to be credited as being written by "Hobartt, Davenport and Davenport", even though the malevolent cousins had nothing to do with it.

The injustice of this had apparently been too much for Easy Geary. On his album of Hobartt classics, the credits just read "Hobartt". No one else. Just the man who had really written the music.

Which was the strict truth of it.

But the Davenports' lawyers didn't see it that way.

Of course, they didn't deserve any credit, but contractually they were entitled to it. And even though the cousins were long since dead, AMI, the corporate entity that represented them, was still thriving and promptly launched a lawsuit.

And, much worse, they unleashed Ox on the owner of the offending record label, poor Bobby Schoolcraft.

It's not clear what he did to Bobby Schoolcraft, but in the past Ox had not been above blackmail, beatings and even death threats. Perhaps it's not surprising that Bobby Schoolcraft took the way out he did. There was evidently a suicide note specifically naming Ox and detailing his campaign of persecution, but it was suppressed by the police.

Fanny ceased her frightened pacing and jumped back up onto the sofa with me. She had provisionally concluded she wasn't about to be devoured by a large carnivore. She settled against me again, warm and solid, as I resumed my reading.

The last Hathor album, the much sought-after *Easy Come, Easy Go*, was recorded knowing that it would be the last album the company ever released, knowing that Bobby Schoolcraft was dead, and knowing that it was all over.

Perhaps that's why Geary and Miss Pollini put their autographs in the dead wax when the record was pressed. As a kind of memorial.

There is a legend that Ox stopped by at this recording session to gloat. That apparently didn't stop it being a stupendous album, musically speaking, by all accounts. If you find a copy perhaps you will play it for me. (I do listen to the occasional bit of jazz!) Good luck in your quest to find it.

Well, that's all I've got for now. I'll let you know if my research turns up anything further. I'll pass it along when I next see you in the shop.

I have to go out later tonight and I shall drop this in the postbox on the way.

See you soon.
All the best,
Jerry

I folded the letter up neatly and put it back in the envelope. I was obscurely grateful that I had taken such care opening it. When he had gone out later that night he had met the person who'd killed him. Dropping the letter in the postbox had been just about the last thing Jerry ever did.

6. JUMBLE

I didn't see Nevada until the following evening.

It was raining when she arrived. Once again she was wearing her white knit hat with the strawberry embroidered on it.

"Nice hat."

"Oh, get stuffed."

"No, really, I like it. It looks very fetching."

She looked at me warily, as if to determine whether I was on the level. "It keeps the rain out."

We walked to the main road and started looking for a taxi. I said, "What's happened to Clean Head?"

"Who is Clean Head?"

"Our taxi driver."

"Why do you call her Clean Head? Her name is Agatha."

"I rest my case."

"*Agatha* has taken the night off because she has a hot date." We both spotted a taxi approaching—from the direction of the Abbey, naturally—and simultaneously began to flag it down. "And I could be on a hot date too, if I wasn't stuck here in the rain with you."

"Don't sulk," I said. "You'll be in a nice, warm, dry taxi soon." The black cab pulled up beside us and I held the door open for her and we hopped in. Nevada had left her shoulder bag on the pavement and when I reached down to pick it up for her, she leaned back out of the cab and snatched it up.

"Well, go on, get in," she said, looking at me. I climbed in, gave the driver the address and sat down opposite her. The taxi pulled away into the night.

"I can't believe it," she said, clutching her bag in her lap, staring out the window at the streetlights flashing past. "I'm going to spend the evening going to a jumble sale."

"You were moaning that we hadn't been to one. Now you're moaning because we're *going* to one."

"I could be on a hot date," she repeated.

"And learning lots about serving coffee." The taxi was speeding towards the gate to Richmond Park. She looked away from the window, at me, puzzled.

"What do you mean?"

"You said you were dating a barista."

"A *barrister*," she snarled, then realised she had taken the bait. "Oh, very funny." She glanced away, but not before I caught a gleam of amusement in those sardonic blue eyes.

And for some reason, from something in her reaction, I got the sense that the dolt in question, be he shyster, java jockey or Cistercian monk, would not be in the privileged position of receiving Miss N. Warren's favours for much longer.

And I rejoiced in this.

The traffic eased once we got through Putney and we made good time to our destination in Wandsworth. Nevada paid the driver and the cab sped away into the night. She turned to me. "Our driver was rather disappointing, wasn't he? I mean, compared to old Clean Head. I rather miss her."

"So do I."

She stared at the complex of buildings in front of us. They were block shaped, with white stucco walls that had over the years acquired a grey porridge colour and texture, where the surface hadn't scabbed away entirely. The green painted trim around the doors and windows looked like it had received some more recent attention. In the last twenty years or so, say.

"So what is this place?"

"A Scout hut."

"Like the Boy Scouts?"

"Yes. Exactly like that."

Light shone through the opaque pebbled-glass lavatory-style windows and indistinct shadowed shapes could be seen moving around inside the building. "Why don't we go in?"

"It doesn't open for almost an hour," I said.

"What? An hour? Why have you dragged us to this, this garden spot, an hour before we need to be here?"

"We want to be the first in line."

"Do we? Why?"

"How would you like it if some guy in front of us in the queue got to the records first and found a copy of *Easy Come, Easy Go* and bought it?"

"How would I like it? I wouldn't." She looked at me. "I wouldn't let it happen. And I hope you wouldn't either."

"And what exactly would we do about it?"

"Wrest it from his grasp. And, failing that, insist he sell it to us."

"Why would he agree to do that?"

"He—this hypothetical interloper—wouldn't know

what it is. Or what it's worth. He'd be bound to sell it for a reasonable price."

"Don't count on it," I said.

"Then we'd just have to take it from him."

"Steal it from him, you mean?"

"I don't see why you have to throw around words like 'steal'," she said.

"Well, in any case, it's just a lot easier to get here a bit early."

"An *hour* early." There was still a certain amount of vexed nostril flaring, but she seemed to reluctantly accept my logic. She stared at the shadows moving inside the hall. "Do the Boy Scouts still exist? I thought they'd all been buggered to death by evil perverted scoutmasters who had groomed them on the Internet."

"You have a very dark view of humanity."

"I get out more than you do."

"Anyway, that's the Girl Guides you're thinking of," I said. She giggled.

Luckily the rain eased off and we were joined a few minutes later by other early birds who queued impatiently for the place to open. As soon as she saw these, Nevada realised I hadn't been kidding. "My god, they're arriving already," she whispered. "I had no idea jumble sales were such a cut-throat business."

"Mind some granny doesn't put an elbow in your eye fighting over a high fashion creation."

"Don't be absurd," she said. Then—"Do you think they'll actually have some high fashion creations?"

"I'm counting on it, to keep you off my back."

About ten minutes before the sale was due to start, the

door opened and a middle-aged man and woman in matching brown and white checked sweaters set up a small table with a coin tray from an old-fashioned cash register on it. By now the line of waiting customers extended down the block, back into the darkness, and there was a certain amount of restlessness manifesting itself, not just from my companion.

Nevada looked at the coin tray and said, "They charge us to get in?"

I laughed. "I thought I was the one who didn't get out much."

"Not to jumble sales," she said, "I don't get out much to jumble sales. Why would I?"

When the door opened I went straight for the records.

There were three boxes of them. Not exactly boxes, though. They were in those purpose-built carrying cases that every self-respecting 1960s record owner had once possessed, red faux leather designs with handles on the lids and cheap tin locks. This was a good sign. It meant the albums had probably come from a decent collection and been properly looked after.

I kneeled down in front of the record cases, as though about to commence an act of worship.

I could feel Nevada standing at my back, as if to shield me from the swarm of jumble sale enthusiasts who were now pouring through the door in a flood. I lifted the first case. It was inordinately heavy and a quick glance inside confirmed my suspicions. It was full of 78s. I shoved it to one side.

"Aren't you going to look through it?" asked Nevada.

"It's all shellac," I said. "We're looking for vinyl."

"I'll take your word for it."

The hall was now packed with people, going at the goods

heaped on the tables like a swarm of locusts. You could feel the heat in the place rising. The second case was stuffed with LPs, so many that I couldn't flip through them, they were that tightly packed. I lifted out a wedge of records and set it to one side. There was now enough clearance for me to flip through the rest. "Shall I look at those?" said Nevada. She indicated the records I'd removed.

"Help yourself." I was already halfway through the first case. It was all classical, by the look of it, mostly Deutsche Grammophon. Nevada finished flipping through her pile and set them down beside me again. I could sense she was bored already. "Why don't you go and check out the other merchandise?" I said. "I saw some shoes over there."

"Shoes?" she said. "Second-hand?"

"Second foot," I said.

"Won't they give me verrucas or planar warts or something?"

"*Plantar* warts," I said. "A small price to pay for a pair of Jimmy Choos, surely?"

"Do you really suppose they've got…" she said, but she was already moving away, into the crowd. I double-checked the pile she'd looked through—all classical—and set it aside. I reached for the third case. It was full of LPs. I took out a handful to give myself manoeuvring room, glancing through them. Jazz; all Dixieland, but jazz nonetheless. Not my cup of tea, but they looked immaculate and would no doubt make some New Orleans fan very happy. I delved into the crate, flipping through the albums. There was enough late Louis Armstrong to choke a horse. Some Acker Bilk. Some Chris Barber.

And suddenly, there it was, in my hands.
Easy Come, Easy Go.

* * *

I stood up, the blood abruptly rushing to my head, and experienced a strange dreamlike swaying. There must have been something in the expression on my face because Nevada saw me from across the room and immediately fought her way back through the crowd to join me. "What is it? What is it? Have you got it?"

I held the album up. The cover was heavy cardboard, the kind they printed in the 1950s, and I could feel the weight of the record inside. It definitely was not a flimsy piece of modern vinyl. It had to be the real thing. Nevada was staring at me. My hands were shaking as I lifted the sleeve and slid the record out.

Two pieces of paper came with it. One was dense with Japanese text. I said, "Shit, shit, shit."

"What's the matter? What's wrong?"

The record itself was in a rice paper inner sleeve. This also was not a good sign. I carefully eased the vinyl out. It was nice and heavy all right, and the label was the proper red and white Hathor design. But in the fine print on it, just barely discernible, was the Jasrac logo.

"What is it?" said Nevada. She could see from my face that something was wrong.

"It's a reissue," I said.

She stared at me as if I'd let her down. In a funny way, I felt that I had. I made myself get back down on the floor and go through the rest of the records, but my heart wasn't in it. I bought the replica album and left the hall with Nevada walking along, uncharacteristically subdued, at my side.

"Why did you buy it?" she said finally.

"It may not be what we're looking for, but it's still a nice record."

"What is it, exactly?"

"A reissue. A replica. A Japanese release from the 1970s."

"Japanese?" she said. "Then he definitely wouldn't be interested."

"Who?"

"My boss." She looked at me. "I feel utterly drained."

"A jumble sale will do that," I said. But I knew exactly what she meant. The adrenalin flood of discovery followed by the bitter and abrupt let-down of utter disappointment.

"And I'm famished," she said. "I want something to eat."

"We could go back to my place and I could cook you something."

"I want something to eat now."

I looked around. It was starting to rain again. "We could find a restaurant."

"Did you hear the word *now*?"

"Well, we could get something and drop in on Tinkler. He lives nearby."

"Won't he mind us just dropping in?"

"Tinkler's life is such that any interruption is welcome."

We ended up buying a selection of pizzas from a minuscule late-night supermarket, with Nevada carefully vetting the ingredients before she put them in the shopping trolley, along with her shoulder bag and a bottle of wine she'd spent ten minutes choosing from the shop's tiny selection. When we got to the checkout I went to take her bag out of the trolley but she snatched it away from me for the second time that evening.

I waited while the sleepy clerk scanned our pizzas and the wine and Nevada counted out the cash to pay him. She let me carry the bag of groceries without protest as we searched for a taxi. Once we found one it took five minutes to reach Tinkler's house, where we stuck the pizzas in the oven and retired upstairs to his listening room. Nevada bundled onto the sofa and sat hunched up with her knees tucked under her chin, her shoulder bag beside her. She looked small, sad, and a little beaten. Tinkler was on fine form, though. He studied our acquisition, chuckling. "So near and yet so far, huh?"

"Why isn't it good enough?" said Nevada.

I looked at her. "What?"

She gestured exhaustedly at the album. "That. Why isn't it good enough? Why does it have to be the original?"

"Ah well, now," said Tinkler. "That's a question that cuts right to the heart of being a collector. If it's not the original it's just not the original and that's that."

"It's crazy," she said.

"It's not entirely crazy," I said. "This is a Japanese pressing, so it will be as good as they could make it, but there are limiting factors. They may not have had access to first-generation master tapes. And for the last track, the vocal with Rita Mae, they wouldn't have had any tapes at all. Because the originals were destroyed. So they must have remastered that from a vinyl copy."

"So someone, somewhere, must have a copy of the record."

"Or a tape of the record," said Tinkler helpfully.

I said, "And then there's the physical aspect."

"Ah, the physical aspect," said Nevada, staring at the ceiling.

"The original pressing had the signatures of Easy Geary and Rita Mae Pollini in the dead wax," I said.

"Really?" said Tinkler. "That would make it a collector's item, all right." He took out the Japanese insert, looked at it briefly, then shoved it back in the sleeve and took out the other piece of paper. "Do you reckon this came from the Unknown Jazz Fan's collection?"

"Actually I do," I said. "Why?"

"Because this is an invoice with his name and address on it." Tinkler looked at me, shaking his head and smiling wistfully. "It's a bit of a shame, isn't it? He isn't unknown anymore. It's the end of an era. It's the end of an enigma. It's the end of an enigma era."

I was about to ask what the guy's name and address was—not that it would mean anything to me—when Tinkler took his dragon box down from the mantelpiece and said, "Shall we?" Nevada suddenly looked up with the first real sign of interest since we'd arrived.

"Shall we what?"

"Nothing," I said hastily, moving towards Tinkler.

But she was alert now, sitting up straight on the sofa. "Nothing what?"

"Put the box back, Tinkler," I said.

He waved a hand at me. "Oh, he's such a prude."

"What is it?" said Nevada. "Is it dope? Here, let me see." Tinkler handed her the box and she opened it. "My god," she said. "Smell that!"

"It's good stuff, all right," said Tinkler proudly. He took the box back and started rolling a joint. "Would you like some?"

"Does the Pope shit in the woods?" said Nevada.

Tinkler chuckled and looked at me. "You're

outnumbered," he said. He licked the cigarette papers and sealed the joint.

"Fine," I said. "Just remember when you're rolling around drooling in your padded cell that I warned you."

"He is so conservative," said Nevada. She accepted the joint from Tinkler, and a light, taking a deep inhalation. After a moment she let the smoke out and said, in a small croaky voice, "My word, that really is something."

Tinkler chuckled again. "Isn't it just?" They swapped it back and forth and the room was soon so full of smoke that any abstention on my part was highly theoretical. After an indeterminate interval Tinkler said, "Hey, what about those pizzas? They must be ready by now."

"Christ yes," said Nevada. "I'm famished."

"I'll go down and serve them up." Tinkler headed for the door.

"I'd better accompany you," said Nevada. "For health and safety reasons." She followed him out and I heard them giggling as they went down the stairs.

Nevada had left her shoulder bag on the sofa. I went over and picked it up. It was strangely heavy. I looked inside and found out why. I took it out.

It sat oddly comfortably in my hand.

But then it *was* a handgun.

7. A NIGHT AT JERRY'S

Jerry's funeral was two days later.

I had phoned Nevada the night before and told her I wouldn't be available for record hunting. To my surprise, she not only accepted this immediately, without any argument or complaint, but also insisted on attending the ceremony herself.

She turned up at my house looking like something out of *Vogue*. French *Vogue* at that. She was wearing a sleeveless black dress, stockings that glistened like dew on a spider web, and a sort of elegant long black wool coat that reached down almost to her ankles. At her throat she wore a grey silk scarf and under it I could see the glint of pearls. Her jaw-dropping beauty, to which I thought I had become immune, was commended to me anew with a clarity that was almost painful; I particularly liked the stockings.

She was carrying a parcel wrapped in dark blue paper. "Here," she said, "this is for you. You need to open it before you go. And put it on."

Our taxi drove us to Putney where we picked up Tinkler, who had also insisted on coming. On one memorable occasion Jerry had sold him a spectacular collection of blues LPs—original black label pressings of Muddy Waters and Bo Diddley on Chess—at a very reasonable price. And Tinkler had never forgotten this. Actually I think memories of the occasion still brought tears to his eyes.

I waited impatiently for him by his front door as he finished getting ready. Tinkler's place was even more of a shambles than usual. I pointed this out to him, shouting up the stairs, and he shouted back in reply, "My sister is coming to visit."

"So you messed your place up specially?"

"My place is in the *process* of becoming *tidy*."

"Good luck with that," I said. I checked the time. "Come on, Tinkler." I could hear tentative squirts of cologne, then the thunder of his footsteps. "Don't run down the stairs," I called. "One funeral this week is all I can handle."

He loomed into view, wearing a navy blue suit and tie; the nearest thing he had to black, I guess.

He was halfway down when he froze on the stairs and stood staring at me. I have to admit, it was quite gratifying.

"Great Scott," he said. "What happened to you?"

"It's an Ozwald Boateng black wool suit with a silk tie from Woodhouse and, let me see, the shirt is a Ralph Lauren linen cutaway, whatever that is. Nevada made sure I was thoroughly apprised of all of this."

Tinkler stared at me. "She bought you that stuff?"

"She apparently went on an epic adventure combing the shops for them. The charity shops, that is."

"Charity shops? She goes into charity shops?"

"Yes. I'm afraid I've created a monster."

"Holy shit."

"Then, Nevada being Nevada, she had everything laundered."

"She did one hell of a job of choosing your size. Did she measure your inside leg?" Tinkler patted me on the shoulder. "Sorry. My mouth's just an open sewer."

"Come on, we'd better get a move on. I wouldn't want to be late."

As he opened the door, he said, "We look like something out of *Reservoir Dogs*."

I said, "We look like something out of *The Blues Brothers*."

Both Nevada and Clean Head shot us looks of impatient reproof as we finally emerged onto the street. Clean Head had obviously been briefed by Nevada about the day's destination. She was dressed sombrely but stylishly in a chic black single-breasted jacket and a white silk blouse with a plunging neckline. I saw Tinkler give her a hastily suppressed double-take. He had even greater difficulty concealing his reaction to Nevada when we climbed into the back of the cab.

"Could you have been any slower?" she demanded. "We're liable to be late." Not much chance of that, I thought. The taxi was already in motion, sweeping towards the main street in a high-speed turn before I could even close the door behind me.

"Oh, for heaven's sake, Tinkler," said Nevada. She leaned forward and straightened his tie, then set to work adjusting his collar. I thought for a moment she might take out a comb and have a go at his hair, or spit onto a handkerchief and clean his face.

But she contented herself with merely working on tie and collar, with a final bit of brisk lapel-straightening to conclude.

All the while she was doing this, Tinkler was having trouble not staring at her legs. I didn't blame him.

* * *

We buried Jerry Muscutt in a vast cemetery in Waltham Abbey beside a particularly busy stretch of motorway, with the endless and unremitting drone of traffic in the distance suggesting that eternal peace might be a big ask around here, or indeed anywhere these days.

After the coffin went into the ground the assembled mourners clustered together, all of us staring at the fresh mound of earth, suddenly at a loss and perhaps experiencing a shared sense of emptiness.

That's what I felt, anyway.

A little black and white dog came bounding towards us and darted in and out of our group, frisking happily. The owner, a small worried-looking man in a yellow windbreaker, hurried after it. He caught the dog. "Come on, Dolly," he said. "No one wants to make a fuss of you here."

He smiled apologetically, not quite looking anyone in the eye, clipped a lead to Dolly's collar and led the dog away.

We left Jerry's graveside and the funeral party began to break up. Nevada and Tinkler and I wandered among the headstones. There seemed to be no end to them. Row after row of markers for the dead. Nevada drifted closer to Tinkler and said in a low voice, "Did you bring the stuff?"

"Oh yes," chortled Tinkler, patting the breast pocket of his jacket.

"What stuff?" I said, although I already had my suspicions.

Nevada turned and looked at me blandly. "I asked your friend Tinkler to help me out with some of that spectacular inflammable contraband he had."

"Inflammable contraband?"

"Just for personal consumption."

I looked at Tinkler, who had the good grace to hang his head sheepishly. "Now *you've* created a monster," I said. I felt a hand on my arm and turned around, a little startled, to see Glenallen Brown and Kempton from the shop standing there.

Kempton, looking a bit embarrassed, handed me a small square of pale blue paper. "See you soon," said Glenallen, and they both hurried off. I glanced at the paper. It was a flyer announcing the reopening of Styli. I remembered hearing that Glenallen had raised the money from somewhere to take over the shop. I was glad it wouldn't be closing. Jerry would have been pleased. I folded the paper and put it in my pocket.

"What now?" said Tinkler.

"We can go back to my place," I said. To my surprise, they both eagerly agreed. The taxi made good time getting back and in just over an hour we were getting out in front of my bungalow. I headed for the front door, taking out my keys and shaking them so the cats would hear and know we were home.

Nevada was behind me and, for some reason, Tinkler was still back at the taxi talking to Clean Head.

Nevada called to him, "It's all right, Tinkler. I've already paid." After a moment he caught up with us. "What were you doing?" said Nevada.

"Just asking her if she wanted to join us."

"What?" I said. "Clean Head? You did what?"

"I invited her in, to join us."

Nevada gave a low, admiring whistle. "You asked her out?"

"I asked her in," said Tinkler, blushing furiously.

"You old dog." Nevada dug an elbow into his side and

winked at him. He looked as pleased as Punch.

"What did she say?" I said.

"What?"

"When you asked her."

"She said she'd love to but she's got a job on."

"She's a busy girl," said Nevada. I opened the front door for her, and the cats came streaking in to join us.

"She said perhaps another time," added Tinkler.

I stood holding the door for Nevada and the cats and then Tinkler to go in. He paused beside me, grinning. He punched my arm jubilantly. "Perhaps another time!"

Nevada was already pouring biscuits for Fanny and Turk by the time I got into the kitchen. She tended to overdo it and spoil them. A fat cat is not a healthy cat. But it wouldn't do them any harm this once. Turk stuck her head into her brimming bowl, unable to believe her luck, and began to eat like a machine. Fanny made a few coy feints, passing her bowl in little trotting semi-circles, and then, protocol observed, settled down to the serious business of crunching away at the brown pile.

Nevada watched them fondly as I went through to find Tinkler sprawled on the sofa in my front room. He smiled at me. "I switched your amps on," he said. "To warm up."

"Good idea."

"And while they're warming up, I'll *skin* up."

Oh Christ, I thought, *why can't they just drink coffee like me?*

Tinkler began to expertly assemble a joint. "Good job old Dolly wasn't a dope-sniffing dog," I said. "Or she would have torn your throat out."

"What?" said Tinkler absently, as he licked the joint to seal it.

"Nothing."

He tucked the joint behind his ear at a rakish angle. "Did you hear what Clean Head said?"

"Yes," I said.

"Another time!" I noticed that in his mind this had moved from the provisional to the definite.

Nevada came in from the kitchen. "I'm famished," she said.

I recognised my cue. I went into the kitchen and took some pasta sauce out of the fridge. I'd made it the previous night: plum tomatoes baked in olive oil and garlic with basil and thyme. I warmed it up and cooked some orecchiette, little ears of dried pasta, in boiling water. I drained the pasta and stirred in the sauce. I didn't have any parmesan but there was a wedge of very good Cornish cheddar languishing in the refrigerator.

I grated pale yellow crescents of cheese over three plates of pasta mounded under the rich red sauce, waited for it to melt, decorated it with bright green dashes of fresh basil, and carried them through to the sitting room.

All this had taken almost twenty minutes, during which time Tinkler had somehow mustered enough restraint not to light the joint, which still jutted jauntily above his ear. It dropped into his pasta while he was eating, though, and Nevada fished it out, scolding him as she wiped it with a paper towel. "I'd better look after this," she said, confiscating it.

"Were those the tomatoes I gave you?" said Tinkler. "In that sauce?"

"Which was delicious, by the way," said Nevada.

"Thank you."

"No, thank you."

"It was largely due to my donation of the tomatoes,"

said Tinkler. "He insisted on taking them all from me. Several kilos."

Nevada looked at him. "What was a devoted junk-food fan like you doing with several kilos of fresh vegetables, Tinkler?"

I said, "Our friend in Wales grows them along with that loco weed you like so much. He thinks it helps to conceal the true nature of his agricultural endeavours."

Tinkler nodded. "And he grows so many of them he always has a problem getting rid of them. So he encloses some tomatoes with each shipment."

"Speaking of the loco weed," said Nevada. She produced the joint, still stained pinkly with tomato sauce and a bit sorry-looking. "Shall we ignite it?"

Tinkler waved his hands in the air. "No, no, not yet. Let me put some music on first."

"While you're still able to move," I said.

"Exactly."

"What shall we listen to?" said Nevada.

"What else?" Tinkler held up the copy of *Easy Come, Easy Go* we'd found at the jumble sale. The Japanese reissue.

"I don't know if I can stand the pain," I said.

"Now, now." Tinkler slipped the record out of the cover. "It will be good for you. Therapeutic."

"I'd like to hear what all the fuss is about," said Nevada.

I took it from Tinkler, slipped the LP out of the inner sleeve. The black vinyl gleamed as I put it on the turntable. I switched on the motor and lowered the arm. The complex insect head of the cartridge kissed the playing surface, the diamond-tipped stylus finding the run-in groove and riding smoothly towards the music. I looked at Tinkler. He was grinning at me.

"Listen to that," he said.

"What?" said Nevada. "I can't hear anything. It's completely silent."

"That's the point," I said. "It means it's a good pressing. On virgin vinyl."

"I'm glad someone around here can lay claim to being a virgin," said Nevada.

Then the music started. It reminded me of those late fifties sessions by Monk and Coltrane with the piano and the saxophone seeming to come from the same place and speak in the same voice, with a perfect shared language. But this had more structural complexity, more apparently unplanned design, like Mingus. It was beautifully recorded.

"It doesn't sound any better than my iPod," said Nevada.

She was still sitting at the table where we'd eaten our lunch. "Come over here," I said impatiently. "Sit on the sofa." She got up and approached, a little warily.

"Where do you want me?"

"Exactly where this opportunistic buffoon has planted himself." I nudged Tinkler and shoved him over so that the spot in the middle of the sofa was free. "Sit here."

"All right."

Nevada sat between us. Her perfume distracted me for a moment and then I said, "Here, lean forward a bit."

"What am I doing?"

"Looking for the sweet spot," said Tinkler. "The perfect place to hear the music. From the point of view of imaging."

"From the point of view of imaging. I see."

"These speakers, his Quad electrostatics, aren't really designed for use as near-field monitors," explained Tinkler.

"No, of course not," said Nevada. "Everyone knows that. Near-field monitors, hah!"

"But if you get just the right placement the imaging is fantastic." This was true.

"Put your head here," I said.

"This is like being at a rather highly regimented orgy," said Nevada. But she leaned forward. "Not that I'd know." She sat patiently yet sceptically listening. "I don't think I can hear anything special," she said.

Tinkler leaned impatiently towards her. "Light that thing, take a few hits and then see if you can't hear anything special."

She duly lit it. After a few moments, and much puffing, Nevada said, "Good lord."

"There? You see?"

"My sweet lord." She moved her head out of the sweet spot, then back in. She let out a low whistle, then turned to give me a sidelong look. Her pupils were dark and enormous. "But you know what," she said. "I think it's just the drugs."

It wasn't just the drugs. I wasn't smoking and I could hear it.

I manoeuvred myself into the sweet spot, jostling her warm thigh against mine, pressing her gently back across the sofa towards Tinkler. "I'm being crushed," he cried. "I'm being crushed against Nevada Warren! For god's sake don't stop."

He and Nevada giggled. Long gurgling giggles. It sounded as if their intellects had already dropped by dozens of IQ points. But they kept smoking.

I leaned forward and listened. It was like I was in the room with the musicians.

"Why don't you roll us another one of those," said Nevada, at length.

"I've got the cigarette papers," said Tinkler. "All I need

is some roach fodder. A business card perhaps?" He looked at Nevada.

"You're not using one of my business cards, sport," she said.

"Oh well, then how about tearing the cover off one of these rare and expensive-looking records?"

I knew he was bluffing, but he still succeeded in putting a twinge of apprehension in me. My precious records. "The cardboard is too heavy for your purposes," I said. I reached in my pocket and found the square of paper Kempton had given me at the funeral. "Use this instead." As I handed it to him I happened to notice that there was writing on the back. It said:

As of midnight tonight the police will allow access to Jerry's house. You can go there first thing tomorrow morning and look through that collection we're selling. You can have first refusal on all the jazz.

Tinkler was flapping his big pale hand in the air, trying to get hold of the paper, which I had snatched back. I fended him off and passed it to Nevada. "Let me have it," he said. "I need to complete assembly of this torpedo."

"Quiet, Tinkler," she said as she read the handwritten message. She lowered the paper and looked at me. "We have to go immediately. Tonight."

I looked at her. "Tonight?"

"At midnight. As soon as the police are gone."

It took three phone calls to track down Kempton, and the keys to Jerry's house. Kempton lived in north London, about half an hour from Jerry's. We arranged for Clean Head to drive us around to his place and collect the keys at half past eleven sharp. I apologised for the ungodly hour, repeated the story we'd cooked up—I was going on holiday, this was my only chance to look at the stuff—a lie that was beginning to take root in my mind as some ghostly semblance of the truth.

I told myself if we found the record, my first order of business would be to indeed go on holiday to celebrate and so it wasn't really a lie at all.

Kempton handed the keys to me with some evident reluctance, despite our earlier conversations on the phone.

He said, "If you find anything you want, just leave it there with a note, all right? Don't take any records away."

"Of course not," I said. Although if I did find *Easy Come, Easy Go* nothing on earth would stop me taking it immediately into safe keeping and removing it from the premises. But equally, if I did find the record, I had every intention of seeing that it was paid for in full. Or, rather, that Nevada paid for it in full. I took the keys, warm from the long time they'd spent clutched in Kempton's reluctant hand, and headed for the taxi.

He watched me unhappily from his doorstep as I climbed on board and Clean Head started the engine.

Sitting beside me in the back, I could feel Nevada literally quivering with excitement. "Did you get the keys?" she said.

"Yes. Of course."

"Tally ho!"

The taxi roared through the dark streets towards Primrose Hill. All the way Nevada drummed her fingers impatiently on the window, staring out. As if in a continuation of the day's funeral theme she was dressed in a black roll-neck sweater, black ski pants and all-black Converse sneakers.

The drumming of fingertips was winding me up. "By

the way," I said, "what's with the ninja assassin get-up?"

She stopped drumming and turned to look at me. "You said it was a dirty business grubbing through these records. I've dressed for dirty business."

"You look like a cat burglar." She turned away again, sulking. "A very high class cat burglar," I added. This seemed to mollify her.

We were making good time, as per Clean Head's usual driving, and only hit traffic once, on Belsize Road in St John's Wood. I was worried about getting to Jerry's before the police had a chance to clear out, but even though we were there at fifteen minutes to midnight, they were already evidently long gone. The only sign of them was a piece of blue and white police tape hanging limply from the doorframe.

"Maybe they knocked off early," I said

"Not too early I hope," said Nevada. "I'd hate to think anyone had a chance to ransack the place before we did."

She paid and the taxi hummed off into the night, leaving us standing on the pavement. We looked at the house. It was a thin, handsome semi-detached Georgian. The front garden was covered with cracked concrete, a slender but flourishing plum tree rising triumphantly from a dark patch of earth in the middle. The wrought-iron front gate creaked as we opened it. Apart from the distant buzz of traffic, it was eerily silent. I paused as we stepped through the gateway. There was the sudden sound of footsteps.

I looked around, but it was just a his-and-hers pair of sports freaks out jogging.

Jogging in the middle of the night.

They ran along the pavement outside the gate, not even glancing our way, their panting breath just audible.

I watched them go as we walked up the narrow stone steps to a narrow green front door. On either side of it the police tape hung down. It looked like it had been cut through the middle. By the police themselves, I hoped. I sorted through the keys, jingling them on the ring, until I found the right one to open the door. It seemed strange not to have a rush of cats accompanying us as we entered.

It was dark and cool and damp inside. "I can't see anything," said Nevada.

I switched on the light, to reveal a scene of chaos. The small front entry hall, staircase leading up from it, and room to the right were all completely covered with LPs. Or at least they had been before the police had begun their crime scene investigation. A narrow pathway had been cleared through the hall, and up the stairs, with the records shoved to one side. I picked up one album. There was a size 12 boot print on it.

"Our British police," I said. "Aren't they wonderful?" In fairness, though, it was almost impossible to move in the place without stepping on a record. They were piled everywhere in toppled heaps like frozen waves. "It's like sand dunes," I said.

"Vinyl dunes," said Nevada. We looked around at the apparently endless mess. It appeared an impossible task. "Well, let's get cracking," she said. Under her jauntiness I already sensed an edge of despair. She looked at me. "Where should we start?"

"Right here, I guess." I crouched down and commenced looking through the records starting with those nearest the door and working my way in. "Luckily I remembered to wear my crate-diving shoes. I mean crate-digging. You've got me doing it now."

"It's more like diving," said Nevada, "the way you launch yourself at them."

She went off to explore the house and I set to work, pacing myself. Even with the right footwear, grovelling around on the floor like this for half the night would prove pretty taxing on the muscles in my legs and my lower back.

And half the night looked like an optimistic estimate.

I moved quickly through the records, checking the covers then stacking them in neat ranks against the wall, out of the way. A few had been badly mangled by people, presumably cops, treading on them. But most had escaped unscathed.

The records, at least those near the door, were all proving to be classical. Mostly on smaller European labels like Hungaroton and Supraphon. The light in the hallway wasn't great, coming from one dim bulb in a floral glass bowl suspended from the ceiling, moths battering it as I worked. Nevada came back down from the upper levels of the house and perched on the steps, watching me. She was showing uncharacteristic levels of patience.

I reached the staircase and started working my way up them, step by step, going through the records and stacking them neatly. Nevada retreated to the landing above and sat there, watching me again, feet dangling, her shoulder bag squeezed between her legs. There was a fluorescent tube affixed above the stairs and the light was better here. I sorted through the records quickly and efficiently. She stayed put as I moved up towards her. By the time I was working beside her legs, my chin on a level with her knees, I had reached the last of the records on the stairs.

We looked at each other.

"Nothing?" she said.

"Not yet."

She sighed. I said, "I'd better go back downstairs and work through the rest of the ground floor."

"All right." She remained sitting disconsolately at the top of the stairs, drumming her heels, as I went back down and started again. I finished checking the hallway, the whole place becoming gratifyingly more orderly and accessible as I stacked the records neatly, and I worked my way through the hallway into the front room.

This was a sitting room with an ornate fireplace, which had seen frequent use by Jerry if the set of fire tools, heaps of ash and large box of kindling were anything to go by.

I pulled the curtains closed and switched on a desk lamp that had been set up on the mantelpiece, to supplement the feeble light from the ceiling fixture. It was cold in the house, the heating not surprisingly having been switched off, but I was sweating from my exertions.

The records in here were, at least, getting more interesting. They were classical still, but some collectable labels—RCA and Mercury. I flicked through them more slowly. I found a copy of the Mercury Living Presence stereo pressing of Gunther Schuller's *Seven Studies on Themes of Paul Klee*. It was in wonderful shape and I set it happily aside. If nothing else, the night's mission had yielded this.

Nevada came running through, as though she had a sixth sense. "Have you found something?" she said excitedly.

"Yes. But not what we're looking for." I handed her the album.

She set her shoulder bag down and accepted the record, studying it unhappily. "I didn't think you listened to classical music." She handed it back to me.

"Occasionally they let me up to the big house," I said. "Providing I remember to wipe my boots."

"Whatever that's supposed to mean."

"How did you know I'd found something?"

"I heard you stop flipping." That made sense. She looked around. "How much longer do you think you'll be?"

It was a small room but the floor, a sofa and two armchairs were virtually covered with records. "Quite some time," I said.

"I think I'll continue snooping."

"Good idea." Her impatient presence in the room was already making the search more difficult. Also, she was standing in my light, and her dark angular shadow shrouded the pile of records I was inspecting. Nevada picked up her shoulder bag and went back out again. I resumed flipping through the records. I appeared to have exhausted the seam of classical and I was now finding vocalists and jazz. A distant beat of excitement started up inside me.

I found an excellent run of early Reprise Sinatra albums that would gladden the heart of some collector. I made a mental note to look out for anything with arrangements by Johnny Mandel or Robert Farnon. Then I was on to the jazz. It was all from roughly the right period and the excitement began to grow.

Suddenly Nevada was in the doorway again. "Look at this," she said excitedly. She was holding a long, thin white cylinder with a smooth, curved head, clutching it in a two-handed grip like a lightsaber. It took me a moment to realise what it was. "Oh Jesus," I said.

"*En garde*," declared Nevada, holding the dildo like a duellist flourishing a rapier. She advanced on me and I took a step back. She cackled.

"Nevada," I said, shading my eyes from the sight of the object. It appeared to be made of ivory and now that I had identified its function I realised it was enormous. "For Christ's sake…"

"Look at the size of the thing," she said, waving it around admiringly. "And it's not at all flexible. Rigid is the word. I mean, can you imagine?"

"I'd rather not. Please…"

"What's the matter?"

"Just put it back wherever you found it."

She went over and set it down on its base on the mantelpiece beside the lamp. It sat there, stable and balanced, pointing up at the ceiling. *Maybe it's purely decorative*, I thought forlornly.

Nevada stood admiring it. She said, "Isn't it magnificent?"

"It's loathsome."

"Why?"

"It's made of ivory. It's from an endangered species."

"Yes, because that's what really bugs you about it." She began to move it around on the mantelpiece. When she was satisfied with its position she began to move the lamp beside it. I saw what she was up to. At the new angle, with the lamp shining on it, it cast a monstrous diagonal shadow right across the room.

"I can't work with that thing looming over me."

She grinned at me. "Feel threatened? Inadequate?" But she laid it down on its side on the mantelpiece, with a resonant clunk, and headed for the door.

"Where are you going?"

"Further explorations beckon," she said and scampered off again—this was more fun than a clothes rail full of second-hand Dolce and Gabbana. I resumed looking through the records. The room was becoming more orderly and inhabitable as I sorted them. I'd worked out where the piles of jazz were and I was going through those first.

I found half a dozen Woody Herman albums on CBS, from the period in the 1960s when Duško Gojković was playing trumpet with the band. They were in beautiful condition and I put them aside with the Gunther Schuller. My spirits were lifting both with the growing order of the room and with my discoveries. What had seemed a Herculean task was swiftly diminishing to human proportions and as I rescued the small neat house from the chaos that had come over it, I felt I was doing something for Jerry.

Nevada came back in. This time she was holding some neatly folded sheets of paper, pale blue and white. She was reading them as she entered. "I've found some love letters," she said, "and they're *torrid*."

"Have you no shame?"

"I'm sure Jerry wouldn't mind me reading them. He seems like one hell of a guy. And *busy*. Obviously very popular, too. Inspired quite the hot epistle."

"Don't feel obliged to commence any excerpts."

She sat down in one of the armchairs that I had cleared and studied the letters with fascination. "You've been turning off the lights as you go?" I said. She nodded absently, enrapt with whatever she was reading. I was far from convinced she'd actually heard me. "You remembered what we said?" I said. "To only have lights on in a room when we're actually in it?"

"Mmmm."

"Because we agreed we didn't want the house lit up like a beacon in the middle of the night. What with the police having only departed and it being a murder scene and all."

She looked up from the letter and stared at me distractedly. "What was that?"

"I was saying, you did remember to turn off the lights? You didn't leave upstairs ablaze with illumination?"

"No," she said, setting the letters aside. "Quiet." She was looking away from me now. "What was *that*?"

Then I heard it, too. A rattling from the far end of the house.

We looked at each other. It was now about three in the morning and London was dead and quiet around us. The night beyond the windows was silent except for the distant murmur of a passing car. Nevada got up from her chair, took a step towards the door, then froze.

The sound again. A metallic rattling. She looked at me. The rattling was followed by a brisk scraping sound. By now I recognised what we were hearing. The rattling had been a doorknob being turned. The scraping was the sound of a key in a lock.

Someone was coming in at the back of the house, through the door from the garden.

I moved to the window and opened the curtain a crack. The street was quiet and dead. There was no sign of any police vehicles. It suddenly hit home to me that this was the place where someone had killed Jerry.

The scraping stopped then started again.

Nevada was looking frantically around the room. I knew what she was thinking. She'd left her shoulder bag upstairs.

She looked at me.

I reached down to the fireplace and grabbed a heavy pair of brass tongs. "I'm going to turn out the light," I whispered. She nodded and turned and seized the long cylinder of ivory off the mantelpiece. It suddenly looked like a solid, lethal weight in her hands.

"When I give the word, turn it back on."

The scraping stopped as the lock popped open.

I turned off the desk lamp and then the overhead bulb at the switch by the door. We were plunged in darkness just as, far down the hall, the door creaked open.

There was a pause and a long strange silence. I felt the shadowed weight of the house all around me. The door creaked slowly shut again and then there were footsteps, moving slowly from the back of the house towards us.

I stood tensely in the darkness. I couldn't see a thing but I could sense Nevada standing at my side. My heart was thudding in my ears. My chest felt like someone had sewn it into a shirt that was too tight.

The footsteps were coming down the hallway. They were getting closer. I sensed the presence of the walker through the wall of the room, as if I glimpsed his shape on an X-ray. The footsteps got closer. They reached the open door of this room and stopped.

I tried not to breathe.

My heart was beating so loudly I thought it could be heard. Someone stood filling the space of the doorway. The cool darkness flowed all around us. Somewhere, miles away, a dog barked. A floorboard creaked. The figure moved towards us. I remembered the plan. I raised the fire tongs in my right hand, high in the darkness above my head and snarled, "Now!"

Nevada hit the switch and light blazed all around us.

Glenallen Brown was standing in the doorway, mouth open and eyes wide. He was holding a bunch of keys in his hand and gaping at us. He might well have gaped. I was now clutching the tongs like a baseball player preparing to swing. Nevada was holding the ivory dildo high, ready to strike.

"Right," he said, looking from Nevada to me. "Right… Okay…"

Two hours later, with no sign yet of dawn in the dark sky, we waited outside the house for our taxi to come. "Did you see the way I handled him?" said Nevada. "I *owned* him."

"Yes, the charm offensive did cheer him up, particularly in contrast to our earlier attempt to smash his brains out."

"There was never any chance of us smashing his brains out. And what was he doing there anyway, turning up in the middle of the night without warning?"

"Kempton must have called him after we collected the keys. I could see he was getting cold feet about our whole nocturnal foray here." I looked back at the house. "So he called Glenallen."

"What an extraordinary name. It makes him sound like a Scottish golf course."

"Anyway, he obviously couldn't sleep for worrying about how many records I was stealing."

She looked at me. Fast-moving shadows approached across the street. But it was just another pair—or perhaps the same pair—of fanatical late-night joggers.

Pre-dawn joggers now.

They ran past, on the opposite side of the road. Nevada said, "Do you really think that's what he thought? That you'd do that? That *we'd* do that? Steal from him?"

I watched the joggers disappear into the distance. "He

obviously couldn't stand the possibility, and since he had a spare set of keys he decided he had to come and see what was going on."

"He was ever so nice about it."

I nodded. "I think he felt bad for not trusting me."

"Well, anyway he was very decent. Saying you could take all those away and pay for them later." She nodded at my bag full of LPs. Unfortunately *Easy Come, Easy Go* was not among them. She must have read my mind because she said, "You couldn't have missed it, could you?"

"Shall we go back and look through them all again?"

"Seriously, though. Could you have missed it?"

"No." I shook my head. I suddenly felt empty and profoundly exhausted. "It wasn't there." The sound of a diesel engine puttered loudly in the bare, quiet street, and headlights swept across us. It was a black cab with a familiar figure at the wheel. I wondered how much we were paying her. We climbed into the back, me carrying the records and Nevada with her shoulder bag.

It was cold in the taxi and we huddled together on the back seat. Outside it was misty and the streetlights passed us in blurs and streaks. "I was impressed with your reflexes," she murmured, her voice low and sleepy.

"Likewise."

"I always wanted to brandish a dildo," she said. She chuckled softly and snuggled against me. The taxi purred through the quiet, misted streets. Sitting there on the big back seat with her at my side, I felt like a baby in a cradle. Nevada went to sleep with her head on my shoulder, snoring gently.

Clean Head dropped me at my house and then drove off, conveying Nevada to wherever she was when she wasn't with me. The Connaught Hotel, or Castle Dracula perhaps. I rubbed my eyes and yawned as I opened the front door. No sign of the cats, but then I had never come home at this time before in their experience and they were nothing if not sticklers for tradition. This sort of unprecedented dawn arrival would probably meet with strong feline disapproval.

I shut the door and wandered into the living room, flicking on lights. Turk looked up at me sleepily from a chair and Fanny was lolling on the sofa. I set the records on the floor and sat down beside her. I leaned back and stared vacantly at the quiet room, too tired to go to bed. A pale pink light was spreading over the sky outside. It was quietly beautiful.

Then I noticed something on the coffee table. It was the cover of the jumble sale *Easy Come, Easy Go* reissue, propped up where Tinkler had left it. And I remembered the record itself was still on the turntable.

I went over and put it back in its sleeve, then returned to the sofa and studied the cover. I slid the record inside, and as I did so two pieces of paper fell out. One was the insert printed for the album, with sleeve notes in Japanese. The other was an invoice.

I remembered what Tinkler had said that night. "It's a bit of a shame, isn't it? He isn't unknown anymore."

Finally we knew who the Unknown Jazz Fan was.

The invoice was in German. It was from a record store in Frankfurt called Jumpin' Jive. I had almost said to Tinkler that the customer's name on it wouldn't mean anything to us. But I was wrong.

I recognised his name.

He'd smoked a cigar in my garden, many months ago. My uninvited visitor who had gone walkabout from the

Abbey. The architect Tomas Helmer.

The man who had fallen off his own roof, with fatal consequences.

I stared out the window, at the garden where I'd met him. I could hear in my memory the music that had been playing that day. I could smell his cigar. I looked at the invoice again.

Under his name was an address in Richmond.

The house where he had died.

How do you manage to fall off your own roof, anyway? I wondered. Then I put out some biscuits for the cats and went to bed.

8. THE BOOT FAIR

The address on the invoice was a quiet street in Richmond overlooking a strip of parkland that led down to the river. It was a big white house set back from the road behind a dense green hedge. A fence of black iron railings rose from the waist-high white wall and ran along to join a tall wrought-iron gate big enough to let a bus through. Well, a minibus.

We didn't have any kind of bus. We were on foot. The gate was open and we walked right in, crunching on the pale gravel that led up to the house. The garden was thick with conifer trees and they shadowed the driveway. As soon as we entered, it was like we'd left London behind. It was quiet and cool and green and a little otherworldly.

I looked at the house and estimated its worth at many millions. That wouldn't make it unique in this neighbourhood. Mick Jagger lived around here, or so Tinkler never tired of telling me.

"Nice gaff," said Nevada.

We pressed the doorbell and somewhere deep in the house it rang and rang and rang. We looked at each other.

"No one home," said Nevada.

"We can't just give up," I said.

"Remind me why we're here?"

We wandered back down onto the driveway. There was no car in sight but a ramp led down to a garage with twin doors, which looked like it could easily conceal a fleet of vehicles. I said, "For months I've seen signs of this guy's record collection turning up, here and there, unmistakeable. And it's been great stuff. The records were like traces of gold being washed downstream from the mother lode and I was like the wily prospector, squinting upstream and looking for the source of the riches."

"Though perhaps over-clad with pelts," said Nevada. "I could easily buy into this whole folksy woodsman fantasy of yours. Keep going."

I stared up at the pale house in the cool shadows of the trees. "Well, this is it. The mother lode." Somewhere in there was an amazing record collection, or what was left of it.

She started to say something, but it was drowned out by the ghastly screaming of a drill.

"Someone is at home," I said.

We went down the steps and along the paved path, around the corner to the side and the back of the house. At the rear there was a wide paved area leading to an outdoor swimming pool, now covered with a sagging, leaf-strewn sheet of dark blue plastic. By the back door of the house was a pinewood table and chairs, obviously situated for al fresco dinners on a summer evening.

Right now, though, the table and chairs were covered with a variety of greasy-looking tools. Propped up against the wall of the house was a metal ladder, and halfway up the ladder was a young woman.

She was coming down, descending slowly with something in her hand. She looked to be in her twenties. She had pale skin and long red hair, tied back in a scarf. She wore blue denim dungarees, a white t-shirt, and sandals.

The woman noticed us as she was reaching the bottom rung, but she didn't seem unduly surprised, and certainly not alarmed.

I saw she was holding an electric drill in her hand, the kind that's powered by a battery pack in the base of the handle. She set the drill down on the table among the other tools and gave us a half smile.

"Hello," I said. "We tried knocking at the front door."

"I wouldn't have heard," said the woman. She lifted the drill again. "I was up there, cleaning the gutters."

"With a drill?" said Nevada.

"Some masterminds did some work up there last year. Some repairs to the chimney." She looked upwards. "They had to mix some cement. And when they finished mixing it they had some left over, in fact quite a lot left over, and they had to get rid of it somewhere. Guess where?"

"They poured it into the gutters."

She nodded. "That's right, they poured it into the gutters. It was just liquid enough to spread through the entire system. And just solid enough to set completely before it could drain out, with relatively little damage, at ground level." She smiled at us. "It takes real talent to fuck something up so completely."

I said, "I think I know those guys who worked on your roof. They once renovated the boiler on my estate." She turned her smile on me.

"So, you don't live here?" asked Nevada, getting to the point.

"Nope. Just getting the concrete out of the gutters."

"And the owner isn't in residence?"

"The owner is dead," said the young woman.

"So I heard," I said. "He fell off the roof." I looked up the high white walls to the roof. It was covered with flat green tiles and it looked an awfully long way up.

"That's right. I'm working for his wife. Ex-wife." She looked up at the house. "I guess she's the owner now. She hired me to try and sort things out. If those gutters aren't fixed soon there's going to be problems with water coming through the roof."

I hated to think of that. The poor records would be ruined. I said, "We would like to speak to her. The ex-wife."

"She isn't around."

"Do you know when she will *be* around?" said Nevada. Even an expert might have said she sounded polite.

I said, "The thing is, we're interested in acquiring his record collection."

The woman laughed. "Well, you're out of luck. She's already got rid of half of it." Half of it, I thought. My heart began to hammer.

"She's sold it off?" I said.

The woman laughed again. "Oh, hell no. She's been giving it away. For free. That's her way of getting back at him. I get the impression it wasn't a dream marriage."

"Apparently not," said Nevada.

The woman nodded. "So she's taking his priceless collection that he scoured the world for and is dumping it at charity shops. Nifty piece of revenge, huh?"

"But she's still got some of the collection to dispose of? The records, I mean. The ex-wife."

"I guess so." The woman shrugged. She lifted the drill and squeezed the trigger. It buzzed to life. She was ready to get back to work.

"Well, listen," I said. "Could you please ask her to get in touch with me?" I took a business card out of my pocket and handed it to her. "I'll be happy to save her any more trips to the charity shop."

"I think she kind of likes them," said the woman. "The trips." She turned to the ladder, sandals slapping as she stepped onto the lowest rungs.

"Aren't those things slippery when you get up there?" said Nevada.

"When I get up there I take them off."

She disappeared up the ladder and we turned and walked back up the steps to the shadowed driveway.

As we walked out the front gate and into the road, we moved apart to let a jogger pass us on the pavement. A woman, serious-looking and sweaty. "What now?" said Nevada. She took my arm and we walked down the hill towards the river.

I said, "Have you ever heard of a boot fair?"

At four o'clock the next morning the alarm went off. The cats flinched at the unaccustomed noise, never before heard in their furry little lifetimes, and reluctantly stirred and jumped off the bed as I got up.

Sitting stunned and blank in a hot bath for the next half hour brought me to something resembling full consciousness and a cup of real coffee finished the job. The cats fled at the sound of the grinder, of course, but I felt I owed myself at least this. I made enough to fill a thermos. It gurgled happily and grew warm to the touch as I poured the fragrant coffee into it.

Out the window I imagined I could see the first hint of pink tendrils spreading across the sky. I was beginning to warm to the whole dawn patrol aspect of today's mission.

I was just tightening the lid on the thermos when the doorbell rang.

Nevada was standing there. She gave me a malevolent look and said, "I'm out of my mind."

"Well, you're in the right place for expensive psychiatric care." I nodded at the elegant white outline of the Abbey, just beginning to make itself seen against the dark sky. She sprawled in a chair, setting her bag down between her feet. She rolled her head and looked at me. Her face was pale and there were lilac shadows under her eyes. She looked like an undead beauty in some erotic Euro horror flick.

"Where are the kittens?"

I hadn't seen them since they'd fled the grinder. "Through there, I think. They've probably gone back to bed."

"Sensible girls." She closed her eyes and for a moment I thought she'd gone to sleep herself. Then she sighed and began to rise, laboriously and bonelessly from the chair. "Well, I suppose we'd better get going." She slung her bag over her shoulder and headed for the door. I followed her, picking up the thermos. She glanced at it.

"Coffee?" she said.

"Yes."

"The proper stuff?"

"Yes."

"Good."

The boot fair, or car boot sale, or—if you were American, car trunk sale— was being held at a green field just off the

A205 where the Mortlake Road becomes the Kew Road. It was evidently a sports field that someone didn't mind hundreds of cars being parked on. Maybe the meandering muddy ruts in the turf made athletic confrontations all the more piquant. Clean Head dropped us at the main road and we walked up to the entrance gate. There were already a dozen people there.

"You see?" I said. "Early birds."

"Early vultures," said Nevada. She was still more than a little pissed off.

"If we'd left it any later we would have been swamped with competition."

"It looks like we're going to be swamped anyway." She was looking unhappily at her boots, which were squelching on the wet grass, mud oozing up around them.

"I told you to dress sensibly."

"For me, this is sensibly. And anyway you didn't quite convey the backwoods nightmare which lay in store."

"This isn't the backwoods. It's Kew." We were at the gate now. "There it is," I said. The stall holders were busy setting out their wares, taking stuff out of the boots of their cars and loading it onto a rickety variety of folding tables. There was one table covered with boxes of records. It was situated at the far end of the field. "As soon as the gate opens, we have to get way over there," I said.

I bought tickets from a sullen man in a day-glo yellow vest and then turned and walked back towards the road.

"Where are we going?" said Nevada. As we walked away from the field, people were beginning to pour in from all directions. A flock of early vultures. She glanced nervously over her shoulder at them as we walked past.

"Won't we lose our place in line?"

"We're not going to wait in line," I said. She glanced at me in surprise then grinned.

"A bad boy. I like that."

Beside the sports field there was another field, consisting of allotments used by the local gardening enthusiasts. Access to this was through a narrow alleyway which was open to the public. I had also noticed several places on the far side of the cultivated area, adjacent to our objective, where it was possible to cross into the sports field. We made our way gingerly across square plots of vegetables and flowers. "Don't step on any cabbages," I said. We came to a row of low green sheds. Behind them was a wire fence. Beyond that was the field and the boot fair. The fence was a low, half-hearted effort and at several points it was quite possible to simply step over it.

"Excellent," said Nevada. She looked at me. The smudges under her eyes were fading now and colour had come into her cheeks. "Commendably devious." She started towards the fence but I caught her by the elbow.

She looked at me in puzzlement.

"We have to wait," I said.

"Wait for what?"

"Opening time." I checked my watch. "Ten minutes to go."

She sighed. "What is the point of us sneaking in here if we aren't going to get in there *early*?"

I indicated the stewards patrolling the field in their day-glo vests. They were escorting a cute young blonde woman off the site. I could see she was trying to sweet-talk them and making absolutely no headway. If they would kick *her* out, what would they do to me?

I said, "If we go in there early they'll chuck us out. And they might not let us back in." At the gate the blonde was propelled off the premises, the crowd watching her departure with unabashed hatred.

"Plus we'd attract the opprobrium of the crowd," said Nevada, watching with keen interest. "So what's the point of being here? Where we're standing. Where you dragged us."

"The point is that when it is time to go in, we can just hop the fence here and, oh, look what happens to be right there on the other side."

"Ah," said Nevada. The table with the records was directly in front of us. It would take us about three seconds to get there. "There is method in your madness after all." She seemed grudgingly impressed. "Let's drink some coffee while we're waiting."

"Sorry."

"What do you mean, sorry?"

"I left it with Clean Head."

"Oh, for fuck's sake," said Nevada.

"Poor girl looked like she needed it."

"That 'poor girl' has got me paying her approximately the gross fiscal output of a small nation for the privilege of chauffeuring us on this early-morning jaunt. And now she's also got the fucking coffee." These and other complaints filled the time and before I knew it, it was six o'clock and time to cross the fence.

I climbed over it, holding a strand of wire down for Nevada, then both of us were running to beat the sudden influx of customers, who were like a stampede. Nevada disappeared into the throng, presumably in search of high-fashion bargains, and I made a beeline for the table with the records.

Half of them were in cardboard boxes on the ground and I was glad I'd got to these early. Within a few hours the damp from the earth would have soaked up through the cardboard and begun to attack the records. It wouldn't have much effect on the vinyl, but all the covers would soon be write-offs.

I squatted in front of the boxes, comfortable in my dawn patrol crate-digging shoes, and started flipping. The first box had no jazz, just a lot of European-inflected easy listening, including a fairly astonishing number of LPs by Nana Mouskouri.

I made a mental note to go back and look for the one on Philips produced by Quincy Jones, and hurried on to the next box.

This was full of budget classical records. Nothing there for me. There were two more boxes. The next one was mostly twelve-inch singles and hip-hop. Onwards.

As soon as I began flipping through the last box I knew this one had come from the Unknown Jazz Fan. Or rather Tomas. Or rather his wife. It was all jazz, all immaculate. But it was uniformly New Orleans and Dixieland. Laudable stuff, but not my cup of tea.

Too early, pre-swing. There wasn't even any Fats Waller. I flipped past the last record and reluctantly accepted the truth.

It wasn't here.

I moved back to the first box to look for the Quincy Jones Nana Mouskouri opus—was it called *The Girl From Athens*?—when something hit me so hard it knocked me off my feet. I found myself lying on my back on the damp grass, winded and staring up at the thug who had done it.

He had shoved me aside and now he was going through the box with intent mechanical speed. He had close-cropped blonde hair and wore a brown rough-woven sweater, khaki combat trousers and some expensive-looking running shoes. His big shoulders rose and fell as he flipped through the records. He was large and burly, built like an athlete. And he had an athlete's physical arrogance.

My shock and incomprehension were now giving way to a murderous rage. I struggled to my knees and began to rise from the ground. A hand caught my arm and helped me up. Nevada was standing there. I said, "That fucker knocked me over." My voice was shaking.

"I know. I saw." The blonde hulk finished looking through the box and turned and walked swiftly away from us. He hadn't found anything, anyway.

Now that I was on my feet I was incandescent with rage. Watching him go, I said, "I'd like to…" I fell silent. I'd been meaning to say "put a bullet in his head" but I decided I'd better not, for all sorts of reasons. Nevada looked at me.

"Well, don't you want to finish looking through that box?"

"I already had," I said. "I was just going back to double-check on something by Nana Mouskouri."

"Is that the girl with the glasses?"

9. INTERLUDE

To my surprise, when we got back to my house Nevada dismissed the cab and came in with me. "I thought you were knackered," I said, as we opened the front door.

"Delightful expression, that."

"I thought you'd want to crash." I walked into the sitting room with her. She looked around the place, and then looked at me.

"I thought I could crash here."

For an instant you could have heard a pin drop but then Fanny emerged scrabbling from under an armchair where she'd wedged herself and came to join us, emitting a series of ingratiating squeaks. Nevada instantly dropped to her knees. "Oh look who's here! Aren't you lovely? Yes you are. Shall we rub your chin? Yes we'll rub your chin. We'll rub it. Where's your sister? Not that we don't love you, but where's your sister?"

"Would you like some coffee?" I said. I was keenly disappointed that the cat had appeared just when she had. I felt like some moment of monumental importance had come and gone and I'd blinked and missed it.

"No thanks," said Nevada, rubbing Fanny's head. "Coffee will wake me up. I want to get a couple of hours sleep. Do you mind?" She shot me a look.

"No, no," I said. "It's just through…"

"Through here," she said. "Right. Thanks. Wake me in a couple of hours." She walked through to the bedroom, Fanny following her. I stood in the sitting room feeling abandoned, conflicted, exhilarated and a number of other things I couldn't even put a name to.

"Right," I said, "I'll just wait here and, and, uh, and…"

The bedroom door closed.

"I'll wake you in a couple of hours," I said to the closed door.

The next two hours may not have been the longest of my life but they were certainly contenders. I busied myself making lunch, then tried to read, which was impossible, and ended up cleaning the kitchen, then tidying the living room, then sorting out my recently acquired LPs. Finally, when two hours had passed, virtually to the second, I went and knocked gently on the bedroom door. There was no reply, so I opened it quietly and looked in.

Nevada's clothes had been unceremoniously piled in a chair.

She was sprawled on the bed, under the quilt. One bare arm was flung out across the covers, the other tucked under her face on the pillow. The two cats were on the bed with her, happily curled up close beside her as if this was standard procedure. Together they made a jigsaw puzzle of warm, sleeping bodies.

I lowered myself to sit gingerly on the edge of the bed. Nevada shifted slightly as the mattress moved with my weight.

She turned her face to me and opened one sleepy eye. "Hello," she murmured. Then she closed the eye and, to all intents and purposes, went back to sleep.

I sat there for a moment then reached out and touched her bare shoulder and gave it the most gentle of shakes. Her skin was warm. I could smell her scent in the bedroom. She stirred lazily at my touch and rolled over and looked at me, both eyes open now. The cats rolled with her, keeping themselves luxuriously curved against the contours of her body. She smiled up at me. "Time to get up?" she said.

I cleared my throat, "You said to…"

One of her hands drifted up and fell lightly on my shoulder, moving to my neck. It rested there for a moment and then seemed to apply just the slightest pressure. I wasn't sure whether I had imagined this or not, but nonetheless I leaned forward, moving my face down towards hers.

Then the doorbell rang.

The sound caused both the cats to jump off the bed and flee as though pursued by demons. They raced out of the room and Nevada and I stared at each other. The doorbell rang again, then again, then again. I rose from the bed, feeling a vertiginous sense of unreality. This couldn't actually be happening. I walked out in the hall where the cats were waiting tensely, watching me, and went to the front door. I opened it.

Standing there was Stinky.

"Hey there, hipster!" he said, grinning at me. Some distant corner of my brain tried to decide if this was some would-be catchphrase he was trying to popularise. He stepped past me, into the house.

"Stinky," I said.

Perhaps there was something in my voice, or my eyes,

because he stopped dead and gave me an odd look. He said, "You weren't busy, were you?" I noted the presumptive use of the past tense.

I glanced outside. The plant pot wasn't disturbed. "You didn't look for the keys then?" I said. "And try to let yourself in?"

"I always ring first," he said virtuously.

There was a movement from the direction of the bedroom and Nevada wandered out, dishevelled and sleepy, wearing one of my baggy t-shirts. She peered at us and then said, "Oh, it's just him," and went back in.

But that glimpse of her, emerging tousled from my bedroom, was enough to cause Stinky to rock back on his heels as if from a physical blow. He looked at me, rendered, for the moment at least, speechless. "Look, Stinky," I said. "This isn't a good time." I stepped back to the door and held it open wide. "If you don't mind…"

Stinky shook his head, like a prize fighter shaking off a punch, and then turned and left without a word. I closed the door behind him and sighed. For a long moment I stood in the hallway, a man becalmed, then I went back into the bedroom.

Nevada was in the bed again, the cats curled up beside her. She even looked like she had gone back to sleep. I had an eerie, but by no means unpleasant, jolt of déjà vu.

It was as though the clock had been set back.

I sat beside her on the bed again. She stirred and the cats moved with her, clinging to her body. I reached down and put my hand on her warm bare shoulder and left it there. She half rolled over and lifted a hand towards my face. I moved down to meet it, towards her face. She turned to me, eyes closed and mouth open.

The doorbell rang.

The cats leaped off the bed again in a scandalised convulsion. The jangling clamour of the doorbell repeated itself, frenzied and idiotic. I stared down into Nevada's face but she wouldn't open her eyes. I didn't blame her.

She rolled over and I thought I heard her sigh. Her body seemed to shrink under the covers. The doorbell continued its mad merry pealing.

I got up off the bed and, moving like a man wading through slowly setting cement, went to the door and opened it.

Tinkler was standing there, holding a shopping bag. He looked a little anxious. "I was beginning to think you weren't in," he said. "I was ringing and ringing," he added. "Have your listening habits finally rendered you deaf?" He brushed past me and walked into the house. "Or maybe it's incessant acts of onanism. Wait a minute, that only makes you blind." I turned to him and tried to say something, but found I had temporarily lost the power of speech.

The cats were greeting Tinkler, wheeling happily around his ankles. "It's the twins," he said. "Hello!" He turned to look at me, his face happy, open, expectant.

"Tinkler," I managed to say. "What are you doing here?"

Nevada came out of the bedroom. She was dressed now and wide awake and combing her hair. "Is that Tinkler? Ah yes. Hi."

"Hi."

All I could say was, "What are you doing here?"

"I invited him," said Nevada. I looked from one to the other.

"Sorry I'm a bit early," said Tinkler. "But you know public transport. So unpredictable."

Nevada shrugged. "No problem."

I said, "You invited him here?"

Tinkler grinned and reached into his shopping bag, drawing out a jumbo pack of Kettle Chips, cheddar cheese flavour. "Provender." He dropped them back into the bag then delved into his pocket and drew out a familiar-looking small plastic pack full of dense green herbage. "And I'm making a delivery."

I looked at Nevada. "You've used up your last consignment already?"

She shrugged. "What can I say, I'm a party girl."

Tinkler went and sat down on the sofa, throwing the bag down on the coffee table. "I'm just as glad to have the stuff out of the house. My sister arrives tomorrow." Nevada went and sat down beside him.

"Does she take after you, Tinkler?"

"She's a devout Christian and championship tennis player," I said. "They're like two peas in a pod."

I was gradually recovering my mental faculties, but I still felt like someone had taken my brain out of my head, used it as the ball in a vigorous round of Alice in Wonderland croquet, and replaced it. I went into the kitchen and re-apportioned the lunch so it would serve three, then returned to the sitting room with it. We ate, and after lunch I put *Easy Come, Easy Go* on the turntable.

Then I sat on the sofa with Tinkler and Nevada and we all listened. I moved into the sweet spot.

It was like I'd stuck my head through a hole in a wall, and on the other side was 1955. I was there at the time and place the music was being made. I looked at Tinkler. "This is really good."

"It's stunning."

And then Rita Mae started singing.

"This is beautiful," said Nevada.

"But listen to this bit," I said. "There's some kind of imperfection here." I looked at Tinkler. "Did you hear that?"

"I didn't hear anything," volunteered Nevada.

"That little pop?" said Tinkler. "I heard it. Do you think it's a flaw in the vinyl?"

"Actually," I said, "I've a listened a few times and I think it's on the original master tape. In fact, I think it's some kind of artefact from the microphone they used."

Tinkler said, "You mean like when the singer gets too close to the mike? That's why they have pop shields."

"Perhaps you're right. Perhaps there was some kind of rogue plosive or something."

"Rogue plosive," said Nevada. "That's a good name for the hero of a swashbuckler. Rogue Plosive, scourge of the seven seas."

The record had ended and the needle was riding in the run-out groove with a slow rhythmic thunk. I took the record off the turntable and put it carefully back in its inner sleeve. Then back in its outer sleeve. Then I put the whole thing in one of the resealable plastic covers I buy from Japan for this purpose, and sealed it.

"What's that for?" said Nevada.

"To protect the record," I said.

"From what? Venereal disease?"

"From Tinkler's greasy little fingers, for a start." Finally, after a protracted interval and much scrunchy noise that sounded like a scary synthesiser soundtrack, Tinkler had succeeded in tearing open the foil bag and getting at his cheddar Kettle Chips. It wasn't a pretty sight.

"Also," I said, "it helps it slide into place more easily." I went to my shelf of records and after much peering at the hard-to-read spines, found the right spot just between Russ Garcia and Stan Getz.

"Slides in more easily, does it?" said Nevada from the sofa, and Tinkler spilled his Kettle Chips. She got up and came over. "Here, let me have a go." She took the record from me and moved to slide it into place on the shelf. But she'd already blown it.

She was holding it the wrong way round.

"For shit's sake don't do that," cried Tinkler. "It's back to front."

She peered at him suspiciously. "What difference does it make?"

"If you slide it in like that the open edge will be pointing out, with the record in it. And the spine, with the name of the record on it, will be shoved out of sight. And it will get lost between the records on either side." Tinkler shook his head solemnly. "Which in a big record collection like this pretty much means you'll never see it again. It will have vanished, like a fish diving back into the ocean."

A little later, the taxi came and picked Nevada up. Tinkler caught a ride back to Putney with her. He rang me later that night. "I figured out why you were so pissed off to see me."

"When?"

"When I turned up today. It was because you thought I was interrupting something."

"What do you mean?"

"Do you actually think you have a chance?"

135

"What are you talking about?" I said.

"You do! You do! You actually thought you were going to get laid."

"I don't know what you're talking about."

"With Nevada! I mean by Nevada. I mean on Nevada. Whatever. You know what I mean."

"Sorry, you lost me back at hello," I said. He sighed and hung up.

It was twenty minutes before he called back. "*Was* I interrupting something?" he said. "I mean, *did* you have a chance?"

"I'm going to switch my phone off now, Tinkler."

"You're going to have to switch it on again sometime. *And then I'll be there.*"

The next morning, almost from the instant that I awoke, Tinkler was ringing me. I didn't answer his calls. He continued ringing after breakfast as I headed out of the house and caught the 493 bus. Despite her nap at my place yesterday, Nevada had declared herself exhausted and decided we couldn't commence operations until two o'clock today. But I saw no reason to waste the morning, so I hopped on the bus and went hunting.

It felt good to be flying solo and it was even pleasant using public transport instead of Clean Head's taxi. Plus I felt a certain relief that I was actually making use of my travel card which I had, after all, paid for.

The 493 was a very useful bus, going south into Wimbledon and passing the charity shops of virtually every obscure hamlet on the way. I got off the bus at each one of these, pausing for a thorough search of the crates. This made it a slow and often interrupted journey, but the weather was nice and I found an excellent little stash of albums on ECM, including the Jimmy Giuffre reissue. They were all in immaculate shape and I fully suspected them of having washed downstream from the Tomas Helmer mother lode. I bought them, bagged them and caught another bus.

Tinkler rang constantly. And each time I looked at his number flashing and, with a mixture of affection and malice, ignored the call.

It was about twelve thirty and I was just thinking of heading homewards when I got a call from Nevada. "Where are you?" she demanded, dispensing with any formalities or greetings.

"I'm in Wimbledon. I thought I'd make an early start. We're covering more ground this way."

"*We* aren't doing anything, because *we* aren't together. I am standing here in your house…"

"In? Oh, right." I remembered she had the key. "How are the cats?"

"I am standing here and you're in fucking Wimbledon."

"It's a nice little village. There's more than the tennis."

Her voice was cold. "This is not funny. You should not be out there on your own."

"I see," I said. "Because I'm not to be trusted."

"It's nothing to do with that," she said. There was a note of exasperation in her voice.

"Then what is it to do with?"

She was silent for a moment and then she said, "Are you coming back?"

"Yes, right now."

"All right. I'll wait for you. But I want this understood. If you ever strike out on your own again, our arrangement is at an end." I thought this was a spectacularly idle threat. But she sounded convincing enough.

She hung up before I could reply. I stared at the phone and it started ringing again almost immediately, but it was Tinkler. I decided to take the call, if only so I could moan to him about Nevada and her behaviour, which had left me more than a little angry. Tinkler would understand.

"Hello."

A woman's voice, tight with tension, said, "I've been trying to reach you all day."

I realised it was Tinkler's sister. "Maggie?" I said.

"I'm using Jordon's phone."

"Yes, of course. I'm sorry, I—"

"You'd better sit down," she said.

10. GLASGOW COMA SCALE

The Charing Cross Hospital is, confusingly, not located anywhere near Charing Cross. It is in fact many miles west of there, in my neck of the woods, in Hammersmith. I have no idea why this is. And, just to add to the confusion, there is also a Hammersmith Hospital, which of course isn't anywhere near Hammersmith but lies adjacent to Wormwood Scrubs, far to the north.

The ambulance took Tinkler to the Charing Cross Hospital. Thanks to Maggie's status as a member of the medical fraternity we got the VIP treatment. They even vouchsafed us a glimpse of the patient lying in the Intensive Therapy Unit.

I wish they hadn't.

His long hair had all been shorn and there was a large dressing on one side of his head.

Monitor wires were stuck all over him and rose from him in a frightening hedgehog effect. His face was so pale it was almost grey and his features were scrunched up, like some poor miserable sleeping creature.

We stood in a brightly painted corridor in the accident

and emergency unit. The whole place was colour coded, with coloured footprints and lines painted on the floor to tell you where to go. Nevada said, "What happened exactly?" She'd arrived at the hospital just before Maggie and I were given the shocking tour of the ITU ward, and I have to say she seemed as shaken as I was.

Maggie said, "Thank god I had my set of keys, and thank god I turned up when I did."

"You just found him… at the bottom of the stairs?"

"Those fucking stairs," I said. She flinched at the obscenity but she nodded.

"I don't think he'd been lying there long. Thank god."

"And he what, just fell down and landed on his head?"

Maggie nodded again. "As you saw, he's now stable but in a coma."

"When is he going to wake up?"

She gave me a long, serious look, making lots of eye contact in a way that somebody had probably trained her to do on a course once and said, "There's something called the Glasgow coma scale. It's scored from three variables. Eye function, motor function and verbal response from the patient."

"It tells you how bad the coma is," said Nevada. She was as impatient with this exegesis as I was.

Maggie nodded, but evidently wasn't to be hurried. "The patient is given a cumulative score from three to fifteen. It used to be fourteen but now it's fifteen."

These details were driving me mad. "How bad is he?"

Maggie frowned and nodded again so we'd know how serious it was but be reassured that there were positive aspects to be weighed up, too. "Jordon is a seven."

Nevada gave a big sigh of relief and said, "That's great."

Maggie stared at her and she hastily added, "Isn't it great?" Maggie shook her head. No, it wasn't great.

"Eight or anything under is considered a severe brain injury."

"Oh shit," said Nevada contritely.

"But he may improve. We hope he will improve. We'll pray that he improves." There was a long silence during which we all stood in this candy-coloured corridor staring at each other.

Then Nevada said, "Because it went up from fourteen to fifteen, the scale, does that mean people are more conscious now than they used to be?"

Maggie looked at her for a moment and then said, "There really isn't anything we can do here. They've got my number and will let me know as soon as anything changes." She glanced at me. "I'm going to the hospital chapel. You're welcome to join me there."

"No thanks, Maggie. Thank you for everything, though. Thanks."

"All right," she said and turned and walked away.

Nevada and I were left standing there, staring at each other. She said, "I'm sorry I was such a bitch earlier. On the phone. I was just worried about you." I looked down the corridor to the room where they had Tinkler wired up.

I said, "It turned out it wasn't me you should have been worried about."

Nevada had told Clean Head not to bother waiting for us, since we had no idea how long we'd be, so now we walked the short distance along the Fulham Palace Road and under the shadow of the flyover to the Broadway mall where we could try to gather our thoughts and have a coffee. My one lucid decision of the last three hours had been to avoid drinking anything that came out of a machine in the hospital pretending to be coffee.

But the coffee we bought at a franchise outlet in the mall was pretty dreadful, too. And we didn't have much luck gathering any thoughts, either. Nevada looked at my cup, which I hadn't touched after the first sip, and said, "Do you want something else?"

"No, it's fine."

"Listen, I'm really sorry to do this and it's going to make me sound like a heartless, evil witch, but—"

"We have to keep looking."

"That's right."

The show must go on, I thought.

We left our coffees on the table and left the shopping mall. We walked up King Street until we came to the neighbourhood full of Polish shops that bordered on Chiswick, then we began to work our way back, hitting every charity shop.

We started with the Amnesty International bookstore, which usually has some records in the back. Today they had plenty, but nothing to interest us. It took about twenty minutes to eliminate them all, though, and without any garment rails to distract her, Nevada was getting pretty antsy by the time we left.

They had one crate of records at the next charity shop and as I crouched to look in it I was suddenly overcome with a wave of hopelessness and depression. What was the point of what I was doing? I was just a pathetic man on a ludicrous mission, squatting over a box of mouldering LPs. I couldn't bring myself to begin flipping through them. Nevada must have read something in my face because she put a hand on my shoulder and said, "It's what Tinkler would want."

Hilariously enough, she was right. Assuming that the cruelly battered vegetable that was now Tinkler could have formulated an opinion and uttered it, he would have told me to keep looking. You never knew what was in the next crate.

I sighed and leaned over the records. There was a rail of coats hung inconveniently close above and they tickled my head as I worked. I found myself wondering if lice were jumping down onto my hair and realised that I'd been hanging out with Nevada too long.

I flipped carefully through the albums, inspecting every one. It turned out what was in the next crate in this instance was Hawaiian guitar and church organ music with a liberal sprinkling of rugby songs. Onwards.

At the next shop, though, I found a solid slab of jazz that must have come from the Helmer collection. The holy grail was not amongst them but I pulled out half a dozen for my personal use and went over and set them on the counter. There was a rotund middle-aged man and a small birdlike woman standing behind it. The man had Einstein-style wacky grey hair, a custard-coloured jumper, and reading glasses hanging around his neck on what looked like a really long black shoelace. I asked him if he had any more records and he said he had some in the back. Would I like to look at them?

The old excitement began to rise up in me. Nevada was busy flipping through the clothes rails with a sneer on her face, obviously gainfully employed, so I left her there and followed the man. There was a heavy brown curtain hanging over the doorway at the rear of the shop and we pushed through its dusty folds into the gloom of the back room. "I'm not really supposed to let customers through here. Health and safety regulations," said the man dryly. "So try not to do a somersault and break your neck." He began moving several cardboard boxes full of crockery, to expose some big square leatherette carrying cases, the kind specifically designed to hold records.

He flipped them open for me and the disappointment was instant and total. It was nothing but shellac. "I'm really sorry," I said.

"Not your cup of tea?" said the man.

"I don't have any means of playing 78s." Just then there was a burst of angry speech from the front of the shop. The heavy curtain muffled it so that all I could discern was that it was Nevada, in what sounded like a spirited altercation with another woman. *Making friends again*, I thought. The man looked at me in amusement.

"Handbags at twenty paces," he said. "Sounds like your missus is getting into it." I hurried back through the curtain, warmed by his mistake, to find my "missus" standing there looking both triumphant and scandalised. She had the pile of records I'd left on the counter and was holding them to her chest protectively. The nervous little lady behind the counter was staring at her and I just glimpsed a third woman disappearing out the door of the shop.

"She tried to steal your records," said Nevada.

"She was just looking through them," said the little old lady.

"She was going to buy them," said Nevada, "given half a chance. Her eyes lit up when she saw them."

"A woman who likes jazz," I said. "You didn't happen to get her number?"

"I'm not your lonely hearts service," said Nevada frostily, shoving the records at me. Over her shoulder I saw the man smiling. He made a small lashing gesture with his right hand—the international sign language for "pussy-whipped". I paid for the records and we left.

There was nothing of interest at the other charity shops on King Street, until we hit the last one. It was brightly lit and modern, not like some of the establishments. The guy in charge was young and chubby with the sort of retro long hair that reminded me—with a painful tug—of Tinkler. I wondered if Maggie had heard anything yet? But she would have rung us.

They didn't have any records on display so I asked the guy.

"Vinyls, you mean?" he said.

"We don't say vinyls," said Nevada. "We say albums or LPs or records." I thought this was a bit snotty, even though I recognised where she'd got it. He didn't seem to mind, though. Pretty women can get away with murder.

"We had some," he said, "but it's all gone."

"All of it?" I said.

He nodded. "We had one of those big plastic boxes..."

"A crate."

"Yeah, it was full of the stuff. Full of records." He smiled and leaned across the counter as if letting us in on a confidence. "The manager wanted me to get rid of them. We had only put them out yesterday, but she said it was making the place look messy. Said it was old-fashioned. So she told me to throw them out."

"You threw them out?" I said.

He shook his head, grinning broadly. "No. We sold it. The whole crate. For a hundred quid. A hundred pounds for some vinyls! We were going to throw them out. The manager, she had just ordered me to throw them in the rubbish, and then this woman comes in."

"What, just now?" said Nevada.

"Yeah, just now, this woman comes in and offers us a hundred quid! She didn't even look through them. Took the lot. And gave us a hundred pounds."

I had a hollow feeling in my stomach. "Do you happen to know if there was any jazz?"

"Oh yeah, it was all jazz. Miles Davis. John Coltrane. That sort of thing." He smiled happily at us. "I'm going to be the under-manager of the month," he said. "A hundred quid!"

I didn't tell him there might have been a record in there worth several thousand times that much.

"What did she look like, this woman?" said Nevada. "Was she a blonde?"

"Yes, that's right, a blonde."

We walked out of the shop. "It was the same bitch," said Nevada.

I got home, emotionally drained and exhausted, and flopped on the sofa. Turk was nowhere to be seen, probably asleep on the bed, but Fanny was pacing restlessly in the kitchen and tapping her bowl with her paw to tell me she was hungry. I poured out some biscuits for her and Turk came pelting through. I poured some for her, too, and returned to the sofa.

Nevada and I had visited the hospital once again before calling it a day. But there had been no change. Not in Tinkler's condition, nor in his sister's. Maggie was still camped out in the chapel and quietly and patiently guilt-tripping us for not joining her. For one wild second I wondered if maybe I *should* be there with her. Maybe god would punish me and Tinkler would never regain consciousness because I was hunkering down in front of crates of records instead of the altar in the hospital chapel.

To put a stop to thoughts like that I got on the phone. I called Alan at Jazz House in Leicester and then, in desperation, Ken at Dusty Groove in Chicago. The record was supposed to be somewhere in southwest London, but you never knew.

But when they heard what I was looking for, they both laughed at me. It was good-natured laughter, and I deserved it. Alan said if he'd found an original copy of *Easy Come, Easy Go* he would be sitting on a beach in southern India instead of a drafty industrial estate in the Midlands. We chatted for a while about other things and then said our goodbyes.

I hung up the phone and stared at it blankly for a moment. I had no idea what to do next. Then the phone rang. I picked it up and said hello. A woman's voice said, "Do you know who this is?"

It took me a moment, but then I got it. "Cement in the gutters."

"You can't beat it," she said. "Listen, I've got some news for you."

My heart was beating double time. "Oh really?"

"Yeah, I spoke to her, the ex-wife, and she said okay."

"Okay?"

"If you want the rest of the records you can have them."

"What?" I said.

She laughed. "Try not to fall out of your chair. She isn't just going to *give* them to you. Or maybe she is. She didn't exactly say. She just said you can come over tomorrow morning if you like, have a look through them, see if there's anything you want."

"Tomorrow," I said. "In the morning? Tomorrow?"

The woman laughed again. "That's right. This is how it must feel to be Santa Claus."

"At the house in Richmond."

She grew serious, all business. "No, at the flat in Turnham Green, I've got to give you the address. Have you got a pen?"

"Yes, no, yes, no, shit." The cats were staring at me in wonderment as I frantically scrabbled through the piles of junk on my coffee table, looking for the pen I knew must be there, somewhere.

She chuckled. "It's okay. Don't panic."

I found the pen and wrote down the address.

There was a gourmet chocolate shop that I knew on Turnham Green Terrace called Theobroma. They also served high-calibre coffee, so I arranged to meet Nevada there the next morning before we went to meet Mrs Helmer, whom I'd learned was called Aisling, pronounced Ash-ling.

I caught the bus to Hammersmith and then a District Line Tube, heading west. I'd talked Nevada into meeting me there. It was about halfway between us—I'd learned she was staying not at the Connaught or Castle Dracula but a flat in Maida Vale—so this made more sense than getting Clean Head to drive all the way down to me in the taxi and doubling back.

Plus, to be honest, I was enjoying using my travel card again.

I caught the Tube to the next stop beyond the address, so I could scout the location before meeting Nevada. I like to look as if I know where I'm going, especially when I'm with a companion as acerbic as her. I walked out of the Tube station into the sunlight and fresh morning air. I had the guarded feeling that this was going to be it. We would find the record today.

I had checked twice with Maggie about Tinkler since I'd woken up, but I still felt guilty because he wasn't the only thing on my mind. I felt in my pocket for the map I'd printed off the Internet, paused to orientate myself, then set off.

It wasn't hard to find the address.

The whole street was full of police vehicles.

I met Nevada at the café ten minutes later. She looked up as I came in and said, "You're right. The coffee at this place is really good." Then she saw my face. "What is it?"

I sat down opposite her. "I went around to her flat before I got here," I said. "The place was crawling with police. The whole road was sealed off. I asked a neighbour what was going on. They said a woman had been killed."

She looked at me. "It wasn't…"

I nodded. "It was. It seems there was a break-in last night and Mrs Aisling Helmer interrupted the burglar." I shook my head. "She was beaten to death."

She stared at me.

I said, "Sound familiar?"

11. SPOOK STORE

The room they'd given Tinkler was a private one in a pleasant location, high up in a corner of the hospital. There was a nice view from the window, over rooftops, and even a glimpse of a distant patch of green. I imagine Maggie had somehow exerted influence, or maybe they were just treating her brother really well out of professional courtesy.

Or maybe it was an index of the seriousness of his condition.

There were grapes in a bowl beside his bed, which I thought was a particularly cruel touch. His face was naked and beaten and vulnerable. Somewhere under that unhappy slackness was my friend. I felt bad staring at him. If I'd been in his place I wouldn't want to be seen like that. I'd be ashamed of anyone seeing me in that state of helpless absence.

I felt a sweet burst of flavour in my mouth and realised with some degree of embarrassment that while I was staring glumly at my savagely wounded friend, I was also absentmindedly stealing, and eating, his grapes.

Nevada was staring at me. "Those are his. You are eating his grapes."

"I was hoping he'd wake up and fight me for them."

But she was genuinely angry. She seized the bowl from me and put it back down with a loud clank on the bedside table. "You can't behave like that," she said. "So callous. It's despicable."

"It's just the shock," I said. "Seeing him like this."

"I know," she said, the anger draining out of her. She sat down and I sat down. The only sound was Tinkler's laboured breathing.

"Well, we'd better get to it," I said.

As we walked down the corridor, away from Tinkler's room, I got my bearings and I realised the distant patch of green that could be seen from his window was Fulham Palace Cemetery.

Clean Head pulled out of the hospital parking lot onto the main road and turned left. "Wait a minute," I said. "I thought we were going to Goldhawk Road."

Nevada shook her head. "We're not looking for records just at the moment." We drove south past Parsons Green, down Broomhouse Lane to cross the river at Wandsworth Bridge. Ten minutes later we were skirting the traffic at Clapham Junction to chug up Lavender Hill and finally stop outside a discreet and ultra modern-looking shop front with the words SPOOK STORE in sober white letters above it.

The street address was evidently 7, but this was ostentatiously rendered on the shop's door as "007".

I looked at Nevada and said, "What fresh madness is this?"

"You just come along now and don't interfere." She led the way into the store that turned out to be an odd cross between an upmarket jeweller's, with its carpeting, quiet and tasteful display cases, and your average techno nerd emporium. All the gear on display was electronics of various kinds, mostly in boring grey boxes. A young man appeared through a door at the back of the shop.

He was slim and tanned, wearing an expensive-looking well-cut light brown suit which I imagined rang Nevada's bells. His hair had been cropped down to a dark stubble and so had his beard, in a kind of permanent five o'clock shadow. This matching minimal hair and beard had been carefully shaved into a series of curves. The effect was that his face and head seemed covered with a kind of swirling symmetrical pattern, which at first glance looked like a Maori tattoo. It came across as both trendy and creepy. I suspected any points he'd gained from Nevada for the suit he had promptly lost with this aberration.

"Good morning," he said. He had a Birmingham accent, which sounded so incongruously workaday that he promptly ceased to be creepy.

"I phoned," said Nevada, "earlier."

"Ah yes. You were interested in…"

"Counter surveillance."

He nodded and said, "Please come to the counter surveillance counter."

As we followed him over to a display case I restrained myself from asking who's on first. He said, "I got your call and have selected a range of bug busters for you to look at."

"Bug busters?" I said in what I thought was an entirely neutral and innocent tone of voice, but Nevada gave me a you-stay-out-of-this look. The man removed two handheld devices from the display case and set them on the counter for us to look at. One was twice as big as the other, but either of them would sit comfortably in your palm. The larger one looked like a walkie-talkie and the smaller like one of those battery packs people wear when they're fitted with a radio mike. The man lifted the smaller one and smiled his best salesman's smile.

"This is the Stone Circle 48 digital radio frequency monitor. It provides high quality bug detection at an affordable price." He patted it. "This model costs just over five hundred pounds including VAT."

"What does it do?" said Nevada with what I thought was admirable bluntness.

"What *doesn't* it do?" He smiled his false salesman's smile again and I sensed stale patter. "In fact it will detect any device emitting a radio signal between one megahertz and four point eight gigahertz. That includes telephone, video, small battery and mains powered transmitters and—"

"Tracking devices?" said Nevada.

"Oh yes, certainly, tracking devices too. Very much so."

"Okay, what about the other one?"

He smiled again, but this time it looked sincere. He put the small device down and picked up the larger one, handling it with reverence. "This is the Stone Circle 10. It retails for fifteen hundred pounds."

I said, "Fifteen hundred pounds!"

Nevada nudged me to shut up. "What's the difference," she said, "between that one and the other one?"

Our guide waxed lyrical. "This model covers a truly staggering frequency range, from zero to ten gigahertz." I repressed the urge to ask him if it went to eleven. "Which covers all bugs which have recently become commercially available," he concluded.

Nevada nodded. She'd got it. "So that one goes to four point eight and this one goes to ten."

"That's correct." He looked lovingly at the device in his hand. I thought he was going to tickle its tummy. "Yes. All the way to ten gigahertz. It also has an optional beep tone."

Nevada nodded decisively. "We'll take that one."

"Which one?" His Brummie accent spiked excitedly, as if he could hardly believe his luck.

"The more expensive one with the truly staggering frequency range." Nevada nodded at it. "That will be fifteen hundred pounds, I believe you said?"

"Eighteen hundred, including VAT."

"What!" I said.

Nevada stepped on my foot and handed the man her credit card. "That will be fine." I had thought the guy would be reluctant to put down his beloved Stone Circle 10 but he discarded it like a hot potato and grabbed Nevada's card quick before she changed her mind. He completed the transaction and wrapped our purchase for us. At that price I expected it to be sealed in an origami swan fashioned from handmade linen paper, but he just stuck it in a plastic bag with a dismayingly chunky instruction manual. The bag had the Spook Store logo on it, which turned out to be a cheesy angular double S motif that I probably wasn't alone in thinking was tastelessly close to a certain well-known Nazi insignia.

As we walked out of the store I said, "Was it the optional beep tone that sold you?"

"Don't be sarcastic." As we got into the taxi she handed it to me and said, "You take charge of this."

"What?"

"You're the technical one."

I reluctantly took the thing out of the bag and began trying to make head or tail of its instruction manual. We drove west down St John's Hill, then Clean Head switched to the back roads, following some abstruse formula that only she knew, until miraculously we came back out onto the A3 by Huguenot Place.

By now I had worked out that, luckily, the manual featured instructions printed in a number of languages, which reduced the relevant English section to a more manageable size.

We turned left into Garratt Lane opposite the shopping centre and drove down it until we came to Sainsbury's. Clean Head signalled for a left turn and pulled into the supermarket parking lot.

She ignored any number of available spaces and drove to a distant, lonely corner of the lot where only a few other vehicles were parked. She cut off the engine as we approached the painted rectangle of the parking space she'd chosen, and let the taxi drift the last few metres on momentum, coming to a stop exactly in the middle of the rectangle.

"She's such a show-off," said Nevada. Then, looking at me expectantly, "Well?"

"What?"

"Have you assimilated the manual?"

I had, as it happened. "I suppose so, sort of, yes."

"Then let's get started."

I looked at her. "Do you really think this taxi is bugged? That they're listening to our every word?" Whoever "they" might be.

"It's a tracking device I'm concerned about. And let's just say I want to exclude the possibility."

"You think someone stuck a tracking device on us?"

"As I said, let's exclude that possibility."

I switched the device on. To my relief the little black and green screen came to life right away. "Looks like batteries were included. All that for just eighteen hundred pounds." The front door of the cab opened and Clean Head got out. She opened the back door and climbed in with us. She sat down and smiled.

"This is a little bit humiliating," she said.

"Why?" said Nevada.

"Because it's my cab." She shrugged. She did seem a bit embarrassed. "It's like going to the STD clinic to be checked out."

"Not that you'd know," said Nevada.

Clean Head grinned. "Not that I'd know."

The instruction booklet had actually been written in an imaginative variant of English, just similar enough to lure the casual reader into a false sense of security. But I had managed to glean the basic facts, and we scanned the inside of the rear of the cab. Then we got out and Clean Head let me into the driver's compartment. I was a little surprised that she hadn't insisted on checking this private space herself, and felt a bit privileged. I noticed that she drank San Pellegrino mineral water and had a Françoise Sagan paperback on the go.

No bugs anywhere, though.

We stood outside the taxi and I ran the device all over its surface. Nothing. We stood and looked at each other. "That's it, then."

Nevada shook her head. "No. Now we have to check underneath."

"By we, we mean me?" I said. Both the women looked at me.

"You're doing so well," said Nevada. She didn't quite bat her eyelashes, but she might as well have done. "I wouldn't want to interfere."

"Well, that's a first."

Clean Head plucked the lapel of her jacket, by way of explanation. "And this is new."

"Well, you're just lucky I'm not wearing my Paul Smith," I said, and got down on my hands and knees on the grubby tarmac and set to work with ill grace. The idea was to do it from several angles so as to make sure everything got scanned. I started at the front of the cab. After a few seconds I had to roll over and change hands. "I'm getting a cramp in my shoulder."

"Poor darling," said Nevada. "We'll give you a massage afterwards."

"We'll get some baby oil from Sainsbury's," added Clean Head and they both cackled. It was a big vehicle and to make sure I covered every centimetre I had to get down on the ground at six separate points—once at each corner of the vehicle and once on each side in the middle.

A family of shoppers were walking past and they paused to gaze at us curiously as I pawed under the car. Nevada called to them, "He's such a cheapskate. It's only a pound coin."

"Two-pound coin," I snarled. But the light on the monitor screen stayed green, the RF readout didn't flicker and the optional beep tone didn't beep. I got stiffly to my feet. "Nothing."

Nevada looked at Clean Head. "The STD clinic has given you a clean bill of health."

We got some coffees from the Starbucks around the corner and all sat in the back of the cab. It smelled wonderful with the three cups of coffee in there. "All right, we've ruled out a tracking device," said Nevada. She was at her most businesslike and I was a little surprised she wasn't asking us to take notes. "But is it still possible we're being followed."

"If we were," said Clean Head, "we wouldn't know it."

"Why not?"

"If they were any good at their job, they'd be almost impossible to spot."

"Well, they're not that good. We managed to spot them once." Nevada looked at me. "You remember? Coming back from Brompton, across Putney Bridge. But we managed to shake them off."

"That doesn't mean they stayed shook off," said Clean Head. "And perhaps they've got more careful since then." She sipped her coffee. "I know how *I'd* do it."

"How?"

"I'd have one in front and one behind. Not too close. That way if one lost you, the other could keep you in sight. It wouldn't be hard."

"What kind of vehicles would they use?" said Nevada.

She shook her head. "Impossible to say. But definitely silver."

I said, "Why silver?"

"Look around you." Nevada and I looked around the car park. At least every second car was an almost identical shade of silver grey. I'd never noticed it before, but she was right.

"But now I know what to look for," said Clean Head. "And I know what to do about it." She was buzzing, and not just with the coffee. This was clearly more fun than *Bonjour Tristesse*. We pulled out of the car park, turned right and headed for Armoury Way. We were bound for Goldhawk

Road, our search for the record resumed.

As we crossed the river again, heading north, a thought suddenly hit me. "We didn't shake them off."

"What?" Nevada looked at me.

"That night crossing Putney Bridge. We didn't shake them off," I said. "We led them to Tinkler's."

12. PEOPLE CARRIER

You wouldn't believe how many silver vehicles there are on the roads of London, once you start looking for them. I lost count of the number we passed, or were passed by, as we drove across the river to Hammersmith and then north to the Goldhawk Road.

I hit all the charity shops there. It didn't take long, because they didn't have much in the way of records. Then we drove past Shepherd's Bush Common and stopped on the corner of Wood Lane. Now I'd work the Uxbridge Road. The first shop here had an impressive selection of accordion music on LP, mostly from Germany for some reason, but no jazz in evidence.

There was a plump woman sitting behind the counter trying to thread shoelaces into a pair of old-fashioned ice skates. I smiled at her and said, "You don't happen to have any jazz records at the moment, do you?"

The woman looked up from the pair of ice skates and said, "We did have a box. But we just sold the whole thing."

"To a blonde woman?" said Nevada.

"Yes. A pretty little thing. Bought the lot."

As we left the store, I saw her.

She was wearing matching dark blue ski jacket and ski

pants, practical enough for the chilly weather but also as close to anonymity as you could get in a plausible city outfit. She was also wearing a pair of sunglasses. They did a pretty effective job of concealing her features, but if anything they helped me. What I immediately recognised wasn't her face but purely an animal sense of her. The way she moved.

"It's the woman from the boot fair, the one who got chucked out," I said.

"And it's definitely the jazz bitch," murmured Nevada. "The one I had the wrestling match with over those records of yours." We had stepped into a doorway and stood there watching the woman. She hadn't seen us. She looked up and down the street then turned left, heading towards the Tube station. There was a promising cluster of charity shops in that direction and it was where we were headed, too. As soon as the woman turned away and set off, Nevada started to step out of the doorway. I stopped her.

"What are you doing?" she said. "If we let her get ahead of us she will have cleaned out every store before we get there. We have to get ahead of her."

"No, we have to *follow* her."

"What are you talking about? She'll buy the records."

"We want her to. We want her to buy a shitload of records. More than she can carry."

She looked at me like I was nuts, but only for a moment. Then she got it. "And she'll have to put them in her vehicle."

I nodded. "So we get to find out what her vehicle looks like."

She frowned for a second, then said, "All right, but if as a result of this initiative she scoops up the record we're looking for…"

"She won't," I said. "I mean what are the odds?" I was

far from certain about this though. It was a chance. But one I thought we had to take.

"If that happens I'm going to want your head on a plate."

"Way to motivate the staff." We stepped out of the doorway and went after the blonde. I knew the location of the next charity shop and I made sure we stopped short of it, which was just as well because she popped back out of the door a few seconds after she'd gone in. No records, evidently. The same thing at the next shop.

At the third shop she stayed in for a couple of minutes then came back out with a big canvas bag, which could have contained two dozen LPs. It must have been heavy but she didn't have any trouble carrying it. A strong woman. I tried to stop myself from speculating fretfully about what might be in the bag. We stayed out of sight at a bus shelter until she moved on to the fourth and final charity shop. She remained in there quite a long time.

Nevada and I were standing in the concealment of an open-fronted telephone booth. It was a minimal structure, but enough to break up our silhouette. "I didn't know they still had telephone booths," said Nevada. "How reassuring. And how reassuring to know they still stink of urine."

"Here she comes," I said.

The woman came out of the shop. She was still only carrying the same bag she'd had when she went in. So had she found nothing? She had been in the shop some considerable time. That would make sense if she'd been flipping through the crates. But that wasn't her style.

She was of the sledgehammer school of record hunting. Buy everything now and look at it later.

She remained standing in front of the charity shop,

scanning the street both ways. Nevada and I pressed ourselves behind the phone booth. "How long is she going to stand there?" said Nevada. Just then a vehicle pulled out of the traffic stream and up to the kerb opposite the shop front.

It was a big sports utility vehicle, or people carrier as they're called.

And it was silver.

The woman went back to the door of the charity shop and opened it and said something. She stood back and two skinny teenagers came out of the shop, each carrying a yellow plastic crate of records. I guess that the kids worked in the store and had been enlisted to help. They'd evidently thrown the crates in as part of the deal. The woman in the ski suit had just bought everything. She looked sufficiently well heeled to have no trouble coming up with a generous purchase price… for pretty much anything she wanted.

The big side door of the people carrier was thrown open. A brawny man got out and helped the kids put the crates into the vehicle. I got a good look at the guy's face and his short cropped blonde hair.

It was the jerk from the boot fair. The knucklehead who had knocked me off my feet.

I was surprised at how unsurprised I was.

They loaded the records, the kids went back into the shop, and the man and woman got into the people carrier and drove away.

We told Clean Head to drive us back to the hospital, going by the most circuitous route possible and taking at least an hour to get there. We wanted to visit Tinkler one more time and on the way there we wanted to have a good look for our new friends. But knowing what their vehicle looked like turned out to confer surprisingly little advantage to us.

From time to time we spotted the silver people carrier, or a vehicle very similar. Sometimes it was in front of us, sometimes it was behind us, and a surprising amount of the time it wasn't in sight at all.

After about twenty minutes Clean Head opened the sliding window that sealed her off from the passenger compartment and said, "I think you're right. A silver SUV is definitely tracking us. But that doesn't really help us until we know what the other vehicle is."

"You think there's definitely another vehicle?" said Nevada.

"It's the only way to do it properly."

I glanced out the window to our right and watched a small figure on a lightweight motorcycle dart past. The rider, who looked like some kind of courier with a shoulder bag, was sexless and anonymous behind a full-face helmet. Bike and rider vanished into the traffic flow ahead of us. I said, "I've been seeing a lot of those small motorcycles. You know, trail bikes, around 60cc, that sort of thing."

"There's a lot of them on the road," said Clean Head.

"It could be that," I said, "or it could be someone changing their helmet and their jacket and looking like a bunch of different riders on different bikes."

"A motorcycle?" said Nevada. "I'd been looking for a car. But a motorcycle, they could pack it up and put it in the people carrier and carry it around with them."

"If it was small enough," said Clean Head.

"Around 60cc," I suggested. There was silence while this sank in.

I said, "They could even alter details on the bike. Use decals, make it look like a different colour. Switch the number plate. We'd think it was a different one but every time it could be the same bike."

"It could be," said Clean Head. "Or it could also just be that there's a lot of small bikes on the road."

I said, "Let's review what we know. There are two of them. A man and a woman. Both blonde. Both athletic types. Kind of Germanic-looking. For the sake of discussion let's call them the Aryan Twins."

"I like it," said Nevada. "The Aryan Twins. Heinz and Heidi."

"And they're also looking for *Easy Come, Easy Go.*"

"We don't know that for certain. I'm playing devil's advocate here. All we know is that they are buying up all the jazz they can find. How can you be certain they're after that one record?"

I'd been thinking about this. "When I was at the boot fair that guy..."

"Heinz," said Nevada.

"Right. He pushed me away from a box of records I was about to look through. What he didn't know was that I'd already given it the once-over."

Nevada shrugged. "So what?"

"You see, he just shoved me aside and looked through that one box and then he went away."

"So?"

I said, "He didn't bother with the others." Nevada was looking at me now. I could see her mind working behind her blue eyes. "I think that's because he'd seen me go through the first two boxes. So he wasn't interested in them."

"Because you'd already been through them," said Nevada.

I nodded. "That's right. He didn't check the other crates because he didn't have to. I'd done it for him."

"Because we were looking for the same thing."

"Exactly," I said. "But the good news is, they haven't found it yet. We haven't found it, but neither have they."

Nevada looked at me for a moment, processing this, then nodded. "Otherwise they wouldn't still be looking," she said.

"Exactly. So we're all looking for the same thing and they haven't found it yet."

"But they're certainly proving to be a nuisance."

"I agree," I said. "So I'm going to fix their wagon."

"What do you mean?" said Nevada.

I said, "When it comes to vinyl in London, don't fuck with me."

13. VINYL CRYPT

The next day I put the plan into action.

We drove north, making judicious use of the bus lane through Barnes and speeding across Hammersmith Bridge. I looked down at the birds wading in the water. The sun glittered on the Thames. The birds picked their way delicately across the mud.

"Don't let the other vehicle lose us," I said to Clean Head.

"If there is another vehicle."

We went to visit Tinkler in hospital, staring at his absent face and trying to think of encouraging things to say to each other. Then we drove to the Vinyl Crypt.

The Vinyl Crypt is located in what used to be a bus garage in north London, near Highgate. We took a fairly discursive route there, zig-zagging from Victoria to Ladbroke Grove to Regent's Park. I leaned forward in the taxi and said, "It's good that you're not making it too easy for them, but make sure you don't lose them."

There was just a disgusted sigh from the driver's compartment. I looked to Nevada for support, but she wasn't offering any. Instead she gazed at me languidly and said, "What are we doing, exactly?"

"In a word," I said, "sabotage."

"French is such an expressive language."

Lenny's Vinyl Crypt was a legend among record collectors. You might once have found a gem at Cheapo Cheapo in Soho or even stumbled on something no one else had spotted at the Record and Tape Exchange in Notting Hill. But no one has ever found anything of value at Lenny's.

A few times I'd thought I'd got something—some wonderful treasure—but when I got it home it was always knackered. I persisted, foolishly, for years buying stuff from there. Always thinking I had beaten the jinx, but always finding some hidden scratch or pressing glitch that would ruin the listening experience.

"It was like a dolls' hospital for damaged records," I told Nevada. "No one who had any good or interesting LPs to sell would ever take them to Lenny's. It's for the unwanted, the cast-offs. If a charity shop can't sell its records or if you hold a jumble sale and you've got some real dross left over, you go to Lenny's and dump it for a few pennies." I looked at her. "It's where bad little records who didn't say their prayers at night or brush their teeth end up."

"Poor bad little records," said Nevada. "But why would any of this have prevented Tomas Helmer's ex-wife dumping the records there?"

"It wouldn't," I said.

"Then why the hell haven't we been to this place?"

"Because we only just found out that was her *raison d'être*."

"Great," she said. "More French. It should be *raison d'agir*, actually, since we're talking about her motivation to action."

"I stand corrected."

"At least, anyway, we're racing there now."

"That's right."

"And they might have the record."

I smiled. "Even if they don't, we can make good use of the place."

Lenny was wearing a beret that might have looked jaunty or hip on somebody else. Somebody who wasn't also sporting the swamp-varmint long grey hair and long scary beard combo as popularised many years ago by ZZ Top. He also wore a smart-looking camelhair coat and a tartan scarf, both of which made absolute sense given the icy temperature in the Vinyl Crypt.

It was a big damp concrete space, lit by the merciless glare of long fluorescent tubes hung by chains from the high curved ceiling. The walls of the building were green corrugated steel reinforced by girders sunk at intervals into concrete blocks in the floor. The space was big enough to accommodate several double-decker buses, which of course it once had. It always made me think of an aircraft hangar and there was a ghostly smell of fuel that had never left the place. Lenny had fitted it with narrow rectangular tables that had once served a school refectory. They lined both walls of the long structure.

The tables along the walls were stacked with crates of records. There were additional crates underneath. There were more tables, of various shapes and sizes, dotted in the centre of the cement floor, enough of them to make the big space seem almost cramped.

One of the tables was an elegant old walnut antique that had at an earlier time enjoyed the loving attentions of a French polisher. God knows how it had fallen into Lenny's hands. Now it was chipped and battle-scarred and served as his shop counter. He sat behind it and watched me go through his NEW ARRIVALS, JAZZ bins.

There was a small white portable refrigerator grumbling away beside Lenny's table, and he sat in front of it sipping from a glass of pale pinkish-purple fluid. No one knew what was in the fridge and Lenny, who was notoriously unfriendly, wouldn't tell anyone. No one knew what he was drinking, either, although guesses ranged from Ribena to the blood of newborn infants.

Now Nevada was standing in front of his table with a doubtful expression on her face. She could be outside, sitting in a nice, warm, comfortable cab. "I understand you want to see me," she said.

"He wants to see your platinum card," I said, glancing up from the table where I was flipping through the records.

"Doesn't he trust you?" Nevada was looking over her shoulder at me.

"He trusts me but not necessarily my buying power." I resumed my search through the bins. My nose was twitching with the spicy smell of some exotic fungus that was attacking the grubby heaps of vinyl.

I heard Nevada say, "What on earth is that you're drinking?" The muscles of my shoulders tightened as I prepared myself for one of Lenny's rudest put-downs. But, to my astonishment, he said, "Mineral water with a little Crème de Cassis."

"Cassis?" said Nevada. "That's lovely. Have you tried it

with champagne? Lovely with champagne."

"Sadly, I don't have any champagne here," said Lenny.

"Disgraceful," said Nevada, and for the first time in living memory I heard Lenny chuckle. "Have you tried Crème de *Framboise*?" she said. "That's very tasty too."

"Yes, I sometimes drink the Framboise. It depends how I'm feeling."

"It depends on how *fruity* you're feeling."

"That's right!" Now they both laughed, him sounding like a rusty hinge on a seldom-opened door, her gurgling with merriment. I couldn't believe it. I drifted over to the table where they were talking, under the guise of looking through some boxes of appalling Euro disco junk. I had never seen Lenny like this. She totally had him where she wanted him. If he'd been a cat he would have purred.

"I don't have any champagne," said Lenny. "But I do have this." He spun around on his chair and opened the refrigerator. He took out a tall green wine bottle with a white label and set it on the table. Nevada let out a meretricious squeal of delight and Lenny said, modestly, "It's a Chablis."

"It's a very good Chablis," said Nevada. "My god, the Valmur."

Lenny nodded and took two glasses out of the fridge. Unlike the tumbler he'd been drinking from before, these were proper wine glasses made of slender, shapely crystal. The neck of the bottle chinked against them musically as he poured the white wine. "It's the Grand Cru, isn't it?" said Nevada.

"Yes, the Moreau-Naudet," said Lenny happily as the wine glugged.

"The 2007?"

"Yes, the 2007." He filled two glasses carefully. I felt

left out, like the hired bumpkin flipping through my smelly vinyl on the other side of the room. But I knew what response a request for a glass of my own would get.

"You can taste the limestone!" cried Nevada.

I looked on the bright side. If she couldn't cater to her clothes fetish here, at least she could indulge her wine obsession. And that would keep her out of my hair while I looked.

"I generally save the wine," said Lenny. "Until the end of the working day, or for a special occasion."

"The end of the working day *is* a special occasion, I always say," said Nevada. They drained their glasses and were working on a refill by the time I finished looking through the bins. I strode over purposefully and joined them.

"It isn't here," I said.

"Are you sure?" said Nevada.

"Yes," I said. "And nobody resembling Helmer's ex-wife, or indeed anyone else, has brought any interesting jazz records here for months, if not years."

"That's right," agreed Lenny happily, sipping his wine.

I looked at Nevada.

"It's just perfect."

As we drove away in the taxi Nevada said, "All right, explain to me what we just achieved."

"Apart from you drinking Grand Cru Chablis?"

"And spending a huge fortune in my funds, yes."

"It isn't a huge fortune," I said. "It's less than you spent on the Stone Circle 10 bug buster."

"But at least I saw some return for that. Some value. I don't see any value in buying a huge quantity of rubbish vinyl that you yourself assure me does not contain the record we're looking for."

"You haven't bought it yet," I said.

"I've agreed to buy it, in principle," said Nevada. "And he's seen my platinum card as a token of our earnest."

I gave her my best confident smile. "If things pan out, you won't have to buy anything."

"And just how likely are things to 'pan out'?"

"Ask Clean Head," I said.

"Clean Head? Why? Ask her what?"

"If she's sure she didn't shake off our tail completely."

"I'm not going to ask her that," said Nevada. "She'll bite my head off. You only reminded her about twenty times on our way here." She didn't look convinced and I could feel my best confident smile beginning to slip a bit. Just then my phone rang. I answered it.

It was Lenny. "I tried your friend's number, but there was something wrong with her phone, so I'm phoning you instead, to tell you."

"Okay," I said, repressing the urge to tell him to get on with it.

"Well," he said, "it went down exactly like you said." And he told me all about it. When he finished talking I hung up and looked at Nevada. She was smiling at me.

"It worked, did it?" she said. "Whatever this evil scheme of yours was?"

"Yes," I said. "It worked. How did you know?"

She shook her head. "It's written all over your face. Well, go on. Tell me what happened."

I leaned back in my seat and sighed. We were speeding through Belsize Park, on the way home. I said, "About ten minutes after we left, they turned up."

"Who did? The Aryan Twins?"

"Yes. Apparently they were very friendly and charming."

"Hard to believe."

"Or at least she was," I said.

"Heidi."

"Yes. Heidi wanted to buy up his entire stock of jazz albums. Lenny regretfully explained he'd just sold, or promised to sell, the whole lot, including all the dire rubbish in the basement—he didn't say dire rubbish, you understand—to us."

Nevada was watching me. "And they made a counter offer."

I nodded. "That's right. And Lenny said he couldn't do that to a friend. So they doubled the offer."

Nevada squealed and I smiled. "But Lenny stood fast. And they kept raising the ante. In the end they paid him five times what we'd agreed."

"Five times!"

"That's right. Now apparently they've gone off to rent a truck big enough to haul the records away."

"A truck!" Nevada exploded in laughter. She laughed until she cried. She laughed so hard that Clean Head looked over her shoulder at us, a little surprised and anxious, and then returned to watching the road. Nevada gradually subsided and wiped her eyes. "Five times," she said. "So that's the going rate for selling out a friend these days."

"That's the going rate."

She sighed and rubbed her face. "All right. But what have we actually achieved, besides making Heinz and Heidi waste their morning doing this transaction?"

I counted on my fingers. "We've also wasted their money. A great deal of their money."

Nevada nodded in agreement. "A shit load of their money."

"And we've given Lenny a significant boost to his income."

"He's such a nice chap. He can buy some more excellent Chablis."

"And," I said, "we've helped him get rid of one of the largest collections of dodgy jazz records in the world."

"All very well, but…"

"But we've also lumbered the Aryan Twins with the task of picking up and then looking through every single fucking one of those records." I looked at her. "That should keep them out of our hair for a while."

Nevada chuckled. "You really do have a twisted mind, don't you?" She peered contentedly out the window at Fulham rolling past. We were heading for Putney Bridge. A thought struck me. I took out my phone and dialled a number. "Who are you calling?" she said.

"Lenny again. I just thought of something." Lenny answered and I said, "Listen, as soon as they've collected the records I think this would be a good time for you to take a holiday."

He wasn't slow. "You think there might be repercussions?"

"I think it would be a good idea if you were out of the country and unable to be found for a few weeks." There was a long pause at the other end. I said, "You've got plenty of money for a holiday now, haven't you?"

Lenny seemed to gradually warm to the notion. "Yeah, maybe Greece, eh? Mykonos will be nice this time of year."

"That's the spirit."

Lenny's tone grew jubilant. "Would you ask your friend if she's ever been to Mykonos? And if she hasn't, would she like to go? And even if she has, would she like to go again? Would you ask her that? If she'd like to go with me?"

"You know what, actually, Lenny? I won't."

"Okay, fair enough, I quite understand."

When we got to my house Nevada asked if she could come in. "I'm expecting a call and my phone's packed up. So I gave them your landline number." She walked through the front door with me and the cats rose lazily to greet us. Nevada settled comfortably on the sofa and the cats went to join her. "They should call about five o'clock," she said, glancing at the phone beside the sofa. It was now five to five.

"Who?" I said.

"My office."

Try as I might, I couldn't visualise Nevada having an office, or working in one. I perched on an arm of the sofa and watched her caress the cats. "Would you like some coffee?" I wondered if I had the energy to make the good stuff. The phone suddenly rang, causing the cats to jump off the sofa. I looked at the clock. The office was a little early.

Nevada scooped up the receiver, listened for a moment, then covered it up and looked at me. "Would you mind?" she hissed. "I know it's terribly rude, but I'm supposed to make a confidential report."

"No problem," I said, although in fact I was little stung to be turfed out of my own house. I went out the back door into the garden. The sky was dark and heavy with the early evening of winter. The air smelled cold and clean and distantly of burning leaves. I remembered Tomas Helmer standing here and the smell of his cigar. The cat flap rattled behind me and Fanny came gliding out to keep me company. Turk, the traitor, stayed indoors. Through the window I could see Nevada playing with her absent-mindedly while she spoke on the phone. Then she hung up and waved to me.

I went back in. Fanny stayed out in the garden, crouched on one of the flat stones that formed a footpath leading to the back gate.

In the sitting room Nevada rose from the sofa, stretching. "Sorry about that. Thank you for being so understanding."

"No problem. How are things back at the office?"

"Ticking over." She sat back down on the sofa, looking up at me. "Listen would you mind if I used your bathroom? I mean, to take a bath. I feel filthy after grubbing around in that dreadful warehouse place."

I was startled by the request. "No, of course. Help yourself."

"Thanks," said Nevada. She wasted no time, scooping up her shoulder bag and carrying it into the bathroom with her. I heard the door click shut and then the squeak of the taps being turned and the thunder of water. I stood in the sitting room staring down at the phone.

I picked it up and dialled 1471. I fumbled to find a pen and a scrap of paper. The recorded voice gave me the last incoming number and I wrote it down. Then I switched on my laptop and typed the number into a search engine.

The country and area code were 0081 956.

The city of Sasebo in Nagasaki Prefecture, Japan.

The sound of running water had stopped some time ago and was replaced now by some quiet, desultory splashing. Fanny wandered up to the bathroom door and stared at it curiously. She wasn't accustomed to seeing it closed. She reached up and began to scratch at it. She scratched vigorously and continuously and showed no signs of quitting. I was about to get up and try and get her to stop when the door popped open a cautious couple of inches and Fanny promptly insinuated herself into the opening and disappeared inside. The door closed behind her.

Turk, having watched this, now walked over to the door and began to scratch on it herself. It opened again and she darted inside. The door closed and I heard the low, indistinct cooing sound of Nevada's voice as she addressed the cats.

I stared at the closed door and felt left out.

About ten minutes later the door opened and released a warm waft of moist, fragrant air and the cats ambled out, followed by Nevada. She had covered her hair in a towel and I was surprised to see she was wearing my bathrobe. She must have found it hanging on the back of the door. Her shoulder bag was dangling from one hand and she put it down in the only armchair that wasn't covered with records.

"That's better," she said, settling down on the sofa. She took the towel off her hair and draped it over the arm of the sofa, swivelling around so she could turn and look at me. "The girls kept me company," she said.

"So I see."

"Turk perched on the edge of the tub and Fanny lay down in the sink, all curled up. She was ever so sweet."

"They like the steam."

"So do I." Nevada yawned and stretched. Not looking at her long bare legs was one of the more difficult things I've ever had to do. Her skin was very pale and startlingly smooth. I cleared my throat.

"We have to talk," I said.

She looked up at me, her eyes innocent and without guile. "Of course," she said. "About what?"

"About this, the whole situation. The Aryan Twins and Jerry and Tinkler and everything."

She stared at me. "What do you mean?"

I sighed and sank down on the sofa beside her. She wasn't going to make this easy on me. "Who are these people who are competing with us to find the record?"

She shook her head. Her hair was damp and the gleaming black fringe of it swept over her eyes with the motion. "I have no idea."

"You have some idea."

"No more than you. I don't know who they are, I just know they seem to be, as you say, competing with us."

I looked at her. "You don't know where they come from, who sent them?"

She tucked her legs up under her. Her bare feet were pressed on my thigh. She shook her head again. "All I know is that we're not the only ones who want this record. It's worth more than you can imagine."

"I can imagine quite a lot."

She hesitated. "We were aware… I was aware of the possibility of this eventuality."

"Talk like a human being."

She sighed and hugged her knees. I couldn't see her eyes now. "It was almost inevitable that someone else would come after the record."

"Did they kill Jerry?"

She shrugged. "I don't know."

"What about Helmer's wife? His ex-wife?"

She shrugged again and looked up at me. "I don't know. Possibly."

"What about Helmer himself?"

She looked startled. "But he fell off the roof. That was an accident, wasn't it?"

"Was it?" I said. "And what about Tinkler?"

She sat up straight, looking me squarely in the eye. "Listen, I know you're upset about Tinkler and so am I. But you mustn't blame yourself for what happened to him."

"We led them to him. They followed us and we led them to him."

She shook her head. "You don't know that. For all we know Tinkler just fell down the stairs. God knows it seems likely enough." That was true. I hesitated. She seemed to sense that she was gaining ground and looked me in the eyes again. "I don't think we led them to him. I don't think they did it." She reached out a tentative hand and let it rest on the back of mine. "But if we did, it was *my* fault. All my fault. Not yours."

I felt the cool touch of her hand on mine. I could smell the shampoo and soap on her. I looked away from her, at the shoulder bag she had placed in the armchair. I said, "Why do you have—"

She reached up and touched my face. Then she shifted position on the sofa and leaned forward and put her mouth to mine. I kissed her and her lips opened and I tasted her mouth. She opened the bathrobe and I reached inside and put my hand on her breast, her nipple as hard as a pebble.

We got up, moving like a single organism with four legs and, without breaking the embrace, moved into the bedroom. I shed my clothes on the way, with her helping me, tugging at them impatiently and throwing them aside. We fell down on the bed together and she wrestled her way out of the bathrobe. We threw that aside too and then her warm naked body was pressed against mine. I moved my hand down from her breasts to the small precise socket of her navel in her taut belly, then I moved it further down and put my fingers in her.

She was slick and wet and opened for me. I moved on top of her and she caught me between her fingers and guided me inside. She was smooth as silk, frictionless, slick and infinite. She hooked her legs over my shoulders as I moved into her and she said, "Yes, yes, sweet, yes, sweet, yes, love, like that, yes, like that, there, like that, yes, yes, honey, honey, honey." She bit my ear and whispered in it, "Who's lovely? Yes, you're lovely."

14. AWAKENINGS

Tinkler said, "So she talks to you just like she's talking to the cats?"

"Yes."

"While you're…"

"In the throes of passion."

"Don't get circumspect with me," he said. "You mean while you're having sex?"

"Yes."

He whistled tunelessly. He'd always whistled tunelessly. It wasn't as though the concussion had cruelly robbed him of a great gift.

In fact, allowing for external physical damage, including the brutal shearing of his abundant locks, he looked much like his old self. He'd been awake for three days now. On the first day they wouldn't let me anywhere near him, but Maggie had been allowed into the inner circle. She sat with him while he'd aced his cognitive tests.

"The only thing he got wrong," she told me later, "was that he said giraffe when they showed him a picture of a zebra." Considering how much dope he smoked I thought it was unlikely he could ever have got that one right, though I didn't say as much to Maggie.

"So what's it like?" said Tinkler, lolling back in his bed and eyeing me with frankly amused curiosity.

"Her talking to me like the cats?"

"Yes."

"The terrible thing is, I find it quite exciting."

"What!"

"I find it strangely arousing."

Tinkler howled with laughter. "This is priceless," he said.

I could feel my ears getting hot. "I'm only telling you this stuff because, you know…"

"Yes?"

"I've only been so indiscreet because of your…"

"Near brush with death?"

"I was going to say incipient role as a vegetable, but I'll go with that." I leaned back in my chair. "Anyway, from now on don't expect to hear anything in the way of intimate details."

"What intimate details? You've hardly told me anything."

"I told you plenty," I said. "I told you everything."

"When I was unconscious! That doesn't count."

"Well, you're not getting any more after today. We're drawing a line under it."

Tinkler sighed and settled back on his pillows. "Okay," he said, finally. "I'll agree to that, but with one proviso. If she starts dressing up in a cat suit complete with whiskers and tail, I have to know *right away*."

There was a brisk knock and the door opened and Maggie came in and looked at us with disapproval. "What were you two talking about? I could hear the laughter from halfway down the hall."

"Nothing," said Tinkler.

Maggie looked at me. I said, "Nothing." She shook her head and came over to the bedside table and put some fresh grapes in the bowl. Tinkler watched her with interest. Lying in his hospital bed, receiving visitors, Tinkler had become something of a connoisseur of vine fruit.

"Those better be seedless," he said.

"You're certainly getting through them," she clucked, fishing out the dry gnarled grape stems from the bottom of the bowl and dropping them, rattling, into the metal waste bin on the floor.

"It's my so-called friends," said Tinkler. "Eating my fruit while I was in a coma."

At the mention of the word "coma", Maggie looked at him fondly and came over and kissed him on the cheek. She was so transparently happy to have him back that I was willing to forgive her any quantity of her usual bossy officiousness. We stayed for another twenty minutes and then Maggie said something anodyne about not wanting to tire the patient, and we both got up.

Tinkler looked sad to see us go. As we left, he called, "Don't forget. *Cat suit. Instant notification.*"

We walked down the corridor. Maggie took me by the arm and said, "Thank you so much."

"What for?"

"For Jordon. For everything." She squeezed my arm. "These little chats of yours have really gingered him up. He's so alert and suddenly full of life. As one of the consultants put it the other day, it's almost as though he was jolted back to consciousness."

"Jolted?"

"I don't know what you said to him when you came to see him in his coma, when you were sitting alone with him talking, but it certainly seemed to do the trick. As the consultant said, it was almost as if he had been shocked awake. 'Dumb outrage and astonishment' was the way he described it. And then Jordon started laughing."

"Laughing?"

"Yes, they were a little worried at first, until he calmed down and they did the cognitive scoring." She looked up at me, happy tears welling in her eyes. "And then everything was fine."

"How was Tinkler?" said Nevada.

"Really good. Improving all the time."

"Good." She put an arm across my chest and dug her head into my shoulder. "I'll go and see him tomorrow." We were lying on my bed. The cats had just jumped up to join us. While we'd been making love they'd maintained a dispassionate, respectful distance, watching us inscrutably and silently from vantage points on the windowsill and the top of a dresser. They hadn't previously known this behaviour pattern in their little lives, but they seemed to be adjusting.

"See if you can dress up in a cat costume," I said.

"What?"

"Tinkler. When you visit. It would mean a lot to him."

She kissed my neck. "Listen," she said, "I know it's been a tumultuous few days, with him waking up and…" She propped herself up and looked up at me. "And us getting together and all. But…"

"But now we've got to get back to work."

She kissed me again. "We mustn't drop the ball. So to speak."

"And by now Heinz and Heidi will have dug through the mountain of duff vinyl from Lenny that we lumbered them with, and they'll know they haven't got the record."

She got up and began shrugging on her bra. "And they'll know we screwed them."

"Quite possibly."

She put the bra on backwards, fastened it, then twisted it around and slipped it over her breasts. I could have watched her doing this forever. "I'm going to have a shower," she said. She found her panties on the floor and pulled them on. "And then we're going to come up with a plan of action." She came back and sat on the bed and kissed me. "And perhaps you could make us some dinner."

"Perhaps I could."

"Those chicken pieces were really nice. The mini drumsticks? The ones you did the other night with the lemon and the garlic? I couldn't help noticing that you've got a freezer full of them."

I said, "That's because I buy chicken wings for the cats."

She leaned over and began stroking Fanny and Turk, who had established themselves on the bed now. "I thought chicken was bad for them. I thought the bones splintered and made them choke."

"Only if it's cooked. Raw they're fine. They're evolved to eat rodents and birds, which are full of bones. They're small carnivores."

"Are you a small carnivore, are you?" she said, patting Fanny. "Are you, are you, are you?"

"The raw wings are good for their teeth. Essential, in

fact. Have you ever tried to brush a cat's teeth?"

"Do you have lovely teeth?" she said, turning her attention to Turk. "You do, don't you?"

"But they only eat the two smallest joints on the wings. So I have to trim the other one off. Which is why I'm always left with a freezer full of the drumsticks. So I casserole them with olive oil and lemon and garlic."

"Oh, okay, I see," said Nevada, getting up. "I thought it was your signature dish. Lovingly prepared especially for me. And now it turns out it's the cats' leftovers."

"That's right."

She started for the door. I said, "I think we have to change our tactics." She stopped in the doorway and looked back at me.

"What do you mean?"

I sat up. "This random searching of charity shops and boot fairs and jumble sales, I just don't think it's going to work." She came back and sat down on the bed again, peering at me. She looked concerned.

"What are you suggesting?" she said.

"The more I think about it, the more I'm convinced the record's still in Helmer's collection. After all, she only got rid of half of it."

"The ex-wife?"

"Yeah, I think she still had the record when she died. She hadn't got rid of it yet."

"Why do you think that?"

"Call it a hunch."

Nevada swivelled around so she was sitting beside me on the bed, her back to one of the pillows that was propped against the headboard. "But that's going to present some difficulties. If we try and go after it, I mean. Her flat in Chiswick will still be a crime scene. The police wouldn't let us anywhere near it."

"I don't think the records are in the flat in Chiswick."

I could feel her looking at me. She said, "But she arranged to meet us there, so we could have a look at them."

I nodded. "That's where she arranged to meet us all right. But why would the records have been there? That was *her* flat. I had the impression she bought it after she split up with Tomas. So why would any of his records be there? Helmer would have kept them at his house in Richmond."

"She might have moved them," said Nevada. "She might have taken them to the flat in Chiswick."

"Why? The only thing she wanted to do with those records was to get rid of them. If she'd taken them from the house in Richmond she might as well have gone directly to the charity shops with them. Why take them to Chiswick? Why move them twice? It doesn't make sense."

She lay down beside me, rolling over onto her side so she could look at me. She took my hand. "So you think she just wanted to meet us at the flat so she could vet us?"

"Right."

"And so the records…"

"They're still in the house in Richmond."

We were coming home in the taxi the following morning when Clean Head said, "There's something I have to tell you." She glanced back at me in her mirror. "You were right about the light motorcycle."

"What?"

"You were right about them putting it in the SUV and everything."

"What?" said Nevada.

"I had a friend of mine, another cabbie, take a look." She paused to concentrate on a tricky traffic manoeuvre then resumed. "They were parked outside a shop and my friend happened to be driving past. I'd asked him to keep his eyes open for a silver SUV in the area. So when he saw it he stopped and parked nearby then went for a coffee and walked back past the SUV and gave it the once-over. He said they had a lightweight scrambling bike in the back." She glanced back at me. "You were even right about the size. It was a 60cc."

"Holy shit," I said.

"He only took a quick glance, because he didn't want to attract attention."

"Good," I said.

"But he said they had a lot of other kit in there."

"What kind of kit?"

"He didn't see. He didn't have time. He didn't want to attract attention."

"What sort of a shop was it?" said Nevada.

"Shop?" said Clean Head.

"You said they'd parked outside a shop. Did your friend say what kind of shop it was?"

"Health food."

"It figures," said Nevada.

"It's the Aryan fitness programme," I said, and she giggled.

* * *

We got home and unloaded the bags from the Spook Store, where Nevada had spent many more thousands of pounds. Mr Five O'Clock Shadow Maori Tattoo had been very pleased. I said, "Do we really need all this stuff?"

Nevada shook her head. "We can't cut corners. We don't want to end up behind bars."

"Good point."

She put the bags on the table in the living room and the cats jumped up and prowled around them in fascination. "Here you go," said Nevada and handed me a particularly heavy bag. It turned out that it contained all the manuals, a little library unto itself.

"These are for me to read?"

"Yes, and you better make a start." She checked her watch. "We want to arrive late enough so there's not too much activity in the neighbourhood, but not so late as to be conspicuous."

"Tonight?" I said.

She looked at me. "Of course tonight. We have to get in there before the Aryan Twins think of it."

I weighed the bag of manuals. "You have great faith in my abilities."

She kissed me. "You built those amplifiers, didn't you?" She nodded at the monoblocks, crouching on either side of my record player. "Your old thermionic valve amplifiers." She had me there. "You're my electronics wizard," she said.

I dropped the bag onto the sofa. It made enough noise to cause the cats to jump. "And it looks like I've got a lot of fucking new spells to learn."

"Look on the positive side," she said. "You'll acquire a

new skill set."

"Breaking and entering."

She smiled at me. "You never know when it will come in handy."

"I think we should go in through the garage."

"At the house in Richmond?"

"Yes."

"Go in through the garage? Why?"

"Because it will be easier to break into. And once we're in the garage we'll be out of sight and we can then disable the house security system at our leisure."

"Well, I wouldn't use the word 'leisure'," said Nevada, "but I know what you mean." She thought for a moment, then said, "How do you know the security on the garage won't be even more formidable than it is for the house?"

"Why would it be?"

"Maybe he was a vintage car nut and has valuable antique automobiles parked in there."

"He wasn't a vintage car nut," I said. "He was a vintage vinyl nut."

"Well, maybe you should ask your friend," she said.

"My friend?"

"The girl who gets cement out of the gutters. The simple barefoot roof worker."

"Yes," I said. "And while I'm at it I might as well ask about the alarm system for the house. That wouldn't be at all suspicious."

"I suppose you're right," said Nevada. "We'll go in through the garage."

* * *

By late afternoon I had as deep an understanding of the manuals as I was going to get with my current brain. "Okay," I said.

"Okay?" said Nevada.

"We need to go out to the shops."

She studied me. "I thought we agreed we'd keep a low profile until it was time to head into Richmond tonight for the job."

"I love the way you call it a job," I said.

"I've even got us some black ski masks," she said.

"We still need to go to the shops."

She was sitting at the table examining all the kit she'd bought, which was spread out in front of her. Now she looked up at me sceptically. "What could we possibly still need? I bought up half the shop. Everything required for detecting, accessing and neutralising alarms." I could discern the echo of old Five O'Clock Shadow's sales pitch.

"That's right," I said. "You have. And what's more, once we drill into the system, I actually now believe we have a pretty good chance of deactivating whatever kind of alarm they have."

She looked up at me blankly. "So what do we need?"

"We need the drill. For drilling in."

"Oh shit. That's right. The bloke said we could buy one at any hardware store."

"And we can. But we need to get moving before our friendly neighbourhood hardware stores start to close."

"I'm right with you," said Nevada.

The cats came out to see us off, following through the estate for a while then fading into the shadows as we walked towards the main road. Here we turned left and headed for the local high street. It was only a short walk away but I had my travel card and Nevada had the financial might of some enigmatic industrial titan behind her, so we caught the bus.

We got off by a little DIY store I knew. There I went through the various drills available and chose a heavy-duty one with several rechargeable battery packs. It made me think of the woman up the ladder. I wondered if she would guess who it was when she found out about the break-in. Perhaps, if we were sufficiently careful, she'd never find out about it.

I stopped beside Nevada, who was looking up and down the high street. "Do you want to go home yet?"

"Not particularly. I've prepared as much as I can and I'll just start climbing the walls with tension as zero hour approaches."

"You'll be fine," I said.

"Thanks." She touched my arm.

"Let's get a coffee."

"Do you know somewhere? What am I talking about? Of course you do, this is your neighbourhood."

In fact, there was a little coffee shop I liked near the railway crossing at Mortlake Station. On the way there were four charity shops and, out of sheer force of habit, I hit them all.

Out of sheer force of habit, Nevada went through the clothes racks.

In the third shop we went to, in the first box I looked through, I found it.

Easy Come, Easy Go.

I lifted it up and as soon as I did so, I knew it was the real thing. It had a heavy old-fashioned sleeve, slightly yellowed with age. I flipped it over and checked the fine print on the back to make sure it wasn't a Japanese reissue, but I knew it wasn't. Nevada was looking at me now. She was standing beside a spinner of tank tops, her hand arrested in the act of reaching for a clothes hanger from which dangled a shapeless golden garment.

I stood up, as though moving in slow motion. I thought my hands would shake as I slipped the record out of the sleeve. But I was perfectly steady. Nevada was standing beside me now. The inner sleeve was of heavy polythene, the kind they used in the 1950s. You could see the record label through it.

It was the wrong label. Instead of being a Hathor LP from the fifties it was an Arista LP from the eighties. Nevada was looking at my face. She could see something was wrong. "Is it a reissue?"

"No," I said. "It's the wrong record." I read the label. Instead of *Easy Come, Easy Go* by Easy Geary it was something called *2:00 AM Paradise Café* by Barry Manilow. I didn't know whether to laugh or cry. I went to the counter and paid, on autopilot. I walked out the door, holding it open for Nevada. She was staring at me worriedly, as well she might.

"For a moment I thought we'd found it," she said. I said nothing. "So I suppose we just have to continue with our plan for tonight."

"No," I said. My voice sounded dry and strange.

"No?"

"It's all over," I said.

We didn't say a word on the bus. Nevada didn't take my hand as we walked from the bus stop to the house. She seemed almost frightened of me, or perhaps of the total defeat that had settled over me. Finally, as we opened the front door, and the cats came rushing to join us, she said, "I don't understand."

I held up my purchase from the charity shop. "It's the right sleeve," I said.

"So what?"

"With the wrong record in it."

Nevada sat down on the sofa and Turk promptly jumped up to join her. "I understand that."

I sighed and sank down beside her. "No, you don't understand."

She twisted around to look at me. "Then explain to me."

I held up the album. "This is it. This is the record we're looking for. Or at least the cover. It's authentic. It's American. It's from the fifties. There's no question that it's the cover of the record we want. But the record is gone. Somebody swapped it." I looked at the Manilow album. "And I don't think it was Tomas Helmer. He didn't strike me as the kind of man who'd misfile an LP."

Nevada was staring at me with concern. "So…"

"So record and sleeve were united when they were in his collection. But at some point since then they've been separated." I looked at her. "Without the record the sleeve is no good to us. And the record could be anywhere, literally anywhere. At least when it had the cover on it, it was easy to spot. But now our problem has been increased by an order of magnitude. The record could be anywhere. In any sleeve. Or in none. If it was in the wrong cover, it could have been one of the thousands of records we've already looked through and discarded." I couldn't look her in the eye anymore. I couldn't see the disappointment and defeat come swimming up into her gaze.

I looked down at the coffee table and for some reason a pile of CDs caught my attention. They were the CDs Stinky had been playing that day when he let himself in and waited for us to come back from the record fair. Fucking Stinky, I thought…

I shot to my feet.

The two cats and Nevada all flinched at the suddenness of my movement. But I was already running for the door. Behind me I could hear her calling, "Where are you going?" but I couldn't stop. I headed out onto the main road and then to the bus stop. There was no bus in sight, and anyway the road was solid with rush-hour traffic. I checked the time, cursed and starting running.

I reached the charity shop in ten minutes of alternately walking and running. It was twenty-five past five and the sign on the door said they were open until five thirty, but the lights were already off inside, except for one shining dimly through a doorway at the very back of the shop. I knocked on the door. I knocked long and loud and with what I hoped was restrained politeness and finally the guy who ran the shop appeared. He was plump with thick spectacles and wiry hair. He wore a loose purple jumper and jeans over a bulging paunch.

He wiped his hands in the air and mouthed, "We're closed." I stared at him helplessly. I could see by his face that there was nothing I could do. Here was a man who was through for the day.

I heard footsteps beside me. I turned to see Nevada standing there.

She had pressed her hands together in a gesture of

prayer and was gazing soulfully at the guy in the purple sweater. She fluttered her eyelashes. He stared at her for a moment, with a fixed, surly expression. Then the expression, and everything else about him, sort of melted. He sighed and shrugged and I knew we had him.

He unlocked the door and opened it for us with a jingling of keys. Then he went to the wall switch behind the till and flicked the lights on. He looked at me.

"She's like that bloody cat in *Shrek*," he said.

I was at the records in about half a second while Nevada waited, apparently keeping the proprietor sweet behind my back. They were talking, but I was concentrating so hard I couldn't make out their words.

There were three boxes of records. Four including the one where I'd found the cover. I'd already looked through that one thoroughly—but not knowing what I knew now.

I started with the first box again, going through every record.

I was halfway through the third box and starting to get seriously worried when I found it: *2:00 AM Paradise Café* by Barry Manilow. As soon as I picked it up, I knew I was on to something. It was way too heavy. I slipped the record out. It was in a white paper inner sleeve with a hole in the middle. Through the hole I could see the red and white Hathor label.

Easy Come, Easy Go.

I slid it out of the sleeve and flipped it over. There they were, the autographs of Easy Geary and Rita Mae Pollini in the dead wax, slightly contorted to fit the curvature of the record. Nevada was looking at me and smiling quietly. She knew.

I paid the guy. Now my hands *were* trembling. He glanced at the record as he put it into a bag for me. "I have a lot of respect for Barry Manilow," he said.

I walked out the door with Nevada at my side.

We had it. In our hands.

15. SUNDAY

Back at my house we reunited the record with its cover and then we put it triumphantly on display on top of my wardrobe in the bedroom. It's a bit embarrassing to admit, but it was a big turn-on, seeing it there. The visible essence of our victory. We spent most of that night alternately making love and lying exhausted together on the bed staring up at the LP.

We only took it down in the early dawn when it looked like the cats might knock it over.

We woke up late, ferociously hungry, and while Nevada was taking one of her marathon baths—which were sheer pleasure for the cats—I cooked breakfast. Cheese omelette. I was still working my way through the Cornish cheddar.

Nevada came out of the bathroom drying her hair. She hung the towel on the back of the orange plastic chair. I remembered when she'd sat in that same chair on her first visit. She smiled and came over and hugged me, arms encircling me from behind as I worked at the stove top. She smelled good.

"Let's play it," she said.

"What?"

"The record. *Easy Come, Easy Go.*"

"We can't," I said. "It's unplayable."

I added the grated cheese to the omelette. There was a lengthening silence as Nevada gradually came to realise I wasn't joking. Then her arms loosened around me. She went over and stood with her back to the sink, so she could see my face.

"Unplayable?" she said. Authentic alarm had flared in her eyes. "That can't be right. That's no good. My boss isn't going to accept that."

She seemed genuinely worried, so I immediately turned down the heat under the omelette then took her by the hand and led her into the living room. Here I opened the curtains and fetched the record and put it on the turntable. In the daylight she could see that the playing surface was thick with dust and also tiny white star-shaped patches here and there of what looked like some kind of tenacious mould.

I said, "It's unplayable. At the moment. But don't worry."

"What do you mean don't worry? My boss is definitely going to want to play it and he'll be expecting a high fidelity audiophile experience." She looked at me. "And what do you mean, at the moment?"

I said, "There's two kinds of damage to records. There's the kind that's permanent and irreversible—wear and abuse and scratches. And then there's the kind that's just due to neglect and lack of care. Like leaving a record lying around and allowing it to collect dust. I think that's what we have here."

She was getting what I was saying, but she was also getting impatient. So I cut the explanation short. "Irreversible damage usually happens to a record that's been played hundreds of times."

"But that's not the case here, correct? This is not

irreversible damage. Correct? Please, sweetie, this is like riding a fucking rollercoaster."

"I'm sorry. I'm just saying that this…" I held up the record. "This looks like exactly the opposite problem." I tilted the record to the light and inspected the thick grey layer of dust that had accumulated on the playing surface. "I suspect that the record has hardly been played. Perhaps it was played once, or never. After that, I think someone left it lying around, perhaps on a turntable, for months or maybe even years." I turned it over. This side was a lot cleaner, which supported my turntable hypothesis.

I looked at Nevada. "But I think, under the dirt, it may well be perfect."

She was watching me intently, as if her future hung in the balance. "And the dirt can be removed, correct?"

I nodded. "By cleaning with a proper record cleaner."

She relaxed. "Well, you've got one, haven't you?"

"No."

She shook her head. "Yes you have. I remember, the first time I was here."

"Shit," I said. "The omelette." I hurried back into the kitchen and caught it just in time. I turned off the heat under the pan. Nevada had followed me into the kitchen.

She said, "I remember it with great vividness. You were banging on about coffee filters in the record cleaner box, or some such lunacy. But the point at the centre of this lunacy was you had one, a record cleaner."

I took the plates out of the oven, where they'd been keeping warm. "I do. But it's just a primitive wet bath system."

"I think I'm still with you so far, but I'm suppressing an urge to scream." I cut the omelette in two and transferred it onto the plates. "Here, let me take those." Nevada took the plates out and put them on the table, and set cutlery around them with a clatter while I buttered the toast and stacked it on the breadboard. When all the food was on the table I showed her the record again.

"For this you need a proper record cleaning machine, one with a vacuum cleaner built into it to suck the gunge off the surface of the record as it cleans it."

"Suck the gunge, right, that's audiophile terminology is it? I must say it isn't very appetising." But she didn't display any lack of appetite as she tucked into the omelette. It was cooked to perfection, despite all the to-ing and fro-ing.

"They're really noisy too," I said, between devouring forkfuls of omelette. The cheddar was just right. "That's another reason I never got one. The vacuum cleaner is unshielded you see, and they make such a racket that you have to wear ear pads when you're using one. To avoid damaging your hearing." I grinned at her.

"Yes, I get the irony. Losing your hearing in pursuit of audio perfection."

"Plus the cats would hate it."

Nevada reached down and patted Fanny, who had become excited by the sound of us happily eating and was now inward bound for her food bowl. "And we wouldn't want to hurt your little ears, would we, would we, would we? Little ears, little ears."

"Plus I could never afford to buy one."

She looked at me across the table and smiled. "You'll be able to afford to buy one now." She helped me carry the plates back into the kitchen and dump them in the sink. "So where do we get one of these machines?" she said.

"It's not that simple."

She followed me back into the living room. "No, of course it isn't."

"If we rushed out and bought a very expensive record cleaning machine, and someone happened to have us under observation, don't you think they might find it a tiny bit suspicious?"

She looked at me, the realisation surfacing in her eyes. "Of course. Why would you want a special record cleaner? Perhaps to clean a special record."

I nodded. "We wouldn't want the Aryan Twins to put two and two together." I looked at her. "And get an Aryan four."

She snorted with amusement. I sat down again and reached for another piece of toast, the last survivor lying lonely on the breadboard.

"So we don't buy one of these cleaners. Instead we find someone who already owns one, for business or personal use. Someone we can trust."

"I was going to have that piece of toast," said Nevada. "And do you know such a person?"

I divided the piece of toast with her. "I do, but he lives in Wales."

"I don't want to sound as if I don't immediately love the idea of driving to Wales, but is that the only option?"

"We could send the record to him in the post."

"Right," she said. "Wales it is."

Once she was sold on the idea of driving to Hughie's to clean the record, Nevada wanted to set off right away. "So let's go," she said.

"Not now. First we want to spend the day combing the charity shops."

"What? Why?"

"We don't want to give any indication we've found the record."

"Of course not. So we don't want to change our usual pattern of behaviour."

"That's right. We have to behave in a way calculated to pull the wool over their little Aryan eyes."

"And if they think we're still looking for it, if they see us doing that, they won't guess that we found it." She grinned at me. "You're so sneaky. I can't believe it. You have a natural talent for this."

So we devoted the day to making the rounds of the charity shops, this time in Chelsea. The poshest neighbourhoods of London tend not to have charity shops. Too downmarket. Which is a pity. The King's Road, though, was an interesting exception and the shops here were always worth a look. Today we hit all of them. It was fun. I didn't find anything, but that didn't matter. I was sated, content, like a fisherman who had already landed his limit.

Landed a whale, in fact.

That night in bed I said, "By the way, do you ride a bicycle?"

Nevada rolled over and looked at me. "Do I look like I've ridden a bicycle since I was twelve years old?"

"That's kind of exactly my point."

For someone who allegedly hadn't been on a bike since she was twelve, she did surprisingly well the following day. We slipped through the Abbey grounds, ghostly in the early morning mist.

It was Sunday and we generally didn't go record hunting on Sundays, because so many charity shops were closed for the day. "So if we can just prevent them from discovering that we've slipped off…"

"Assuming they're watching us at all. For all we know, they take Sundays off, too."

I had borrowed the bikes from the two nice women, Ginnie and Sue, who lived next door. Because their bungalow was adjacent to mine, we could step out of my back gate and in through theirs virtually unseen. The two bikes had been left out for us, equipped with rather impressive heavy-duty steel locks. We unlocked them using the keys Ginnie had slipped through my letterbox the previous night and walked the bikes out, ticking and whirring, into the dark and quiet of the foggy street.

We closed the gate behind us and stood in the small access road that paralleled the rear wall of the Abbey. There was an opening in the wall about a hundred metres down on our left, which allowed pedestrian access into one small section of the Abbey complex, a public thoroughfare for centuries. We threaded our bicycles along the footpaths here, guided by the low amber footlights that marked the path, both of us gaining in confidence as we got used to the machines. "It's just like riding a bike." My voice seemed to be muffled in the fog. No one else was around, so I spoke a little louder. "You never forget how."

"So, who did we borrow these from?" said Nevada.

"Lovable local lesbians."

She shifted around on her seat. "Do you think I'll catch being a lesbian from sitting on this bicycle saddle?"

"We can but hope."

Having taken our meandering, roundabout route through the Abbey grounds, we now came out onto the main road about half a mile from the exit of my estate. We would proceed to ride back past that exit, as though approaching from another direction entirely, and hopefully only recognisable as a couple of anonymous dawn cyclists.

We whizzed down Abbey Avenue, towards the Upper Richmond Road. The avenue was silent and empty, wreathed in fog. The amber streetlights were discreet glowing clouds flowing above us. I could sense Nevada relaxing beside me as she got used to the bike. She looked over and flashed me a grin. She was beginning to enjoy the ride. So was I.

The air was damp and cold and clean. You could smell the promise of snow.

Up ahead glowed two soft red circles, ill-defined and floating in mid-air. The traffic lights. We slowed to a halt and waited, balanced on our bikes. The eerie green glow of the traffic lights shone through the fog. We took off and turned right.

There were no cars in either direction. The only sound was the drone of a passenger jet descending towards Heathrow, high above us in the immensity of the morning sky. We pedalled towards the next set of lights. As we slowed, there was a wet whispering sound behind us.

The sound of bicycle tyres.

A cyclist appeared out of the mist and fell in beside us. An indeterminate lean shape with helmet and goggles, dressed all in black with a yellow stripe down the side, he or she stopped and waited poised on his or her bike for the traffic light to change. Through the fog the soft red light shone down on us all.

Just then there was the sound of a second bicycle. It

whispered to a stop on the other side of us. This rider was also dressed in an entirely black outfit with a yellow stripe. This rider was bigger, undoubtedly a man. My heart began to beat raggedly in my chest. The light changed.

We all surged forward together. The two riders in black were tight on either side of us. I could see Nevada was pushing as hard as I was, but we weren't making any headway. Our escort kept pace effortlessly.

We moved down the empty streets in perfect formation. I was going full out now, sweating profusely. My rucksack felt hot where it was strapped against my back.

Inside the rucksack was a box. Inside the box was the record.

I looked at Nevada helplessly. The riders to our right and left kept pace with us like automatons. There was no one else in sight. We were alone in the street. I began to realise just what a miscalculation I'd made.

Then there was the sound of a third bike.

Then a fourth and fifth. They came out of the mist. All wearing the same black outfit as our escort, black with a yellow stripe. They fell in all around us, all identically dressed. More and more until it was finally a dozen cyclists, all with the same team colours.

They were all around us, like a school of fish surrounding two of a different species. They were riding with us, and then suddenly they were gone, pouring on the speed and contemptuously pulling away from us—the two Sunday-morning amateurs—as they disappeared into the mist. Quite possibly on their way to the Olympics.

Nevada and I looked at each other and slowed down.

My heart was pounding, and not just with the exertion of cycling.

* * *

At the car rental place in Putney we loaded the bikes into the back of the Volvo we'd hired and set off towards Hammersmith and the M4.

I was driving, Nevada beside me with a large book of maps, prepared to supplement the in-car navigation system if necessary, and a rather more useful bag of oranges that she was all set to peel on demand, then neatly segment and pass across a piece at a time to refresh the driver.

"Are they seedless?"

"Now you're starting to sound like Tinkler."

Speaking of Tinkler, we had to drive along the Fulham Palace Road and right past the Charing Cross Hospital. But we didn't stop. "They might have it staked out. They might be watching for us."

"Do you really think so?"

"No," I said. "But we can't take the chance." She nodded and started peeling an orange, releasing its lovely scent.

So we agreed we wouldn't stop in to see Tinkler.

It was something I'd live to regret.

The sun was coming up and burning off the mist as we drove west out of Hammersmith and onto the motorway. Nevada napped for a while and then woke up and resumed our conversation as though it had never stopped.

"So tell me about your friend."

"Hughie Mackinaw," I said. "The Scottish Welshman."

"That's what Tinkler calls him."

"That's what everybody calls him. Good old Hughie.

What can you say about a white man with an afro? At least it's not ginger."

"There is that," she said.

"He has a wife called Albina and a boy called Mickey and a little girl called Boo."

"Is that short for something? Boo?"

"I don't know. But she's nice."

"It's a nice name."

"I like her a lot better than the boy."

"Why?"

I considered. "Hughie is one of those macho guys who has spoiled his son completely rotten. So the kid is this sulky, tantrum-throwing, petulant little pudding."

"You paint an attractive picture."

"So, anyway, what I'm driving at is that the son's the antithesis of the guy himself."

"I get it. In what way is Hughie a macho guy?"

"He used to run with a motorcycle gang in Scotland. He was their mechanic. Great precision mechanic—could build spares from scratch. He could make anything. But then he discovered it was safer and more profitable to build turntables."

"Strange career U-turn."

"Not really. He always loved music. Had a good ear. That's the connection."

"And he now makes a living from making these turntables?"

"He sells a few each year. Mostly to the States and Japan. They're not cheap, they're high-end kit, but it's never quite enough to make a living."

"So he now also grows huge swathes of weed, right?"

"Yes, he has rather reverted to type there."

"What's the wife like?"

"Common-law wife actually."

"Nothing wrong with that," said Nevada, "in this day and age."

"She's all right. Nice, but a bit ditzy."

Nevada's stomach suddenly rumbled, dramatically loud in the confines of the car. We both laughed and she said, "I hope we're going to get lunch."

"Oh, we'll get lunch all right. That's going to be a strategic and diplomatic minefield."

"Why? What do you mean?"

I said, "Because she's probably the only pagan earth mother operating in Wales who doesn't know one end of a green vegetable from the other."

"How ironic."

"So lunch is going to be an application of the triple arts of the freezer, the can opener and the microwave."

"Oh joy," said Nevada.

There was a long silence as we watched the landscape flashing past and the traffic, which was sparse but growing as we drove west. Finally I said, "When we get the record cleaned will you have to take it to Japan?"

She looked at me. "Japan?"

I took the plunge. "I checked that number that called you. On my landline. The night your phone wasn't working."

"My, you are sneaky. Yes. My employer is based in Japan."

"But your card says GmbH."

"Yes. Fiendishly cunning ruse, isn't it?" She smiled, staring out the window into the distance. "Made you think it was a German concern, didn't I?"

I said, "Actually, I began to smell a rat when Tinkler

asked you about that German Rolling Stones album he covets and you didn't know what *Sonderauflage* meant."

She looked at me, askance but fondly. "The vinyl detective," she said.

The sun was high and shining down onto a brilliant winter's morning, the trees bare and the fields limned with gleaming pockets of frost. We reached Hughie's just before eleven, feeling a little weary with all the miles we'd driven.

We made our first stop at his factory, as we'd arranged on the phone. Hughie was there to greet us, wearing gleaming black Doc Marten boots, tattered jeans and a navy blue donkey jacket. His only concession to the cold was what looked like a Cambridge University scarf. If it was, it would be a garment he had no right to wear; but then that was the least of Hughie's misdemeanours. He was bare-headed, as if to proudly reveal the afro as advertised.

He was smoking a rollie and threw it aside as he waved to us. He had a lean yellow dog at his side. They were standing in the narrow approach road that came off the main road and ran past the low two-storey building which served as his factory, into the grounds behind. I drove in and around and pulled up by the back door of the old brown building, beside Hughie's battered vintage BMW.

We got out of our car, yawning and stretching, and locked it behind us. I almost forgot to take the record, which was on the floor in the back of the car, safe in its box and rucksack and as far as possible from any sunlight or heat source.

We heard Hughie's footsteps as he came down the road

beside the building. The dog's claws were clicking on the frozen surface.

I looked at Nevada. "Whatever you do, don't mention his afro."

As soon as Hughie came into sight she said, "I love your hair."

Hughie grinned and rubbed his head happily, as though discovering it for the first time, and I knew that, once again, she'd got away with it. "It would make a really good Jewfro," he said, "if only I was a Jew." And he came forward to shake hands with me and give Nevada a rather impertinent hug and kiss on the cheek. On both cheeks, in fact.

I had to remind myself that we were in neo-hippy territory here.

The dog promptly disappeared, clattering through a large dog flap in the factory door, sensibly getting out of the cold and leaving us to our human concerns.

The grounds behind Hughie's factory extended back a long way before coming to a high wall that overlooked parkland beyond. All of which was just as well, given the privacy required for Hughie's agricultural operations on the site. I was familiar with the general layout, having driven down here with Tinkler when he'd had his Thorens restored, but there was now a large new structure looming on the left of the yard.

It was an odd-looking water tank rising from four steel legs like a squat alien giant who had grown tired and given up his attempt to invade our planet.

"What's the water tank, Hughie?"

He shook his head. "It's not a water tank. It's a fuel tank. To feed the generator." He proudly pointed towards a shed near the rear wall. I realised that was new, too. "I'm now energy self-sufficient."

"By burning petrol?"

Hughie grinned. "More importantly, it prevents any spikes on the electricity grid from running the lights or the watering system. To grow you-know-what." He indicated the greenhouses that occupied most of the yard.

"I understand you've had a bumper crop this year," I said. Tinkler always kept me updated on developments at Hughie's.

He nodded his head, his big afro bobbing. I noticed some streaks of grey in there amongst the brown. "That's true. That's how I was able to pay for the generator. Not to mention the fuel." He looked at me, his eyes a little wild, but no wilder than usual. "I got an entire tanker full. I swapped it for a load of weed."

"You're kidding."

"No, it's the alternative economy." He gazed fondly at the greenhouses. "You just plant things in the earth and up they grow and then you can swap them for an entire tanker full of fuel." He nodded at the tank, walking over into its shadow. "And I had to store it somewhere, so I built this." He gazed up at it proudly, then looked at me. "Now we're energy self-sufficient," he repeated.

Nevada was staring at the greenhouses, which were fashioned of heavy-duty transparent plastic. They were big long tunnels sealed at each end, essentially like giant versions of the poly tunnels in which commercial growers cultivate tomatoes. Which was appropriate enough, because all you could see from the outside was the blurry red of tomatoes growing in dense clusters within.

They looked cheerful and festive in the winter landscape.

Of course, behind the screens of growing tomatoes was the real crop, which could just be glimpsed as a rich green background of foliage.

The greenhouses rested on flat rectangles of earth with deep trenches dug all around them, like moats. There was frost in the bottom of these, making a neat white pattern around each greenhouse. You gained access to the greenhouses by crossing the trenches using rather precarious miniature bridges or walkways. These were sheets of corrugated aluminium, which hadn't been fastened down at either end. They were worryingly unstable under foot, as I'd discovered on my previous visit.

But Hughie liked them like that, because he could remove them at will, cutting off access to the greenhouses. Nevada was peering at one of them now.

She said, "Why the moats? Are you expecting to be besieged by knights with medieval battering rams?"

"No rams," said Hughie, his Glasgow accent now going full throttle for some reason, perhaps brought out by his appreciation of Nevada. "Just rats." He smiled at her, nodding in my direction. "I take it our friend here has told you about my little agricultural endeavours?"

"Oh yes. What's more, I've had a chance to sample your produce and may I be the first to assert my belief that the farmer is the backbone of the nation."

Hughie chuckled raspily, his breath fogging on the cold air. Nevada said, "Anyway, you were saying about rats." Hughie's smile faded.

"Oh yes. The little bastards. They were getting into the greenhouses. Didn't matter what we did—we used heavy-duty PVC, we tried putting sheet iron underneath, it didn't matter. They always managed to dig or chew their way in."

"And then they'd attack the, ahem, cash crop?"

"They'd eat the tomatoes and *then* they'd attack the cash crop."

"Really?" said Nevada.

"Oh yes. They'd gnaw through the green stems of young plants, killing them with a couple of bites. It would break your heart. Leaving these nasty little tooth marks."

"Do you suppose they get high, the rats?"

"Not anymore," said Hughie, smiling grimly. "Not on my weed they don't."

"Thanks to the moats?"

Hughie nodded. "That's right. In the spring we fill them with water and the little bastards can't get across."

"They won't swim?" said Nevada.

"It seems to discourage most of them."

"I must say that shows the sort of lack of endeavour and initiative which blights this fine nation of ours."

Hughie grinned at her delightedly, showing his full assortment of mismatched teeth. "You must take some tomatoes home with you," he said.

"Bugger the tomatoes," said Nevada. "We'll take a bale of weed." Hughie gave a hard shout of laughter and did a jaunty little strut back towards the factory. All this talk of illicit hemp farming had fired him up. He was a lot more excited than I'd ever seen him when dealing with a hi-fi. He clapped me on the shoulder.

"Is that it?" He indicated the rucksack with the record in it.

"Yes," I said. "Shall we give it a clean?"

But he insisted on taking us home for Albina to cook us lunch first—an alarming prospect to those in the know.

16. BLACK CIRCLE IN THE SNOW

The meal was as mediocre as expected, and Hughie's son was just as much of a brat. His little daughter, Boo, was charming, though, and Nevada took to both her and her mother, Albina. The feeling was mutual. They actually seemed sorry to wave goodbye to us when we left.

The light was failing as we drove back towards the factory. The sky was clear now, but a lot of snow had fallen while we'd been wasting time at the house. It had come down in silent quantities, clothing the sides of the road in soft rounded white contours. We drove by a different route this time, passing the local railway station. It was only half a mile away. I said, "We could have caught the train down and then walked."

"Wouldn't that have made it easier to follow us?"

"I guess that's why we didn't catch the train."

She looked at me. "Do you think someone could have followed us, after all the precautions we took?"

"If they have, I'll be really pissed off."

I peered at the winding road ahead. Hughie's tail lights started blinking to indicate a left turn, the red and amber glow reflecting off the snow on the road.

He was waiting for us by the open back door of the factory. The dog was beside him, dancing impatiently and wondering why we didn't all go into the nice warm building and close the door tightly behind us. The yard was illuminated by the pearly glow from the greenhouses, all of them lit from within by the growing lights. It was a soft, eerie, suffused luminescence that shone on the snow. I could hear the faint chugging of the generator.

I said, "You switched the generator on?"

Hughie shook his head. "Comes on automatically after dark." The dog was straining at his side, willing us all to go in. We did. Hughie took us through the shadowy, echoing machine shop which occupied the ground floor of the building, to a staircase that led up to the offices, some store rooms and a listening room. The record cleaner was set up in one of the offices, along with some disembowelled turntables and a surprisingly elaborate closed circuit television system.

Two large computer screens set up side by side gave assorted views of the front and back yards of the factory from several angles. Beside them was a heavy-duty metal cabinet fitted to the wall. Hughie unlocked this and took out a double-barrelled shotgun. He took a handful of shells from his pocket and set them on the desk.

I said, "What the hell is that?"

"Is it for the rats?" said Nevada.

Hughie shook his head. "The rats don't bother us in the winter." He proceeded to load the shotgun. Nevada picked up one of the shells and looked at it curiously. It had a yellow case instead of the usual red.

She said, "I've never seen ones like this. What kind of shot is it?"

Hughie grinned his crooked grin again. "Sea salt. Finest Welsh sea salt. Hand loaded. I've had some trouble with kids breaking into the greenhouses. And if I see them, I'm going to give them a little discouragement."

"You're going to pepper them with salt," said Nevada.

Hughie chuckled. He set the shotgun down on the desk in front of the screens. He nodded at them. "We can keep an eye on these while we work. In case those sneaky little bastards try to break in again."

"How serious is the problem?" I said, peering at the camera feeds. The yards were desolate and empty and looked like no one had ever set foot there.

"At first it was just some clusters of buds," said Hughie. "Then entire plants went missing."

"Do you have any idea who it is?"

He shook his head. "No."

"All large-scale crime is an inside job," confided Nevada.

"Well, this is small-scale crime," said Hughie, and he switched on the record cleaning machine. He had built it himself, but its design was the same as most of the top-end machines. Essentially it looked like a bulky turntable, but with a slender vacuum-cleaning head instead of a playing arm.

Hughie held out his hand. I felt a strange reluctance to unpack the record and give it to him, but I did. He put it on the turntable, fitting a small circular clamp to cover the label. Then he took out a plastic bottle of liquid and sprayed it all over the playing surface of the record. Nevada gave me an anxious, questioning look but I just nodded my head and gave her what I hoped was a reassuring smile. The liquid Hughie was using was his own secret formula, but it would be essentially the same as all other record cleaning fluids—distilled water, isopropyl alcohol, some kind of surfactant and perhaps a special something to counteract mould-release agent.

Hughie finished drenching the record and inspected the gleaming wet surface with satisfaction. "Now we let it soak for a moment." He turned away and started rooting around in a cardboard box, eventually producing three pairs of heavy-duty ear defenders. These were like sets of headphones with large foam discs to enclose and cover the ears. He handed a pair to me and one to Nevada.

"Are these really necessary?" she said, inspecting them.

"Just you wait," I said.

"Well, I hope they've been washed." She slipped them on reluctantly.

Now that we were all safe, Hughie set the turntable in motion. The record began to spin. He set the cleaning head on the disc and turned on the vacuum cleaner. As I'd explained to Nevada, a normal domestic vacuum cleaner is insulated to reduce the amount of noise it kicks out. Hughie's record cleaner, like most such machines, dispensed with these fripperies.

It emitted a bellow suggesting dinosaurs fighting in a primordial swamp. Big dinosaurs.

Nevada looked at me in amazement and fitted her headphones a little tighter. She was happy to be wearing them now, dirty or not. We watched the cleaning head travel across the record, slurping up the liquid from the vinyl. When it reached the run-out groove, Hughie guided it carefully back to its resting point and switched the turntable off.

He turned the record over and repeated the process on the other side.

When he was finished we removed our headphones and looked at each other. Hughie unscrewed the clamp from the label and took the record off the turntable. He handed it to me, grinning.

The vinyl was gleaming, a deep rich reflective black with rainbow highlights. The dense beautiful pattern of the microgrooves shimmered, precise and pristine. It looked brand new.

It was perfect.

"Normally I charge two quid for this service," said Hughie.

"I think we can manage that," said Nevada. She was jubilant. "We may even stretch to a bag of your no doubt overpriced cannabinoid greenery."

"Yeah, you mentioned that," said Hughie. "And you must take some tomatoes." He was always eager to get rid of those tomatoes. He turned to me and pointed at the record. "Do you want to play it?"

Hughie's listening room was next door to the office. It was a large, rectangular room with a turntable, amp and speakers located at one end and a sofa at the other. So that was where his sofa had gone. At home his lounge had nothing but armchairs in it. Now we knew why.

The speakers were set up against the far wall to fire down the long axis of the room towards us listeners at the other end. It was an ideal setup.

Hughie switched on his amps while I held the record, still faintly damp, carefully by its edges.

"That's weird," I said.

Nevada was instantly on the alert. "Is something wrong?"

"No, no, not at all." I held the record up to the light. "It's just something in the dead wax."

She was watching me apprehensively. "But there's no question that it's the original?"

"On the contrary, everything about this authenticates it. It's got the autographs by Geary and Rita Mae. It's got the initials DDP, which is Danny DePriest, who engineered it. It's got the right stamper and matrix numbers." I moved closer to the light. "But there's something else here too."

She moved closer. "What?"

"Two more letters. A capital 'B' in a circle on side one, and a capital 'Y' in a circle on side two."

"What do they mean?"

"I have no idea."

"Ready here," said Hughie impatiently. He reached for the record, then smiled indulgently when I insisted on putting it on the turntable and lowering the stylus myself. He winked at Nevada. "He doesn't trust me."

"Very wise," said Nevada.

We went back down to the far end of the room and sat on the sofa as the music began to play. Hughie had aligned his speakers with considerable care and the imaging was excellent. Much more importantly, the record was in great shape. "Sounds good, doesn't it?" said Hughie proudly.

I nodded. "Sounds like it's never been played before."

"Just as you predicted," said Nevada. She moved closer to me on the sofa. She sounded proud as well.

The second side of the record sounded, if anything, even better. I waited with particular eagerness for the vocal track at the end. It was an old Red Jellaway composition, a spooky little number called 'Running from a Spell' and Rita Mae Pollini brought out all its eerie loveliness. But by now

I was taking the sonic and musical qualities of the album for granted and I was specifically listening for the tiny flaw I'd noticed before.

The one Tinkler had diagnosed as the singer being too close to the mic.

This was the first time I'd heard a first-generation copy of the track, direct from the master tape. And there it was, the undeniable popping sound. Nevada looked at me. "Is that good old Rogue Plosive?" she said.

I nodded. "Yes. But I don't think it's anything to do with the singer or microphone anymore."

"Yeah, weird isn't it," said Hughie. He was listening keenly. "It's not dirt on the record." He sounded a trifle defensive.

"No one's suggesting that it is."

"My cleaner would have removed all that."

"Naturally."

"And it doesn't sound like a pressing flaw." Hughie sounded thoughtful now that there was no question of him being at fault. "It's probably a noise from the session." When the track ended he went to the turntable and played it again. I didn't interfere this time, although I had to repress the urge to do so. The song began again, and again we heard the sound. Hughie was listening with the keen attention of a hunting dog, his head to one side. I wondered where his dog had got to.

"It's the sound of someone knocking over a music stand," he said.

"Maybe." I wasn't convinced. The track ended, and with it the record. Hughie went to the turntable and lifted the arm and switched it off. I let him. I was, finally, beginning to realise what we had accomplished. A sleepy sense of triumph was stealing over me, lulling and relaxing me. I reminded myself that I would have to drive back. Nevada had hit the wine a little too hard at lunch.

Hughie came back to the sofa. Nevada was looking at me and smiling a lazy, contented smile. She squeezed my hand and leaned over to Hughie.

"Well, it looks like we owe you two quid," she said.

"I take cash, credit cards or PayPal," said Hughie.

Then the lights went out.

"Oh fuck," said Hughie, sounding irritated but unsurprised. "It's the fucking generator."

"Hughie," I said, trying not to let the tension show in my voice as we all sat there in the darkness, "does this happen often?"

"All the fucking time." He got up from the sofa and starting blundering around. The only light in the room was the distant gentle orange glow of the valve amps, slowly fading now that their power had been cut. Nevada suddenly giggled.

"I've got to go to the loo," she said.

"I'll get some candles," said Hughie. "So you can see your way."

"It's all right," said Nevada. She'd taken out her phone and the spectral glow of the screen created a pool of pale blue light. She offered it to Hughie. "Here, you can borrow this."

"It's all right," grunted Hughie, searching his pockets. "I've got one of my own. I just keep forgetting to use the damned thing." He took out his phone and used it to guide him to the doorway. Nevada followed. She was gone for what seemed an awfully long time. When she returned she was preceded by the ghostly glow of her phone.

"Where's Hughie?" I said.

"He went out to look at the generator, with much cursing." She switched off the phone and we were in the darkness again. The sofa creaked as she sat down beside me. We groped blindly for each other and then held hands. "This is fun," said Nevada. "A power cut in Wales. In the winter. You take me to all the best places."

Before I could answer, the dog started barking. He was downstairs and evidently very excited about something. "Jesus," I said. "What's going on?" But I could hardly hear my own voice. The dog's baleful cries were echoing stridently through the whole building. Nevada said something but I couldn't hear what. We both stood up at the same time, as if synchronised. And at that exact moment the lights came back on.

We heard Hughie's voice downstairs and the dog fell silent. We sat down again. A minute later Hughie was in the room, shaking his head. "Spencer's going spare," he said. "I had to give him some biscuits."

"Look, Hughie," I said, "if you don't mind, we'd better be going."

He looked crestfallen. I suppose he'd envisioned a convivial late session listening to music and smoking dope. "Do you have to?" he said.

I nodded. "Got a long drive back," I said firmly.

"I suppose," he sighed.

Nevada put a hand on my knee and stood up. She yawned and stretched. She hadn't said anything but I knew she was as anxious to get going as I was. The power cut and the malignant cacophony of the dog had put both our nerves on edge. I got up and went to the turntable to get the record.

It was gone.

I turned and looked at Hughie and Nevada. "Hughie," I said. Then I turned and looked at the wall behind the speakers. There was a door there I hadn't noticed before. I opened it and stepped through. Nevada was calling something behind me but I didn't hear what it was. The room I'd stepped into was dark. I fumbled for a light switch and found one. The room was another office, empty except for a desk and some old filing cabinets.

There were footprints on the floor, damp with melted snow.

I followed them out the door, into the hallway, down the stairs. Hughie and Nevada were coming after me now, moving fast and with a sense of urgency. They'd realised that the record was gone.

Spencer the dog was sitting waiting by the back door. He gave me an I-told-you-so look. I shoved the door open and stepped out into the cold night air. I heard the crunching of feet moving quickly on snow and then I saw the figure. Small and lean, moving fast. Wearing a dark ski suit that might have been black or navy blue.

I was sure it was a woman. And I was sure I knew which one.

As she ran, she was trying to slide the record back into its sleeve. She'd managed to steal both. "Wait!" I shouted, inanely, then I started after her. I turned my head as I ran, and saw Nevada and Hughie coming through the door behind me. Hughie raised his shotgun into the air and fired a blast into the night sky.

"Stop!" he yelled.

Instead the woman turned. She had the record in one hand. In the other was something I couldn't make out. It sparkled brightly and then I heard a noise like twigs breaking and behind me a window shattered.

I realised I was being shot at. I stopped dead and the woman kept running. Nevada came up behind me, moving fast. "Get down," she said, and shoved me down, hard, onto the snow. I saw she had her own gun in her hand, the one I had never asked her about.

She stopped and aimed it, using a professional two-handed grip, and fired.

The woman went down.

The record went flying out of her hand, through the air. The record and sleeve separated, the record flying like a discus. It landed on a sloping bank of snow. It made a perfect black circle against the whiteness. In a distant, detached corner of my consciousness I found myself thinking the record would be fine. A nice soft bed of snow was probably one of the best things in the world it could have landed on, provided it didn't have a chance to turn to water.

I got up and started towards the record. Nevada looked back at me. "Stay there," she shouted. "I'll get it." I did as she said.

Suddenly the woman lying on the ground got up again, apparently unharmed. Nevada had hit her for sure, so she must have been wearing some sort of vest. I pieced all this together and it made a kind of sense, but suddenly in my mind it made everything seem like a paintball game. None of it was serious, and no one was really going to get hurt.

So I got up and followed Nevada.

The woman was running away towards the darkness at the far end of the yard, the record abandoned. Nevada glanced back over her shoulder at me. "Stay back!" she shouted. Suddenly Hughie ran past both of us, reloading his shotgun as he went. Nevada cursed and set off after him.

Hughie emptied his shotgun towards the fleeing woman and the darkness at the far end of the yard.

Someone started shooting back.

Nevada was now running beside one of the greenhouse ditches and as the gun went off, she stumbled with the impact of a shot.

I could feel it. It was as though the bullet had hit my own body.

Nevada wasn't wearing a vest.

She fell sideways into the ditch, disappearing from sight.

I ran towards her. There was the sound of Hughie's shotgun again and then a savage burst of fire from what I now realised was an automatic weapon of some kind. Hughie came fleeing back from the shadows at the end of the yard.

Bullets whined overhead. I heard them hitting something metallic, above me and to the left, with a ringing, stitching sound. Hughie came running toward me. "Get back!" he shouted.

"Nevada!" I yelled.

"She's dead. I saw her. No chance."

There was more gunfire. I heard it rattling off metal, ricocheting wildly off something and then punching hard into something else.

Hughie and I were both crouching low, trying to stay under the whining slice of the bullets. Behind us I heard the dog barking frantically. Hughie was staring desperately into my face and I nodded and he ran back towards the factory.

I let him think I was with him, but I ran the other way, the way I'd been heading before.

Towards the ditch where Nevada lay.

But as I moved towards it, there was a fierce sizzling, popping above me and then a dangerous creaking sound. Suddenly the snow was a bright yellow, lit with a hot wavering light. I looked up and saw flames rising out of the fuel tank. It must have been hit by the bullets, and ignited.

As I watched, it began to come apart.

It collapsed, easing down on its four legs like a wounded giant falling to his knees. The tank burst open and decanted its blazing contents across the frozen ground.

A tongue of flame poured into the ditch where Nevada had fallen.

The mass of burning fuel gushed after it. The ditch filled with a hot, bright, crackling flood.

The ditch where Nevada had fallen.

My mind couldn't absorb what was happening. I could feel the heat on my face, like sunburn. My lungs were full of the stink of burning petrol. Shadows twisted on the ground. Black smoke began to pour into the sky, hiding the flames.

I heard a noise and I turned and saw Hughie was standing behind me, the dog at his side. It had gone deathly quiet except for the simmering of the flames. Tiny delicate snowflakes began sifting down from the sky.

The silence and the calm seemed insane, but it only lasted a few seconds. And then the sirens started in the distance.

"Get out of here," said Hughie. "You've got to get out of here."

"Nevada…"

He shook his head. Tears were streaming down his face. He gestured towards the ditch, now brimming with burning fuel, a mass of smoke and flame. There was no hope.

He grabbed me by the arm and began to push me back, away from the fire, towards my car.

As we went I noticed the record lying on the snow-covered ground where it had fallen.

Splashes of burning fuel had reached it. The cover was a scorched fragment, the record a shapeless melted puddle of black vinyl.

The elegant Hathor label was still recognisable in the centre of the distorted black mess.

I left it there.

As I drove away from the factory I looked back in the mirror. The distant glow of the flames cast festive lights into the sky. I realised from this distance it looked like some kind of Christmas display. I left the country roads behind and joined the motorway.

Driving back to England.

Driving home.

Fat white flakes began falling into the beams of the headlights.

Snowfall.

Nevada.

17. KILL FEE

The roads were clear and, by the time I got home, it was still only late evening, but already pitch black with winter darkness. I was on automatic pilot, my mind meticulously and efficiently planning and preparing.

I drove around to my house first, because I had to drop off the bicycles next door, and only then returned the car to the rental place.

I couldn't do it any other way because there were no longer enough people to ride both bikes.

So I dropped off the car and caught a bus home from Putney and unlocked my front door and stepped inside and felt my world fall apart. The cats, who had come running to meet me, stopped and stared as I doubled over with a cry of anguish and gradually went down onto the floor as though forced down by a giant hand. They watched me cautiously as I slowly got back on my feet, weeping. Fanny circled me uncertainly and Turk gave a funny little cry, which seemed to echo my own.

I didn't sleep all night. Every time I tried to close my eyes, all I could see was her body, huddled in the ditch, and then cremated by a flood of fire.

Lying there all alone.

As soon as the sun was up in the sky, I rang Hughie. He answered instantly. "I'm coming back," I said.

"No. Stay away. Please."

"I have to see her. I have to take care of her."

"It's all taken care of. She's gone. It's done."

"What do you mean?"

"She's buried. It's all taken care of." He hung up.

I went to the hospital to see Tinkler as soon as visiting hours began. I had nowhere else to go. As soon as he saw my face he knew something was terribly wrong. When I told him what had happened, he went white. I broke down completely so that towards the end of my account I was almost incoherent, leaning forward, sobbing. His plump hand crawled across the bed sheet and took mine and squeezed it, clumsily and powerfully.

As soon as I returned home I phoned Hughie again. I'd realised I had to go to the place. Wherever she was buried. I had to put some flowers there. I couldn't rest until I'd done that. Suddenly I understood every sad roadside shrine of every accident victim I'd ever seen. "I've got to come down, Hughie," I said.

"Stay where you are. I'm coming to London tomorrow."

"I need to know—"

"I'll tell you all about it when I see you tomorrow. I'll tell you everything."

"What do you mean, tell me about it?" But he was gone. Five minutes later I got a text from Hughie, giving me a time and place to meet.

* * *

I was there waiting for him the next day, at the coffee shop in the Curzon Soho. He came through the door carrying two large shopping bags. He saw me and waved and gave a big false smile and came over and sat down. It was a strange situation. Neither of us ever wanted to see the other again, and yet I had to see him. And he seemed to be under a similar compulsion. Before I could say a word, he started in.

"What a relief. Those sirens you heard. They weren't the cops. Just the fire service. And I have friends in the fire service. They sprayed foam on the petrol and put it out. There wasn't any damage to the greenhouses." He shot me a fast, worried look, as if he realised how uninterested I was in his crops escaping unscathed. "No one had heard any shooting. They just gave me hell about the storage tank. Said they'd known it was unsafe and how I should be prosecuted and so on, but they were just putting the fear of god into me. I gave them some early Christmas presents and everyone went home happy." He tried a smile, then gave up on it.

"When are you going back?" I said.

"Tonight."

"I'll come with you."

He gave me an appalled look. "What for?"

"I have to see the place."

"What place?"

"Where she's buried. I want to put some flowers there."

He was staring at me as though I was insane. Perhaps I was. "What are you talking about?"

"You said you buried her."

"No I didn't. I didn't do that. I wouldn't do that."

"You said it had all been taken care of. That she was buried."

"No I didn't," said Hughie. He had, but what was the point of arguing? Now he leaned across the table towards me and lowered his voice to a hiss. "I said it had been taken care of and her body was gone. When I came back the next morning, just after daylight, it was gone. I think they came back and took it."

"Who?"

"Them. The bastards. The ones who shot her."

"Why do you think it was them?"

"Because they also took that record of yours. What was left of it."

"That melted lump of vinyl?" I said.

"And the cover."

"Why would they do that?"

"I don't know." He shook his head. Then, "She was something, your lady. The way she went after those bastards." He stood up and gripped me manfully on the shoulder for a moment. "Tough it out," he said. Now that he was leaving he seemed to feel he could afford to be genuinely fond of me. He turned for the door. He'd left his bags on the chair.

"Hughie," I said. "Your bags."

"Those are for you." He pushed through the glass door of the café and disappeared into the crowds on Shaftesbury Avenue. I looked in the bags. They were full of tomatoes.

Seeing Hughie had released something in me. Exhaustion spread through my veins like a drug and I realised I would be able to sleep at last. Since the incident I'd been lying in bed in a state of crystalline anguish, every sense sharp and alert. All that was gone now. As I walked through the door I started pulling my clothes off and threw them aside. It reminded me of the times with her, when we'd hurried to the bed together, undressing as we went, and my cheeks were slick with tears as I put my face to the pillow. In the darkness I heard the rattle of small feet on the floor and the cats surged in to join me.

As I fell asleep, at last, I realised why they might have wanted to retrieve the destroyed record.

To prove it no longer existed.

The next morning I woke up with a new determination. I had to tell someone what had happened to her. She had family somewhere and they needed to know. I had no idea how to contact them, but I knew someone who might. I started looking for her business card. The one she had given me on that first day. I searched everywhere, but I couldn't find it. I started throwing things around. The cats watched me, baffled at my bad temper and the fact that they hadn't been given their breakfast.

I forced myself to stop and take a deep breath. I fed the cats. Then I went on the Internet. I don't know why I'd been so obsessed with finding the card. I remembered what was on it, anyway. Just her name and the company name. International Industries GmbH. Any large business was bound to have an Internet presence.

But not this one. The words International Industries GmbH typed into a search engine threw up plenty of results, all right. But they were all companies in which those words were prefaced by some kind of other name.

"Like Krautrock International Industries, GmbH," said Tinkler when I told him about it.

"Exactly."

He wrinkled his brow. "You know, I think you might have given me her business card."

"Don't worry about it," I said.

"And I might have used it as a roach. I'm really sorry."

"Don't worry," I said. "I'm sure that's all it said on it."

He nodded eagerly. "Her name and Industrial Industries GmbH."

"International Industries."

"That's what I meant." He looked at me. "So do you think that means it doesn't really exist? Because you can't find any trace of it?"

"I don't know. Maybe."

But it turns out it definitely did have some kind of existence, because when I got home there was an envelope waiting for me. It was addressed to me and had a logo in the corner that read *i i GmbH* with the I's in fashionable lower case. I tore it open with shaking hands. Inside was just a cheque. Made out to me. For one thousand pounds.

On the cheque was the name "International Industries", but there was no address or other information of any kind.

I stared at it, the implications slowly seeping in. This meant that they must know what had happened to Nevada. How could they? But there didn't seem to be any other explanation.

I looked at the cheque. Why a thousand pounds? Obviously it was a round number, but beyond that it seemed a strangely familiar sum. Then I remembered. It was what they were going to pay me if I'd found the classical record for them. The bogus Stravinsky on Everest.

This is what I was getting paid, for having failed to get them the record they really wanted. The same as if I'd found them one that didn't exist.

I guessed it was what they call a kill fee.

* * *

The winter was suddenly deep and fierce and bitter. Much colder. Or maybe it just felt that way because Nevada was gone. The cats crossed the freezing floor with trepidation, scurrying as fast as they could, or jumping from one handy piece of furniture to another to avoid putting their little paws on the icy surface.

So I knew what I had to do with the money.

I bought an underfloor heating system and installed it. It was a simple carbon film technology with flat copper heating elements in sheets of plastic. I just took up the laminate flooring and laid the heaters down on the concrete. I unrolled the big sheets of film across the floor, fastening them onto a layer of insulation, spreading a membrane across the top to prevent damp, then putting the laminate flooring down again on top of everything. The cats watched in fascination as I ganged the wires from the heating units and attached them to a thermostat on the wall. Then I switched it on. *Voila*. Warm floors.

The cats looked at me like I was a god.

The work had done me good. I hadn't needed to think about anything while I was concentrating on it. Now that it was over, I had to find something else to throw myself into. Another project.

There was enough money left over to buy some lumber to serve as shelves. Now I could address a job I had been ducking for at least ten years. Because it was ten years ago that a clergyman I had come to think of as the Digital Divine, who lived nearby in Barnes, had decided to get rid of his enormous, and wonderful, collection of rare jazz records.

He had taped them all onto DAT and consequently decided, insanely, to get rid of the vinyl. Perhaps god had told him to do it. Although personally I suspected it was more likely the devil.

Anyway, I'd got wind of his decision and I was the first one to approach him about buying his collection. He was agreeable, and he was willing to meet me on price, on one condition.

That I took everything.

Including all the crap and dross, along with the treasures. He just wanted to get rid of it all in one fell swoop. So I'd ended up taxiing everything home and living among the boxes for weeks. I'd managed to get rid of the worst of the junk—to charity shops, where else? And I'd sifted out all the real gems, and there were some astounding finds. Original Tempos featuring Dizzy Reece and Tubby Hayes, and some Shake Keane and Joe Harriott on Lansdowne.

Plus a strong run of California small label releases, including some Marty Paich and Lucy Ann Polk on Mode. The finest records in my library had come from this collection—the cast-offs of the Digital Divine.

But there also remained a stubborn residue of second-rate stuff. Records that weren't bad enough to get rid of at the charity shops, yet not good enough to sell for a profit.

Some of it was worth listening to. None of it was very exciting. But all of it was in a state of chaos. About half the records were on shelves in the cupboard that had once housed my hot water tank. The rest were in crates on the floor of that cupboard.

There were a lot of records. Tinkler had seen them once and whistled and said, "From the crates they came and to the crates they shall return." It was a depressing thought, and one day I'd promised myself I'd sort them out. I just needed to put in some new shelves.

That day had finally come. The demanding, mindless work was my salvation. Buying the timber, measuring and cutting and installing it. And once the shelves were made, the work didn't stop there. I had to get the records out of the crates and onto the new shelves.

And even then there was one more job I could throw myself into.

The records were all on the shelves now, heaved there in batches, but in a random order. I had to sort them out. Go through them painstakingly, one by one. It was a blissful, brainless, painless sedative to me. I threw myself into the task. I escaped into it.

It was a marathon job putting the records in alphabetical order. Looking at them, I guessed it would take me two hours. It actually took twelve, with breaks for meals, and with the cats jumping on each shelf as soon as a cat-sized space was cleared, then being obliged to jump off again as it was subsequently filled with records.

Finally, at three in the morning, feeling weary and empty but also with something resembling happiness that came out of the weariness, I came to the last few records to file away. There were a handful of them, currently on a shelf at eye level.

They needed to be moved to other sections of the shelves, in the correct alphabetical positions.

I had been looking at these records, on and off, for the last ten years or more. The first two were Duke Ellington albums, but not ones I had been in any hurry to play.

While I loved and revered Ellington, I couldn't ignore the fact that his choice of vocalists had been, to say the very least, eccentric. True, he had worked with greats like Billie Holiday and Ella Fitzgerald.

But the regular singers in his band had ranged from the wonderful to the oddball to the chillingly mediocre. Some people theorised that Duke had deliberately made such jarring choices because he never wanted his band to become associated with, or dominated by, a vocalist.

Whatever the reason, this odd tradition meant there were some Ellington recordings that were well worth steering clear of. These LPs were two such.

On a small British specialist label, they were volumes one and two of a collection of air-shots which might have been titled *The Duke's Dodgiest Singers*—gathered here for the first time.

I suppose it was nice to know that someone had preserved them for posterity, but I had never been moved to listen to them and they had remained untouched since the Digital Divine had dumped them on me.

But as I took them off the shelf I realised that there were actually *three* records, not two.

Between the Ellington albums was another LP.

The record had been stored back to front, so its spine was concealed, rendering it virtually invisible all these years. I remembered Tinkler and I describing this very situation to Nevada.

I steered my thoughts away from Nevada. I separated the two Ellington compilations and there it was.

The familiar cover of *Easy Come, Easy Go*.

I knew it was an hallucination. I went down the corridor to the bathroom and splashed cold water in my face. I left the water running. Fanny jumped into the sink and bent over so she could drink from the tap. While she lapped at the water, I looked at my face in the mirror. I knew what I'd seen was just the product of fatigue and shock and longing.

Yet, at the same time, some uncontrollable part of my mind was racing through the options, reasoning and rationalising and weighing up possibilities.

The clergyman had owned a lot of West Coast rarities. Mode and Tampa and Contemporary. It wasn't inconceivable that he'd picked up something on the Hathor label.

Fanny jumped down from the sink, having drunk her fill. I turned off the taps and dried my hands. I went back down the corridor and looked at it.

The record was still there. I picked it up. The cover was in better shape than the one we'd found in the charity shop. This one had been kept away from the light, so there was less yellowing with age. I took out the record. The vinyl was heavy and authentic. And it was sealed in what looked like the original transparent plastic bag.

Sometimes, over the years, these bags begin to stick to the records they're supposed to be protecting. It's something to do with the petroleum-based plastics used in the bag. In the worst cases, they bond with the playing surface of the record, to terrible effect, leaving permanent irremovable ridges of residue across the microgroove.

But this record felt loose in the bag. I tore it open along the neatly perforated line at the top. I slid the record out into my hands and looked at it. It might as well have been brand new. In fact, in a sense, it was. It had never been played. I switched my amps on and set the record on the turntable. I set it in motion and felt dizzy as I watched the Hathor label revolve, the little Egyptian symbols spinning around and around at thirty-three and a third RPM. I lowered the tone arm and the music began.

I sat down on the sofa and listened to it. As far as my life was concerned, I felt like I was sitting at the end of an infinitely long tunnel. As far as the music went, I felt like I was in the same room where they were playing it. The dead came alive around me.

It gradually came to me that the record was in perfect condition. The world where such things mattered seemed so distant that it was hard to remember it. But still I noted the fact with detached interest. When I got to the end of side one I decided to not even bother listening to side two, except for the song 'Running from a Spell'.

And in fact, I wouldn't even listen to the whole song.

As I bent over the turntable I felt light-headed. I carefully cued the playing arm so the stylus would land at the right point on the track. As I did so, I distinctly heard a voice behind me.

"Our old friend Rogue Plosive," said Nevada. I looked up but of course she wasn't there and I knew she wasn't there. It was just the echo of something she'd said once, playing again on some groove of my memory. I was so exhausted I could hear voices surfacing at the very edge of perception, like the subdued mutter of the sea. Fragments of things people had said, scraps of memories from the last few days.

I shook my head. I'd been up all night. I'd hardly eaten. I was light-headed with fatigue.

I lowered the needle onto the record. It was a few seconds ahead of the popping sound. Perfect. I went back to the sofa to sit down and listen. I leaned forward into the sweet spot. And it came.

And with the clarity—and familiarity—of listening to it on my own system, it was obvious what it was.

A gunshot.

* * *

I put the record away and went to bed. I felt my consciousness melt away as I turned my face to the pillow. I was distantly aware that the cats were jumping onto the bed to join me.

I went out walking the next morning, just as the sun was coming up over the Abbey. It was a strange watery yellow colour. Nevada was walking beside me, holding hands with me. She said, "So you found it, then?"

I said, "I had a copy all along and I didn't even know it, because it was lost among all the other albums. It was the classic record collector's story."

She nodded. "So we were searching everywhere and yet it was here. Here all the time. It's like that appalling novel by Coelho."

"I kind of liked it," I said. "That book."

"My god, you couldn't possibly," she said.

We argued about the merits of the Coelho novel until the absurdity of it woke me up.

I sat up in bed, the cats stirring around me. It was noon and the sun was coming in the window and I was sweating and groggy. My sluggish brain realised with anguish that I had only dreamed that Nevada was alive.

But what about the record?

I went into the living room. It was there.

I looked at it for a long time and then I went looking for a scrap of paper where I'd written a phone number. I thought I'd thrown it out, but I'd found it again when I was installing the heating. Now it seemed like it was lost again.

Eventually I found it.

The number with the area code for Japan.

I dialled.

18. JAPAN

I've never been able to sleep on a plane, but I'd always suspected this was because I was a tall lanky guy forced to fold himself into a tiny uncomfortable seat. I assumed if ever I got to fly first class, or business or whatever they called it, I would be able to sleep just fine.

It turns out that this assumption was entirely correct.

On the flight to Omura I slept dreamlessly—which was a first in recent days. My wrist was a bit uncomfortable, of course, but that was still preferable to the alternative. It felt a bit strange to take the briefcase with me even when I went to the loo but the stewardesses were very nice about it and no doubt had seen similar contrivances before.

It also, weirdly, gave me a certain cachet among the other passengers. It was difficult to wash my hands, though.

The briefcase was actually really nice. It had been couriered over to me within hours of my phone call. It was matte black leather, backed with a thin layer of steel and lined with a considerable thickness of what might have been heavy white cotton. There was a big square carefully hollowed out of the cotton, just the right size to accommodate LPs.

There was very little that could damage a record once it was in there. I suspected that the thick cotton layer would even protect it from some fairly extreme temperature changes.

It was the ultimate record bag.

I wondered if they would let me keep it after the transaction.

Without the handcuffs, of course.

I was met at the airport by a quiet young man in a mustard yellow roll-neck sweater and brown tweed jacket. He was holding a sign with my name on it. I identified myself, but he had already spotted me because of the briefcase. Having shown me his documents, which confirmed him as Atsushi, Mr Hibiki's personal assistant, he led me to the car.

Nagasaki Airport is located on an island in the middle of the city of Omura. The airport is connected to the mainland, and the rest of the city, by a long bridge with a two-lane road running along it. As we drove towards the mainland I looked out at islands and clouds in the shadowed distance across the bright water.

We drove through the city and crossed the Nagasaki Highway onto what my map told me was Route 444, which carried us out of the city and into the countryside with surprising rapidity. We were soon climbing into what looked like parkland. I was surprised that in a country this densely populated I could feel so suddenly out in the lonesome wilderness.

Just past a little settlement of white houses called Nakadakemachi we turned off onto a secondary road that took us up into the mountains. The roadside was thick with green trees.

Mr Hibiki's house lay behind a low rambling wall made of natural stone that seemed to rise organically—or rather minerally—out of the landscape. Beyond the wall there was a slope of white pebbles, then a dense band of trees. Past this there was a large pond full of lilies and the darting orange shape of fish. The tyres hummed as we passed over the pond on some kind of pontoon bridge. Then we were on another pebbled slope but one that was terraced and dotted at intervals by small circles of black earth with glistening green shrubs growing in them.

It was all very minimal and elegant but I could also see hardware lurking among the shrubs. Garden lights, but other things, too.

The house was built into the hillside with big picture windows facing out. On the windows there were the cut-out shapes of birds in black crepe paper. These looked elegantly decorative, but I recognised them as raptor silhouettes. They were designed to scare off birds and thereby stop the poor enthusiastic things flying into the windows—thinking the glass was thin air—and breaking their silly little necks.

Apparently they worked pretty well.

In the centre of the windows was a heavy slab of handsome wood. I thought it was some kind of reinforcing structure or central pillar of the house, but Atsushi just walked straight up to it and pushed it open.

It was the front door.

He stood aside to let me in. We took off our shoes in a sunken white atrium and donned paper slippers then walked up some polished cherry-wood stairs to a hallway and more polished wood, a beautiful shining length of it. It was warm under foot and I thought of my own underfloor heating and my cats happily asleep on it. They'd love it here. And just as I thought this we walked past a room with a grey cat lying in it. Nothing else but a dark bare wooden floor and the small pale cat sprawled in a corner. Maybe it was his room.

Past this, on the other side, was a room with nothing in it but a grand piano, a piano stool and some big cushions. We came to a short stretch of corridor with floor-to-ceiling windows on one side, which looked out into a little Zen garden with a cherry tree and a tiny water sculpture.

It looked very tranquil and peaceful.

We came out at the end of the corridor into a room that seemed to span the whole back of the house. The walls here were stone. Cement stairs built into the far wall led up to another level. We went up these, our slippers whispering on the rough cement steps. I realised they had to be rough. If the steps were smooth and polished this kind of footwear would see people slipping off the steep staircase into oblivion, Tinkler style.

At the top of the stairs we turned to our left and found ourselves in an alcove with a painting on the wall. It was the Leo and Diane Dillon portrait of Miles Davis. I had no doubt that it was the original. Through the alcove was a small cosy room. We went in.

Mr Hibiki had short, cropped black hair streaked with grey. His eyes looked like he was just remembering something that amused him. He was dressed casually but immaculately in moccasins, chinos and a sharp pale blue shirt.

He looked like a well-heeled preppie hipster who had just got back from Newport, circa 1958.

He shook my hand, the one that wasn't handcuffed to the case.

"Please sit down." If he had any accent, it was faintly American.

I sat down on one of the low charcoal-coloured chairs that matched the sofa where he'd been sitting. It was a small, intimate square room with a thick white carpet. The chairs and the sofa were the only furniture. The walls were lined with shelves that were densely but neatly filled with—what else?—records. Above these, the high ceiling was made of wood and rose above us in a graceful curving arch.

I looked around me. The solid walls of records on all sides were occasionally broken up by an alcove or deeper shelf, discreetly illuminated and containing hi-fi components. I saw a turntable and two groups of very expensive-looking valve amplifiers.

I couldn't see any speakers, though.

Mr Hibiki reached in his pocket and took out the key and handed it to me. I unlocked the handcuffs and gave him the case. While he opened it I massaged my pale, chafed wrist. "Very nice," said Mr Hibiki, looking into the case. He looked up at me. "Would you like something to drink?"

"Some coffee, please." I rubbed my wrist.

Atsushi the assistant went over to another little alcove I hadn't noticed, which contained a flask and some cups and saucers. He took the lid off the flask and instantly I could smell the coffee. I perked up as soon as it hit my nose. He poured two cups, set them neatly on saucers, then gave one to me and one to Mr Hibiki, who ignored it.

He had taken the record out of the case.

I'd sealed its cover in a mylar sleeve, which he now carefully peeled open and removed.

I sipped the coffee. It was excellent, and fresh. It couldn't have been made more than a few minutes earlier. Mr Hibiki weighed the cover in his hand, admiring it. "Flawless," he said.

"I think it spent most of its life sandwiched between two other albums and never even saw the light of day." I said.

He nodded and carefully slid the record out of its plastic bag. He leaned closer to a standing lamp and examined the vinyl in the discreet pool of light it threw. I realised there were no windows in the room.

His face grew serious as he squinted intently at the label, then he turned the record over and checked the other side, carefully inspecting the label again. Finally he grunted with satisfaction and slipped it back into the plastic bag.

He fingered the little irregularities left by the torn perforation strip at the top of the bag. He looked at me. "It was sealed when you got it?"

"Yes, sorry about that." In some ways the ultimate collector's experience is to get the sealed copy and open it yourself. It's the holy grail. Any tasteless comparisons to deflowering virgins are to be vigorously avoided. "But I had to open it. To check that it was okay."

"Of course." He smiled to show it was all fine. "What kind of cartridge do you use?"

"Ortofon Rohmann." This was a top of the line thousand-pound-plus cartridge that I'd got in a complicated swap including a mint original copy of the Beatles' White Album I'd found at a boot fair. But basically the thrust of his question was to check that I hadn't played the record using a rusty knitting needle. He seemed satisfied.

"Very nice," he said. He set the LP aside and sipped his coffee. "How was your flight?"

"Fine."

"That's good."

I said, "Do you mind if I look around?"

He smiled. "No. Be my guest."

I went to one of the alcoves and inspected the turntable. It was a Roksan Xerxes, a British machine. I'd heard one at a hi-fi show once. Its rhythmic accuracy was unsurpassed. The cartridge was Japanese, a dizzyingly expensive Koetsu. I went to the alcove containing a set of valve amps. They were WAVACs, also Japanese, using directly heated 833As. The highest of the high end.

I still couldn't see any speakers, though.

I looked through his records. All jazz, of course. There was one shelf that was full of just original Blue Notes. "May I?" I said.

He waved his hand. "Please."

I took out a few albums and looked at them. A thought occurred to me. I said, "What do you do about playing flat-edge LPs?"

"That's the flat-edge turntable you were looking at. The regular turntable is over there." He pointed across the room where, I realised, another alcove housed another identical Roksan Xerxes. Well, why not? If you had the money. In an adjacent, smaller alcove was the small black control box that switched one turntable or the other into the signal path that fed the amps. I examined it. It was a passive unit made by David Heaton.

Still no sign of the speakers, though. I scanned the room as I returned to my chair. Mr Hibiki smiled at me politely. "Is there anything you'd like to hear?"

"Everything," I said, and we both laughed.

"Well, perhaps later," he said. "But now let's listen to

this." He picked up *Easy Come, Easy Go* and handed the album to Atsushi who took it and went over to the turntable. He took the record out of the sleeve with the skill of a man who had done it before.

As he cued the LP up on the turntable, I was still searching the room with my gaze. Where were the bloody speakers?

"So you've had a chance to listen to it?" said Mr Hibiki.

"Yes, sorry, but I had to."

"No, that's fine. I understand." He sipped his coffee and set the cup down again. "So how did it sound?"

"Absolutely mint. High-quality vinyl with no noise, no pressing flaws. Just perfect."

Atsushi switched the turntable on and lowered the tone arm onto the record. It began to play.

The noise that came out was the most grotesque, shrieking cacophony imaginable. It sounded like someone had gone over the playing surface with a professional sander, obliterating the microgrooves.

We all stared at each other.

The din continued. Sizzling distortion. A galaxy of white noise.

Atsushi had quickly stepped back from the turntable as though it was an animal that might bite him. I got to my feet and went over to the turntable and lifted the arm off the record. Silence. They were both staring at me. I could distinctly feel the force of their gaze, at the nape of my neck, between my sweating shoulder blades.

I bent down and inspected the tone arm.

As I had suspected, there on the tip of the stylus was a tiny ball of grey fluff that had accumulated from playing dozens of records over a period of weeks. I put my mouth near and blew gently. The puff of air carried the dust ball floating serenely away. I lifted the tone arm again and lowered it onto the run-in groove.

First, smooth silence as the stylus rode inwards, and then music filled the room. Warm, rich, beautiful music.

Mr Hibiki was staring at Atsushi who was looking distinctly seasick.

I sensed a restructuring of the chain of command some time soon.

The music sounded wonderful. As I sat down I realised it was coming from above. I looked up and finally I got it. The graceful curving panels of wood rising upwards from the walls formed an enclosure for a horn-loaded speaker. The whole ceiling was a speaker.

In fact the whole room was one.

Ask not where the speaker is. You're sitting in it.

Perhaps at some signal from his boss, Atsushi made himself scarce. Now it was just Mr Hibiki and I sitting in the room, listening. I could see him relaxing, enjoying the music. When it reached the end of the side I went to the turntable and turned it over.

"This is very good," he said, watching me. "In fact, it could hardly be improved."

"There is one anomaly." I thought I'd better bring it up before we got there. "On the last track on this side, the vocal by Rita Mae Pollini. There's a tiny rogue… noise." He was watching me politely, attentively, taking it all in. "But it's a noise from the original session. Not damage or any kind of pressing flaw." He nodded.

"I think it's a music stand falling over," I lied.

We listened as it arrived and he nodded again. "It's

definitely on the master tape," he said. "I believe you're right. A music stand falling." He smiled at me. "If anything, it adds to the charm of the recording. As if we're there during the date."

"I'm glad you like it," I said. The record ended and Mr Hibiki got up and switched the turntable off. He put the LP back in the sleeve and went over to one of the shelves of records. I'd noticed earlier there was a thin strip of paper sticking out here. He removed this marker slip and slid the record into its correct place on the shelf to join the complete run of Hathor recordings, all thirteen of them. Fourteen now.

As he did so, an odd thing happened. I could see his whole body visibly relax, his shoulders sagging luxuriously in relief. He sighed, a long, low, quiet sigh, and a strange wild smile spread over his face. It was my first glimpse of the unguarded Mr Hibiki, and I could see the child inside the man. It was gone in an instant, but I'd never forget that smile, a mad savage smile of victory.

With *Easy Come, Easy Go*, he had the complete set. A collector's dream come true.

I wondered when—or if—he'd ever play it again.

He sat down and nodded affably. "Well done. Thank you." Atsushi came back into the room holding an iPhone. He gave it to me. The website for the money transfer had been set up ready. I typed in my bank details and accessed my account. Then I passed the phone to Atsushi who gave it to Mr Hibiki.

Mr Hibiki entered his own details and then got up and handed the phone to me, bypassing Atsushi, who was looking more and more unhappy. I studied the screen. The transfer was in progress. Quite rapidly a message appeared, indicating that the transaction was complete. I stared at it. The total was given there on the screen.

My head swam. I couldn't absorb the figure. I had to put my fingertip down on the screen to cover up two zeros, then move it along and cover up two more zeros, and slowly count them in this way.

When I finally had the number straight in my head I went to a currency conversion website and with a push of a button I converted the sum from yen into dollars.

It came to just over a million.

I pushed a few more buttons and converted it into the sterling equivalent. Then I left the browser and used the phone as a phone. I called Tinkler's number, including the international dialling code for England. It only rang twice, sounding hollow and distant, before he answered.

"Hello?"

"It's me."

"Okay," said Tinkler. "I'm ready. Right. Right. Yup. I'm ready."

I waited patiently. He was lying in his hospital bed with my phone, his own phone and a crib sheet giving him all the information he needed to access my bank account. I waited while he made the call, hearing his nervous voice responding to the security questions from the bank. Basically, he had to pretend to be me.

Finally he finished the other call and came back on the line. "The money's come through," he said. "My god, there's a lot of it isn't there? Even the girl at the call centre was impressed. I'm in love with her, by the way."

"Glad to hear it."

"Right," said Tinkler. "Now I'm going to use all that

information you gave me to access your account and siphon off every penny and steal it for myself. Steal it, do you hear me?" He laughed maniacally, then added, "I hope that's all right."

"Good luck with all that."

"Right. Okay. You take care." He hung up.

I switched the phone off. My palms were damp. I looked at Mr Hibiki, who was watching me with polite interest. "Sorry about that," I said.

"No problem. It's perfectly all right."

I handed the phone to Atsushi, who took it and left. I breathed deeply and relaxed. On one level the whole thing had been a complete farce, of course. If they'd actually wanted to rob me, they could have just taken the record and hit me with a baseball bat. I was alone in this house, in an unknown part of an unknown country.

"Would you like something to eat?" he said.

I shook my head. "They fed me pretty well on the plane, and I imagine they're going to feed me pretty well going back."

He checked his watch. "There's plenty of time. But it's quite a long drive back to the airport. If you're like me, you may want to get there early." He smiled. I'd been dismissed. I stood up. We shook hands again. I turned and looked at the shelf where the record now stood. I experienced a sudden strange, painful pang of loss.

I felt like I'd gone to the vet and left a beloved pet there to be put down. I steeled myself and turned away. Perhaps he read something in my face because he said, "You should stop in the Zen garden on your way out. It will make you feel better. There's plenty of time." He patted me on the arm. "Goodbye."

Atsushi was waiting for me in the doorway. He escorted me out.

Now it was over I felt a tremendous let down. It was weird. Even getting paid turned out to be a disappointment. As I walked away from that small room where Hibiki sat, all I had was a frustrating sense of things unresolved. Questions unanswered.

Questions that would never be answered now.

First there was the matter of the money. The amount of it. No piece of vinyl, in and of itself, was worth what he'd paid me. Yet he'd paid it happily. If anything, he had the air of a man getting a bargain. What he'd received from me was clearly vastly more valuable than what I'd just received from him.

Why?

I wanted to know. I *needed* to know. I had a sense of huge, tumultuous events going on around me, but just beyond the edge of my vision, just out of range of my hearing.

Some matter of enormity was transpiring, brushing past me, close enough to touch. Like an invisible ship sailing by on a silent sea. Vast and ghostly. And I had no idea what it was. And now I was never likely to.

Plus there was that small matter of the "session anomaly", the rogue noise that haunted side two.

Music stand falling over, my ass.

It was now very clear in my mind that it was a gunshot.

We went down the stone staircase, through the wide hall that spanned the house, into the corridor beyond. Here on the right was the glass wall looking out into the Zen garden.

There was a young woman standing in the garden. A woman with short black hair in a black dress. For one aching second I thought she looked just like Nevada.

Then she turned.

It was Nevada.

19. ZEN GARDEN

What had appeared to be floor-to-ceiling windows were actually a series of sliding doors. I slid one of them open and stepped into the garden. The air was cool and damp. A faint, fine mist hung in the air as if a phantom rain was falling. She looked at me through the mist. Then she came over and touched my lapel. "You're wearing your suit. The one I got you. It looks good on you."

I pulled her towards me and put my arms around her and squeezed for dear life. She was warm. She was real. She was hugging me back. I was breathing in her perfume. It was all true. My heart was beating so fast I thought I might be having a medical emergency. But a good one.

I pushed her back so I could look at her. I said, "You were wearing a vest. When they shot you. A bulletproof vest."

She shook her head. "Nothing that complicated. I saw the muzzle flash in the dark. I guess it must have been Heinz. Because Heidi was running away from us. He was firing towards us, towards me. But he had to be careful not to hit her. So when he started shooting I had time to get out of the way before he could range in on me. When I saw the muzzle flash, what I actually tried to do was gracefully duck out of the line of fire, but I'd forgotten that I was running beside that ditch. That fucking ditch. The anti-rat ditch. And I fell into it."

I was beginning to put it together in my head. "And you climbed out of it before the…"

"Before the torrent of flaming oil flowed into it. Ouch. Yes, luckily I scrambled out before that."

"You climbed out on the other side of the greenhouse. That's why I didn't see you."

"That's right." She nodded towards the house. "What happened to old Atsushi?" I looked through the window and saw that my escort had disappeared. "He was looking quite sick."

"He forgot to blow the fluff off his boss's needle," I said.

"I'm not even going to begin to ask what that might mean."

This garden was a strange place. Neither indoors nor outdoors, it was a cube in the centre of the house, walled in by glass on all sides but with the roof open to the elements. It was heated just like being inside the house, though. Which is why she could stand there in that dress, not shivering and no gooseflesh on her smooth skin. But beneath the rounded white pebbles underfoot I suspected there was a man-made floor. At the centre, the water feature was a little pile of flat black stones with a trickle of water flowing through them, emanating from an unseen source and vanishing to some unknown destination, also presumably in that floor.

I looked at the cherry tree. That at least was planted in a bed of real earth. But it was surreal to see it in blossom in the middle of winter. Yet the little leaves were vivid and pink. Perhaps wealth could buy you even that.

I said, "And you've been here ever since?"

"Pretty much," said Nevada. "How could I stay away from good old Nakadakemachi? Once you've learned to pronounce it, you just can't stay away."

"Yes, because you've invested so much time and energy in it," I said.

"Exactly." A petal fell onto my shoulder and she brushed it off. "Who's looking after the girls while you're over here?"

"Maggie promised to look in and feed them while I'm gone."

"Tinkler's sister?"

"Yes."

"And how is old Tinkler?"

A petal fell into her hair. Pink on black. I didn't touch it. It was perfect. "He'll be pleased to hear about this," I said.

She took a step towards me.

I took a step back from her.

"Listen," she said.

"How could you not tell me?" I said.

"Listen." She put her hands on my shoulders. I shook them off.

"How could you let me think you were dead?"

"I'm sorry."

"Sorry? Do you know what it felt like? How could you not tell me?"

She shook her head. The petal floated to the ground. "It wasn't like that."

"What was it like?"

"At first, all was confusion. I was chasing the Aryan Twins. I heard the fuel tank collapse and I heard the fire. But I had to be sure that they, and their Aryan guns, were gone.

So I followed them as they made their retreat. They were parked in the road outside. In the good old silver SUV. They drove off and by that time I heard sirens in the distance. So I hurried back into the factory yard, or should I say the great cannabis greenhouse conflagration and I saw…"

"You saw that the record had been destroyed."

"Yes," she said. "And I saw that you'd driven off."

"What?"

She said, "You were in a bit of a hurry, weren't you?"

"Hughie told me you were dead. He said he saw you lying there dead."

"Lying is right."

"And then he told me you'd been buried. That your body had been buried."

"Good old Hughie. The Scottish Welshman. Still, he's raised a nice daughter so he must be doing something right." She glanced at me. "How is Boo?"

"Like the rest of us. She'll be relieved to hear that you're not dead."

"Look, I'm sorry."

"How could you not tell me you were alive?"

"I'm telling you now, aren't I?"

"Yes, because I'm here."

"What do you mean?"

"I'm only here because I found the record."

"Yes," she said. "That was amazing, wasn't it? I can't get over you just finding it like that, in your house. I mean, having it all along." She looked at me through the mist. "It's just like that dreadful Coelho novel."

And the surface of my brain rippled with the sensation of déjà vu.

"I thought it was sort of okay," I said. "That book."

"Really? Anyway, it was a good job I brought back the fragments of good old *Easy Come, Easy Go*. What was left of it, that is, after the great cannabis conflagration."

"That was you?"

"Yes, there wasn't much left of the sleeve, and the record was just this melted blob. But enough survived to authenticate the find. Luckily for me." She looked at me. "Because Mr Hibiki might otherwise have been tempted to think that you and I were in league."

"To do what?" I said.

"To fake the record being destroyed and then you pretending to find another copy. And getting all the money for it."

"But we're not in league," I said.

"No we're not," she said, gazing at me as if she was searching for something in my face. I suppose she didn't find it, because then she said, "You're not looking at this in the most positive light."

I stared at the cherry tree. On second thought, maybe it wasn't real, either.

I said, "Let me tell you what I think. I think that once you confirmed that the record was destroyed, you didn't think there was any point in getting back in touch with me. I'd outlasted my usefulness. Because the project was over. So you just came back here to give Mr Hibiki your report. And that was the end of that. If I hadn't found the record and ended up flying out here, you would never even have told me you were alive."

She looked at me. There were tears in her eyes. She said, "When I didn't tell you right away, it just got harder and harder, the longer I waited."

"If I hadn't found the record, I'd still think you were dead." I looked at her. "You would have let me think that."

I turned my back on her and walked away. Back through the sliding glass and down the corridor. Atsushi was waiting impatiently by the front door. He drove me to catch my flight.

All the way back to London I could smell her perfume.

SIDE TWO

20. CALL ME REE

I jerked awake so abruptly that Fanny jumped off the bed with a little cry of protest. My heart was slamming in my chest.

The noise that had woken me was still ringing in my ears.

I lay there listening for it to come again. I was still disoriented with the jet lag of my flights to and from Japan. All I could hear was the early-morning chatter of birds outside. Fanny paused casually in the middle of the floor to wash herself, just to demonstrate that she hadn't really been spooked. What was it that had woken me? A sudden, violent sound. Whatever it was, it had scared the hell out of me. I was soaked with sweat.

Fanny had apparently decided to relocate to the chair in the corner of the bedroom, and hopped onto it. She curled up on the cushion, gave me a pointed stare for having disturbed her, and went back to sleep.

Turk sauntered lazily in, hard little paws tapping on the floor. She jumped up on the bed. I was surprised to see her. Despite being the intrepid explorer and implacable mouse-killer, she was amazingly skittish. Any sudden noise should have sent her fleeing for the high timber.

If the sound I'd heard had been real, she would be hiding in a distant corner of the house right now.

Instead she ambled across the bed, insolently treading over me on her way to the windowsill. She paused, then hopped up, neatly ducking under the curtains. Only her tail protruded as she took up her position there, staring out into the big world.

So I must have dreamed it. The sound. My mind had conjured it with hypnagogic vividness. And I knew what it was now. I recognised it.

The gunshot from the record.

I was even dreaming about the damned thing.

Seeing Nevada had driven all the other questions from my mind, but now they were crowding back in on me. There had been a message from the bank waiting for me when I'd got back from Japan yesterday. It confirmed the transfer of funds from Mr Hibiki.

And once again I thought, no record was worth that kind of money. So what was going on? I lay in bed, staring at the ceiling. Turk stirred on the windowsill. Fanny snuffled in her sleep.

Why was it worth so much to him? And not just to him.

Someone else had also wanted it, badly enough to be willing to kill for it.

But the one thing I couldn't get out of my mind was the smile Mr Hibiki had been smiling when he slid the album in with the others. He hadn't smiled like that when he had first got his hands on it, or when he first listened to it.

Only when he had filed it safely away with the other thirteen Hathor albums.

It had been a smile of triumph.

Ever since I'd seen it, I'd been trying to convince myself that this was just a case of an obsessive collector finally completing a set. Filling an annoying gap. Crossing it off his mental list.

But I didn't believe that. This was about more than a man and his record collection.

Behind the curtain, Turk chattered as she spotted a low-flying bird. I rolled over and tried to find a comfortable spot for my head on the pillow. My mind kept turning the question over and over. I needed to know. What the hell was Hibiki up to? Who were his competitors—the people behind the Aryan Twins? What was going on?

Of course, there was one person who might be able to tell me.

But I was damned if I was going to phone her.

I rolled over and tried to get back to sleep. Fanny snored on her chair. Turk stirred from time to time on the windowsill, to get a better vantage point. My mind kept turning over and finally I gave up and got out of bed. I checked the clock.

This morning I had to collect Tinkler.

Some people come out of hospital addicted to the painkillers. Tinkler came out addicted to grapes. The first thing we had to do when they discharged him was go to the local Marks and Spencer and buy him some to take home. We got Clean Head to drive us into Hammersmith.

She had opened the panel that separated driver from passengers and asked me about Nevada, and I told her she was away in Japan on business. This seemed to satisfy Clean Head and she even made some remark about what a lucky girl. She had completely missed out on the whole period when Nevada had been dead, which was an odd thing to contemplate.

Tinkler's phone buzzed. He glanced at it. "It's Maggie. A text message." He frowned. "It says, 'Have you seen the papers?'"

"Well, that's a silly question," I said. There were probably no two other grown men in London less likely to pick up a newspaper. Tinkler frowned at the phone.

"She's also sent us some links." We looked at each other. "Better click on them," he said.

They were both newspaper sites. The first headline read DJ FINDS MILLION DOLLAR LP.

The second one, CRATE DIGGER STRIKES GOLD.

The first article featured a photograph of me taken by some nonentity at a record fair years ago, in which I managed to look both pretentious and educationally subnormal. Of course, this rogue picture over which I had no control was the only one that had crept out into cyberspace to announce my presence to the world.

But that wasn't my worry at the moment. We looked at each other.

"How the hell did they find out?" he said.

"Nevada's people must have let it leak."

He was frowning at me. "Why?"

I shrugged, but I was beginning to guess. I said, "What's the point of beating the opposition if the opposition don't know it?"

"Ah, I see." Tinkler nodded.

"Plus it will have the effect of calling off the dogs." I

realised that now I'd got over the shock of this exposure, I was oddly relieved.

"You mean the Aryan Twins."

"Yes."

"You mean now they can just pack their bags and slink back off to… Arya? Is that a place?"

"No."

"So that's the last you'll see of them," said Tinkler. After a moment he added, helpfully, "Assuming they're not vengeful types." He put the phone away and settled back in the taxi seat. "Speaking of Nevada…"

"Yes?"

He sighed. "So… she's alive and we're all rejoicing that she's alive."

"Correct."

"But you don't want to go out with her anymore."

"Correct."

"Even though she gave every sign she wanted to."

I said, "I couldn't. How could I? After what she did."

Tinkler sighed again and said, "Not everyone has your high standards of moral conduct."

"Look, she never cared about me."

"She seemed quite fond of buying you nice clothes."

"She was just *managing* me. They needed me to find the record. So they put her in to sweeten the deal."

Tinkler sighed again. "Well," he said, "she sure was sweet."

When I realised I actually, for the first time in my life, had some serious money, one of the first things I did was to blow a small fortune on some very high-end *ca phe cut chon* coffee beans from Vietnam. These would arguably make a cup of the finest coffee in the world. I should have been excited about this, but for some reason as I prepared it at home, carefully grinding the beans in my little kitchen, all I could think was how much work it was. Maybe I should have just bought a jar of instant.

Nevertheless, now that I was back from Tinkler's I was glumly determined to set about making my first pot of the stuff. And it was almost ready when the doorbell rang.

The cats scooted into hiding, as they tended to do, and I went to see who it was.

It was a slender young woman, medium height, in her twenties. She was wearing suede boots, faded jeans and a quilted jacket with an unusual black and white check pattern that looked vaguely Indian. Her vulpine features were so striking I would have made the same blunder as with Nevada—assuming she was another model–stroke–starlet stumbling around looking for rehab—except that hanging from her shoulder was a black bag with a bold red and yellow logo that read AMOEBA MUSIC, HOLLYWOOD.

I knew Amoeba. It was one of the biggest record stores in America.

She looked at me. Her skin was the colour of *ca phe cut chon* with a generous splash of cream stirred in. Her eyes were a disconcerting shade of bronze. The large mass of curly hair framing her face was brown, with broad streaks of a tawny golden shade that made me think of lions.

She looked tired, but oddly alert. She smiled. "That smells good," she said. She had an American accent.

"Just making some coffee, the hard way."

"How hard can it be? Look, I'm really sorry if I've got

the wrong address, but is this you?" She handed me a copy of one of the newspaper articles I had seen on Tinkler's phone. It was the one with the picture, of course. I looked down at it, at the girl holding it in her hand, eager and a little hopeful.

And so it begins, I thought. "I'm afraid it is," I said.

She folded the piece of paper. "Your photo doesn't do you justice."

"That photo wouldn't do the Hunchback of Notre Dame justice."

"You know, that really does smell good," she said, looking over my shoulder. She smiled again. She wanted a cup of coffee. I didn't blame her. So did I.

"Look…" I said.

"Oh listen," she said, "I'm not going to put the arm on you for money or anything." She held up the folded piece of paper. "Because of your sudden new wealth or anything." She had read my mind. Now she smiled at me. "That's just not me."

"How did you get my address?"

She took out another piece of paper. Here was printed out a web page, where some joker had posted a scan of one of my Vinyl Detective cards online, helpfully displaying my contact details, including my address, to the world at large.

"Is this why you've come here?" I said. "You want me to find a record for you?"

She shrugged. "Look, can we talk inside?"

I shook my head. "I'm sorry," I said, "I've retired."

She gave me a droll look. "Isn't it a bit early to retire?"

"It's been a short but eventful career."

"Maybe I can convince you to come out of retirement." She smiled at me. She wasn't giving up. I sighed. The coffee was getting cold. "I came all the way from LA to see you," she said.

That was it. Even if she was a total nutcase I had to talk to her now. "All right, come in."

"Thanks." As she brushed past me I caught a whiff of her perfume, a smoky, insistent spiciness. I poured coffee for us and she sipped appreciatively. "The real stuff is always better than the instant," she said, as if she had been sent by the fates as a caution to me.

Then she looked around the kitchen. "Holy shit. Where did you get all those tomatoes?"

"It's a long story. If I said, 'from Wales', that would be the short version."

"Okay." She drank her coffee and I finished mine. The caffeine hit my veins and I began to feel impatient and a little testy. "So…" I said. She looked up from her cup.

"So anyway," she said. She took out the piece of paper with the news story. "I've come here because you found my grandmother's record."

My heart sank. I could see the way this was shaping up.

I said, "Even if the record did once belong to your grandmother, any claim she had to ownership would have lapsed long ago."

She stared at me for a moment, then started laughing.

"What's so funny?"

"When I said it was my grandmother's record, I meant she sings on it."

"Rita Mae Pollini was your grandmother?"

"Sure."

272

She must have read the doubt on my face because she snapped her fingers a few times, her hand going up and coming down with metronomic regularity and began to sing 'Running from a Spell'.

The hair on my arms went up. The voice was very similar—but what really gave it away was the rhythmic quality, the fast-moving bebop inflection she brought to the piece.

Two things were for certain. She could really sing. And she could have been the reincarnation of Rita Mae Pollini.

I sat and looked at her. I didn't know what to say. She finished her coffee, set the cup aside and took out what looked like a silver cigarette case with the initials REE engraved on the top.

I said, "Does the other side say FER?"

"What?" She looked at the case. "FER. Oh, I get it. Reefer. That's funny. But this is just tobacco." I supposed that this was a relief, after recent high jinks, but the last thing I wanted was a cigarette stinking up my house. She must have read my mind, because she said, "Okay if I smoke in your yard?"

"Be my guest, I guess." She headed for the front door, but I showed her to the back, where the garden was larger, and nicer. I led her through the sitting room.

"Hey, cats." She nodded at Fanny and Turk, who were sprawled on the floor in a square of sunlight and then paid them no more attention. Not a cat lover, then.

I opened the back door and went out with her. It seemed only sociable.

We stood in the garden together, our breath fogging on the cold bright air. It was a sunny winter morning with the frost gleaming as it melted on the stones of the footpath. She removed a cigarette from the case and one of those lighters that is like a miniature butane torch. It hissed and spat out a tiny blue flame, almost invisible in the daylight, and she lit her cigarette.

Breathing in hungrily, she exhaled a cloud of smoke then put the lighter back in the cigarette case and closed it. She looked at the silver case, then at me.

"It stands for Rodima Eden Esterbridge," she said, indicating the engraved initials.

"Quite a name."

"That's why my friends call me Ree for short."

"Look," I said. "It's very nice to meet you…"

"Likewise."

"But if you want me to find a record for you—"

"Not a record."

"What then?"

"A whole bunch of records."

"It all started at my grandma's birthday one year. She decided she was going to write her memoirs. She'd been talking about writing her memoirs ever since I can remember, so no one paid her much attention. But this particular year she actually went up in the attic to get what she called her 'memory-bilia'. And she discovered that some bees had built a huge nest in the corner of the attic."

I said, "Bees? Honey bees?"

She nodded. "Very definitely honey bees. This huge nest, right on top of all her stuff. So she got these insect-control guys in to deal with it. They said they'd have to spray."

Ree looked at me. It was cool in the garden and the sky was high and blue and empty, with just a few tiny white wisps of cloud, promising that it would soon be colder still. "Grandma didn't want to be around when they sprayed the poison, so she got out of the house."

"Very wise," I said.

"Maybe not so wise. Because next thing you know, we've not only got an attic full of dead bees, there's also about half a ton of honey which has melted and poured all over my grandmother's things." She gave me a rueful smile. "Turns out the bees keep the honey cool by fanning it with their little wings. Kill the bees and you turn off the natural air conditioning in the hive."

"And the honey melts."

"Right. You would have thought these dedicated insect specialists, the exterminators, might have been aware of this interesting fact about our friend the honey bee."

I said, "We have the same company here. They do boiler maintenance."

"Anyway, the contractors figured everything that got buried in the honey was ruined, so they just threw it all in the garbage when they cleared the honey out. By the time my grandmother got back, all her 'memory-bilia' was gone. Gone forever."

"I guess she wasn't too pleased."

"She was hysterical. She turned blue in the face and we thought she'd had a heart attack. When finally we got some sense out of her, it turns out that the only things that were really crucial, that she couldn't afford to lose, was her set of Hathor LPs." She looked at me. "She had the entire run, original copies. Fourteen albums."

"I'm impressed. A girl who knows her West Coast jazz discographies."

"How could I forget? Those fucking fourteen albums haunted my teenage years." She tried to take a puff on her cigarette, but it had gone out while she was talking. She took out her lighter and relit it. "Anyway, after the big honey disaster we looked for the records she'd lost. And, without telling her, we eventually found a complete set of those fourteen titles. It wasn't easy. We searched every record store in southern California. We surfed the net. We bust our asses. We spent a lot of money. It took us a year, but we found them. And we gave them to grandmother on her next birthday." She took a drag on her cigarette, exhaled and squinted at me through the smoke.

"She wouldn't even listen to them. She just took one quick look at the records, said they weren't the originals, then she threw them in the shit-can. Well, all except two of them. But we found those later."

"Not the originals?"

"No," she said. "It seems that was the deal breaker."

A passenger jet trundled in the sky high above us, coming in to land at Heathrow, leaving a white contrail against the blue. Ree studied the streaks of vapour, then looked at me. "We were all in tears, but she didn't care. She was furious. I rescued the records from the garbage, but she said I ought to just burn them."

"So, not a brilliantly successful birthday present, then."

Ree shook her head and smiled. "No. She said if they weren't the originals, they were no use to her."

"I wonder exactly what they were," I said. "These non-original albums."

"I've got them here."

"Here? The records?"

She looked at me. "Oh yeah."

I felt the first stirrings of an old familiar excitement. "Can I see them?"

She stubbed out her cigarette and we went inside. As we went through the kitchen she said, "What are you going to do with all these tomatoes?"

"I'm using them to make sauce for pasta and pizzas. It's the world's easiest and tastiest sauce."

"Well, man, give me the recipe."

I said, "You just casserole the tomatoes with garlic and basil and thyme. And olive oil."

"Hang on, hang on." She wrote it down, asked me about cooking times and temperatures, took the note and folded it and put it in her pocket. "Thanks," she said. "Now, those records. The funny thing is, Grandma didn't seem that interested in playing them. She wanted them, but she didn't want to *listen* to them."

"No?" Intriguing.

And who did that remind me of?

Mr Hibiki.

He'd been extremely eager to get hold of Easy Come, Easy Go, but hadn't been particularly interested in playing it once he'd got it. I'd tried to put that down to him being an obsessive-compulsive collector type. Plenty of record nuts were. But I couldn't see Ree's grandmother fitting that profile.

Nor Mr Hibiki, for that matter.

"My grandmother was furious," said Ree. "Because for years you could have picked up those records for like a dollar ninety-nine. Now they were priceless collector's items and impossible to find. Sometimes she'd get drunk and cry on my shoulder just thinking about it." She started to rummage through her bag.

"She used to say it was my birthright, my inheritance, my destiny. And then she'd curse like hell. She wanted me to know, she said."

"Know what?"

She paused in her search, a rolled pair of pink socks in her hand. "I don't know. She said she didn't want it coming out until she was dead. But then she wanted me to know. Told me I had to know. She said it was proof."

"Proof of what?"

She shrugged. "I don't know that either." She took out a pile of LPs, loosely swathed in bubble wrap. "These are the ones she shit-canned. And the other two."

She handed them to me. I removed the bubble wrap carefully and flipped through them. They were mostly reissues on V.S.O.P., Fresh Sound and Jasmine, but two were originals. I said, "You found some Hathor pressings."

She nodded. "And my grandmother was as happy as could be about those two. But that was all we ever found. We were still looking for the others when she passed." She looked at me. "She got really sick. It took hold suddenly. She was in and out of consciousness in hospital. She made me promise I'd try and find them for her. The rest of the records. I did try, but I didn't find them. Not before she was gone, anyway. She was sure she was going to get better, you know. But it turned out she was wrong."

I looked at the Hathors, the two original pressings. They were the Jerry Fielding, HL-005, and the Russ Garcia, HL-006. The Fielding was in good shape but had no cover. The Garcia, on the other hand, had a cover but the vinyl was a disaster, like a relief map of the moon.

I sat down and looked at them. "She was pleased with these?" I said.

"Sure." She watched me as I sat there, going through the logic of it. "What are you thinking?"

I considered. "I'm thinking that we know quite a lot."

She went and sat down in the only armchair that wasn't full of records. "Like what?"

"Your grandmother said there was something crucial, some vital information in the fourteen Hathor releases."

"Yes."

"And she needed all fourteen of them."

"Yes."

I remembered the neat little rank of LPs, pristine and complete, on Mr Hibiki's shelves. I remembered that smile as he'd added the last one.

Now suddenly, for the first time since Japan, I felt my spirits lift. I could begin to sense an answer. There was something about all fourteen albums, when you had them together…

She grinned. "Well, she didn't put it quite as neatly as that. But that was it, more or less, yeah."

"And she was happy with these two."

"I'd say so. She laughed like the devil in hell when we found them for her."

I held up one of the records, HL-005, the Jerry Fielding. "Well, one of these has no cover, so we know whatever this information is, it's nothing to do with the cover."

And Mr Hibiki hadn't been interested in the cover of *Easy Come, Easy Go.* He'd been politely appreciative that it was in such nice shape, but that was as far as it went. He'd hardly glanced at it.

I held up the other LP, HL-006, the Russ Garcia. "And

this is so scratched that it's unplayable—it looks like some idiot has played Frisbee with it in a room full of broken glass—so it's nothing to do with the ability to play the music on these records."

Just like Hibiki had listened with polite satisfaction to the Easy Geary album, but it clearly hadn't been what really interested him. Not the music.

She looked at me. "So, what's left?"

I took the Garcia out of the cover. It didn't have a protective inner sleeve, and it was much too late for one. I looked at the red and white label with the little Egyptian symbols on it. "Well, the labels for a start."

I remembered the way Mr Hibiki had stared with such intensity at the label on each side of the record.

"I hadn't thought of that," she said. "So you think it's something to do with the labels?"

I sat and thought about it for a moment. "No." I indicated the stack of records beside her. "You say your grandmother threw those in a trash can?"

"Oh yeah. 'Shit-can' is actually what I said."

"Okay, well the thing is, most of these reissues are exact replicas, especially the Spanish ones. Visually they are virtually identical, right down to the labels."

"So it's not those," she said.

"No." I remembered Hibiki's intense gaze. He hadn't necessarily been looking at the label at all. Instead he could have been studying something *adjacent* to it.

"So what is it?"

I said, "I think it's what's written in the dead wax."

"Okay, what's that?"

"It's after the run-out groove, where the needle ends

up at the end of the record. There's a space there where information is written, etched into the vinyl itself."

"Information," she said.

I nodded. "Music is the principal information on a record, but this other stuff is a kind of information too. There's a matrix number, which identifies the master tape that was used. And the stamper numbers that tell you where and when the record was manufactured."

I paused, thinking. "And sometimes there are other things in the dead wax, too."

She was looking at me. "What sort of other things?"

I went to her pile of records and eased out the copy of *Easy Come, Easy Go*. It was a Japanese reissue like the one I'd found at the jumble sale, ten million years ago. "Take this for instance. Easy Geary and your grandmother both signed it. If this was the original pressing it would have their autographs in the vinyl. Which was very unusual."

She took the album from me and looked at it. "But they're not here on this copy?"

"No. Only on the 1955 original. But that wasn't all there was."

"What, you mean there was something else… written in the dead wax?"

I nodded, going back to the Fielding and the Garcia. I could feel my pulse racing steeply. I thought, *Hibiki you bastard, I've got you now*.

I said, "On *Easy Come, Easy Go* there were these two other weird letters."

"Weird?"

"They were nothing to do with the stampers or matrix. They weren't even the initials of the engineer. We identified all those. These were something else. On side one there was a B. On side two there was a Y. So, BY."

She was staring at me. "What does it mean?"

I looked at the Fielding album and the Russ Garcia, albums HL-005 and HL-006. "And on these we have YI and ST."

She came over and stood beside me, looking down at the records. "So what does that tell us?"

I got up. At last I began to feel I was getting somewhere. The frustrated turmoil I'd felt since flying back from Japan was leaving me. Lifting off me like a heavy burden. "It tells us this. There are fourteen albums." I thought of them, sitting there on Mr Hibiki's shelf. "Each, I'm guessing, with two letters in the vinyl, one on side one and one on side two." I found a notebook and turned to a blank page. "Putting them in sequence, this is what we get."

- - - - - - - - -YIST- - - - - - - - - - - - - -BY

"The dashes indicate the missing letters from the other eleven albums."

She nodded, studying the letters while I poured some more coffee. She looked at me as I came back to the table and put a cup down in front of her. "You think there's a message here?"

"Your grandmother certainly seemed to think so."

She examined the paper again. "It's a full-on puzzle."

"Why didn't she just leave you a letter?" I said.

She looked up at me. "What do you mean?"

"Instead of the big mystery, why didn't she just leave you a letter explaining everything."

"She did," said Ree. "Well, she left me a letter telling me everything was in her diary."

"And did she leave you her diary?"

"She did. But it disappeared."

"Disappeared?"

She looked at me. "Yeah. It was all very shady."

"You think it was stolen?"

She shrugged. "It was there and then it was gone. Maybe it slipped through a rift in the universe." She sipped her coffee. "Or maybe, yeah, it was stolen." She looked at me again, holding my gaze steadily with hers.

"Who would have taken it?"

"There was this creepy guy who was supposed to be writing her biography. He disappeared about the same time as the diary."

"That sounds pretty conclusive."

"I thought so. And I'm working on tracking him down. Anyway, can you help me? To find the records, I mean."

I thought, *Is the Pope Catholic?*

"Sure. Of course. I guess."

She took my phone numbers and left.

That night, as I got ready to go to bed, I noticed my mobile phone sitting where I'd plugged it in to recharge. It was back at full power and the screen was flashing. I had a message. Several messages.

As I unplugged it from the charger, it started to ring. It was Clean Head. I answered.

"Where the hell have you been? I've been trying to reach you since this morning."

"Sorry. My battery was dead."

"I didn't want to tell you in front of Tinkler," she said.

"I mean him being just out of hospital and all. I didn't want to give him any shocks, but…"

"But?"

"When we were driving today. When I picked you up from the hospital…"

"Yes?"

"Someone was following us."

21. THE BULL'S HEAD

"I told you Clean Head would get us here on time," said Tinkler.

"Don't call Agatha 'Clean Head'," I said, aghast. I glanced nervously at where she was sitting, in the front of the cab.

"It's all right, she's given me special permission. Isn't that right?"

"That's right," she said, peering out into the night as the wipers swept the windshield. "So long as he doesn't make a habit of it." We had reached the mini roundabout between Barnes High Street and The Terrace and the Friday traffic had suddenly come to a standstill. Snow was drifting down in a soft white curtain over the river.

"And anyway," said Tinkler, looking at me pointedly, "you're one to talk. It was you who gave her a nickname in the first place."

This was true.

"How would you feel if someone did that to you?" he persisted. "Gave you a silly nickname?"

"Funny you should say that."

Clean Head dropped us off by Barnes Bridge Station and

we walked back, feet crunching on the snow, for the short distance along the Thames to the pub. "Gustav Holst lived there," I said, pointing at a handsome red-brick house with a white lattice-work balcony and blue plaque on the wall.

"I know," sighed Tinkler. "You've only told me fifty times."

The front of the Bull's Head is a spacious open bar with a high ceiling and, according to Tinkler, a "dangerously excellent" selection of malt whiskies. "Are you sure you should be drinking so soon after a serious head injury?" I said as they served him a Cragganmore.

"The only thing they said I should try to avoid was falling down the stairs."

"They're clearly not aware of your substance abuse issues."

He sniffed the whisky happily. "I should have made it a double." I ordered a glass of red wine, even though I felt sad whenever I thought about wine—it made me think of Nevada.

We went through the pub and into the small auditorium at the back, paying at the door. A teenage girl with a pint glass full of pound coins and a roll of fivers sitting there on a stool took the money. Tinkler insisted on paying. I had noticed that people did that now I was suddenly wealthy. This was in stark contrast to the custom previously, when I'd been broke, and when it would have made some sense, in addition to being really useful.

Tinkler also insisted that we sat right at the front, our feet virtually touching the low stage where a gleaming Yamaha grand piano, a drum kit and a variety of microphones stood, with colourful cables snaking around them. He then set about putting in earplugs. I said, "Why don't you just sit further back and not use the earplugs?"

"What?"

"Why don't you just sit further away from the stage and not use the earplugs?"

"It wouldn't be the same. You'd lose the sense of immediacy. Here, do you want some? I have a pair spare."

"Maybe later," I said. A door clanked open at the side of the building, behind the piano, and Ree stepped through, flanked by a pair of paunchy middle-aged men who had the affable, slightly ironic look of musicians. I was surprised at how glad I was to see her. She smiled at me.

"Hey, Chef," she called and waved as she and the musicians walked to the small bar at the back of the room.

Tinkler was staring at me. "Chef? Has she given you a sassy nickname already?"

"She liked my pasta sauce."

"That's stupendous." He was grinning like the Cheshire Cat as they shut the doors and the gig began. When Ree came on and sang, Tinkler looked at me and whispered, "She's good." Then he took his earplugs out. "She's really good." Then he looked at me and hissed, "She sounds just like…"

"Her grandmother. Now shut up."

She ended the first set with 'Joy House Blues', a Professor Jellaway number.

The song allegedly commemorated Jellaway's stint as a whorehouse pianist in New Orleans and its ironic title alluded to how this giant of the music had felt about that situation. But he had turned the tables on those who exploited and demeaned musicians when he'd turned it into a hit popular song and one of the first small masterpieces of jazz.

In the interval most of the audience and all of the

musicians decamped to the bar at the back of the hall or went out into the pub proper. Tinkler and I stayed put. "That was… amazing," he said.

He took out a pale blue plastic lunchbox with a snap lid and opened it. Inside nestled a glistening, dewy bunch of grapes. They were plump and so purple they were almost black. He began to pluck them off the stalks and eat them.

"Tinkler, for Christ's sake." I looked around to make sure nobody had noticed. "You're supposed to buy snacks on the premises, not bring your own."

"Well, they're not likely to sell grapes, are they, on the premises?" He was talking with his mouth full. Then he swallowed and smiled and said, "Hey look, here she is!" He beamed as Ree came over carrying a drink and joined us, sitting on the low podium amid a mass of cables, her knees pressed against ours.

She put her drink down on the stage. "Are those grapes?"

"Help yourself," said Tinkler magnanimously. She did so, munching them happily.

"Were you wearing earplugs?" she said.

"He didn't want to lose any immediacy," I explained. She nodded, as if this made sense, then reached into a pocket and took out a small roll of banknotes.

"Here's the money," she said proudly. "I've got it for you already. I've been doing a load of gigs."

I waved my hands in the air. "Don't pay me until I've actually got hold of the records for you."

"What's going on?" said Tinkler.

"She's hired me to find some records. To collect all of the Hathor originals for her."

"And he's found some," said Ree.

Tinkler leaned forward eagerly. "Really?"

"Well, Ree had two to start with and I've found two more."

"Already?" said Tinkler. "Nice going. How did you find them? Internet?"

"No, Alan at Jazz House had HL-003, the Richie Kamuca, and they've got a copy of HL-012, the Pepper Adams, at Jerry's. I mean at Styli." I still couldn't quite wrap my head around Jerry being dead.

"I spoke to them on the phone today." I glanced at Ree. "I told them we'd pick it up at the shop this weekend."

"So, do you have a list of these damned records?" said Tinkler. "Maybe I can help you find them."

Although I doubted that, I pulled out my notebook and showed him the list. We needed all the help we could get.

HL-001 EASY GEARY (PLAYS BURNS HOBARTT)
HL-002 MARTY PAICH
HL-003 RICHIE KAMUCA
HL-004 JOHNNY RICHARDS
HL-005 JERRY FIELDING
HL-006 RUSS GARCIA
HL-007 CY COLEMAN
HL-008 HOWARD ROBERTS
HL-009 RITA MAE POLLINI (SINGS BURNS HOBARTT)
HL-010 RITA MAE POLLINI (SINGS PROFESSOR JELLAWAY)
HL-011 MANNY ALBAM
HL-012 PEPPER ADAMS
HL-013 CONTE CANDOLI
HL-014 EASY GEARY (EASY COME, EASY GO)

At this point the musicians trooped back to the stage with their pints of beer and took up positions by their instruments. People hurried back in and the doors were closed and they started to play. Ree sat out the first few numbers, then she rejoined the band. As she stepped out onto the stage the crowd responded enthusiastically.

Tinkler clapped like a performing seal.

The set concluded with a hair-raising version of 'Running from a Spell'. When the song reached a certain point, it seemed strange not to hear a gunshot.

Ree was sitting in the pub garden on the bench of a green plastic picnic table. The table was dusted with snow and so was the bench. We brushed it off as we sat down.

She said, "Thanks for being here, guys. The electric bass player wants to hit on me. For some reason it's the electric basses who do that. The acoustic bass players are pretty much always perfect gentlemen." She took a drag on her cigarette. Snowflakes in her hair sparkled in the glare of the floodlights that lit the garden.

"Maybe that's because their instruments are bigger," said Tinkler.

She looked at him.

Tinkler turned bright red. "I mean," he said, "the acoustic bass players. Maybe they don't get around quite so much, or with quite such nimbleness because they have to carry around these enormous acoustic basses, you know like a double bass, like an oversized cello, you know?"

I patted him on the shoulder. "When you're in a hole, stop digging."

"Here he is now," said Ree, nodding towards the pub. A thin man in leather and denim was walking towards us. It was indeed the bass player from the set. He had a rooster's comb of dark hair shot through with grey. His whippet-like leanness was at odds with the comfortable potbellies of the rest of the band. I wondered if he was a speed freak. That would account for his relative emaciation.

He came and sat with us. "This is Jimmy Genower," said Ree. We introduced ourselves and shook hands. I noticed he had tattoos that started on his thin hairy wrists and ran thickly back in dark swirls under his shirt sleeves.

After the introductions he proceeded to ignore us, focusing all his attention on Ree. I began to feel bored, and cold. As he leaned hungrily towards Ree, his intent was clear. Equally clear—it seemed to me—was that he didn't stand a chance and that Ree was making this as obvious as she could, both verbally and physically, in terms of body language, without actually sticking her cigarette in his eye.

"That last number," he said, "now that was by Professor Jellaway." He announced this as though it was a startling revelation. "They say he sold his soul to the devil in New Orleans in exchange for his enormous talent."

He then began a potted history of Professor Jellaway, based on any number of popular accounts with which I was familiar. Jellaway had been a tireless—and tiresome—self-mythologiser and most of the startling and sensational facts that studded his life story simply didn't check out. Some of it was just harmless ornamentation—like Louis Armstrong pretending he'd invented scat singing when he'd happened to drop the sheet music. And some of it was more than that.

Boasting, or what would more cruelly be called lying,

had been part of the weave of life for the early jazz musicians. It also didn't help that subsequent generations of biographers had felt obliged to add to these tall tales.

In the end, all that was certain about Jellaway was that he had been a genius.

"His life story is a very scary story," said Jimmy Genower. "He was born at the stroke of midnight on Friday the 13th. In 1917, although he was too young to enlist, he came over to France with the US Army, in Jim Europe's 369th Infantry Band." He paused significantly and confided, "Their regimental nickname was the Hellfighters. The Hellfighters."

Tinkler gave me a flabbergasted who-is-this-guy look.

"They say he sold his soul to the devil on the blood-soaked battlefields of World War One, in exchange for his life."

"Hang on a minute," I said. "I thought you said that he sold his soul to the devil in New Orleans in exchange for his enormous talent."

"Yeah," piped up Tinkler. "Were there two deals with the devil? Surely that's not fair."

I said, "Maybe he renegotiated his first deal."

Jimmy Genower was glowering at us with disgust. We were spoiling his carefully crafted atmosphere. Ree, on the other hand, was regarding us with barely concealed amusement.

She said, "Do you want to hear the really scary story about Red Jellaway?"

We all said we did, even Genower, whom I'd thought to be incapable of listening to any voice but his own.

Ree said, "Professor Jellaway was a gambler. Always had a lot of paper out there. You know, gambling debts. 'Markers' we call them. Anyway, one day two white men who called themselves the Spike brothers bought up all his gambling debts. Which was a lot. And once they did that, once they owned all the markers, they thought they owned him, too."

She stubbed out her cigarette. "The Spike brothers were sharp businessmen. They had the company all set up already. A music company, imaginatively called Spike Brothers Music. They were going into the publishing business and Professor Jellaway was going to be their house slave. He'd write the songs and they'd grow rich on the fruits of his labours."

She took out another cigarette and lit it. "When he heard what they had in mind, the Professor laughed in their faces. He told them they could have one song. Just one. To pay off all the markers. They turned him down. Said their deal was the only deal on the table."

She smiled. "But it turned out it wasn't. Professor Jellaway took that song to another publisher and it was a substantial hit and he used the money to pay off all the debts the Spike brothers had been holding over him."

She looked at us. "You see, he had a more realistic estimate of his worth than they did. Isn't that amazing, this guy bred in the ghetto was smarter than these big capitalist jerks who were trying to tie a rope around him."

"Power to the people!" said Jimmy.

Ree didn't dignify this with a response. "So, like I say, he paid them off with the one song. But that proved to be a fatal move. Because the Spike brothers now saw his earning potential. They knew what he was really worth. And they weren't going to let him get away."

Her gaze met mine. "Besides gambling, Professor Jellaway's weakness was women. So the Spike brothers got this beautiful prostitute…"

"Beautiful prostitute," repeated Tinker happily. He looked at us. "I just like saying it."

"Anyway," said Ree, "they hired this working girl and they used her as a honey trap. And Professor Jellaway walked right into it. He had this hot weekend with her and the Spike brothers made sure the happy couple were photographed in all the clubs and every joint they visited. On Monday morning Red Jellaway discovered he'd acquired a 'wife'. This woman was claiming she was married to him. And she had documents to prove it. And she wanted half of the money for anything he'd ever written, or ever would write."

She took a drag on her cigarette. "The white judge upheld this total fraud—it was Los Angeles in 1924, remember—and so this prostitute ended up owning the rights to half of all his earnings on his songs, which she signed over to Spike Brothers Music."

"I hate this beautiful prostitute," said Tinkler. "Which is odd because usually I really like them."

Ree breathed out a luminous cloud of smoke. "Anyway," she said. "Sorry if I'm ranting. But to me the really scary story is the one about a musician getting screwed by the suits."

"Right on, sister," said Jimmy. We all tried to ignore him and Ree did the best job, just continuing with her account, addressing Tinkler and me.

"It was all a total and shameless scam. If Professor Jellaway was alive today, he could walk in and demand justice and they'd have to rearrange the corporate universe for him. But this was white America in the early twentieth century. And so they had him just where they wanted him. And the Professor couldn't stand living with this fact. With what the Spike brothers had done to him."

"I don't blame him," I said.

She nodded. "He had to do something about it. And soon a rumour started going around that the Professor had hired some hitmen to kill the brothers."

She looked at the smoke from her cigarette, rising to meet the snowflakes. "So the brothers decided they had to strike first. The story is they found the Professor in Chicago where he'd gone to ground and beat him to death with baseball bats and threw his body in the river. But the body was never found."

She sucked on her cigarette and it glowed, a tiny spot of red in the night. "But within a year, both the Spike brothers were dead themselves by violent means."

I said, "Maybe Professor Jellaway really did hire some hitmen."

She said, "Or maybe it was what they would have called the coloured community, getting even."

We looked at each other.

"Or maybe it was the curse," said Jimmy Genower, trying to get back into the conversation by any means possible. He suddenly spotted Tinkler's lunchbox. "What's that, mate? You brought your fucking sandwiches? That's priceless."

"Grapes, actually," said Tinkler.

Jimmy announced that he was going in to get another drink. He offered to buy one for Ree, and rather pointedly not for us, but she declined. As he stood up, she said, "Jimmy's got something to tell us."

Jimmy looked blank for a moment and then he said, "Oh yeah, that's right. I'm going to sell you that record."

"What record?"

"One of the ones by my grandmother," said Ree.

"*Rita Mae Pollini Sings Professor Jellaway*," said Jimmy, grinning.

I said, "Not the original Hathor pressing."

"Oh yes."

We agreed to meet Jimmy Genower at his house—which was near the pub—at lunchtime on Monday. I would have a look at the record and if I gave the go-ahead, which privately I thought was unlikely, Ree would pay the inflated sum Jimmy wanted for it.

And then we'd have secured five of the fourteen albums she needed.

But first we had to collect the record I'd found at Styli.

I'd arranged with the guys at the shop to pick it up on the weekend and I went in on Sunday to collect it. To my astonishment, the shop was shut. That would never have happened when Jerry ran the place. A staunch atheist, he'd been open all day, every Sunday.

On Monday I was at the shop ten minutes after it opened. I would have been there waiting on the doorstep half an hour earlier but Clean Head's cab had got hopelessly ensnared in traffic around Waterloo. I'd had to get out and catch the Tube, which proved to be equally problematic with three cancelled trains in a row. It probably would have been quicker for me to walk across Hungerford Bridge.

When I got to the shop I raced upstairs to the jazz department. Kempton was behind the counter with Gilbert, the new kid they'd taken on to make up the numbers now that Jerry was gone. Kempton and I waved to each other. He was busy on the phone so I turned to Gilbert. I smiled at him. "I've come to collect the Pepper Adams album."

He stared at me as though I was speaking a different

and unrecognisable language. "The one on Hathor," I said. "Catalogue number HL-012. I phoned about it. You're holding it for me."

"No we're not," said Gilbert.

I took a deep breath and tried starting again. "It's by Pepper Adams. He plays baritone sax."

"I know who he is. I know the record. It's sold."

"What do you mean?" I said. "What do you mean, sold?"

"I just sold it. Just five minutes ago."

"You can't have sold it," I said, my voice rising slightly. "You're holding it for me."

At this point Kempton hastily concluded his phone call and joined us. "What's the matter?" he said.

"He says the record is sold."

"But we were holding it for you," said Kempton.

"I didn't know anything about any record being held," said Gilbert, a whiney, high-pitched don't-blame-me note entering his voice.

I couldn't believe this was happening. "I told you I was going to pick it up this weekend."

"Ah well," said Gilbert. "It's not the weekend anymore." I could have throttled him with my bare hands.

Instead I turned to Kempton and said, "This is unacceptable. It would never have happened under Jerry's regime."

Kempton seemed genuinely upset. "Look, I'm sorry. We're sorry. Here's a ten per cent coupon. Let's call it fifteen per cent. As a discount on your next purchase. I mean *off* your next purchase."

I ignored this. "Who bought it?" I said. "Who bought the record?"

"Was it that woman?" said Kempton, looking at Gilbert.

"The one I saw coming down the stairs?"

Gilbert nodded. "She's the only customer we've had today."

I said, "What did she look like? Was she blonde?"

"No, she had red hair," said Kempton. "I passed her on the stairs."

"Definitely not blonde?"

"No. Red hair. Long red hair."

"It was a wig," said Gilbert suddenly. We both looked at him.

"What?"

His face took on a stubborn set. "A good one, but definitely a wig."

"I defer to your greater knowledge of women's hairpieces," said Kempton, rather bitchily, I thought. Then he said to me, "Listen, we'll make it twenty per cent. Twenty-five per cent…"

I met Ree at the Bull's Head at noon. We'd agreed to rendezvous there before going on to Jimmy Genower's. I hadn't been able to reach her on the phone that morning and I was dreading giving her the news about the record at Styli having disappeared. I hadn't wanted to leave a message. That seemed cowardly. So I told her in person.

She took it philosophically, shrugging. "Just a piece of bad luck."

"Luck had nothing to do with it. I suspect it was the Aryan Twins. Heinz and Heidi. Or in this case just Heidi."

She said, "Who are they?"

"Matching blonde his and hers hitmen… hit persons? Hit people?"

"Blonde?"

"Except now she's wearing a red wig."

"And you say they're hitmen."

"Men and women."

"Have they actually killed anyone?"

"I am very inclined to believe so. And made a damned good try on other occasions."

Ree took this in with no apparent reaction. Maybe she didn't believe me.

"I think this may be my fault," I said.

"What is?"

"Them getting to the record before us."

"Why do you say that?"

"They were hired by somebody to try and stop me getting hold of *Easy Come, Easy Go*. The pre-emptive buy was the Aryan Twins' trademark trick. Getting in just before me and snatching up the merchandise."

"But you *did* get hold of *Easy Come, Easy Go*. So why are they still trying to stop you?"

This was a good question. Was it possible that they hadn't seen the press coverage announcing my find? Or perhaps, rather more likely, they hadn't believed it? My speculations were interrupted at that moment because Ree looked at her watch and said, "We'd better get moving. Even someone like Jimmy should be awake by now."

Jimmy Genower's house was in Elms Avenue, just the other side of the traffic roundabout. Like much of Barnes, it was an odd mix, with council tenants in social housing jostling beside very wealthy homeowners. Here you could find a millionaire stockbroker ensconced next door to a colourful local who was indulging his god-given right to leave a motorcycle half dismantled in the front garden.

Which is exactly what Jimmy seemed to be doing.

"Nice place," said Ree ironically. "Very trailer park." We walked across the oil-stained gravel, dodging motorcycle parts, towards his front door. I got there ahead of her and knocked, good and hard, with the black iron lion's head knocker. I had decided I was going to take charge of this encounter, and make damned sure that Jimmy Fucking Genower didn't manage to charge Ree the ludicrous sum quoted for his second-hand record.

I'd be amazed if it was even the right album.

Ree stood beside me on the front step. There was no sound from within the house. The entire street was quiet. I thought about knocking again—then I noticed the garden gate. It was just over to our left. "Maybe he's in the back garden," I said.

The garden gate opened with a screech and we walked into the narrow shadowed walkway between the two houses, Ree just behind me. She was following me so closely that she walked right into me when I stopped suddenly.

Jimmy Genower was there all right, sitting in the back garden in an old black and white striped deckchair. There was a can of beer between his feet and he was looking at us.

Or at least, he would have been, if he had been able to see anything with his eyes.

I hustled Ree back through the gate. "What is it?" she said. "What's the matter?"

My stomach felt cold and bruised. "He's dead," I said.

"What?"

"He's sitting there in a chair, dead."

"Are you sure?"

I nodded. I was never more sure of anything.

"Let me go have a look," she said.

"No, we've got to get out of here."

"Why?"

"Not least because the people who did it might still be around." I was trying as hard as I could to think straight. "Give me your lighter, please."

"The people who did it?"

"Your lighter, please."

She reached into her pocket, dug around for a minute, then handed it to me. She was looking at me strangely. I was figuring out how to work the lighter.

"You press the thing on the—"

"I've got it." I went back to the garden gate and ignited the lighter, playing the blue flame over the metal handle where I'd touched it. Then I went to the front door of the house and repeated the procedure on the lion's head knocker.

She was looking at me. "DNA?" she said.

"Yes." I finished and gave her back the lighter.

"Seriously?"

I led her back to the street and looked both ways. The street was still empty. Ree was reluctant to go but I took her by the arm and walked her away from the house. We marched briskly down Elms Avenue, just a couple out for a bracing stroll on a winter day. When we reached the main road I began to breathe again. We turned right, towards my house.

"I should have taken a look at him," said Ree suddenly.

"We want to get the hell out of here," I said.

She began to slow her pace. "Maybe he wasn't dead."

"He was dead."

But she had stopped, so I had to stop too.

We were standing outside the little local supermarket with the occasional shoppers hustling past us and snow starting to come down from a clear sky. Ree was getting a stubborn look on her face and I realised with a sinking feeling that I might be in for a battle here I couldn't win. "Maybe he's just sick," she said. "He might be in bad shape and need our help." I took a deep breath before I replied, and just then we heard the sirens.

They were coming from the direction of the river. Approaching from Hammersmith. They came around the bend in the road by the Bull's Head, shot across the mini roundabout and turned right into Elms Avenue. There was an ambulance and two police cars. A group of children ran past us and followed them.

I looked at Ree. We followed the kids. By the time we turned left into Elms Avenue there were a dozen neighbours and passers-by stopping to take a look, in addition to the kids. A big enough crowd for us to get lost in. We stood there and watched as the police and medics got out of their vehicles and hurried towards Jimmy Genower's house. Ree looked at me.

"Okay," she said. "There's nothing we can do. Let's get out of here."

The snow began falling heavily as we walked back past Barnes Pond, white flakes disappearing into the cold black water. She looked at me. "They got here fast. The cops."

"Yeah," I said. "Almost like someone wanted us to get caught there with him."

22. A RED WIG

I phoned Tinkler as we walked home and he was waiting for us when we reached my estate. "What's the matter?" he said as he fell in step beside us. Ree and I looked at each other. "Well?" said Tinkler.

I cleared my throat. "You remember that bloke we met the other night at the Bull's Head?"

"What bloke? Oh the moronic prick of a bass player with his fucking silly stories? The arrogant, brainless, boorish tattooed wonder?" Something in our faces must have cued him, because he went quiet.

"He's had an accident," I said.

Tinkler peered at us. "Just before he could sell you the record?"

"That's right."

"Christ."

We walked the rest of the way in silence.

The sun was low in the winter sky and threw the angular shadow of the crane across us as we entered the square and crossed it, heading towards my house. The crane was recently arrived, a hefty red and white piece of equipment on the back of a truck with the name REDGEAR CRANE HIRE on it. It was parked in the alley leading off the square where it was being used in the dismantling of the boiler.

We paused for a moment to look at the work in progress. The boiler room was in a sunken area, a basin adjacent to our square, about twenty feet below us where there had once been a car park. We couldn't get too close to the edge because the first thing the contractors had removed was, of course, the handrail which had previously served as a safety barrier.

The boiler had been dismantled and was lying around in the form of giant steel components severed from the whole. I remembered how I used to think of that vast boiler as a sleeping dragon.

The dragon's bones, I thought.

The cats heard us coming and streaked through the door as we opened it, back from their adventures in the snow. I took off my shoes, hung up my coat, and excused myself, going into the bathroom where I vomited violently and noisily. I was thinking of Jimmy Genower's dead eyes. I flushed the toilet, brushed my teeth and came out to find Ree and Tinkler looking at me with concern.

I avoided their gaze and went into the kitchen to feed the cats. I poured out some biscuits into their bowls, only for these to be ignored after a quick tentative sniff, as was the custom of late. "They've lost their appetite," I said to Tinkler, who had wandered in to join me.

"What?" The concept of not having an appetite was utterly alien to Tinkler.

"They just don't seem to be eating," I said.

"They must be eating something."

"Not nearly enough. In the winter they need a lot of calories."

"They're not the only ones," said Tinkler, opening the fridge and peering into it. "Have you got any grapes?"

Before I could reply, the doorbell rang and I went to answer it. Standing there was Tanya, my postwoman. She looked agitated. "You won't believe this," she said. "But I've just been robbed."

"Christ," I said.

"Shit," said Ree, peering over my shoulder. "What happened?"

"I was just doing my walk, just headed for your place in fact, and I'd taken out the post ready and this bloke came running past."

"Big?" I said. "Athletic build?"

She gave me an odd look. "Yes. At first I thought he was just a jogger. I had my headphones on so I didn't really notice him. But then he ran right past me and snatched something from me. Right out of my hand, he did. Cheeky bugger." She was obviously angry, and a little shook up.

"What did he get?"

"What?"

"You said he stole something. What was it?"

"A calendar, I think."

"A calendar?"

"Yes. It was addressed to one of those ladies who lives next door to you. Why would anyone want to steal a calendar?"

I said, "Did you see what colour his hair was? The runner?"

"No. He was wearing a woolly hat."

At that stage I wouldn't have been surprised if he had been wearing a long flowing auburn wig. Tanya was looking a bit pale now, with the aftershock of the encounter. "Are you all right?" I said.

"I'm fine."

"Do you want a coffee?" I said. "A cup of tea?"

"No, I'm fine." She gave me a crooked smile. "For a moment I thought it was one of your LPs, but thank god, I reckon it was just a calendar. Probably had meerkats on it." She handed me my post and left. I closed the door and looked at Ree.

"You know, it does look like an LP," she said. "A calendar." She shook her head. "Is there an LP coming to you in the mail?"

"Not yet," I said. "And I think we're going to have a little change of plan about that." I hurried to my laptop and sent an email to Alan at Jazz House, asking him not to ship the record of HL-003, the Richie Kamuca, just yet, but to hold it for us. I then asked him if he would do me a favour and outlined what I wanted. Then I settled back on the sofa. Through the window I could see Ree in the back garden, having a cigarette. It was dark now and the streetlights had come on. I watched the smoke from her cigarette glow strangely in their yellowish sodium light.

And I sat thinking.

Tinkler wandered in from the kitchen and said, "About those grapes?"

"Bottom shelf at the back," I said.

"Are you sure?"

"Yes."

He gave me a sceptical look and went back into the kitchen. I returned to my thoughts. Ree came back inside with a gust of cold air, closing the door behind her and taking off her shoes. Tinkler came back in munching away at a bowl of grapes.

I said, "Does anybody need to use the bathroom?" They both gave me a strange look, but shook their heads in unison as though operated by the same puppeteer.

"Okay." I took out my phone and holding it carefully in full view, went into the bathroom with it. I set the phone on a shelf beside the window and came out again, closing the door behind me. I came back into the sitting room where Tinkler and Ree were waiting. The looks they'd given me before were nothing compared to the strangeness of the ones they gave me now.

"What was that about?" said Tinkler.

"Let me explain."

"Okay. Would you? It would be nice."

I took a deep breath. "These fuckers are always one step ahead of us," I said.

"This would be the Aryan fuckers," said Ree.

"Correct."

"And I want it to stop. I want to be one step ahead of them for a change."

"Okay," said Tinkler.

"Good," said Ree. "But how do we achieve that?"

I sat down. "Well, to start with, we figure out how they've managed to *be* one step ahead of us."

"You left your phone in the bathroom," said Ree.

"You think it's bugged," said Tinkler.

I nodded. "I'm sure someone is picking up my calls. But for all we know…"

"They might also be able to listen in," said Ree, "even when the phone is off."

I nodded. "If they installed some kind of microphone."

"Man," said Tinkler, glancing towards the bathroom,

"your phone is seriously bugged."

"But are you sure it's the phone?" said Ree.

"No." I could have checked it using the hardware we'd bought at the Spook Store—if I still had it. But I'd thrown it all away when I'd thought Nevada was dead. It had been just too painful to look at, so I'd simply thrown it all in the communal rubbish bin, thousands of pounds' worth of electronics, rattling into oblivion.

Just then my email dinged. It was Alan at Jazz House getting back to me about my query. He'd checked the record and provided the two letters from the dead wax.

Ree watched over my shoulder as I took out my notebook and added the new information.

- - - - EG - - YIST - - - - - - - - - - - - - - BY

"What now?" said Tinkler.

"Now we go to the big record mart at Wembley."

"You think you'll find something there?"

"There will be at least two dealers who're likely to have something for us. So we go see them tomorrow. And we go very carefully. We especially don't mention anything about it on the contaminated phone."

"What do we do with the contaminated phone?" said Tinkler.

Ree raised her hand. "I'll put it somewhere safe. Until we think of a way of using it. Against them."

"Carry the fight to the enemy. Nice."

After dinner Ree settled down on the sofa and curled up, like a cat deciding it had found a place to sleep. "Sorry," she yawned, "jet lag."

* * *

The next morning I made real coffee. I'd discovered the trick for enjoying this every day. On waking you have a cup of instant to give yourself the energy to embark on the ordeal of making the real stuff. I'd just finished grinding the beans—always the most stressful part—when the doorbell rang.

I opened the door.

It was Nevada.

"Can I come in?" she said.

I couldn't think or, for a moment, speak. I said, "Okay."

She stepped past me. I smelled her perfume again and my heart started beating raggedly. I closed the door and turned to face her. I said, "Look—"

"Don't say anything," she said. "Just let me say my piece."

"But—"

"Please."

"But, listen—"

"No. You listen to me. Just listen." She went into the kitchen and sat down. That had always been her favourite chair. She looked up at me. "A lot of the things you said in Japan were true. I did behave unforgivably."

"Nevada—"

"Just listen, please. This isn't easy. I know you should never forgive me for letting you think I was dead. But I just want to try and explain. I don't want you to forgive me. I just want you to understand." She looked at me. "Can you do that?"

"But, Nevada," I said.

"Just listen. You have to try to understand what it was like. It was dark, and they were firing guns at us—

remember?—and I was shit-scared, as who wouldn't be. But I was chasing them. And they got away. They roared off into the night and I came back and found the whole place in flames. And you were gone. I thought you'd run out on me." She looked at me. "I didn't know you thought I was dead. It was only later that even occurred to me." She looked down. "After I saw you in Japan, I phoned Hughie. To tell him, and to tell everyone, that I was still alive."

She looked at me again, and there was anger in her eyes now. "And I also wanted to know why he told you I was dead. Do you know what he said? He said he saw me lying in the ditch and it just looked to him like they'd shot me and I was done for. Well, he certainly didn't stick around to find out, did he? I was out of that ditch in about two seconds flat. But good old Hughie already had the idea firmly fixed in his mind, such as it is."

She reached over and took my hand. "So thanks to him, you thought I was dead and I thought you'd run out on me. I was in a state of shock. I retrieved the record and the cover, what was left of them, and I walked to the station and I caught the first train back to London. All the way there I thought I was going to come back to you, to confront you, to see what had happened. But when I got to London I just kept going, to Heathrow, and there was a flight just getting ready to board. For Japan." She gazed up into my eyes. "Everything just fell into place, as if that was the way it was meant to happen."

"Listen," I said, "I've got to tell you—"

"Not yet. Just let me finish. I flew back with the fragments of the record in my bag and I knew that the mission was over and we'd failed. And I knew that all I'd done was bring danger into your life. I'd nearly got you killed. It didn't seem right to go back to you, because it might just put you in danger again. I didn't want to do that." She squeezed my hand.

"You see," she said. "I just thought you'd be safer without me."

She looked up as the bedroom door opened. Nevada fell silent and watched as Ree walked into the kitchen. She was wearing one of my baggy, oversized t-shirts.

As it happened, it was one that Nevada had been fond of wearing.

Ree came over and kissed me and put her arm around my shoulder.

Nevada stared at us. "I didn't know you had company," she said slowly.

"I tried to tell you," I said.

"That's right. I suppose you did."

Ree sat down and poured herself a cup of coffee, taking her time. The air in the kitchen crackled with tension, like static electricity before a storm.

The front door opened and a familiar voice called, "Hey there, hep cats!" Footsteps approached down the hall and the same voice said, "The door was open so I just—"

Stinky came into the kitchen and froze. He looked at Nevada, then at Ree, then at me, then at Ree again. Ree looked at me and said, "Friend of yours, Chef?"

"Stinky," I said. "This isn't a good time."

I walked Stinky back into the hall. He immediately began speaking in a low, urgent, confidential tone. "Listen, Chef," he said. "Why don't we go out some time? Bring your girls and I'll bring mine. We can double date. Or quadruple date. Or actually quintuple date because I'll bring three girls."

"Stinky, please." I urged him out the door and felt my entire body relax as he finally left and I closed the door behind him. But you almost had to admire the way he had instantly picked up on the nickname. In his need to be in with the in-crowd, Stinky was always the first with a new piece of slang or catchphrase.

I went back into the kitchen. "You managed to get rid of him?" said Nevada.

"Stinky had to hurry off to phone an escort service."

Ree drained her coffee and stood up. "You guys can finish your talk. I'll get dressed and go out and have a cigarette."

"You smoke?" said Nevada.

"Yeah."

"And your face is so beautifully unlined, for a smoker. That's so unusual. But then, there's plenty of time."

"Plenty of time for all sorts of things," said Ree, and she went into my bedroom. As the door closed Nevada looked at me.

"You slept with her?"

Was there any point in denying it, or dissembling? "Ah," I stammered. "Yes?"

"Is she good in bed?"

"What?"

"Is she?"

"Please, Nevada."

"Better than me?"

I shook my head. "No."

"As good?"

"No."

She stared towards the bedroom. "Well, at least I know she's lousy in the sack."

"I didn't say that," I said. She glared at me.

"What, then?"

"Things were better with you because I loved you."

She looked at me. "So you don't love her?"

I shrugged. "I've only just met her."

"Well, give it time. Plenty of time for all sorts of things," she quoted. She stood up. "I suppose I'd better be off." Then she paused. "I almost forgot. Here's a souvenir for you." She took it out of her bag and set it on the counter. It was the scorched cover of *Easy Come, Easy Go* and the melted misshapen piece of vinyl.

"Good luck," she said. "With everything." She went out and the door closed behind her and she was gone.

Ree and I travelled to the record mart in Wembley separately. I went in a taxi with Clean Head and Ree got a cab driven by Clean Head's friend. They both took great pains to avoid being followed, and were in radio contact with each other all the way. So we reached the exhibition centre with a clean bill of health.

I was familiar with the floor plan of the record mart from previous visits and I knew all the shortcuts. As we made our way through the crowd, a skinny guy in frosted denim with a large badge that identified him as the official event photographer stalked us, repeatedly taking our picture with his bulky digital camera.

When I say "our picture", I actually mean Ree's picture.

"Am I a celebrity?" she said.

"Sort of. He's not accustomed to having an attractive woman to photograph. They're a bit of a rarity at this kind of event."

"Maybe I should take off my top."

"That would probably cause his brain to melt and run out through his ears."

I'd decided there were three dealers worth visiting and by cutting around on the walkway behind the exhibition area, and avoiding the crowds, we were able to hit all three in swift succession. The first was a total bust, but at the second one, run by a guy called Florien, we struck gold.

A copy of *Easy Geary Plays Burns Hobartt*, HL-001, the very first of the Hathors. I checked and nodded to Ree. It was a genuine original pressing.

"Okay," she said, and reached into her pocket. "How much?"

Florien scrutinised her, then the record, then her again. "Two grand."

"Two what?" I said. "Florien, are you out of your mind?" This was the least rare of the Hathors, having been produced in the greatest numbers.

Ree tugged at my arm. "No, we'll just pay him. I'll have to cash some traveller's cheques, though."

"Wait a minute," I said. I looked at Florien. "Shall we try playing one track?"

"What?"

"Oh look," I said. "There's a turntable over there." I took the record from Florien. "Surely you have no objection?"

"Look, don't worry about that…"

"You know what? For two grand I think we will."

He watched me unhappily as I went over to the Rega deck one of the other dealers had set up nearby. It was connected to a phono stage and small pair of active speakers. Not exactly an audiophile setup, but it would do. I put the record on the platter, started the motor and lowered the tone arm. There was a rustling from the speakers and then the music began.

It sounded like Satan playing a barbed wire banjo during a particularly noisy thunderstorm.

Florien quickly backed away, as though expecting a blow. He certainly deserved one. I looked at him and said, "This is supposed to be one of the most beautiful recordings in the history of jazz."

"All right, all right, all right."

"I think the price needs to head south in a dramatic fashion."

"All right," he said. "One thousand—"

I looked at him.

He cleared his throat. "Nine hundred."

I looked at him.

"Five hundred. Four hundred."

I continued to look at him.

"Ah, two hundred and fifty?" This was uttered in a newly tentative tone. I began to think we could drive him even lower.

"Done," said Ree hastily, stuffing the bank notes into his hand.

We bagged the record and moved away, Ree at my side. I said, "I think we could have beaten him down some more."

"It doesn't matter."

"But it's in really bad shape. You heard how it plays."

She leaned towards me and said, "It doesn't matter how it plays. My grandmother didn't care about that. And neither do we." She patted the bag. "This has got what we need."

She was right, but it still rankled. It was the principle of the thing. "That doesn't mean I'm going to let someone rip you off."

"I know," she said. "Thank you, Chef."

We found our way to the last dealer, a lady called Mrs Kitchener whose husband had run a record shop in Brighton specialising in jazz. Since he'd died she'd taken over and taught herself all about vinyl and the music. Her prices were high but her records were scrupulously graded.

When I told her what I was after, she looked stricken. "I've just sold one, dear. The Johnny Richards. HL-004."

"Who bought it?" I said.

"A girl. Pretty. Long red hair."

There was a refreshment area on the upper level where you could buy cardboard sandwiches and drink crankshaft coffee and look down on the crowd milling around the dealers' stalls like insects below.

We did all three of these things.

I felt the ache of the record we'd missed, like a bruise where someone had punched me in the chest. Ree took it in her stride, though. She was more concerned with being pleased about what we'd found, than upset about what we'd missed.

I understood the superior virtue of this attitude, but I still couldn't stop smarting about the setback.

"How did they know we were coming here? They couldn't have known. We didn't use the bugged phone."

She nibbled at the corner of her stale cheese sandwich and looked at me. "Couldn't they have just found out about it on their own? The record mart, I mean. Is it possible?"

I made a noise that sounded vaguely like a laugh. "It's

only the most widely advertised vinyl event of the year. So it's very possible."

She put her sandwich down. I was glad to see her give up on it. I'd make her a real meal when we got home. "So it was just bad luck, then," she said, and touched my hand. "And good luck too. We did find the other one."

I took the album out of its bag and looked at it. "This is the record that started it all," I said.

"In more ways than one," said Ree. "It sealed all their fates. That's what my grandmother used to say."

"Because of the lawsuit?"

She nodded. "Yeah."

I slid the record out of the inner sleeve and looked at the label for the composer credits. Sure enough there it was. The works of Burns Hobartt, all attributed to… Burns Hobartt. No mention of the Davenport cousins. Nasty pieces of work, Jerry had called them.

Then suddenly I remembered. I held the record up to the light and studied the vinyl. Then I got out my notebook and a pen and wrote in the letters from side one and side two. I showed it to Ree.

EA--EG--YIST--------------BY

A shadow fell over the paper. I looked up and saw Mrs Kitchener there with the photographer in frosted denims. She said, "You wanted to know about that girl? The one who bought the record? Well, Ian here has some pictures of her." She nudged the photographer forward. "Show them, Ian." He kneeled beside our table and showed us the back of his camera.

There was a good-sized screen on it and the images were very sharp. "Here she is," he said, clicking through the pictures of her. There were a lot of them. "This is the girl who bought the record."

The red hair threw me off for a second, but there was no question.

It was Nevada.

23. FEED THE CATS

I zipped my bag, slung it over my shoulder and turned to start for my front door. But it was as if my feet were rooted to the ground. "Have we gone over everything?" I said.

Tinkler sighed. He lifted a finger and said, "Food. Make sure I keep an eye on them when I give them food because Fanny tends to take a few bites and then take a break and wander off to smell the roses. Meanwhile, if she gets the chance, Turk will wolf down her own meal and then eat all of her sister's too. So to stop that happening, I put Fanny's bowl in the fridge until she comes back. Fanny, that is."

He lifted a second finger and said, "Water. Make sure there's always a bowl of water for Turk, but Fanny likes to drink from the tap. So if she jumps up on the sink I run the tap for a while and let her drink. Also, in the bathtub. If she jumps in the empty tub and goes scratchy-scratchy-scratch that means I run the bath tap for a minute and she drinks from that, because human beings are her slaves and vassals since she's a cat and she's in charge." He frowned at me. "Have I got that right?"

"More or less," I said. "I told you all that already?"

"Oh yes. So *bon voyage!*" He started pushing me towards the door. "Have you got your tickets and passport? Remember you have to check in an hour earlier for international flights."

"Before I go, just a quick word about the hi-fi."

He stopped and sighed a deep sigh. "I know how to handle a hi-fi. I'm not going to scratch your records or damage your stylus or drop an anvil on your valves. Though, come to think of it, that might be fun with the 300Bs."

"Okay, okay. But see that you also resist the impulse to swap components around and start experimenting with my system…"

"Who, me?"

"And if you do, if you must, just make sure you don't blow the Quads by overdriving them with a pair of Krells or something."

"I wouldn't do that. I understand about the Quads," he said.

As I was on my way out the door, he added, rather alarmingly, "Anyway, haven't they got that protection device fitted?"

Clean Head was waiting outside in her cab and she drove me to Heathrow where I met Ree in the departure lounge. "How's old Tinkler? He all set to house-sit?"

"I briefed him in detail, and I left him some notes."

"Saying what?"

"Saying, 'Don't smoke the catnip by mistake'."

I'd suggested buying us both seats in first class but Ree wouldn't hear of it. So I ended up sitting back in coach with her. She took the aisle seat, I had the window. I tried not to think of Nevada. I had the strange conviction that if I did, the girl sleeping beside me would know it. So I stared out at the clouds and reviewed our strategy.

At LAX we separated into our respective passport streams. I was bleary-eyed with lack of sleep and, I imagined, looking like an international terrorist. But evidently not too much, because after I'd submitted my thumbprints, fingerprints, and retina scan for scrutiny, I sped through immigration and customs and found myself outside a few minutes later, blinking in the warm exhaust fumes, in record time. Ree was at my side. We collected her car from the long-term parking.

"It's a 1968 Plymouth Barracuda. Arguably the fastest production car ever made in America."

"I won't argue with you."

"It's got the 426 Hemi V8."

I looked out the window at our reflection rippling by in the copper-coloured glass of a fashionable storefront as we drove past. The muscular lines of the dark grey car made it look like a powerful crouching beast. "Is it the car from *Bullitt*?"

She snorted with amusement. "That was a Mustang."

"Just trying to take an interest," I said.

"I guess it *does* look a little like a Mustang. But they're completely different in the long-hood short-deck dimensions." It was hot in the car, and smelled of leather and Ree's perfume, and I could feel myself drifting off in the unreal sunshine.

"Am I boring you?" she said.

"There must be a diplomatic answer to that," I said.

She laughed. "You got your hi-fi, I got my car." Then the lights changed and we pulled away at speed.

* * *

Our first stop was at the Westfield Century City mall. We went to a tiny store tucked into a corner between a shoe boutique and a self-defence emporium full of legal weaponry, with a poster boasting THIS WEEK'S SPECIAL: KROWD-KLEAR 6OZ TEAR GAS GRENADES TWO FOR $20! The only staff in our shop was a skinny teenage girl with braces on her teeth wearing a baggy black t-shirt that read BYTE ME. I told her we wanted to buy a bug buster and she said they had a whole range.

When I asked for the Stone Circle 10 by name, she gave me a disconcerting look of adoration.

Ree grinned at me as the girl went to the back of the store in search of stock. "You made a conquest there." I could feel my earlobes grow hot.

The girl came back with the model I wanted. "You can just rent it, if you like," she said.

"No, I'll buy it." Ree looked at me. I shrugged. "I'll take it back to England with me. Then I can sweep my place."

"If they'll let you take it onto the plane."

I paid for the bug buster, which cost about a quarter of what Mr Maori Tattoo had charged for an identical device, and we left.

We went back to Ree's small house on Acacia Avenue in Mariposa and swept it, looking for any kind of covert transmitter. Nothing. Then we went outside and swept her car. Again, nothing.

Her next-door neighbour came over and joined us, a portly black woman in a yellow tank top and shorts. She said, "Hey, Ree. Some guy was looking for you."

"Who was it?"

"Some white guy in a suit."

I said, "Was he heavily built? Muscular? Like an athlete?"

She shrugged. "I don't know. He was a white guy. In a suit."

Ree put a hand on my shoulder. "This is Chef. He's staying with me."

"Hey, Chef."

"A little geek girl fell in love with him at the mall today."

She looked at me. "Congratulations."

Ree and I went back inside and made coffee. Her house was cool and comfortable and full of pale wood. I could hear wind chimes in the back yard. We reviewed the situation. We had swept her house, her car, and both our phones—I had a new, hopefully un-bugged one, with many no doubt wonderful functions that I didn't know how to use yet—and come up with nothing.

"I kind of wish we had found something," I said. I stared at the bug buster.

"Because then at least we'd know it was working."

"Exactly."

We got back in the car and went out for some Mexican food, which was a revelation. Then we headed on to our next destination. Air flowed through the window, whipping at my hair. I squinted into the brightness of the afternoon. *I have to get some sunglasses*, I thought.

I said, "Who is this guy again?"

"Dr Tinmouth."

"That can't possibly be his real name."

But apparently it was. Jeremiah Tinmouth, professor of music, blogger, jazz historian, broadcaster and late-night DJ. "But he lost that gig a while ago," said Ree. I suspected his outlandish name explained why he'd had less than a meteoric career in the media.

"I made an appointment to see him before I went to England. He's got a houseful of books and tapes and DVDs. It's like a research centre for the history of jazz."

"Will he help us find the Hathor LPs?"

"Maybe. But what I'm really hoping is that he'll know something about my grandmother and help us figure out what the hell this is all about. He sounded really interested when I contacted him."

We drove past Griffith Park and along Glendale into Atwater Village. At Cerritos Park we turned off. An industrial area gave way to a shopping strip. We turned again, onto what became a leafy residential street called Princeton. Ree braked sharply.

"Oh no."

To our right, beyond a screen of trees was the scorched shell of what had once been a small pink stucco house. It was now charred and black.

It had been burned virtually to the ground.

We parked and walked across the road. We could smell the stink of the fire as soon as we got out of the car. We stood and Ree stared at the ruin. I didn't say anything. I didn't know what to say. She turned to a woman who was standing in the garden of the house next door, pruning a rose bush with a pair of secateurs.

"Excuse me," said Ree. The woman looked up at us. She was wearing a straw hat and headphones. She took the headphones off. She had a pale, wary face.

"Hello."

"When did this happen?"

"Two nights ago. It was awful."

"Was anybody inside?"

"Yes, the doctor. It was awful."

"Did he make it out?"

"No." I thought she was going to tell us it was awful again, but she just shook her head. "Poor Dr Tinmouth. The fire department said we were lucky the flames didn't jump across to our roof. I have to go inside now."

"Okay. Thanks." Ree looked at the burned-out house, then at me. "Well, shit," she said.

Neither of us said anything as we drove along the freeway, coming off onto South Arroyo Boulevard. We were running parallel to another park. I hadn't realised Los Angeles was so green.

The trees thinned out and we found ourselves on Chestnut Avenue. It was an incongruously English-sounding name. The residential area gave way to a business district. We turned onto a side street and parked beside some dusty palm trees.

We got out and I followed Ree across the road to a small square white building with a wide tarmac parking lot. I recognised the address. It was the one we'd used for all our web purchases before we left England.

We walked around the back of the building to a large open garage housed in a military-looking concrete building which might have been a small fortress. Men in blue overalls were working on vehicles. Mostly cars, but also a few motorbikes. A neon sign on the front of the fortress said BERTO'S. Ree led me inside, amid the noise and heat, saying "hi" to the guys working on the cars as we passed. A man came out of the shadows at the back of the garage.

"I thought I heard that hemi," he said and grinned at Ree. This was an idle boast because in the garage we could hardly hear each other speak, let alone the distinctive signature of an engine across the road.

Ree introduced the man as Berto. He was so corpulent that he couldn't fit into his blue overalls. Consequently, they were unzipped with the top half hanging, arms tied around his waist where the rolls of fabric supplemented the rolls of fat. But his bone-crushing handshake suggested that there was muscle lurking somewhere under all that adipose tissue.

He led us through a small doorway to the back of the building, where the noise thankfully diminished and it was cooler. To our right there was a short hallway with doors opening onto offices. To our left was a large storage area protected by vertical steel bars with a chunky central door. He unlocked the door, using a key hanging around his neck, and led us in. The door was very big and very sturdy and the bars looked impressively solid.

The room inside was stacked with gleaming, expensive-looking auto parts, the cost of which no doubt more than justified all the security measures.

Berto led us to an old-fashioned green strongbox at the back of the room. "You're welcome to keep your stuff in here as long as you want," he said. He spun the dial in cryptic patterns and opened the strongbox. Ree gave him the LPs we had collected so far and he put them inside. "Do you want to put the new one in, too?"

"The new one?"

"Just came in the mail today." He nodded at an LP-sized cardboard box sitting on top of an oil drum. I went over and examined it. Sure enough, it was one of our Internet purchases.

"That was quick," I said. I opened it, or tried to.

"Here, dude," said Berto. He took a clasp knife out of the pocket of his overalls and handed it to me. Even with the knife it wasn't easy getting into the box and once I did I found another package, sealed in a ridiculous swathe of sticky transparent tape.

"Like a fucking mummy," opined Berto. He was right, too.

I sighed and set to work. I'd seen this before. For some reason, some people had a great belief in the protective qualities of sticky tape. The more, the better seemed to be their philosophy. I carefully cut it away. "Okay," I said. "It looks like there is a record in here after all."

"Finally," said Ree. She held out her hand for the knife, and I gave it to her. "You mind if I keep this, Berto?" she said. He shrugged and she folded the knife and put it in her bag as I freed the record from the last of the packaging. It was HL-008, by the great guitarist Howard Roberts. I showed Ree the dead wax and we filled in our chart.

$$EA--EG--YIST--FA---------BY$$

It was dark and the cool of evening had come on by the time we got back to Ree's house on Acacia Avenue. As we stepped out of the car we saw there was a man waiting on her porch.

A white guy in a suit.

He stepped forward and said, "Miss Esterbridge?"

Ree hesitated and moved imperceptibly closer to me. Night was coming on fast and it was hard to see the man's face. "Yes," she said.

"My name is Gordon Hallett. I did some legal work for Dr Tinmouth."

I felt Ree relax beside me. "We just heard," she said. "About the fire. We just heard today."

The man nodded. "It was a terrible tragedy." I had the sense that he felt it was late and he wanted to get out of here, but he was being polite.

Ree said, "So what can I…"

The man quickly reached in his pocket as though he had been waiting for this cue. "If anything happened to Dr Tinmouth I was instructed to make sure that you got this." He took out a small padded mailing bag and handed it to her.

"What is it?" said Ree.

"I have no idea." He turned to the street. "Now if you don't mind I've got a family function to get to."

"Of course. Thank you."

We watched him as he left. As soon as he was out of sight she handed me the mailing bag. It fitted snugly into the palm of my hand and weighed nothing. Ree was looking in her bag for something. She took out Berto's clasp knife.

She gave it to me and I slit the package open and shook it. Out came a small piece of paper with an address written on it.

And a key.

24. TWELVE BOXES

The storage unit was in a district called Alhambra. It was in a dusty industrial park just off Mission Road. We used the key we'd been given and opened the creaking door and took one look inside. Then Ree made a phone call to Berto. He sent a van from the garage and we transferred everything from the storage unit, which proved to be enough boxes to crowd the van.

Ree did her share of carrying as we loaded up the boxes and took them back to the garage, where we unloaded them all again and transferred them to the high-security storage area, where Berto kept his auto parts. Berto looked at us sceptically as we schlepped back and forth, and said, "You really think someone's going to be interested in stealing a bunch of books and papers? Okay. I got plenty of room. I don't mind. Put them in the cage."

Berto was right. The boxes were full of books and papers but also photographs, letters and journals—mostly jazz magazines, including copies of *The JazzLetter* by Gene Lees which I earmarked for special attention later, purely from a point of view of personal pleasure. But no records, sadly. I went through the boxes and took out a selection of books. I had no idea what I was doing, but I had to start somewhere. Berto watched in puzzlement until Ree explained.

"Chef here's going to be taking the material out, going through it and bringing it back. Maybe like one book at a time, one magazine at a time."

"So now I'm a public library."

"Listen," said Ree, "If you mind…"

"No, no, it's fine. You can keep your shit here. I'll make sure nobody steals it. I've got plenty of room."

Each time he said this it came out with less conviction. I looked at the boxes. It was clearly an impossible task, but I said, "Just until I get it into my head."

"Then you got to watch somebody doesn't come along and cut off your head," said Berto. "And then steal that."

Everybody laughed.

Except me.

"Okay," said Tinkler. "So tell me more about this Mexican food. Can you bring some back with you?"

"Are you sure you don't want me to bring grapes?"

"No, just Mexican food and Rolling Stones albums. Anyway, you were saying that you think this jazz scholar knew something important."

"Dr Tinmouth. Yes."

"He sounds like somebody from *The Wizard of Oz*."

"I know."

"Anyway, you think because of what the doctor knew, whatever it was, someone bumped him off. Burned his house down with him inside."

"Yes, I'm afraid it looks like that."

"And they made sure they did it before he could talk to Ree."

"Exactly."

"But he left you a clue."

"No. He left us twelve fucking boxes of clues."

"How many? Twelve?"

"Yes. That's the problem." I stared across Ree's living room. A wide selection of books and magazines from those boxes was strewn on the bare wooden floor. There were also piles of newspaper clippings and photographs and what I'd learned to call "tear sheets"—pages that had been torn from magazines. While working on this lot it seemed strange not to have a cat around to get in the way. If I'd been at home Fanny would have been sitting on any open book within about thirty seconds.

"But he arranged for you, or at least Ree, to get the key. So he wanted her to have this stuff. There must have been something he wanted her to know."

I said, "It was a classic academic's solution. Leave us all the necessary research materials so we could work it out for ourselves."

"Or not."

"Or not, as it certainly feels at the moment."

"So it's just a completely random mess of documents."

"Documents about jazz, yes. Random except for three things, which might be significant."

"Actually, come to think of it," said Tinkler, "*do* bring me some grapes. Californian grapes. Organic would be nice. What three things?"

"Well, all of the material deals with 1955 or earlier."

"Ah," said Tinkler. "The year that Hathor Records came and went."

"And the year that Easy Geary died."

"Okay, nothing later than 1955. What else?"

"Well, at first it looked like it was just an undifferentiated mass of books and magazines and so on, but I found markers in the articles."

"Okay, that helps. What sort of markers?"

"Sometimes a section of text has been highlighted. Sometimes there's a sticky note or a piece of paper stuck in, to indicate what page we should start reading on. Like a bookmark."

"Well, great."

"Not so great. I've been ploughing through it and unfortunately this marked text seems to refer to just about everyone who ever played a jazz instrument, including a few who never got any further than just thinking about it."

"Bummer."

"But on closer inspection, most of the material seems to relate to either Burns Hobartt or Easy Geary."

"Him again."

"Yes. And the photographs are almost exclusively of those two, plus Rita Mae Pollini of course."

"Ree's grandmother."

"Right. Which you would have expected, since Dr Tinmouth was going to be talking to Ree. So I'm not sure how significant that is. Some of the documents are about her, but again they may just be some nice souvenirs he wanted to show Ree."

"You said three things."

"Say again?"

"What was the third thing that wasn't random?"

"Oh, yes." I looked at the papers again, stirring gently in a breeze from the back window. "Like I said, they're all documents about jazz, naturally enough, except for one item."

"The suspense is killing me."

"A Los Angeles medical directory for the years 1948 to 1950."

"Good luck with that."

Ree came back with food and we ate in the kitchen. Just as we were washing the dishes we got a call from Berto to tell us another package had arrived. We drove over to the garage and found it waiting for us in the cage. It was one of the LPs we'd ordered while we were still in England. This one was from Times Square Records in New York. It was Hathor HL-010, *Rita Mae Pollini Sings Professor Jellaway*.

It was the one the late Jimmy Genower had wanted to sell us. I did my best not to think too much about Jimmy, sitting dead in his garden. I studied the cover. The photograph on it depicted a woman of almost unreal beauty. And I could see an echo of Ree in the bones of her grandmother's face.

But we didn't even look at the cover until after we'd taken the record out, studied the dead wax, and filled in our chart.

EA--EG--YIST--FA--ER------BY

As we walked back through the garage Berto called us over and said, "You remember you said to watch out for a red-haired girl? Good-looking?"

"Nobody said good-looking," said Ree.

"Right, well, anyhow there was this girl came in today.

333

Had some story about bringing her car in for a service."

"What kind of car?" said Ree.

"Carrera 911. Said she was having problems with the oil seals."

I showed him the picture I'd got from Ian the photographer at the record mart in Wembley. He nodded. "Yeah, that's her."

"So Nevada is in Los Angeles?" said Tinkler when I phoned him. "You understand I don't mean in a geographical sense. That would be a map maker's nightmare."

"Apparently. Apparently she is."

"She just can't stay away from you."

"Yes, that must be the reason," I said.

"So, how's the mystery of the Tinmouth archives progressing?"

"It isn't. How's the search for Christian porn?" Tinkler was staying in Maggie's flat and was convinced, despite his sister's religious nature, that she had a stash of pornography somewhere. And he wouldn't rest until he found it.

"Equally a washout. You know, I'm beginning to think my sister doesn't have a dark side. She's just not interesting enough."

"I need your keen analytical mind," I said. I looked at the stacks of books, magazines, tear sheets and photos. Different from the landscape of data I'd been looking at last time I'd phoned him, but equally enigmatic.

"Oh-oh."

"Here's the situation. Virtually all the material points at two men, Burns Hobartt and Easy Geary."

"You said that last time."

"Well, trust me, since then I've become obsessed with the pair of them." Across the room a square of morning sunlight fell on the faces of Geary and Hobartt. I had printed out a large black and white photograph of each of them and put it up on the wall.

Burns Hobartt's face was elegant, haunted, marked with the almost tribal scars, bequeathed him by a dancehall fire, which had earned him his cruel nickname. Easy Geary's was smooth, serene and nearly Asian. Buddha-like.

"So almost all the marked material concerns the two of them," said Tinkler.

I picked up a paperback of Gunther Schuller's *Early Jazz*. "Plus a smattering of background reference on the early history of jazz."

"Well, that right there doesn't make sense," said Tinkler. "That's what my keen analytical mind tells me. Because neither Geary nor Hobartt belong to that period. They came much later."

I said, "Well, Burns Hobartt was performing with territory bands in the late twenties and early thirties. But he only began to make his mark around 1935, after he'd recovered from the injuries he sustained in a fire. And Easy Geary was playing in US Army bands in remote postings like the Philippines in the thirties and forties. He returned to the States after World War Two and only rose to prominence around 1949."

"So basically neither of them has anything to do with early jazz."

"No, you're right. They don't."

"Okay, so that's an anomaly right there. And then you've got the other one."

"The other what? The other anomaly?"

"That's right. The medical dictionary."

I stared at the thing. "It's not a medical dictionary. It's a medical *directory*." It was a massive hardcover book with an orange jacket. "And it's big enough to stun a proverbial ox."

"But its very presence is significant. There must be some vital information in there."

I sighed. "That's what I've been telling myself. At least some of the time. Other times I wonder if he didn't just pack it in the box by mistake."

"Dr Tinmouth?"

"Yes, he seems to have thrown this stuff together in a hell of a hurry. Like he just pulled out the relevant literature, marked everything the best he could, then tossed it all into the boxes and put it in storage. And you know what the worst thing is? When I go through the books sometimes there's a loose piece of paper lying around—to commemorate the fact that a bookmark has come accidentally and permanently adrift and that we'll never read what piece of text it was supposed to bring to our attention."

"Total bummer," said Tinkler.

"All the more so when it turns out that the medical directory is one of those books that's lost its marker."

"I guess you'll just have to look at every page, then."

I stared at the huge orange tome. "I don't seem to have adequately conveyed the scope of the problem. This book is thousands of pages of small text. It's the size of several telephone directories. It seems to list information on every registered professional physician who worked in the continental United States, plus Alaska and Hawaii, in the years 1948 to 1950."

"And there's quite a few of them?"

"It would take days just to flip through it," I said.

"Have fun."

A few minutes after I finished speaking to Tinkler I came upon a classic example of the adrift bookmark I'd been talking about. Between two books was pressed a narrow scrap of paper. It could have come from either of them, or from somewhere else entirely.

I put it aside with a pang of despair.

It was only a couple of days later that I turned it over and I realised it was a compliment slip from a firm. The name and address of the firm was printed at the top of the slip. Beneath these, in sprawling, vivid handwriting it read:

Jerry, by all means tell the girl to get in touch with me. It would be good to meet her. Does she have a decent rack? I certainly hope so. Her grandmother definitely did. All the best.

I couldn't decipher the scrawled signature but I didn't need to. The name was printed clearly above. Ron Longmire.

When Ree got in from her gig that night I said, "Have you ever heard of Ron Longmire?"

"No. Who's he?"

"A record engineer. Along with Rudy Van Gelder and Roy DuNann he was one of the geniuses who created the sound of jazz as we know it." I looked at her. "Most importantly from our point of view, he worked with your grandmother at Hathor Records."

"And he's still alive?"

I held up the slip of paper. "More than that, I think we've got an introduction to go and have a chat with him." I handed it to her. "This letter, or note, is from him. I thought about not showing it to you."

"Why not?"

She took it, read it, and laughed.

We phoned Ron Longmire and made an appointment to see him the following day.

His house in Woodland Hills was a Frank Lloyd Wright-inspired stack of redwood and glass boxes arranged on a slope of the hill with a breathtaking view of the dirty brown haze hovering over the San Fernando Valley. As we pulled up outside, Ree was singing quietly to herself. The tune was familiar to me and after a moment I was able to identify it.

"Grandma's Hands", by Bill Withers.

Except Ree was singing, "Grandma's Rack". I didn't hear any other words, but I didn't necessarily feel this boded well. She switched off the engine and we got out. Ree broke off singing when she saw the car parked outside the house.

"Holy shit," she said.

It was a streamlined silver 1960s creation, its powerful curves built low to the ground. Ree went over and touched its gleaming surface. "A Shelby Cobra," she said. "The 427. From 1966."

"Careful with the paintwork."

We turned to see a suntanned, hawk-faced man with

silver hair cropped short in a military style. He was dressed in a safari shirt and khaki shorts. He was of medium height but barrel-chested, and his bustling vigour made him seem bigger than he really was.

He trotted down the steps and shook hands with us. "Ron Longmire. Call me Ron. I guess the first thing you'll want to see is my recording studio. Everybody does."

The studio was located in the basement of the house, or rather the lowest of the stacked boxes. We descended to it down a stone staircase in the side of the hill and entered through a small door at one end. It was warm and calm inside, and very quiet. The most surprising thing about it was that it wasn't a single big open room. Instead, only half of the studio was open space, while the rest consisted of sudden cubbyholes and corners and arbitrary spaces that reminded me of a hedge maze.

"Each of these areas has its own acoustic properties," said Ron. "If we wanted to reduce the sound level for a given instrument we'd simply choose the right place to put it."

"Why not just lower the level on the mixing desk in the control room?" said Ree.

"Purity of sound," I said.

Ron grinned. "Plus we didn't have a mixing desk in those days."

On the floor was a vast Persian carpet with an elaborate abstract pattern. Ree was staring at it. "I love this carpet," she said. Ron shot her a searching glance.

"Do you?"

"Yeah, it's just my thing."

"Well, isn't that interesting? It was just your grandma's thing, too." He looked at her and smiled. "In fact she chose it."

"You're kidding."

"No. She had it put in without me knowing about it. A surprise gift. To celebrate the end of recording on *Easy Come, Easy Go*. We all knew it would be the last Hathor album and we felt it was kind of a special occasion. So she got this for me."

He stared down fondly at the carpet. "She even got rid of the old one for me. An orange monstrosity of a carpet, all stained with beer and cigarette burns and puke." He smiled at us. "Speaking of beer…"

We tramped back up the stairs to the living room of the house where a highly polished baby grand piano crouched gleaming. We walked past it into the kitchen, where we sat at the breakfast counter, blinking in the sunlight as Ron poured us Mexican beer from chilled brown bottles.

There were pictures everywhere of Ron with a sprightly platinum-haired woman. "Is that your wife?" said Ree.

Ron nodded solemnly. "That's Ladybird," he said. "She's gone."

"Oh, I'm sorry."

He grinned, his face crinkling. "Don't be too sorry. She's only gone to the store. She'll be back in about half an hour." He set the beers in front of us and sat down on the other side of the counter with his own. "Okay," he said, leaning forward on his suntanned elbows. "What can I do for you?"

I said, "It seems that Dr Tinmouth thought it would be a good idea if we met. Or at least, if you and Ree met."

"Poor old Jerry."

"You don't have any idea why he wanted you two to meet?"

Ron shook his head. "None."

I glanced at Ree. "Well, there are a couple of questions I want to ask you."

"Fire away," said Ron.

"First of all, do you have original copies of any of the Hathor albums?"

"No."

"None of them?"

"No, sorry. I got rid of all of that stuff years ago."

I felt a stab of loss. "Got rid of?"

"Yeah, I sold them." He took a sip of beer. "To collectors here and in Europe and Japan. For what seemed a lot of money at the time but was about a tenth of what I could get for them now." He shrugged.

"How could you just get rid of them?" I said.

For the first time his good-natured grin faded and I saw how fierce that hawk face could look. "Listen, kid, they were my records and I could do what I liked with them."

"But they were beautiful. They were your masterpieces."

He shifted uncomfortably. "I made those recordings over fifty years ago. That was another lifetime. And anyway, I copied all of them onto DAT."

Ree chuckled and said, "That won't cut any ice with the Chef. He's strictly an analogue man. A vinyl guy."

Ron made a non-committal sound and sipped his beer. I cleared my throat. I felt a little awkward, but I pressed ahead. I said, "The other thing is the gunshot."

He stared at me. "The what? The gunshot? What gunshot?"

"On one of the Hathor sessions. There's a noise in the background. I'm sure it's a gunshot."

Ron laughed a dry rasping laugh and took another hearty sip of his beer. He set the glass down and looked at me. "Listen, kid, I think I'd remember if somebody fired a gun on one of my recording dates."

"But it wasn't your date. It was *Easy Come, Easy Go*. That was engineered by Danny DePriest, wasn't it?"

His face clouded over. "Danny DePriest? That kid was a genius. I let him do that record on his own. It was going to be the last album from the label and I wanted him to get the full credit for it. To launch his career. Which I guess it did." He shook his head. "He was a hell of an engineer."

"What happened to him?" said Ree.

He looked at her bleakly. "Somebody killed him, in Seattle in 1967."

"Killed him?"

"Slipped him a Mickey Finn. He was in a bar and somebody spiked his drink with some narcotic and killed him." He shrugged. "Hell, I don't know. I can't prove it was murder. Maybe he put the dope in his own drink. Maybe it was a drug thing. I just don't know. All I know is that kid had a hell of a talent, as an engineer, as a producer, as an arranger. What a waste." He shook his head.

"But you've got the master tapes for that session," I said. "The ones Danny did for you."

He looked at me like a man coming out of a reverie. Coming back from Seattle, in 1967. "Of course."

"Would it be possible to listen to them?"

"I don't see why not." He grinned at me. "And check for a gunshot?"

"That's right."

"Sure, kid. We'll put paid to this little fantasy of yours." He rose from his chair. "Which track?"

"The last track, side two. Ree's grandmother sings on it. 'Running from a Spell'."

He sat back down again, suddenly looking tired. "Sorry, kid. Forget it."

I had been half expecting this, but the disappointment was still woundingly sharp. I said, "Why?"

"Because the master tape for that track doesn't exist anymore."

"I'd heard that. But I was sure you must have a copy somewhere."

He shook his head. "Not me, not anybody." Ree was staring at us. She was smiling a quizzical half-smile.

"What happened to it?" I said.

"Nobody knows." He abruptly picked up his beer and drained it, then set the glass aside with an air of finality. "Well, you can forget about your mystery gunshot. I've got the DAT from the vinyl but that will be third generation. And anything less than first generation and we're pissing into the wind."

"Are you sure?" said Ree.

Longmire and I both nodded the same decisive nod. We looked at each other. He turned to Ree and said, "There's no way we can draw any real conclusion without the master tape." He picked up his empty glass and got up and put it in the sink, shaking his head. "And I have no idea where the hell it is."

"I've got it," said Ree.

25. A LITTLE DEAD

We both looked at her.

"You've got it?" I said.

"I knew it." Ron smacked his fist into the palm of his hand triumphantly. "I knew it had to be somewhere." He'd certainly changed his tune.

I looked at Ree. "We're talking about the original 1955 master tape? From the session itself?" She nodded.

"My grandmother kept it. And luckily she didn't keep it in the attic."

Ron glanced up quizzically and we explained the great honey calamity. He nodded smugly and said, "You fuck with Mother Nature at your considerable peril. But our problem isn't going to be that the tape's too sticky. It's going to be that it's not sticky enough. Where is it?"

"At my house," said Ree. She looked at me. "We could go get it now."

"Yes," I said. I stood up. My heart was beating hard in my chest. Ree stood up too.

"We'll go now and get it and we'll bring it right back and you can play it for us."

Ron shook his head. "I'm afraid it's not going to be that simple."

"What do you mean?"

He shrugged and said, "What do you expect? We're talking about a tape that's over half a century old. We can't just *play* it."

"Why not?"

He sighed. "A tape is made up of three things. There's the iron oxide particles, which record the sound, right? And then there's the carrier, which is made of a kind of plastic. In those days it was mostly acetate, which was a bitch because it gets brittle and stretches. But we used an early polyester compound." He glared at us to see if we understood.

"And what's the third thing?" said Ree.

I said, "The glue that holds them together."

Ron grinned and nodded. "That's right, kid, and it's the glue that's our problem." He nodded at Ree. "By now the stuff on your grandma's tape will have let go."

I said, "That's what you meant about it not being sticky enough."

He grinned toothily. "Correct. If we tried to play it now, the iron oxide particles would just come off it, they'd shed in a miniature grey blizzard, and you'd have a blank strip of polyester and a pile of iron oxide." He chuckled. "And then the only thing you could do is get some glue and a microscope and try to put all the oxide molecules back in the right place. And to do that you'd have to be god's smarter older brother."

He smiled into our silence.

"So we can't play my grandmother's tape," said Ree.

"Oh hell," said Ron cheerfully, "of course we can! But first we have to reactivate the glue on it."

"We can do that?"

"Oh yeah, sure." He beamed at us. "You just take the tape and bake it."

"*Bake* it?"

He nodded. "Yeah."

Ree and I stared at him with identical aghast expressions. I said, "You just take the tape and stick it in an oven?"

Somehow he managed to laugh heartily while simultaneously sneering. "Hell no, kid, of course we don't just stick it in an oven. Do you really think we'd do that? We've got a *special device*."

We drove to Ree's house, getting there with miraculous speed and fetching the tape from the top shelf of the cupboard where it had sat, undisturbed in a shoebox, for years. I couldn't believe it was still there, that nothing had gone wrong. I was a little shellshocked with relief, looking at it. Then we set off back and sat in traffic for two hours, with me holding the box gingerly in my lap.

I expected absolutely anything, including an attack by ninjas from a flying saucer.

But nothing happened. Except the traffic crawled.

When we finally got to the Longmire house Ron was standing on the drive, putting an industrial vacuum cleaner back into the garage. He paused when he saw us. He was now dressed in white tennis shorts, a lime green polo shirt and navy blue blazer. He looked the picture of health, like a man luxuriating after a workout.

"Welcome back!" he said.

"You look like you've been busy."

"What you said got me thinking. If somebody fired a gun in my studio then there'd be a bullet hole somewhere. So I went down there with a strong light source and inspected every inch of the place. Every wall. The entire ceiling." He nodded at the vacuum cleaner. "Even the floor. I rolled up the carpet—had to vacuum the whole place first and wear a mask. You don't want to breathe in any dust at my age. At any age, really. Anyhow, it was quite a project. Pretty good exercise, though. Where was I? Oh—I even rolled up the carpet and examined the floor. You know what I found?" He looked at us expectantly.

"A bullet hole?" I said, without much hope.

"Nothing?" said Ree.

"Nothing!" Ron snapped his fingers. "That's right. No bullet hole nowhere." He looked at me. "You almost had me going, kid. I was actually thinking somebody might have fired a gun during one of my sessions."

I said, "I still think somebody did."

"Okay, kid, so what happened to the bullet?"

"It left the studio inside somebody."

He looked at me. "Inside some… body?"

I nodded at the vacuum cleaner. "When did you say you got the new carpet? Right after that session?"

"That's right."

I glanced at Ree. "I think that's how they got rid of the evidence."

"Evidence?" said Ron.

"Yes."

"And who would *they* be?"

"Rita Mae and Easy Geary and whoever else was on that session."

Ron's eyes became distant for a moment as he considered something. "Including Danny DePriest." His gaze sharpened again and he gave me a hard predatory stare. "So what are you saying? That they got rid of my old orange monstrosity of a carpet because it was covered with blood?"

"That plus it had a body rolled up in it."

"A what?" he said. He stared at me for a moment, and then he pounded his thigh and started to laugh. "A body rolled up in a carpet? Is that what you think?" He punched me on the arm good-naturedly. He had a considerable punch for a man of his age. I resisted the urge to rub the sore spot. "I'll say this for you, kid, you've got a vivid imagination. So vivid you had me going for a while. But anyhow, one good thing came of it." He beckoned to Ree, looking hungrily at the box she was carrying.

"Come on into the kitchen. We've got us a tape to bake."

He led us through the big living room with its baby grand. Nodding at the piano he said, "Who needs recordings? These days if I want some music, I just get Ladybird to play me something."

In the kitchen there was a domestic appliance standing on the counter. It was a shiny, squat white cylinder. At first glance I thought it was some kind of salad spinner, but it had a power cable running to it. Ron looked at it proudly, then looked at us.

I went over and examined the apparatus. I said, "The Smoky Snack Chef 500?"

He nodded happily. "Yeah."

"This is the 'special device'?"

"Yes."

"It's a Crockpot!"

"No, it's a professional food dehydrator. Great for my

348

beef jerky and it also makes some mean sun-dried tomatoes for Ladybird. Although they're not actually *sun* dried."

Ree and I looked at each other, then at the thing, then at him. "You're actually proposing we put the tape in there?"

He opened the box and examined the reel. "Yeah, for about ninety minutes at one hundred and thirty Fahrenheit."

"You're serious. You're going to bake it in the Smoky Snack Chef?"

He grinned at us. "You wouldn't want to try it with acetate, true. But, like I told you, this is a polyester carrier."

I looked at Ree. "Do you want to let him do this?"

She shrugged uncertainly. "I guess."

Ron patted the Snack Chef. "I've used this baby plenty of times. It works great for restoring tapes. And it so happens it's also great for making food! Just don't do them at the same time."

While the tape baked we sat in the living room and listened to Ladybird play the piano. She was a small, spry chubby woman with striking platinum hair. "Don't mind Ron," she told us. "His bark is worse than his bite." She proved to be a good musician, thankfully.

After a while Ree began to sing along with her and the two of them performed so well together that, at several points, I almost forgot to worry about the priceless audiotape being slowly cooked next door in a branded kitchen appliance.

And after it was baked it had to cool, of course.

Then finally we got to play it.

Ron had a listening system consisting of a classic Revox tape deck, vintage solid-state Quad amps and some superb

BBC LS3/5a speakers. I would have gone for the valve Quads myself, but the system was compact, high quality and no-nonsense. Perhaps a little like its owner.

The loudspeakers were small but reproduced vocals beautifully and Rita Mae Pollini's voice made the hairs stir on the back of my neck. Ree stared intently into the soundstage, as though trying to see back into 1955. Then it came.

The gunshot.

I looked at Ron. He frowned at me and rewound the tape. He played the passage again. Then again. Every time it sounded like a gunshot.

"So what do you think, Ron?"

He shook his head. "I don't know," he said. "Maybe." He gnawed at a knuckle, considering, then looked at me. "Only one way to find out." He went out and came back with a laptop. He attached it to an analogue-to-digital cable that ran directly into the Revox. Then he put on a pair of wire-framed spectacles and peered intently at the laptop's screen as he launched some sound analysis software.

We played the tape again and he studied the computer screen, colours flashing on the lenses of his spectacles. Finally he sighed and shut the computer down. He took off his glasses, rubbed the bridge of his nose and looked at us.

"Sorry," he said.

"What do you mean, sorry?"

"Kid, the waveform is all wrong. It's not a gunshot. It can't be."

"It sure as hell sounds like one," I said.

He shook his head, a trifle mournfully, and patted the laptop. "Not to the analyser it doesn't, and the analyser never lies. Whatever it was, it wasn't a gunshot."

* * *

I woke up from a deep sleep to find Ree sitting bolt upright in bed beside me, listening intently. The room was dark and all I could hear was her breathing. Then she murmured softly, "What the hell?"

Thinking she'd been woken by a nightmare, I wrapped my arms around her. I put my face between her warm, fragrant breasts, ear pressed to her smooth skin, listening to her heart. She said, "I heard a car. I heard an engine."

"This is Los Angeles."

"Not just any car. Not just any engine." She hopped off the bed and went to the window. Lifting the curtain, she peered out. "I thought so." I went and stood beside her.

Out in the street, parked in the cone of light under a lamppost, was Ron's gleaming silver Cobra. Ladybird was sitting in the passenger seat, looking immaculate in a headscarf and big movie star sunglasses—despite it being the middle of the night. The driver's seat was empty and there was no sign of Ron, until we saw an angular shadow move under the porch light and the doorbell rang.

I pulled on a t-shirt and boxer shorts and padded out to answer it.

Ron was standing there in a black leather jacket, which made his stout chest look even broader. He was wearing an elaborate pair of eyeglasses that looked like racing goggles. Behind them, his eyes were bright and wide awake. "Look, kid," he said, "I'm sorry as hell about this. I know it's the middle of the night."

"No," I said. "Of course. Come in." We went into the

living room together as Ree came in from the bedroom, knotting a black and red flowered kimono around her. She put on lights and then perched beside me on the couch as Ron sank down into an armchair opposite us. He groaned like a man trying to postpone an unhappy duty.

"Is Ladybird okay?" said Ree. "Wouldn't she like to come in, too?"

"No, she's fine out there. We go out driving in the middle of the night all the time. Neither of us sleeps much these days. We're a pair of night owls. Might as well be high noon out there, as far as we're concerned…" He trailed off, looking at us. "Listen," he said. "I owe you an apology."

"How so?"

He unzipped his jacket about half an inch, as though that was as far as he'd allow himself to relax. "Let me explain. A few years ago these guys in Holland licensed some Hathor tracks to release on CD. They had access to our tapes, all the original elements, but when the CD came out it sounded like crap. No one could figure out why."

I said, "It was a CD, that's why." Ree gave a muffled snort of amusement.

Ron shook his head stubbornly. "No, it should have sounded fine. Those original recordings were great. But these CDs sounded flat, lifeless. It was a mystery." He looked at us, his glasses glinting. "Then I remembered."

"What?" I said.

"Our studio is a wonderful recording environment. But it's a little dead."

"A little dead?" said Ree.

"Acoustically speaking. People are accustomed to hearing music played in a concert hall or a club or a bar.

Compared to those, any recording studio can sound a little dead. Because there's no echo, you see, no reverberation. Now, that's a good thing, as far as it goes. But when we did the Hathor recordings we discovered that they sounded a little dry. A little airless. Think of it this way. The studio made the music sound a bit artificial. And we wanted to put the reality back in. So I got Danny to sweeten the recordings with a little reverb. He added some echo to the mastertape."

He took off his glasses and massaged his face wearily. "That's what I remembered tonight," he said. "And I had to come and tell you right away."

"About putting the reverb on the recordings."

"About *not* putting it on." He stared at me. "I suddenly thought to myself, what if Danny put the reverb on everything on that tape but *not* on the gunshot? He could have done it. The kid was a genius. He could ride the levels, listening with the headphones, and drop out the reverb just for the duration of the gunshot. Do you get it?"

I nodded. "I think so. And if he did that…"

"Then the gunshot wouldn't be identifiable as a gunshot. It wouldn't give the right waveform. It disguised the sound— and it would fool the software. Even though the software wasn't going to be invented for fifty years." He stared off into space. "Danny DePriest was a genius. It's such a pity about that kid." He focused on me again. "What he did could fool the equipment, but it couldn't fool your ears."

Ree kneaded my shoulder. "They can't fool the Chef."

"So, as soon as I thought that," said Ron, "I took the copy I made of your tape, and I dubbed reverb over the section in question, and I ran it through the analyser and I got the waveform." He lifted his hands in a gesture of helplessness.

"And it was a gunshot," he said. He put his glasses on and sighed, leaning forward in the chair.

"Kid, you were right and I was wrong. There I was, laying down the law like I was King Shit and telling you your ears were wrong and it wasn't a gunshot. And I'm sorry as hell about that."

"There's no need," said Ree. "We know now. You've told us."

"Still," said Ron. "I'm sorry. And if there's anything I could do…"

Ree smiled. "You could let me take your car for a drive."

"Okay, well, let me wrap my head around that notion. In the meantime me and Ladybird wanted you to have this. She reminded me that we had it." He unzipped his jacket and took out an LP.

It was the Manny Albam. Hathor HL-011. It was framed like a picture, in glass and black metal. As he spoke, Ron unclipped the back of the frame and took the LP out.

"I thought you'd got rid of all of them?" I said.

"We did. We only kept this one because Ladybird liked the cover." He separated the album from the frame and handed it to me.

"Is it just the cover?" said Ree.

"No," I said, examining it. "It's still got the record in it."

Ron shrugged, grinning at us. "What the hell would be the point of keeping the cover and throwing out the record? Anyway, you can have it."

"Have it?" I said. "You're giving it to us?"

He inclined his head. "It's the least I can do."

"We can pay you for it," said Ree.

"No. Just get a full-colour photocopy of the cover for

us sometime, or a scan or whatever the hell you kids call it, and we'll put that in the frame. That'll be good enough for us." He stood up and re-zipped his jacket. "I better get going before Ladybird gets cold."

His car rumbled away in the night as I checked the dead wax and filled in our chart.

EA--EG--YIST--FA--EROF----BY

26. HOLLYWOD

"Okay, so we know it's a gunshot," said Tinkler. "What does that tell us?"

"Surprisingly little."

"Well, do we know who was playing at the session?"

"The instrumentation is very sparse on that track."

"Talk like a human being."

"It's just a small band. Piano, bass and drums. Plus Rita Mae singing of course."

"So, let me see," murmured Tinkler. "That's four plus whoever was in the control room."

"Which was Danny DePriest, but he was also playing bass on this track."

"So it was Easy Geary on piano. This DePriest guy on bass. Rita Mae on vocals…"

"And the drummer was Moses Gunther. He only died a few weeks ago."

"Is that suspicious? Him suddenly dying, I mean."

"Not too suspicious considering he was over a hundred."

"Wow," said Tinkler.

"Yes. Ree said the old boy and her grandmother used to

see each other occasionally. Not often, but when they did get together they always seemed very chummy."

"Is that what she said, 'chummy'?"

"What she actually said is that they were thick as thieves."

On the other side of the world Tinkler made a thoughtful noise. "Which would make sense if they shared a secret."

"That's exactly what I think."

"So anyway that's four all told. People at the session."

"Yes and unfortunately they're all dead."

"Which is really spooky," said Tinkler.

"No it's not. Moses was over a hundred. And Ree's granny was eighty-something when she pegged it."

"Okay, so four people. It shouldn't be hard to figure out who shot who. Or is it whom?"

I said, "I think it was someone who wasn't there at all."

"You're not making any sense. All that sex and California sunshine is rotting your brain."

"California smog."

"What do you mean someone who was not there?"

"I mean not officially. Jerry told me there was this goon who was putting the frighteners on Hathor."

"Goon? Frighteners? This really isn't you. Maybe we should talk about hi-fi instead."

"It was this guy called Ox. A brutal ex-cop."

"Is there any other kind?" said Tinkler.

"He was putting the frighteners on everyone who worked for Hathor."

"You just had to say 'frighteners' again, didn't you?"

"But that's all I've been able to surmise."

"What about your other clue?" said Tinkler. "I mean twelve boxes of clues."

I sighed and decided to lie down on the couch and give up any pretence of working. I had the phone in one hand and a cup of coffee in the other. "I haven't got any further than last time we spoke." I glanced at the photos on the wall. "It's all about Burns Hobartt and Easy Geary. But I have no idea what 'it' is."

"Let's think about this rationally."

"I'm willing to try anything."

"Now, what is the common factor between them?"

"They both got screwed by the music business. But then so did virtually every other jazz artist, especially if his skin tone didn't happen to be whiter than white."

"Focus. Hobartt and Geary. What *specifically* happened to them?"

I forced myself to think. "Burns Hobartt was operating one of the best swing bands of all time. It was right up there with Lunceford and Ellington. And like Ellington he was also writing for his band. He was coming up with great dance hits and popular songs. But to get his music onto the radio he had to sign a slave contract with AMI—American Music Industries. Which was run by the Davenport cousins."

"The creepy cousins."

"Correct."

"Boy and girl cousins."

"Correct. They took half the money and two thirds of the credit on everything Burns ever wrote."

"That's insane."

"Well, eventually it did drive him insane. Or close to it. There's an urban legend that he flipped out and killed both the Davenports at their house in Lake Tahoe."

"*Their* house? They lived together, the cousins?"

"Yes."

"In a creepy, we're-first-cousins-so-it's-incestuous kind of way?"

"Yes, according to the urban legends."

"Well, what do we know according to urban non-legends?"

"That Burns Hobartt and the Davenport cousins were all in the Lake Tahoe house when it burned down. And none of them got out." This had been the second, and final, catastrophic fire that had marked Hobartt's life.

"So, end of Hobartt. What about Easy Geary? Hang on—can I call you back later?"

I told Tinkler he could indeed call me back later. I went to the kitchen and found an avocado to eat. I was becoming addicted to them. They seemed to attain a state of ripeness here in California that was unknown back home on my chilly island. When I finished, I put the slick skin and giant seed in the compost bin and started making some more coffee. It was ready when the phone rang. Tinkler again.

"I won't tell you what happened during that interruption. You see, all your talk of mouth-watering Mexican food drove me to order in a bunch of takeaways last night. It was like getting in a bunch of hookers for an orgy, but in this case it was an orgy of eating and the fiery prostitutes were nine kinds of chilli and various other spicy, allegedly Mexican, dishes. Anyway, today my guts have basically exploded. It's as though my poor quivering bowels are connected directly to the sewers."

"I thought you weren't going to tell me about it."

"Anyway, we were talking about Easy Geary."

I said, "I was about to say he got screwed by the same people who screwed Burns Hobartt."

"AMI?"

"Yes."

"The company that the Davenports set up?"

"Yes, then as now an unstoppable colossus of American commerce." I sipped my coffee. "Their legal people went after Easy Geary because he recorded an album of Burns Hobartt material."

"I know, I know, and left the Davenports' names off the credits."

"And when their legal people didn't get immediate results, they sent in their *illegal* people."

"Meaning your friend Ox?"

"No friend of mine." I set my empty coffee cup aside. I tried to shape the caffeine buzz into an impulse to attack the stack of books sitting in front of me. But the best I could come up with was a strong desire to crawl back into bed.

"I feel like I'm studying for an exam I can never pass."

"That's right, think positive."

"In fact, an exam I'll probably never even take."

"A little more positive than that."

I picked up one of the books I'd gone through yesterday. "Let me give you an example." I flipped through it. "An entire book and just one word is underlined."

"One word?"

I found the page. "It's a name, actually."

"Tell me what it is."

"I can't."

"You don't trust me?"

I stared at it. "No, I mean I actually can't."

"Why not?"

"Because I have no idea how to pronounce it. Here, let

me text it to you." I sent him the name, *Ysaguirre*.

"That is a weird one. Listen, let me help you out here. I'll set about doing some research of my own and I'll find out who it is." I could hear him eagerly typing on his computer.

I chuckled. "As much as I appreciate your eagerness to sleuth, Sherlock, I already know who it is."

"Oh." I could hear his disappointment.

"It's Red Jellaway's real name. His family name. They came from somewhere in Central America."

"So Professor Jellaway is part of this too?"

I shook my head, which is a stupid thing to do when someone can't see you. "I very much doubt it," I said. "I've been through twelve boxes of books and I've found exactly one sentence in one book that relates to him."

"One sentence in one book?"

"Yes. Referring to that family name."

"You're right."

"Am I? About what?"

"It does sound like an exam you're not going to pass."

"Thanks."

"Any time. Listen, could you get me something from LA?"

"Mexican food?"

Tinkler groaned. "No. Please."

"Grapes? Rolling Stones albums?"

"Well, all those too, of course. But I'd also really like a postcard from LA. To impress people. And the more tacky the better."

"Okay," I said, "I'll do that for you. And you do something for me. If you come up with a theory that might explain all this, no matter how wild or weird, call me. Any time of the day or night."

"My day or night, or your day or night?"

"Both. Either. All four."

The rest of the week passed. Ree was singing in clubs and I was working my way through the archives that Dr Tinmouth had bequeathed us. When she was home we settled into a rhythm of sex, food, sleep and chess, which was very much her game.

I must say that chess, like proper Mexican food, had been a real eye-opener for me. I'd never really played before. Now I played badly, but with total attention and a kind of fierce analytical joy I'd never experienced anywhere else.

Well, almost never anywhere else.

Staring at the board, imagining the moves, I could feel it doing my brain good. Ree consistently creamed me, assassinating my queen from a sudden ambush or checking my king with subtle insurrections. Out of a blue sky she could turn a game around and suddenly I'd be demolished in three moves, my pieces rolling shamefully as I set them down on the table beside the board. The fallen.

But I was getting better with every game. And I was loving it.

Unlike my research project.

I was growing to hate the piles of reading matter, the constantly changing but always unwanted invasive presence in Ree's little house. Stubborn, defiant piles of books and journals and documents. I stared at them and despaired.

But Ree expected me to figure it out. She never doubted that I would.

Neither, in their own way, did the guys at the garage who had taken to calling me Library Boy, as I came and went, borrowing literature from the high-security storage room. But despite all their derision they seemed touchingly certain that eventually Library Boy would piece it all together.

I wasn't so certain.

Especially late at night, working as I waited for Ree to return. With the faces of Easy Geary and Burns Hobartt looking mockingly down from the wall at me. To my weary brain their expressions were beginning to converge in an identical, pitying disdain for the poor buffoon who was trying to understand what was going on.

One evening Ree came home and said, "I've got something for Tinkler." She showed me an assortment of postcards. "You asked for tacky," she said. The postcards were great. Dogs wearing clothes, freaks of the vegetable kingdom, historical photographs of Los Angeles street life with snarky comments.

I was particularly taken with a shot of the Hollywood sign done in the most garish Bollywood colours.

"I know what I'm going to do," I said. I found a printout with pictures of Burns Hobartt and Easy Geary on it. I chose shots of about the right size and cut their heads out with a pair of scissors. Ree saw what I was doing and got me some glue.

I pasted the faces of Geary and Hobartt onto the postcard, over the two adjacent O's in the WOOD in HOLLYWOOD. Then I wrote on the back:

THIS IS WHAT I'VE SEEN SINCE I'VE BEEN IN LA.

"Poor Chef," said Ree, reading over my shoulder. She kissed me. "Come to bed. I'll show you something else LA has to offer."

That night my sleep was haunted by endless, repetitive dreams from which there was no escape. Sequences of letters kept cycling through my anxious brain. First I saw the letters on our chart, those tantalising fragments gleaned from the dead wax on the records.

But then these got mixed up with the letters from the Hollywood sign. Everything kept shifting and altering as I made frantic, fevered efforts to try and keep up with it. It was like one of those dreams where you urgently need to dial a number on your phone, but the numbers keep changing.

And, sure enough, the letters on the Hollywood sign began to change. The two O's merged into one, so it now read HOLLYWOD.

I opened my eyes. My pillow was soaked with sweat and my heart was pounding. Beside me Ree breathed softly in her sleep. I was wide awake. I had never been more awake. I got out of bed and went into the living room. I switched on a lamp and looked at the photos of Geary and Hobartt on the wall. Then I looked at the postcard with their images pasted onto it.

I thought, *Hollywod*. I went and got a pen and returned to the large photos on the wall. I studied Hobartt, the scars of the fire that raddled his cheeks. Then I looked at Geary, that smooth, unlined, almost Asian face. I checked the scars and started drawing. I drew the lines on Geary's face, copying carefully. Finally I stepped back and looked at it, then at Hobartt's.

It was the same face.

I picked up the medical directory. I knew where to look now and I immediately turned to find the marked page.

Plastic surgeons.

27. BUDDHA ON A BAD DAY

"Okay," said Tinkler, "so they're the same guy. That's fairly interesting. But do you want to hear something that's *really* interesting? This morning Turk came charging through the cat flap with a magpie in her mouth. A magpie! This thing was almost as big as she is. Still alive. Unharmed, in fact. She'd brought it back alive. That's my girl. She let the magpie go and went and ate some biscuits. So I had to open the windows and chase the bird out. Which in all modesty I have to say I did with brilliant success."

I said, "Tinkler, I don't want to sound disloyal to my cats but I think this discovery of mine is even more important than Turk bagging a magpie."

"No, you're right. You're probably right. I guess you're right."

I said, "Ree is so pleased with me, that I worked it out. I don't know what the hell good it does her. Or anybody. But she's as pleased as Punch. Even the guys at the garage are pleased. And they don't know what the hell I found out. But they bought me a bottle of mescal. You know, with the worm at the bottom."

"Yes. Yuck."

"And they gave it to me with a note that said, 'For the Book Worm'. You know, referencing the worm and everything."

"So, anyway, they're the same guy?" said Tinkler. "Easy Geary and Burns Hobartt?"

"The weirdest thing," I said, "is that it makes absolute sense, from a musical point of view. Nobody played Hobartt's tunes like Easy Geary did. He played that music as if he knew it from the inside. Which it turns out he did."

"But Hobartt was the king of swing. And Geary was a bebop cat."

"Hobartt was already moving in the direction of bop when he vanished. And he probably would have moved faster and further in that direction if he hadn't needed to stay popular with a mass audience."

"But to hell with these questions of artistic integrity," said Tinkler. "What about the *money*? Hobartt was rich. Astonishingly rich for a musician. Thanks to his compositions he must have owned a huge chunk of AMI."

"The company that would later become AMI. And it wasn't such a huge chunk because Davenport Music was already a big concern before he came along, thanks to stealing half of everything Professor Jellaway ever wrote."

"Anyway, you're saying that he actually went from being a big-shot millionaire bandleader to some unknown little guy who played in little clubs?"

"Yes."

"And he did it deliberately. He gave up all that."

I said, "Yes. To become a cult genius known only to a few. But it was only a matter of time. That's what he must have figured."

"That he could rise like a phoenix from the ashes?" said Tinkler.

"Exactly. Start all over again, because when you're a genius like that it's only a matter of time before you break through again. In fact, he was already on the rise, with a growing reputation and destined for greatness—again—when he died."

"So he just assumed another identity? Hobartt became Geary. And he walked away from his band and his music and all the publishing rights and royalties?"

"He also walked away from a murder charge. If that story about the Lake Tahoe house is to be believed."

"But didn't they find his body there?"

"They found *somebody's* body there. It could have been anyone. We may never know who it was. Except is wasn't Burns Hobartt."

There was a pause as, on the other side of the world, Tinkler thought about it. "This was the late 1940s, right?"

"Right."

"So it wasn't exactly *CSI: Lake Tahoe*."

"The forensic sciences were in their infancy if that's what you're trying to say, yes."

"So no DNA. So just use the body of some John Doe or skid row bum…"

"That's what I'm thinking."

"So they actually could have pulled it off? I mean, *he* actually could have pulled it off?"

I said, "When I listen to their stuff I can't believe I didn't see it before. It's the same musical mind. So clearly the same mind."

"But there was more to it than just planting a body in a

burning house, surely. How the hell did they do it? I mean, did *he* do it."

"Well, by the late forties plastic surgery had advanced to the point where Hobartt could get his scars fixed."

"You mean, Burns could lose his burns," said Tinkler.

"Tasteless but true. He had the money to get his face repaired and medical science could now repair it. Sort of. If he didn't mind ending up looking like Buddha on a bad day and only have about three facial expressions in his repertoire."

"That explains his face, but what about the rest of it? Creating a whole new identity."

"After the Second World War servicemen were pouring back into the States from all over the world. Hobartt bought or forged papers from a soldier who had been serving overseas for years in far-off exotic outposts and was only now returning to the homeland. Don't forget that he had plenty of money to pull this off."

Tinkler said, "And these were the days before our friend the computer."

"It also explains one of the great mysteries of jazz. How Easy Geary could arrive on the scene as an unknown, but already fully formed, genius. Supposedly he'd been listening to jazz greats on records in lonely military outposts. But this explanation is much more convincing."

"This is amazing," said Tinkler. "Thinking about it, you're right. It's even more significant than Turk's magpie. You should write a book about it."

I stared at the piles of literature that still crowded Ree's living room. "If I never see a jazz book again, it will be too soon."

"I'll remind you that you said that next Christmas."

"Okay."

"And I want to go on record as saying I still think Turk's catch is pretty important."

Tinkler and I said our goodbyes. Ree had also been talking on the phone. When she saw that I was finished she rang off, too.

I said, "Tinkler's been cat-sitting too long. He's gone native."

She said, "That was Berto. Someone tried to break into the garage."

"Did they get anything?"

"No. They never even got as far as the lock-up before all sorts of alarms went off and they had to get the hell out of there."

"Do they know who it was?"

"No."

"I thought they had cameras everywhere."

She shrugged. "They do. But somebody shot them with a BB gun. Do you know what that is?"

I said, "An air rifle. Fires tiny ball bearings. Traditionally given to young boys so they can learn to slay small animals."

"Right," she said. "Also good for slaying small cameras."

We were both silent for a minute. Then I said, "Let's not forget that there might be all sorts of reasons all sorts of people might want to break into Berto's garage. It's full of valuable auto parts."

"Right," she said.

When we first met, Ree had mentioned the disappearance of her grandmother's diary, and her suspicions about the shady character who'd supposedly been working on Rita Mae's biography. The only reason we hadn't gone straight to see this guy when we landed in LA was because we didn't know where to find him.

That changed, however. One day she looked up at me triumphantly from her computer and said, "We're going for a little ride."

So I found myself standing in front of a white stucco house in a shady cul-de-sac of a street in Downey just off Imperial Highway, watching as Ree rang the doorbell. She said, "Don't forget what I told you."

"Let you do the talking and just play dumb."

"Not dumb." She shook her head impatiently. "Silent. Just stand around and kind of…"

"Loom?"

"Right. And don't say anything unless you have to." She was about to add something else but then the door popped open.

He was a small, chubby man with thinning chestnut hair and a goatee. He wore a garish Hawaiian shirt, Bermuda shorts, white socks and sandals.

When he saw Ree, a hastily concealed look of alarm flashed across his face. But he quickly composed himself and smiled and said, "Ree, I haven't seen you for the longest time!"

"You're a hard man to find."

The guy shot a worried look at me. As instructed, I just stood there silently.

"This is a friend of mine," said Ree.

The little man said, "Wilburt Sassman, pleased to meet you." I took the hand he offered but said nothing and my silence seemed to have a profound effect on him. I actually felt his palm grow warm and sweaty as we shook.

He said, "So, ah, what brings you here, Ree?"

"Could we step in for a sec?"

He looked over his shoulder helplessly. I could see he was trying to think of an excuse not to let us in. "It'll only take a minute," said Ree, and smiled. He was trapped by social convention. He shrugged and stepped aside and we went into the house. It was cool inside and I could hear a soft bubbling sound like someone smoking a bubble pipe. One enormous endless soft inhalation.

Wilburt led us through to a heavily carpeted living room with thick overstuffed floral furniture gathered inwards towards the centre, as though huddling together for security. Around the walls of the room were glass aquarium tanks full of brightly coloured darting fish. The bubbling noise came from the air pumps on the tanks.

Thick curtains shut out the sunshine. But emanating from the illuminated fish tanks there was more than enough light to see that the walls were covered with framed photographs of Ree's grandmother.

Rita Mae Pollini.

She was a very beautiful woman and they were striking photos, clearly publicity shots, and any given selection of them would have looked fine and indeed attractive on any wall. But the sheer number of these gave a queasy sense of obsession.

Wilburt gestured for us to sit down. Ree remained standing and so did I. He settled warily into a big soft pale green armchair facing us. Ree moved away from me, so he had to turn his head to look from one of us to the other. He tried to smile and said, "I suppose you're wondering how the biography is going?"

Ree shook her head. "No, Wilburt," she said regretfully. "We're not wondering that at all."

He gave her a sharp look. "Well, I know I haven't been as quick about it as I might have been, but I've had some health issues." He looked at me. "Allergies have compromised my immune system."

I didn't say anything, just expressionlessly returned his stare, and he grew visibly more uneasy. "Who did you say your friend was?" he asked Ree.

She glanced at me. "I brought him with me all the way from England. To see you."

"Me?" said Wilburt. His voice was a squeak. "Why?"

"Because I want what's mine. And he's here to make sure that I get it."

"What do you mean what's yours?" His voice was, if anything, growing more high-pitched. Constricted with tension. "What are you talking about?"

Now Ree sat down. I remained standing, fascinated by what I was seeing. The guy was coming apart in front of us. She was pressing his buttons, and he was self-destructing.

She said, "I think you know exactly what we're talking about."

"I don't understand," said Wilburt. He sounded close to tears. "I don't understand what I've done that makes you think you can come barging in here, making accusations, with your hired muscle."

"You mean Chef?" She shot me a look. "Do you want to know why they call him the Chef?"

Wilburt actually covered his ears. "No, no," he moaned.

Ree went to him and spoke softly, persuasively, lifting his hands from his ears. "You don't need to ever find out, just so long as you give me what is mine."

Their faces were close together, but he wouldn't look her in the eye. "I don't have anything! I don't know what you're talking about." He was so obviously lying that it was embarrassing to all of us. I didn't know where to look. "This is so unfair."

"No, Wilburt," said Ree gently. "What is unfair is you getting unlimited access to my grandmother and using the opportunity to loot things."

"I didn't loot anything!"

Ree made as if to head for the door. "Do you want to continue this interview with just you and Chef? I can leave the two of you alone."

He glanced at me. "No!"

"Then I want it back."

"This is so unfair," repeated Wilburt.

I went and tapped my knuckle against the glass of the aquarium. The fish came and peered at me. "Leave my fish alone!" he cried.

"We want you to give us the diary," she said.

I looked at him. "Now. Or else you'll find out why they call me the Chef."

"Okay," he said, staring at me. "Okay. Take it easy." He rose from the chair. "I'll go and get it." He glanced at Ree accusingly with big wet eyes, then left the room.

We stared at each other. Ree looked like she was going to lose it and start laughing. I started to get worried. He was gone a long time, and the longer he was gone the more she began to shake with suppressed hilarity. But she managed to control herself and pulled herself together swiftly, adopting a grim, blank face as he came scurrying back in with a small red book.

After all the fuss, it didn't look very impressive. But Ree flipped through it and nodded. "This is it."

We took it out to the car. Ree sat at the wheel for a moment, making a bubbling convulsive sound, her shoulders jumping. Then finally she succumbed to laughter. When she finished, she wiped her eyes and turned to me.

"That was fun," she said. "What say we go back in and do it all again?"

We stopped off at Berto's to lock up the diary, and when we got there we discovered another record had arrived in the mail. I unwrapped it while Ree locked the diary in the safe. It was HL-004, Johnny Richards. I felt a particular sense of triumph about acquiring this one, because it was the album we had missed out on at the record mart in Wembley.

When the red-haired woman had beaten us to the punch.

When Nevada had beaten us to the punch.

I eased the record out of the inner sleeve and checked the dead wax. Then I got out our chart and added the information.

EA--EGARYIST--FA--EROF----BY

28. HAMMER MAN

"So you've got the diary now," said Tinkler.

"Ree tracked down Wilburt Sassman, the guy who stole it, through eBay. He'd covered his tracks pretty well in other regards but he couldn't resist buying and selling paraphernalia online. She actually bought something from him, incognito, and got hold of his address that way."

"And now you've got the diary you know everything."

"We know *some* things," I said. "The diary is fragmentary. The earliest surviving page of any interest describes Rita Mae and her husband the dentist holding a party. The dentist had a lot of money and he certainly knew how to throw a bash. Nat King Cole was there, Pete Rugolo was there. Rita Mae sang a duet with Nat, with Pete playing the piano. Then the dentist calls for silence and he makes this big tasteless announcement about how the 'rabbit died' which is his way of saying he's knocked up his sexy young wife and she's mortified with embarrassment, but everybody is toasting her health with champagne and refilling her glass for her."

"Because in those days giving a pregnant woman

champagne was still the done thing."

"Right."

"A simpler, happier age," said Tinkler.

"She's a frustrating diarist, Rita Mae."

"How so?"

"There'll be two pages about getting a new hairstyle she saw in a magazine, and then she'll mention a gig with the cream of the West Coast jazz set, singing at the Lighthouse, and dismiss it in two lines. But there is some crucial stuff. Like when she describes the reign of terror by that cop."

"The cop called Ox."

"That's him. His crusade against jazz musicians, and the more famous the better, is recorded in frightening detail in these pages. So we get to hear how Art Pepper comes out of a session with Marty Paich and finds Ox waiting for him. He busts Pepper for heroin he planted in Pepper's car. Another time it's Chet Baker. Then Ox almost nails Gerry Mulligan. He has absolutely no compunction about planting evidence. And these people go away to prison for *years*. No one is safe."

"Like you said, a reign of terror."

"Exactly. So that's the atmosphere at the time. And then we get to the Hathor sessions."

I could hear Tinkler exhale on the other side of the world. "So there is some stuff about the Hathor sessions?"

"I'll tell you what I'll do," I said. "I've typed up the most important passages on my laptop. I'll email them to you for safe keeping."

"I'll keep them safe. Send them now."

* * *

Thursday January 13th
Bobby Schoolcraft has a brand-new cream Mercedes-Benz 300 SL.

(There then follows a couple of pages on the virtues of this car. Ree certainly got her obsession with automobiles from her grandmother.)

Bobby also has a stunning new girlfriend Tilly, a colored girl. When I sat down with her I discovered there were two dogs under the table, licking my toes. They were the cutest little black and brown dogs. Cavalier King Charles Spaniels.

Easy Geary joined us. The piano in the joint was okay so he agreed to play. Easy said that Bobby got the dogs because this breed are called Black and Tans. He said, "Get it? It's the world's most obvious Duke Ellington gag." He's pretty amused by Bobby.

And then there's a maddening gap that would have covered the entire period we're interested in: the launching of Hathor Records and their first album and everything else we'd give our eyeteeth to know about.

But Rita Mae was a sporadic diarist.

In fact "sporadic" is a polite word for it.

Then she starts writing again. To make sense of what follows you have to remember that by the 1950s AMI had become a multi-million-dollar corporation, having built an empire with the money they'd earned from the music of Burns Hobartt. Though "earned" isn't the word I should use. "Stolen" would be more like it. Anyway, they were now extremely powerful, in all sorts of ways.

By the time of the next diary entry the little record company, Hathor, is already reeling from the legal battle with AMI. But they refuse to quit. At one point Rita Mae writes:

> It's like an elephant stomping on a mouse. And then the mouse gets up and comes back to challenge the elephant again.

But by now Bobby Schoolcraft is almost broke. Rita Mae is working for him as a secretary, without pay, to help.

Wednesday February 16th

A man came in to the office just as we were opening up for the day. His aftershave was so strong I couldn't tell if I smelled booze on him or not. I thought I did. He said his name was Oliver Xavier and Mr Schoolcraft was expecting him. So I let him go back into Bobby's office.

He came back out a few minutes later and smiled and said, "By the way, are you one of our colored friends?" Bobby must have heard him talking because he came racing out of the office. I told the man that my dark skin is due to my Italianate heritage. "Nice story," he said and tipped his hat and left. Bobby was white as a sheet. "Do you know who that was?" he said. "That was Ox."

Thursday February 17th

Something has happened to Bobby's Mercedes. It has been completely vandalised. I saw it, and it's a complete wreck. All the windows and headlights smashed, tyres slashed, dents all over the bodywork. The leather seats are slashed too and somebody peed all over them. I'm so upset. I know how he loved that car.

Friday March 4th

Something terrible happened. Bobby and Tilly were coming home from a club last night and, as they drove up towards their house, they saw something in the headlights of their car. Something on the gateposts, on either side of their driveway. They stopped and got out. It was the heads of their little dogs, Duke and Fantasy. Someone had killed them and cut off their heads and left them there, one on each gatepost.

Tilly had to be sedated.

Those poor little dogs.

Saturday March 5th

I went to Bobby's house. Easy Geary was there too. Bobby said he knows who killed the dogs. It was Ox. He wrecked Bobby's car, too. Ox is trying to intimidate Bobby, to get him to settle the lawsuit with AMI. Bobby is challenging their right to put the Davenports' names on Burns Hobartt's compositions. And it looks like AMI thinks he might win. So they've hired Ox as their hammer man. Tilly wants him to cave in. But Easy is urging him to keep fighting. I've never seen Easy so angry. If he knew where he could find Ox I think he would do something terrible. He has an awful temper. They say he once pulled a knife on Billy Eckstine.

Tuesday March 15th

Bobby's colored girlfriend Tilly is in hospital. She was driving home alone last night and Ox pulled her over. He took her into an alley and beat her up. Bobby wants her to tell what happened but she won't. Ox has two cops who swear she was drunk and attacked him. If she tries to report Ox they will swear charges against her. She's too frightened to ever report Ox.

He beat her up really badly. He kicked her in the stomach, so she miscarried.

He did it deliberately.

He called it "Irish birth control".

Thursday March 24th

Bobby is frantic. Tilly has disappeared. Her family won't tell him where she went. They think it's his fault she almost got killed. I think she's gone to Paris. Poor Bobby is beside himself. He says he can't go on without her.

Thursday March 31st

Bobby is dead. He shot himself.

The phone rang in the middle of the night. Ree woke up before I did. She answered it. "Tinkler," she said, handing me the phone and crawling back under the covers.

I took the phone into the next room, sleep ebbing from my brain, and said, "You do know what time it is?"

"Of course. When you insist on travelling to the other side of the planet the eight-hour time difference is the price you pay."

"Why are you calling me?"

"I read the diary entries you sent. And I can't wait for the next batch. I had to call and get you to read it to me now. Don't worry about typing it up and emailing it. Just read it to me."

"I can't."

"Look, I'm sorry, I know it's late and I probably woke

up and pissed off your sexy new American girlfriend, in fact I know I definitely did, but forgive me anyway and read me the rest of the diary."

"I can't."

"Don't punish me. Don't make me wait."

"No, I mean I literally can't. That's all there is."

There was a pause and then he said, "It can't be."

"Rita Mae never wrote another word. At least not in that year's diary. All the remaining pages are blank."

There was a long silence on the other end of the line as, across the ocean in England, Tinkler came to terms with this.

"Shit," he said.

The next morning Ree said, "What was all that about?"

"Tinkler couldn't wait to read the next diary entry. I had to break it to him that there wasn't one."

I looked at the diary, lying on the table in a square of morning sunlight. It was a strange feeling to have got this far and to know that it was the end of the line. Now we would never get the story of the recording session. We'd never know exactly what happened on that day in 1955.

I picked up the diary. It was warm to the touch. I flipped through it idly.

As I did so, a slight but emphatic smell rose up to my nostrils. Faintly intoxicating, promising a headache, reminiscent of childhood construction projects.

Glue.

The heat of the sunlight had caused the smell to come out of the pages. I stared at the diary, spread open loosely in my hands. I thumbed carefully through to the last entry and studied it. I got up and carried it to the window and held it in the sunlight. Ree was standing in the kitchen pouring cereal into a bowl. She was watching me.

"What is it?" she said.

I held the diary in the sunlight. The pages were made of high-quality paper, which hadn't yellowed much in over half a century. They were ruled with thin blue horizontal lines. There were two pages allotted to each day's entry. The date and the day of the week were printed at the top of the left-hand page.

The final, terse entry only occupied one line of the left-hand page.

I studied the blank page opposite, trying to see any difference in the colour of the paper.

There was none.

As far as I could see, it was exactly the same paper, aged to exactly the same extent of yellowing. It was the same weight and thickness. The pale blue lines were precisely aligned with those on the left-hand page.

Then I noticed it.

There was an extra line at the bottom of the page.

Ree was standing at my side now, drawn over by my intense silence as I scrutinised the diary. "Look," I said. I put my finger beside the bottom line on the right-hand page. On the page to the left of it there was nothing, just the empty space of the bottom margin.

"Maybe it's a printing mistake," said Ree. I flipped through the rest of the diary. The remaining pages were all the same—one extra line.

"If it is, it's a consistent one," I said, pausing with it open at the following day, April 1st.

"Maybe it's an April Fool's Day joke," said Ree, "by the printers."

I stared at the date. That was when I spotted something else.

I flipped back to the previous day, then back to April 1st again. I was right. There wasn't any doubt about it.

The typeface for the day and the date on April 1st were different from the one for March 31st. I showed Ree. "It's almost identical…"

"But not quite."

We stared at each other. She was still holding the bowl of cereal, forgotten in her hands. I said, "Would you be heartbroken if I was to dismantle your grandmother's diary?"

"Dismantle it?"

"We can always put it back together again." I borrowed the clasp knife she had got from Berto. We spread the diary wide and flat on a table, open at the last entry. I ran the knife blade carefully down the join between the left- and right-hand pages. It came apart surprisingly easily.

And a strong smell of glue rose up.

Opened up like this we could see the binding of each set of pages. The pages to the left were bound at the back with red cloth. Those on the right with green cloth. "They're from two different diaries," said Ree.

"The little bastard pulled a switch on us."

"No wonder he was gone such a long time when he went to fetch it. He was busy with scissors and glue."

29. TEARS

We were back in the sun-dappled cul-de-sac in Downey, on Wilburt Sassman's doorstep. Ree was standing beside me as I pressed the doorbell. Nothing. Silence. I pressed it again, looking at her.

"It's dead." The word rang ominously in the silence.

We tried the door and it opened, into the cool, quiet shadows of the house. We stepped inside, the door easing shut behind us on a hydraulic hinge. There was something odd about the silence, and then I remembered. Last time there had been the bubbling of the fish tanks.

Now there was nothing.

The natural thing to have done would have been to call Wilburt's name. But neither of us said anything. There was something about the silence of the house that precluded shouting. And, perhaps, which urged caution. We moved out of the entrance hall into the short corridor that led to the living-room. It was so dark I couldn't see the living-room door. There was a light switch on the wall and Ree fumbled with it, to no effect.

Like the doorbell, it was dead.

We moved cautiously into the darkness of the house.

I found the living-room door by feel, and opened it. The room was dim, in distinct contrast to our previous visit, when it had been illuminated by the eerie glow of the fish tanks. But there was just enough light coming in through a gap in the curtains to see Wilburt.

He was standing, or rather leaning, against one of the aquarium tanks with his hand dangling limply over the side, immersed in the water. Floating beside it in the otherwise empty glass tank was a thin snaking black shape with a gleam of copper at its tip. I realised it was a power cable, and I began to piece together what must have happened. Wilburt was bent over the tank, turned away from us, so we couldn't see his face. But on the carpet, around his bare feet, was a ragged black scorch mark.

"He's been electrocuted," said Ree.

I noticed a flicker of motion out of the corner of my eye and turned to look. The other tanks were a safe distance from where Wilburt had been messing about. In their dark water, fish were moving.

I moved closer. They were still milling around in their coloured hordes, apparently none the worse for wear. That meant their life support apparatus had only been turned off recently.

At the exact instant I realised this, I heard the back door slam.

With no conscious thought at all I was running out of the room, back into the darkness of the corridor, moving the other way. Back through the entrance hall and down the other corridor, towards the other end of the house. I clattered across the tile floor of the dark kitchen, heading for the oblong of pale light that marked the back door.

I threw the door open and found myself in the back yard.

It was a small yard, but deep, with high stone walls. Like a courtyard. Square in section and sunk well below street level, the walls on each side increased its depth. It was a cool, shadowed hollow, lined at the bottom with red and yellow crazy paving. White stone steps led down into it from the kitchen and, on the opposite side, another stone staircase rose up to a gate in the wall.

Standing at the top of those stairs, holding the gate open, was a tall, powerful man wearing a tracksuit and running shoes. Sunglasses, a baseball cap and a hooded sweatshirt concealed his face. Just below me, in the pit of the garden, heading towards him, was a woman dressed in an almost identical outfit. She was frozen where she was standing, staring up at the man. He had his fist stretched out, index finger extended, pointing at something, something back across the yard.

At the foot of my staircase.

I looked down at where he was pointing and saw it. The small white rectangle lying there.

A clump of pages torn from a book.

She must have dropped them.

The woman turned around and saw them. She saw me standing at the top of the steps and jerked with reaction, then launched herself back towards the pages. At the same moment I threw myself down the stairs and grabbed them. Even in the split second as I seized them, I saw the handwriting on the pages and knew they were exactly what I thought they were.

I went back up the stairs with them as fast as I could. The woman came to a halt at the bottom of the steps, staring up at me fiercely, then looking back at the man on the other side of the yard.

He had a gun in his hand.

He was aiming it at me.

A woman's voice spoke, from high on the wall to our left.

"Hey, Heinz," she said.

Everyone turned to look, and I saw Nevada standing there, perched on top of the wall, silhouetted against the sunlight. She had the ridiculous red wig on, but it was her. She had something in her hand and she said, "This is for you," and threw it down into the yard. As she did so, she jumped off the wall, disappearing into the street on the other side.

Down in the pit of the courtyard, the object hit the crazy paving with a metallic clank and began to roll. It was a yellow and black cylinder. It looked like a can of insect spray with the lid removed. But the white cloud that was spitting from it wasn't insect spray. As it rolled I read, in revolving black lettering on the yellow can, the words KROWD-KLEAR.

If you could call them words.

I saw the white cloud engulf Heidi at the bottom of the stairs. Heinz lowered his gun and started down his stairs, as if to help her. But then he stopped, realising he was going to step straight into the rising cloud of tear gas.

I didn't stay to see what he did about this quandary.

As I slammed back through the kitchen door I could hear Heidi coughing and choking. Ree was waiting in the shadows. She'd been watching from the kitchen window. I glimpsed the back yard, now entirely filled by the swelling, gleaming cloud. I could see two dark figures moving in it. I grabbed Ree's hand and we ran for the front door.

In my other hand I had the diary pages.

We punched through the front door and down the steps, out into the street. As we unlocked her car we could hear a gate slam at the back of the house and the sound of violent coughing, approaching fast. Ree gunned the engine and we raced away, bouncing down the tree-shadowed street, taking a left, a right, and then a left again.

Only when we were on Imperial Highway did she begin to relax. By then I was reading the diary.

"Is it all there?"

"Looks like it."

"Good," she said. Then, "Was that your girlfriend with the tear gas grenade?"

"Ex-girlfriend. Nevada. Yes."

She glanced at me, her eyes unreadable. "Is she your guardian angel or something?"

"Or something," I said.

"Well, it's a good thing she turned up when she did. That guy had a gun."

"I noticed."

"And they were the Aryan Twins?"

"In person."

She signalled a turn and began to pull towards the slip road, off the highway. We were still miles from home.

"Where are we going?" I said.

"To find a phone booth somewhere. One that isn't overlooked by a security camera."

"You're going to call the cops?"

"And the ASPCA."

"What's that?" I said.

"They'll look after those poor fish."

* * *

When we got back to Ree's house, we photographed all the remaining pages of the diary and then I typed them up and sent them to Tinkler while Ree glued them back into the binding with the first half of the diary.

This was what Wilburt hadn't wanted us to read.

It was what the Aryan Twins had almost snatched from us.

Wednesday April 6th

The last Hathor session today. Easy and Moses and Danny DePriest. And I'm singing on one track. We all want to do it, in memory of Bobby. There's no money left but Ron has given us the studio for free. He and Ladybird have driven up to Santa Barbara for the day. They left the keys for us. They were gone when we got there.

Ox must have arrived after they left, or they would have warned us.

He was waiting for us.

He had a bottle of whiskey with him and he was drinking out of it. You could smell the booze even over his aftershave. When we pulled up he came over to us.

He had the whiskey in one hand and a gun in the other. He told us to go away. It was all over. Danny DePriest and Moses were scared and so was I.

But Easy Geary just ignored him and made us go into the studio and start recording, like everything was normal. And the session went beautifully. Danny DePriest was very professional, setting everything up in the control room and then running out to play on the takes.

At lunchtime we all went out to get some sun and my stomach sank when I saw that Ox was still there. And he was even drunker. He was waving his gun around and we all went back inside as quickly as we could. But he saw me and I had taken my sweater off. I've started to show and he saw right away that I'm pregnant.

He smiled at me and showed me the gun and said, "Irish birth control."

I was really shaken up but Easy was calm and Danny was still very professional despite it being his first solo session and we all got on with the recording. When we got to my song everything was cooking and we'd forgotten all about Ox.

But then I saw someone moving around in the back of the studio.

It was him.

Ox.

He'd come inside. Easy saw him, too. He waited until a moment came when he could drop out, then he signalled for us to keep playing and he got up from the piano and went into the back. I was singing and I didn't see what happened but I heard a noise and it frightened me.

But I kept singing.

And Easy came back and sat down and played his solo. We all finished the song and it sounded great and only then did we realise that Easy was bleeding.

The sound had been Ox's gun. He had shot Easy. Easy had defended himself with his knife and afterwards we found Ox lying there. It's funny how calm everyone was. I guess we'd known what had happened, even if we didn't admit it to ourselves, while we were finishing the song.

We worked out what had to be done.

We cleaned the place up. I went and bought a new carpet while Moses and Danny got rid of the old one and everything else. Easy went to a doctor that he knew. I stayed at the studio and supervised while the new carpet was installed. Ron and Ladybird got back just as the carpet men were finishing. They were really pleased. They have no idea what happened.

I'm not sorry about what we did.

I'm glad.

Friday April 8th

Danny was making the acetate of the record today. Easy and I joined him, like we agreed, to put our signatures in the wax. I couldn't believe Easy had been able to get there. He was bleeding badly through the dressing on his wound. I told him to stay put and I hurried out and got some bandages from the drug store. But when I got back he was gone. Danny told me Easy had said that we'd done it. We'd made our statement for posterity, if anybody ever needed proof. Danny thought he was talking about the music. I knew he wasn't.

There were no more entries until a week later, when written in big letters across the entire page was:

Friday April 15th

RIP Easy Geary.

The rest of the diary was blank.

Ree read through my transcription before I sent it off to Tinkler. She said, "The part I like best is the way he put paid to that bastard and still got back in time to play his solo. With a bullet in him."

She looked at me. "She was sleeping with him."

"Who?" I said. "Your grandmother? With Easy Geary?"

Ree nodded. "From the way she writes about him in the diary. But also the way she used to talk about him." She nodded again, emphatically. "I'm sure about it."

"You mean, while she was married to your grandfather?"

"Of course," said Ree impatiently.

She went to a cupboard and came back with a gold plastic crown large enough for a child. She held it up and said, "My grandmother gave this to me for my birthday, the first birthday I spent with her after my folks died. She called me her little empress and told me everything was going to be all right for me."

We looked at each other. There was an idea trying to surface at the back of my mind, but every time I reached for it, it slipped away.

We'd made our statement for posterity, if anybody ever needed proof.

I took out our chart and looked at it.

EA--EGARYIST--FA--EROF----BY

I felt a shiver go down my spine, like cold electricity.

30. SOLUTION

There were still five Hathor LPs left to find, but it was as if we'd reached some crucial tipping point. Suddenly in quick succession we tracked down copies of HL-007 and then HL-012, which was a particularly satisfying find because it was the same Pepper Adams album that the "redhead" had scooped up at Styli just before I got there.

That Nevada had scooped up.

We located these records online and bought them, arranging for them to be shipped to the garage.

Then we got a lead on HL-009, one of the two which were headlined by Ree's grandmother. A copy was being sold by a dealer in El Sereno. And then the same dealer phoned to say he'd also dug up the Conte Candoli, HL-013. Lucky 13.

Which left just one.

I got out our chart and stared at it.

EA--EGARYIST--FA--EROF----BY

That morning the garage called to say that two of the records had arrived. We went down to get them. I unwrapped the first, HL-012 by Pepper Adams. I checked the dead wax and filled in the chart.

EA--EGARYIST--FA--EROFMY--BY

"And here's the other one." Ree handed me the second record. HL-007 by Cy Coleman. I checked it and amended the chart.

EA--EGARYISTHEFA--EROFMY--BY

I looked at Ree. "Are you thinking what I'm thinking?" I said. She looked back at me, bronze eyes clear and level.

We drove over out to El Sereno to collect the two records from the dealer. He operated a small store out of his house. He had one of the records—HL-009, *Rita Mae Pollini Sings Burns Hobartt*, waiting for us when we arrived. He went off to get the other one.

Ree studied the photo of her grandmother on the album cover as I filled in the chart.

EA--EGARYISTHEFATHEROFMY--BY

Ree and I looked at each other.

I checked what time it was in England and phoned Alan at Jazz House. While I held the phone and Ree waited impatiently, Alan followed my request. After a few minutes, he came back and gave me the information. I thanked him and hung up.

"He's checked. And it turns out the labels on HL-003, the Richie Kamuca, were glued on the wrong sides of the record."

"On the wrong sides?"

"Yes. They were reversed. It happens sometimes."

"Okay," said Ree. She looked at me. "We both knew it anyway, didn't we?" I nodded, then corrected the chart. Instead of:

EA--EGARYISTHEFATHEROFMY--BY

It now read:

EA--GEARYISTHEFATHEROFMY--BY

The dealer finally came back with HL-013, the Conte Candoli. "I'm sorry. My wife had it filed under 'Easy Listening' with the Al Hirt stuff. Because it has a trumpet on the cover. That kind of reasoning."

I took the record and Ree watched over my shoulder as I added the information to the chart.

We stared at it.

EA--GEARYISTHEFATHEROFMYBABY

I felt light-headed and weightless. We soon found the final album, HL-002 by Marty Paich, on the Internet. A copy in Hawaii. It seemed to take forever to arrive, even by the most speedy of carrier. But it finally did.

I checked the dead wax as Ree watched.

"It's SY."

"Of course it is."

I looked at the chart.

EASYGEARYISTHEFATHEROFMYBABY

I inserted the spaces.

EASY GEARY IS THE FATHER OF MY BABY

31. ENCOUNTER

The implications slowly began to sink in. Easy Geary and Rita Mae Pollini had signed Hathor HL-014 because it was the conclusion of a message. A statement they wanted to preserve permanently. Instead of carving it in stone they'd carved it in vinyl. Perhaps not the finest choice for permanence, but we'd read it in the end.

Easy Geary had gone to great trouble to code that message into the vinyl. I'd asked Ron Longmire what he knew about the cryptic markings in the run-out, but he didn't remember anything about them. "I always left the final stage to Danny," he said. But he did recall that Easy Geary liked to be there with Danny DePriest when he prepared the acetates. "And Rita Mae liked to be with him, too."

So Danny had been in on it. But what was "it"? Why did they do it?

Easy Geary evidently regarded this message as some kind of summing up of his life's work. He dragged himself to sign the final LP's lacquer with a bullet in him, and he died soon afterwards, presumably from that same bullet.

Ree's grandmother, Rita Mae, had also attached a vital

importance to what they'd written in the dead wax. Which is why she'd freaked out when she'd lost her copies of the records. They'd spelled out the true paternity of her child.

And the bloodline of her grandchild.

She understood the implication.

"She called me her little empress and told me everything was going to be all right for me."

We talked about it as we played chess that evening, sitting on the floor in Ree's living room with the board between us. I loved playing here with her but I couldn't help thinking the game would only be improved by a cat attempting to wander across the board, chancing to scatter pawns and kings with equal insouciance.

I said, "This makes you a direct descendant and heir of Easy Geary."

"I know."

"And Easy Geary was Burns Hobartt. And Burns Hobartt owned a substantial piece of AMI. Which means you now own that. A chunk of one of the biggest corporations in the world."

"I know."

"Your grandmother kept the secret at first because she didn't want her husband to find out that another man had fathered her child. Obviously. Later on she kept the secret because she knew it was potentially dynamite and she wanted to keep you safe. You're one of the richest women in America." I looked around at her small, cosy house and wondered what would become of it. "Maybe you can use this place for storing your shoes," I said.

"I'm not really the shoe-buying type."

"Anyway," I said, "the Milkybars are on you."

"The what?"

"It's just an expression. It means, like…"

"The drinks are on me?"

"Exactly. The drinks are on you. And for the foreseeable future. Unless you choose to blow it all in Vegas."

"I don't like gambling," said Ree, scrutinising the trap I was trying to set for her with my bishop. "I like chess." She nimbly avoided the trap and took one of my knights. How could I have missed that? "I think the first thing we'll do," she said, "is take a vacation in Hawaii. Finding that last record there got me thinking. And I've always wanted to go there. My grandmother was always talking about it."

I made suitably enthusiastic noises, but I had the strange certainty that Hawaii would never happen. At least not for us.

Even as we made love that night I could feel her slipping away from me. As if the money, even the remote prospect of it, had put a fatal distance between us.

The following day I borrowed a car from Berto's garage and drove down to Amoeba Music. It was located in Hollywood, just past the corner of Sunset and Vine.

Now that I had concluded the business aspect of my trip—looking for records—I could get down to the pleasure aspect. Looking for records. I searched the LP racks in Amoeba in a state of happy excitement. I found some nice stuff, mostly on Verve and Cobblestone.

I was on my way out of the store when I spotted a striking young woman looking through the rock albums in the vinyl section.

She held a record bag tightly under one arm as if she was

afraid someone might try to take it away from her. She had long red hair. I went over to the adjacent aisle, where I could watch her without being seen. Then I went into her aisle and stood behind her as she searched the new arrivals rack.

I said, "Thanks for the tear gas grenade."

Nevada turned and stared at me for a moment with genuine astonishment. Then she regained her poise and said, "You're most welcome. They were on special."

"I know," I said. "Two for twenty bucks."

"I never could resist a bargain. What are you doing here, by the way? Are you following me?"

"No. Are you following me?"

"For once, no." She hesitated. "Want to have a coffee?"

I said, "They make good coffee in LA."

"Yes, you're in clover here, aren't you?"

We walked through the morning heat past the glare on glass buildings and into the air-conditioned coolness of the Cinerama Dome. Nevada led the way to the balcony café. She'd obviously been here before. We ordered and sat down in a curving, leather-padded booth.

"How is Tinkler?" she said.

"He's house-sitting for me. And cat-sitting."

"Oh, that's good," she said. "The girls will like that. I was going to ask about them next. How is that going?"

"Tinkler thinks his chronic flatulence may have permanently alienated Fanny's affections."

"Oh, I'm sure she'd never be that shallow." Nevada held up the record bag that was on the table beside her. "You keep staring at this."

"Do I?" I hadn't realised I was so obvious.

"Do you want to know what's inside? Of course you do."

"Of course I do."

"Well, you're not going to find out." She sipped her coffee. "Oh, all right," she said. She picked up the bag and took out the record. It was a vintage gatefold copy of *Their Satanic Majesties Request* by the Rolling Stones, with the original lenticular cover. "It's a present. For Tinkler."

"He'll love it," I said.

She examined the album. "You see it's got the hologram cover."

"Lenticular, actually," I said. "That's what we call it."

"Anyway you can see Mick Jagger's little arms move back and forth. Sort of." She tilted the cover up and down, studying it with satisfaction. "Do you really think he'll like it?"

"Oh yes."

"Are you sure he doesn't have it already?"

"Not the American version."

She stared at the record. "Is this the American version?"

"Yes."

"But it says London on it."

"That's right."

"So the one that's marked London is the American version?"

"Yes."

"I'll never get the hang of this." I was startled to realise that she sounded on the verge of tears.

"Listen," I said quickly. "He'll be delighted with it. He will be *unwholesomely pleased* with it."

She managed a smile. We finished our coffees in silence and left the café. Back outside, blinking in the glare of the sunlight, we paused for an awkward moment before going our separate ways.

When I got back to the house I didn't say anything to Ree about seeing her.

The next morning, as I walked out to my car—I had borrowed it from the garage so often that I'd begun to think of it as my own—the next-door neighbour leaned over the fence and beckoned to me. I struggled to remember her name and came up blank. So I just gave her a big smile instead. She was wearing a red tracksuit and sunglasses.

"Good morning," I said.

"Hi. The guy in the suit was around again."

I realised she meant Gordon Hallett, Dr Tinmouth's lawyer. "The white guy in the suit?"

"Yeah. With another guy."

"Another white guy?"

"No. He looked Mexican or Indian or something. But he was in a suit, too."

Armed with this maddeningly vague information I drove to the garage. As I walked back through the heat and noise Berto came over to me. "I saw that chick again," he said. "The one with the red hair."

"She was here?"

"With the Porsche Carrera, yeah. She asked me to give you this."

It was a printout of a map with a spot marked on it. Above the map a phone number had been written in ballpoint pen. Underneath it was printed an address and a time, and the words:

GOOD TO SEE YOU YESTERDAY. CAN WE
MEET? N x

32. RENDEZVOUS

I didn't tell Ree about my rendezvous with Nevada that evening. She was out doing a gig anyway, so there didn't seem much point. As we ate lunch together at her house we talked about the possibility of her inheritance, about the legal battle that would surely commence. I suggested a game of chess but she said that she wasn't in the mood. Once again I felt like a barrier had come down between us, but I had no idea what it was, or how to deal with it.

Shadows were lengthening and evening was coming on as she left for her gig. I waved as she pulled away.

As soon as she was out of sight, my phone rang. It was Berto at the garage. "It was that chick again," he said. "The redhead. She just came around asking for you. She said she had to change the place. The place where you're meeting."

I could feel myself sweating. I was glad I hadn't got this call while Ree was with me.

Berto read me the directions to the new rendezvous and I wrote it all down. The new address was near Westlake Village, in the vicinity of the Malibu Hills. I stared at it for a moment then took out my phone again. I found the piece of paper with the map of the original meeting point and dialled the number written on it. It went straight to voicemail, a synthesised generic American voice inviting me to leave a message.

I said, "Nevada, what's going on?" and hung up.

Then I went into the kitchen and started making coffee. As the water was coming to the boil my phone bleated, announcing a text. I picked it up and read the message. *Sorry about the changes. Safer this way. Malibu Hills! See you soon. Nx*

I drove west along the Ventura Freeway, famed in story and song, and turned off onto Lindero Canyon Road. From there I took a side road sliced into the rock of what at first I thought were tall hills but gradually began to realise were actually small mountains.

The light was fading to a banked orange glow as I reached the rendezvous, an observation point carved out of the cliff face beside the road. There was a small semi-circular area with a low guardrail fitted around it where you could pause to stare out at the sheer drop, then rolling parkland and finally the tiny lights of suburban housing to the east.

Above the observation area, the road rose into the mountain in a precipitous straight line, which suggested a major feat of either engineering or sheer masochism. About a hundred metres below it was a parking area and I left my car there and walked the rest of the way.

Nevada was waiting for me in the observation area.

She waved as I got out of the car and trudged up towards her. She was still wearing the ridiculous red wig. Actually, I thought as I walked up the hill, it wasn't so ridiculous. It looked quite good on her. The air was clean and cool and smelled of pines and sage.

As I approached her she was staring out at the vista. She didn't turn around and now I was almost beside her. I wondered if she was upset about something.

"Lovely spot," I said. She turned to me.

It wasn't Nevada.

It was Heidi.

"Isn't it just?" she said. "I've got to tell you, it's been an education following you around." Whatever her accent was, it wasn't German. Maybe South African. Or perhaps Australian. She smiled at me. I immediately turned around, thinking whatever her game was, I wanted to get the hell out of there.

And he was standing right behind me.

Heinz.

He had come out of nowhere. Or maybe he had simply followed me up the slope. He smiled, too. "You're not leaving already, are you, mate?" His accent was definitely Australian. "You've only just got here." He seemed genuinely pleased to see me. "We weren't sure you'd come, what with all the chopping and changing." He looked happily at Heidi, at me, at the barren mountain slope where we stood.

Suddenly I realised just how alone I was.

"You've picked a nice place for it, anyway," he said.

"Place for what?" I said. I wanted to keep them talking. My mind was racing. I hadn't seen another car go by since I'd arrived here. We were absolutely isolated, and I'd put myself in their hands.

"We have a little bone to pick with you, mate," said Heinz.

I realised that the only chance I had was to run down

the hill and get back into my car. Somehow do it before they caught up with me. I wondered how fast he was. His bulk suggested strength rather than speed.

She would probably be the real threat, but she was some distance behind me now, since I had started moving away from her and the observation area. "A bone to pick?" I said. "About what?" I took a careful step to my side, keeping my eyes on them. It was not enough to alarm them, but increased my distance from her.

"Saddling us with a trailer-load of fucking useless records." I realised he was talking about Lenny and the Vinyl Crypt, the scam I'd arranged. "We didn't appreciate having our time wasted like that, mate. Going through every single fucking one of them."

"I can still smell them," said Heidi.

"That's the mould," I said, trying to relax and sound conversational. "You know what you have to do about that?" Then I threw myself to one side and started running down the hill.

He was faster than I could have imagined. Despite his bulk he got in front of me and blocked the way, moving with great rapidity and no apparent effort.

"Oh, no, no, no," he said. He had a gun in his hand now. "None of that."

I turned and looked back at Heidi. She was holding a pistol, too.

I began to understand that there was no way out.

"Let's get on with it," she said.

He looked at her. "What do you think?"

"Over the edge." She nodded at the abyss beyond the guardrail. "Just one more careless tourist."

"Fair enough." He pointed the gun at me. I backed away from him slowly. He was forcing me towards her.

"Wait," I said.

Heinz shook his head good-naturedly. "That's what they always say." He moved towards me, backing me into the observation area where she waited. I was now on one side of the semi-circle of tarmac. They were on the other, watching me speculatively.

"It won't look so good if I've got a bullet in me," I said. "That's not just one more careless tourist."

"He's right, you know," said Heinz. "You take his left arm, I'll take his right."

"Don't forget to get his phone."

"Oh yeah. Points for remembering, babe."

They moved towards me.

Just then there was the high thin sound of a motor approaching. We all looked up and saw the headlights of a car coming down the steep slope of the mountain road towards us. Above the headlights a blue light was spinning. Then we heard the brief blurting of a siren.

The noise a police car makes when they want you to pull over.

I looked at Heinz and Heidi. They had moved close together and they were both holding their guns out of sight. He looked across at me and said, "If you say anything, we'll kill the cops and then kill you." I backed away from him.

"Hey," said Heidi. But I kept moving until I was as far away from them as I could get, on the other side of the observation area.

Then I realised she wasn't talking to me. They weren't paying any attention to me.

Instead, they were both staring up the mountain road.

Because the car wasn't stopping. It wasn't even slowing down. It *increased* its speed, the engine a rising powerful snarl as it hit the bottom of the steep section of road, bounced up over the kerb and sped headlong into the observation area.

Heinz and Heidi had started to move, but it was too late. The car hit them both full on, with the sound of a sledgehammer striking a side of beef.

Then there was the scream of brakes as it pulled up, just short of the guardrail. Heinz and Heidi both continued over it, however, flung by the force of the impact, sailing out into the darkness.

Heidi was as loose as a rag doll, eyes shut and mouth open. Heinz, on the other hand, had his eyes wide open and was staring at me.

I saw his look of aggrieved astonishment as he flew out into the void.

Then they were gone in the darkness.

Hundreds of feet below them, the rocky floor of the canyon waited, black as night and deep as forever. I stared down, but I could see nothing.

The door of the car opened and Ree stepped out. She took the blue light off the roof.

"Who's your guardian angel now?" she said.

33. BUSINESS CARD

We drove for miles in silence. Back down the mountain.
Back to the freeway. Finally Ree turned to look at me, with
the lights from the dashboard on her face, and said, "It was
kill or be killed."

"You won't get any argument from me." I was still
shaking, as if I had a bad fever. And I kept staring in the rear-
view mirror as though I was expecting something to come
after us. But what? Ghosts? The wrath of God? As the shock
wore off, my brain was slowly beginning to work again.

I said, "You intercepted the messages?"

She glanced over again and gave me a crooked smile.
"You see what happens when you try and sneak off to meet
your ex?"

We were driving through Hidden Hills now, where
Ventura Freeway became Ventura Boulevard. "What about
my car?" I said. I had suddenly remembered, with a sickly
acceleration of my heartbeat, that we'd left it parked back
there, just below the observation area.

"It's all taken care of," said Ree. She peered out into the
traffic. "In fact…" She slowed down at the lights, signalled

and turned right. We were in a residential street. She reversed the signal, turned left, and we pulled into the parking lot of a KFC. At the far end of the building, on the blind side, Berto was waiting for us, standing beside my car.

We pulled up next to him and got out. He came over and slapped me on the shoulder. "Sorry to rat you out to your old lady, bro, but I could tell something wasn't right."

I said, "When she dropped off the message... They were setting a trap for me. By pretending to be Nevada. The redhead in the Porsche that second time was actually Heidi. But you spotted it was a different girl."

"No, dude. All white chicks look the same to me. But I spotted that it was a different *car*." He grinned at us. "Anybody want to split a bucket of wings?"

My stomach turned over. "No thanks." I looked back at the car we'd driven here in. Besides the dents I could see at the front, there was no doubt all sorts of DNA evidence on it. "What are you going to do with the car?"

Ree smiled and shrugged. "By tomorrow that car won't exist."

"Speaking of which..." said Berto. He took the keys from her and got behind the wheel.

"Thanks, Berto," said Ree. He gave a casual wave and pulled away. We looked at each other. The night was cool and there was a steady rumble of traffic passing on the boulevard. Headlights moved across her face. My brain was working now. I couldn't stop it.

I said, "It just happened to be the perfect spot."

"What do you mean?"

"It just happened to be the perfect spot to ambush them. For you to wait up the hill and then come zooming out of nowhere and nail them."

She shrugged. "I think I nailed them pretty good. And just in time, by the look of things."

"You chose the location," I said. "It was you who changed the rendezvous. You sent a message to me and you sent a message to them."

She nodded. "It was the way it had to be. We had to draw them out. We had to deal with them."

"How did you get their number?"

"It was printed on the bottom of the map she gave to Berto. So we trimmed it off."

"And wrote another one on it," I said. "So when I thought I was calling them, I was calling you."

"Right."

"And what did you do, text them using my phone? The bugged one, the one you kept in London?"

"That's right."

I said, "So you set it all up. You laid a trap for them."

"I guess."

"You staked me out," I said. "To lure them there. Like a tiger for a goat. I mean, a goat for a tiger."

She came to me and put her hand on my chest. "You were right the first time," she said, "Tiger."

For a moment, I almost bought it. But then I took her hand away. I didn't say anything, but she must have seen it in my eyes. Her voice trembled a little and she looked down.

"Anything I did, I did to protect us both."

I said, "Thanks for keeping me in the loop," and turned and walked away into the night.

* * *

I found a quiet bar and had a few drinks then caught a taxi back home. I mean, to Ree's house. I didn't know whether she would be there or not. I wasn't sure which would be worse. I just wanted to get my stuff and get out, find a hotel. But when I climbed out of the cab the house was dark and silent. I paid the driver and he pulled away. I suddenly thought longingly of Clean Head and I realised how keenly I missed London. I just wanted to go home.

I turned and walked towards the house.

A man stepped out of the shadows.

He was a small man with angular features, dark skin and a pale suit. I must have moved back very abruptly at the sight of him because he said, "I'm sorry to startle you. I came by earlier, but no one was at home."

"Who are you?" My voice was curt and hoarse in my own ears.

"I'm Easy Geary."

I stared at him. He didn't look anything like Easy Geary of course. He was even the wrong height. Geary had been a huge bear of a man. In addition to which, there was the small matter that this guy was, at most, in his early thirties. Whereas Easy Geary would be over a hundred.

I decided either he was insane, or I'd misheard him.

"I'm sorry," I said. "I didn't catch that."

"I am Easy Geary. My name."

"Okay."

There must have been something in my voice because he scrabbled for a business card and handed it to me. "Gordon Hallett gave me your address. Dr Tinmouth wanted that we should meet. He didn't say why, but he seemed very excited about it."

The card read:

Philip Ysaguirre

"Philip Easy Geary," he said.

I looked at him. I said, "Ysaguirre. So that's how you pronounce it."

I was sitting on the steps when Ree pulled up and got out of her car. "Haven't you got your keys?" she said.

"I've got them. I just don't feel like going inside. I don't feel like going anywhere."

She sat down beside me. "Look," she said, "I'm sorry about what happened."

I watched the moths attacking the porch light. "So am I."

"Once they knew about me, about who my grandfather was, they were going to come after me." She looked at me. "They would have killed you and then they would have killed me."

"I'm sure you're right."

She reached over and squeezed my knee. "I had to take them out. Like I said, kill or be killed. And they were suspicious because we'd changed the place to meet. They would have sniffed it out if you'd known about it. Don't you see? You had to be in the dark when you arrived there. You couldn't know anything." She peered into my face. "When it turned out that it was the Aryan Twins, and not Nevada, your surprise had to be genuine."

"Well, it fucking was," I said.

She took my hand and we both sat in silence and watched the moths. She said, "They found another box at the garage. Of Dr Tinmouth's books. It turns out there wasn't twelve boxes, there were thirteen."

"Thirteen," I said. "Lucky for some."

"It was just a small box. When they put it in the storage area it was set behind some boxes of auto parts. So we didn't notice it until now."

"The thirteenth box," I said.

"It's full of books…"

"About Professor Jellaway."

She stared at me with those disconcerting eyes. "How did you know that?"

"You had a visitor. You just missed him." I turned and gazed at her. "He was some kind of distant cousin of yours. His name was Philip Easy Geary. Spelled like this." I handed her the business card. She read it then looked at me.

"What does it mean?"

"Ysaguirre was Jellaway's real surname. And it means that when your grandfather was looking for a new alias he chose a phonetic pronunciation of his original family name."

"His original family name?"

I nodded. "Easy Geary was Burns Hobartt. But Burns Hobartt was Professor Jellaway."

She put a hand to her head. "Wait a minute. This is all just a little too…"

"Tell me about it. But I've gone over the timeline, and it all fits. Jellaway vanishes from the scene and Hobartt appears. Hobartt makes an exit and Geary turns up." I watched it sinking in. "It explains so much," I said. "Like the reason why Burns Hobartt was content with obscurity, playing in small territory bands, until the fire that disfigured him in 1935." I looked at her. "Jazz critics have always said it was as if the fire triggered something in him. Sparked his genius. People have surmised that perhaps it was because it gave him an awareness of his own mortality. But it was a lot simpler than that. The fire took away his face. It made him unrecognisable. It freed him."

"Holy shit," said Ree. "All three of them?"

"There's a sort of inevitable symmetry to it. Professor Jellaway was screwed by his music publishers the Spike brothers and Burns Hobartt was similarly screwed by the Davenports and Easy Geary was screwed by AMI. But it was all the same corporation. Spike Brothers Music became Davenport Music and Davenport Music became AMI. And it was all the same man—Jellaway, Hobartt, Geary."

I looked at her.

"Which means you don't just own a chunk of AMI."

"No?"

"No. You own a controlling interest."

34. LONDON

I said, "It's incredible. He was a great genius of jazz in three different eras. Every time the music changed, he rose to the top. He was like the Stravinsky of jazz."

"Never mind that," said Tinkler in London. "Tell me about the money."

"Well, there's inevitably going to be a battle-royale in the courts, but she's his direct descendant. So, basically, a cornerstone of the American music and media business belongs to her."

"But *how much*?" said Tinkler.

"Well, the Davenport cousins were the children of the Spike brothers. Davenport was their real name. 'Spike' was a highly appropriate *nom de plume* or maybe *nom de guerre*. The kids were the son of one and the daughter of the other. And their company is the same corporation as their fathers'. Clear so far?"

"Suppose I say yes?"

"Basically, when we discovered Ree's grandfather was Burns Hobartt, she owned a big chunk of that corporation because it was founded on his music. But now we know her grandfather was also Professor Jellaway, that big chunk suddenly gets bigger. In fact, it becomes a majority shareholding."

"But how much does she get? Exact numbers, please."

"Apparently sixty-two and a half per cent. Of everything."

Tinkler whistled tunelessly.

I said, "Don't forget to book Clean Head to pick us up at the airport. International arrivals are at Terminal 2."

"See if you can remind me half a dozen more times."

Clean Head did meet us and in fact Tinkler came with her. He'd brought two bottles of champagne to welcome us back. Ree was very touched.

We drank one bottle on the way home. We dropped Tinkler off at his house in Putney, then headed to my place. As we unloaded our baggage, including the remaining bottle of champagne, Clean Head gave me a sardonic look and said, "Your boy asked me out."

"Tinkler?"

She nodded. "Mmm hmm."

"Did you say yes?"

"I said maybe."

We paid her and she drove away. Ree and I hefted our bags and set off across the square towards my bungalow, and the boiler room where the dragon had once slumbered. The dragon was still having his funeral—indeed the crane was even now delving into the basin and winching up a large piece of what had once been the boiler from what had once been the boiler room. The amount of noise and general commotion was impressive.

I looked down at the work site, cautiously because they

still hadn't replaced the safety rail, and saw to my surprise that some progress had actually been made in our absence. The old boiler room was now well on its way to its new fate as luxury flats, tennis courts or quite possibly a pilates centre.

The cats came streaking to meet us as we stepped through the door. They swirled around my legs, creating a navigational hazard. Ree watched us with amusement. I said, "See how pleased they are to see me after Uncle Tinkler's reign of terror."

"He probably spoiled them rotten." Ree set her bags down on the sofa. "I'll let you have some quality time with your cats." She went into the bedroom. I put the bottle of champagne on the table and then I set my luggage down on the sofa beside hers. Fanny instantly jumped on it. For some reason she had made it her life's mission to try and kill my rucksack and whenever I had it out she gave it another instalment of the old needle-sharp claws and teeth.

She waited impatiently while I unzipped it and searched around inside. As soon as I found what I was looking for and left the bag unguarded, she pounced on it and attacked again.

While she gave the rucksack hell I took the bug buster, the Stone Circle 10, proud souvenir of the Westfield Century City mall, and checked its batteries. Its charge was fine, so I switched it on and started to sweep my house with it. In the same instant the doorbell rang, as if the two devices were wired together.

As I walked towards the door I read the result on the bug buster's screen without surprise.

I set it down as I opened the door.

He was standing in the doorway, almost filling it. He had an expensive-looking black backpack slung over one shoulder. On his left leg there was some kind of medical brace. In his right hand was a gun, which he pointed at my stomach.

He smiled at me and I backed away. He followed me into the house.

"Heinz just walked in," I said loudly. "And he's got a gun."

"I don't know why you keep calling me Heinz, mate."

Ree walked in from the bedroom, drawing a brush through her hair. "What did you say, honey?"

I turned to look at her and Heinz promptly stepped behind me and pointed his gun at her over my shoulder. I could feel the metal of it cold against my neck. He addressed Ree. "Come into the room slowly and sit down. Glad you could make it. No funny business or…" He moved the gun a casual fraction so the muzzle was now against my skull.

Ree came in and sat down. I felt him relax and the gun moved away from my head. I thought that if ever there was a time when I should make a grab for the gun it was now. I had no sooner begun to think this than Heinz shoved me forward, hitting me in the back with an arm like a piston.

I stumbled into the sitting room and had to grab the table to stop from falling. Ree half rose to help me, but he pointed his gun at her. "Sit down. Both of you."

We sat at the table and he sat opposite us. "You should see your faces. I guess you're wondering why I'm still around. Well, there was a tree on that slope. Just the one tree. And I landed in it." He smiled at us. "So I guess it was just meant to be." He put a hand to his forehead and I saw he had some scratches that I hadn't noticed before. "So I just got this. And this." He patted the leg brace. "I've been telling girls I got these trail biking and I have to tell you it's been going down a storm." He sighed wistfully. "It feels funny to be travelling alone again, but I kind of like it."

He looked at the bottle of champagne. "Having a celebration?" Neither of us said anything. It wasn't clear whether we were meant to. It was hard to know the etiquette of being held at gunpoint by a madman. "You can have a glass if you like. I'll give each of you a glass." He looked at us. "Straight up. I mean it. This is an unpleasant business, but if everyone just behaves professionally, in a civilised manner, we can get through it with the minimum of fuss."

The doorbell rang.

The merest second after the doorbell rang, and long before any normal person could have even begun to answer it, the door popped open and a figure stepped in. "Greetings, groovers," he said.

It was Stinky.

He ambled into the living room and looked at me and Ree and Heinz. And at the gun, which was now pointing at him.

"What's going on?" said Stinky. But I could see by his face that he already had an all-too-clear idea.

"Sit down," said Heinz. Stinky sat down. "You're just in time, mate. We were about to open the champagne." He looked at us. "You can all have a glass of bubbly before you go." He smiled at us, friendly but firm. "But whatever happens, you *will* go."

"Go where?" said Stinky in a small voice. Everyone ignored him.

"What are you going to do?" said Ree. "Shoot us?"

"I don't see why not," said Heinz. He nodded towards the front door. "The sound of all that building work should more than cover the noise."

I said, "You can't really believe you'll get away with this." My voice sounded strangely normal.

"Again, friend, I don't see why not." He reached into his jacket and took out a fat plastic package filled with white powder. It was as thick as an overstuffed sandwich. He slapped it on the table. "Cocaine. Very high-grade cocaine. You see, what I'm going to do is spread this all over the place. Just chuck it over everything. You're thinking, *that's a bit of a waste*. And you're right. But here's what it will do. It will convince the cops that there must have been even more cocaine here. So much that someone could afford to just leave this amount lying around. And they'll deduce that this whole thing was some kind of drug deal gone tragically wrong." He looked at me. "The millionaire crate digger got carried away with his newfound wealth and fell in with a bad crowd. I think everyone will buy that."

"You're going to kill us?" said Stinky.

"Yes, mate. Sorry." He was polite, apologetic but implacable. I could see Stinky believed him. He visibly wilted, sinking down in his chair as if his body mass had suddenly dropped. "Actually, you know what, come to think of it," said Heinz, "you could have some of the coke too. I don't see why not. In fact it will help sell the whole thing. There you go. Cocaine and champagne. That's fair enough, isn't it? Takes the sting away a bit."

"We're going to die," said Stinky.

"Yes, mate."

Stinky gave a sharp, anguished intake of breath, then turned and looked at me. "Since we're going to die," he said, "I want to apologise to you, Chef, for ruining your career."

I said, "What do you mean?"

"Your career as a DJ, as a broadcaster. Every chance I got, I did everything I could to sabotage it." There were tears beginning to run down his face. "It was like that Bob Marley song. Every time you planted a seed I killed it before it could grow."

"That's 'I Shot the Sheriff'," said Heinz. We might as well have been having a pub quiz.

Stinky was looking at me, big fat tears running down his cheeks. "It was because I knew you were so much better than I was. You had a better voice. You knew more about music. If you'd got started I never would have stood a chance."

Heinz roared with laughter. His amusement was enormous and sincere and I realised that Stinky had inadvertently bought us all a few more minutes of life. "Will you listen to that?" said Heinz. He looked at me. "When his turn comes, I should let you do the honours, mate."

Just then Fanny, who had been hiding behind the luggage on the sofa, jumped up and came streaking past. She raced through the room, as she always did when she was uncertain of the company, and went clattering out the cat flap. Heinz stared after her, the gun aimed at the door, distracted for an instant.

I picked up the bottle of champagne and swung it at his head.

Heinz swatted it aside, casually, as if it were a dragonfly. The bottle was knocked from my hand. It sailed through the air and bounced onto the sofa, landing soft and unbroken. Heinz turned and hit me.

His fist crunched into my face right beside my left eye and the room vanished in an explosion of white flame. I found myself lying on the floor. There was no pain as such yet. My face felt hot and numb. But the white flames were retreating from the periphery of my vision. I could see that Stinky was cowering in a corner while Heinz was turning in surprise to see Ree coming at him. Her arm was swinging, slicing at him with something in her hand that gleamed.

The clasp knife.

She must have carried that over in her checked baggage because they sure as hell wouldn't have let her have it in her carry-on. These and other thoughts flashed through my mind in a vivid and leisurely fashion as I stood up on rubbery, wavering legs and tottered towards them.

On the way I stooped over the sofa and picked up the champagne bottle again. I continued on my endless journey to reach Heinz, watching helplessly as he laughed and grabbed Ree's wrist and twisted it until she dropped the knife.

"Spunky!" he said to her. I suddenly found I was standing behind him, bottle in my hand.

This time I made no attempt to go for his head. Instead I hit his hand with my champagne bottle, good and hard—the hand that was holding the gun.

He had seen me out of the corner of his eye and tried to move to avoid the blow but it was too late. The gun went skittering across the floor, ricocheted off the base of a standing lamp and bounced into the kitchen. Meanwhile our sturdy friend the bottle rolled across the floor, still unbroken, and disappeared under an armchair.

Heinz slammed Ree against the wall, then turned to deal with me.

I saw the sledgehammer of his suntanned hand approaching my face in dreamy slow motion, like a distant train. I was careful to close my eyes before the blow landed.

The blow didn't land.

I opened my eyes again and saw Ree had grabbed his arm from behind and was pulling it back. Stinky still stood frozen in the corner.

I started looking around for that unbreakable champagne bottle.

The back door opened and we all turned around to see Nevada standing there. My first thought was that she wasn't wearing that fucking wig anymore. My second was that she was holding a gun.

She aimed it at Heinz, who promptly turned and fled. He went straight out the front door. It was so unexpected that we all just turned and stared at each other.

I was out in the square less than a second after Heinz, so I saw it all happen.

They were swinging a section of the boiler above us on the crane.

Its huge shadow swept across the plantings in the middle of the square, and then over Heinz. There was a shout and then a strangely musical metallic twang and the big shadow twitched and shifted and the boiler section came falling down out of the clear sky. Heinz was scrambling through the plantings, retreating in a straight line from my front door. He must have felt the shadow cut off the sunlight because he looked up and saw several tons of metal floating quietly down towards him.

He leapt to one side. His agility was astonishing. He jumped clear across the planter and landed outside it. The boiler component crashed harmlessly down behind him in a crunching shower of leaves and earth. The ground shuddered beneath me.

Heinz had landed just on the edge of the deep basin

created by the excavation of the boiler house. He was staring back at the monstrous piece of metal that had so nearly crushed him. He was grinning at his miraculous escape. He saw me and winked. Then he turned to run.

As he turned he came down hard on his left leg, the one with the brace. The impact caused him to stumble a little and he fell to the side, towards the basin. He reached out to steady himself, to grab the safety rail. But the safety rail was gone.

He fell through the space where it used to be, and straight down.

Into the basin.

I ran and looked down. Heinz was lying on a pile of building rubble twenty feet below. There had been no helpful trees this time. His face, suddenly pale, was staring blindly up at me. He had come to rest on a heap of concrete blocks, each one the size of a shoe box. His head—no longer quite the shape a head should be—rested on one of the blocks as if on a pillow. His neck was bent almost at a right angle. A dark stain spreading out beneath him was turning the grey concrete-dust brown.

Ree and Nevada and Stinky came running up behind me. They looked down. Below us in the basin, work was stopping as people gradually began to realise what had happened.

Stinky turned away and threw up. I didn't feel sick at all. I felt something much worse than that. A deep evil delight.

35. THE RULE OF THREE

I was busy trying out my new coffee grinder. The cats were watching me as I unwrapped the thing, set it up, and put in the beans. I said, "Now, this very expensive new coffee grinder is supposedly completely silent and won't offend the sensibilities of cats. So I hope you like it. Did I mention how expensive it was?"

I put in the beans. I switched it on. There was a faint but discernible and very eerie high-pitched buzzing. The cats fled in mortal terror. I sighed, looked at the price tag and got on with making my coffee. It was just smelling great when the doorbell rang.

It was Nevada.

"My god," she said. "Can I have some of that coffee?"

She came in and settled into her favourite chair. "There isn't a half-naked American meretrix about to spring out at me is there?"

"No. Ree is out shopping."

"Yes, I imagine she's going to be doing a lot of that."

"She's buying presents for the boys back at Berto's garage."

"Yes, they seemed like a fun bunch. They were very eager to inspect the undercarriage of my Porsche. So to speak."

"And, by the way, I know what 'meretrix' means."

"Oh. Sorry."

I poured the coffee.

"My god, that smells wonderful. It didn't come out of a monkey's sphincter, did it?"

"A civet, you mean," I said. "And that stuff is called *kopi luwak*. This is *ca phe cut chon*." I was blinding her with science. They were one and the same. Anything to get her to shut up and try the coffee.

She peered into her cup. "I'm not sure I should trust you."

"Likewise," I said. That killed the conversation for a minute. We sipped our coffee.

Nevada said, "I've been meaning to ask. What happened to Heinz's gun?"

"Call me sentimental, call me foolish. I dropped it off Hammersmith Bridge when no one was looking."

"Really?"

"Yes. It's now at the bottom of a rather large river. I hope you didn't want it."

"No," she said. "Just curious. I'm much more interested in what happened to the cocaine."

"Now, that *is* interesting. After Stinky puked—you remember, when he saw Heinz's mortal remains—he went back into my house to clean up. By the time I got back inside he was hurrying off, looking pretty pale. He didn't say anything, which was unusual for Stinky. It was only after he was gone that I realised the cocaine was gone, too."

"Stinky took the coke?"

"He was never one to miss an opportunity."

"My god. The little stinker."

We sat and drank our coffee. She seemed to be waiting for me to say something. What I eventually said was, "How much did you know?"

"Know?"

"About all this."

"About as much as you did, most of the time, I suppose. I knew that Mr Hibiki wanted this record and he was willing to pay a hell of a lot to find it."

"You knew enough to carry a gun."

"Mr Hibiki was pretty clear that other interests would be after the same item and that they would be, shall we say, highly motivated. And not above doing us harm."

"The Aryan fuckers."

"The late Aryan fuckers. I understand that something very final befell Heidi in LA?"

"It seems probable."

"How sad," said Nevada. She didn't sound any sadder than I was. "Well, anyway, to answer your question, all I knew was that we were after the record, and so were these others. That's what I knew. What I *deduced*, from the money being spent on the project, was that something of considerable value was involved. Of value to men like the good Mr Hibiki."

"Who the hell is Mr Hibiki?"

"Well, he's very senior at one of Japan's largest music and media corporations. One of which occupies much the same market sector as American Music Industries—our old friends AMI. And you might say there's a certain friendly rivalry between the two firms. The way there is between a snake and a mongoose."

"So that's as much as you knew when you met me?"

"That's as much as I knew then. Virtually nothing. In contrast to Mr Hibiki, who knew essentially everything. Or at least he knew the essentials."

"Which were?"

"That if he played his cards right, he could take advantage of a huge shift in the corporate structure of AMI."

I said, "You mean, when it was discovered that Ree held a controlling interest in it."

"Yes. Ridiculous name, that, by the way. Ree. Anyway, this would have big consequences in the global marketplace. And since he knew it was coming, Hibiki was well placed to take advantage of the consequences."

"Profitable advantage."

"Yes. Especially if he knew exactly *when* it would happen and could position himself to get the maximum benefit from it."

"Basically he had to get his ducks in a row," I said.

"Exactly."

"So he actually *wanted* Ree to discover who her grandfather was, and go after AMI for ownership."

"Yes. But not until he was ready. Mr Hibiki wanted to sit tight and wait for the ideal market conditions, so he could make a killing with insider knowledge." She looked at me. "That was pretty much the situation when we saw each other in Japan. At that point, Hibiki just planned to sit back and let his scheme mature. But unfortunately for his plans, your friend Ree was busy in Los Angeles putting two and two together herself."

"She's a clever girl," I said. "Plays a lot of chess. It's good for the brain."

"I can fucking play chess," said Nevada abruptly. "And I could have given you a stupid fucking nickname if I'd known you wanted one."

"It was never a deal-breaker."

"What were we talking about? Oh yes. Good old Ree. She had begun to work out who she was, and what was owed to her. But even then things might have worked out for Hibiki." She gave me a wry smile. "But then you got involved. When she enlisted your help."

"Always happy to help," I said.

"And that was when the shit really hit the fan. Because the Aryan Twins still had you under surveillance when she turned up. And if she had been off their radar before, she was definitely on it now. And the Aryans—or the people who were running them—also began to slowly put two and two together, at a rapidly escalating rate."

"And who were the people running them?"

"Have a wild guess."

"AMI?" I said.

"Or one of its thousands of subsidiaries. Some highly deniable rogue dummy shell front of a corporation."

"Shell front?" I said. "Is that a word?"

"It's two words. But you know what I mean."

"Yes, I suppose I do."

"So Heinz and Heidi worked in opposition to you, as they started to realise what was really afoot."

"They were in opposition to me." I looked at her. "What about you?"

She shrugged. "I was just supposed to act as a spoiler. To get to the records before you did. To stop you piecing it all together." She sighed. "Fat chance."

"So you were working against me," I said. "Like the Aryan Twins."

"There was one significant difference. They were ready, willing and able to kill you. I was just trying to slow you down. And only long enough for Mr Hibiki to be in an ideal position. To get his ducks in a row. Odd expression. Can you imagine how hard that would actually be? With real ducks?"

"So he could make his killing."

"Yes. But you let the cat out of the bag. Another odd turn of phrase. What sort of bastard would put a cat in a bag in the first place? What is it about us and animals?"

"But," I said, "Mr Hibiki didn't make his killing."

"Not a killing. He had to act prematurely. And he had to merely settle for a serious injury, so to speak. Instead of a killing. In other words, instead of the billion or so he must have envisaged making, he only realised a few tens of millions, the poor soul."

"The poor soul."

"So now he's a bit pissed off."

"Pissed off at you?" I said. It seemed unreasonable.

Nevada shook her head. "Pissed off at *you*."

"Oh well," I said. "We can't put the genie back in the bottle."

We sipped our coffee. She said, "One other thing. I have a confession to make. I bugged your living room."

"I knew you had."

"You knew?"

"I knew it as soon as I realised someone was coming in here and feeding the cats."

She laughed. "It's true. I couldn't resist. They're such little *honeys*."

431

"What did you feed them?"

"Lamb chops. Nice meaty ones. With all the fat and bone trimmed out."

"Yes, they would have liked that. You did a pretty good job of concealing the evidence."

She said, "Most of the evidence was eaten by cats. I can't believe you're not more upset that I planted a listening device in your house."

"Did you get Mr Maori Tattoo Five O'Clock Shadow to help you install it?"

"No. Good lord, I would never do that to you. I installed it all by my own little self."

"Then I don't mind. What's more, I was actually counting on it. You might remember me announcing in a loud voice that Heinz had arrived. With a gun. I'd just swept the room with a bug buster and I knew you were listening."

"You knew *someone* was listening."

"I knew it was you, just like I knew it was you feeding the cats. I was just praying you were listening somewhere nearby."

"I rented a room in the Abbey. The rates there are extortionate, you know."

"And you got here in time to save us. All of us."

"Even Stinky," she said.

"I forgive you. For bugging my house. And for saving Stinky's life."

She smiled a ghost of a smile. "It was a package deal. By the way—what happened to it? My listening device. I couldn't help noticing it's gone off the air."

"I'm afraid I stomped on it."

"How appropriate, for a bug. And where is what's left of it?"

"I've lost track. The cats were using it as a toy. Batting it around the place."

"Oh well, at least it's still serving a useful function."

"I've got something else I want to ask you." I paused. "That I *need* to ask you."

"Fire away."

I refilled our cups. I sat down across from her. I looked at her and took a deep breath. "Despite their verifiably complete incompetence, do you really expect me to believe that our lovable local contractors just happened to drop a section of a boiler weighing several tons from a crane at exactly the moment Heinz happened to be standing under it?"

"I'm not asking you to believe anything." Nevada sipped her coffee decorously. I sat there watching her in silence until finally she said, "If I was going to say something about the matter I'd say that obviously any such act would be conspiracy to murder and murder for hire and assorted other really naughty *faux pas* that no one should be involved in. And if anyone was involved in such activity they wouldn't talk about it, would they?"

"I suppose not."

She said, "Although they'd probably find themselves at least compelled to observe that for the sort of sums of money involved—theoretically involved—in bribing someone to commit such a dastardly act—it would be galling that in the end the fucking fuckers fucked it up."

"Perhaps you remember my earlier remarks about gross incompetence."

"Well, anyway, as I say, an entirely theoretical discussion."

"Understood."

She peered into her cup. It was almost empty. "Do you

want another one?" I said.

"No, I have to be going." She stood up and then paused. "When I was listening, when I was eavesdropping, I heard quite a lot of you and her. Together. The two of you. And I realised something. I think she really does care about you." She stared at me. Her eyes seemed suddenly pale, like the sky. "I don't want to stand in the way. Of the two of you. I think you can be happy with her." She bent down and kissed me on the cheek. "Goodbye."

Then she left.

Ree got in about an hour later. "Where are all your bags?" I said. "Your shopping?"

"I left them in the taxi."

"With Clean Head?"

"Yes." That seemed a little odd, I thought.

"Were there a lot of them?" I said. "The bags?"

"I didn't just go shopping. I spent a lot of the morning talking to lawyers."

"That sounds serious. What's up?"

She sat down and looked me in the eye with the unreadable expression I'd seen over dozens of games of chess. "We will win," she said. "In court, we're going to win."

"Of course," I said.

"But AMI are going to put up a fight. We may have to find my grandfather's grave and get a DNA sample, to prove I am who I am. And even if we do that, there's going to be a legal shit storm like you've never seen. You're a lot better off out of it."

My stomach went cold. "What do you mean, 'out of it'?"

She shook her head. "I'm sorry, Chef, I just don't have time for anyone in my life right now."

"What are you talking about?"

"I have to devote myself to this legal battle. One hundred per cent. Twenty-four-seven. Day and night." She put a hand on my face. I couldn't believe what I was hearing. "I'm sorry," she said. "Maybe later. When things settle down." She kissed me on the cheek.

She was packed and gone within half an hour. Clean Head drove her to the airport. It only occurred to me later that she'd kissed me goodbye on the opposite cheek to Nevada.

Perfect symmetry.

They say things come in threes and later that day I got the letter from the bank.

"They can't do that," said Tinkler.

"Evidently they can."

"But how can they possibly justify—"

"You know when you read about these computer errors and some lucky chump discovers that a vast fortune has inadvertently been transferred into his bank account? They're saying that's what happened to me."

"So they just took all the money *out* of your account?"

"Returned it to its rightful owner, they said. Which would be Mr Hibiki."

"I can't believe it."

"Nevada said he was pissed off at me. I guess this is his way of demonstrating it."

"But you can prove the money is yours," said Tinkler.

"No I can't."

"Show them the press cuttings. Crate Digger Strikes Gold."

"I did. And they laughed in my face."

"That doesn't seem possible."

I said, "Did I mention we were talking about a bank here?"

He peered at me, face pale and eyes round. It was funny; he was more shocked than I was. "You mean, someone can just put money in your account and take it out?"

"That's the way it works. In fact, it's a pretty good summary of the capitalist system."

"So they didn't leave you with anything?"

"I've got what's in my pocket."

"This is outrageous," said Tinkler. "What did they say to you?"

"They said they're amazed I'm not being prosecuted for the money I've already spent. Money that wasn't rightfully mine."

"What did you say to that?"

"I said I wasn't so amazed."

Tinkler shook his head. "Can they really get away with this?"

"They already have. The super-rich giveth and the super-rich taketh away."

Tinkler got up and went to the shelf on the far wall of his listening room and took a record down. It was the copy of *Beat Beat Beat* I'd bought for him with my first flush of wealth. It was a ten-inch album issued on German Decca for the Sonderauflage record club in 1965. It had been withdrawn after only two thousand copies were issued. Very rare.

"Here, take this," he said. "You can sell it for a shitload of money." He handed me the record.

I shook my head. I said, "Greater love hath no man than to offer to sell his rare German Rolling Stones ten-inch LP for his fellow man. But things aren't quite that bad." I handed it back to him.

He studied me dolefully. "Aren't they?"

I said, "I've got my health, I've got my house, I've got my cats, I've got my friends."

"I notice friends come fourth," said Tinkler.

"You're lucky you feature at all."

36. OUT OF THE RAIN

The next morning I got up early. Dawn was a faint pink promise in the winter darkness. Fanny and Turk were happy to have me up and around, keeping cat hours almost. I remembered what I had said to Tinkler and I went through all my pockets. I had several handfuls of American currency that had travelled back with me from my visit. I put on my crate-diving shoes—I mean, my crate-digging shoes—and I went into Richmond.

I was waiting outside Marks and Spencer when it opened. The shop had a bureau de change on its upper level and there I converted the dollars into sterling. I now had just enough money to buy a one-week travel card, which I did.

I hopped on a bus and started searching. I travelled to Twickenham and worked my way back, hitting every charity shop, junk shop or antique shop that might be harbouring a box of records. The following day I did the same thing, starting in Wimbledon. The third day it was Chelsea. On the fourth, Shepherd's Bush. On the fifth day, when I began my hunt in Chiswick, I found it.

It was a copy of *Pet Sounds* by the Beach Boys on the

Capitol rainbow-rimmed label—an original mono pressing instead of the fake stereo. A British copy, but immaculate. That night I flipped it on the Internet and made enough money to buy food for me and the cats for the next two weeks.

And maybe even some grapes for Tinkler.

I was just cutting up some lamb chops for the cats—I'd decided to splash out—when there was a knock at the door. I wiped my hands and went to answer it.

It was pouring with rain outside.

Nevada was standing there in a white raincoat, wearing her white hat with a strawberry on it. She had a suitcase with her. She looked at me. "Can I come in?"

I stood back and she brushed past, transferring a fair amount of moisture from her raincoat onto me in the process. "Sorry about that," she said. Her suitcase was on wheels and she wheeled it into the sitting room with a tiny rumbling sound that immediately drew the cats. "Oh, look who's here," she said. "Have you come to hear the suitcase? Have you? Come to hear the wheels on the suitcase? Does it sound silly? Does my suitcase sound silly?" She patted and stroked them. "Your coats are nice and warm and dry. You're sensible girls, aren't you? Inside on a day like this. Not like your Auntie Nevada. *Her* coat is soaking wet."

"Here, let me take it," I said.

"No, it's fine." She hung it up on one of the pegs in the hallway and took off her hat and stuck it on the peg beside her coat. It looked jaunty and disembodied there. We went into the kitchen and sat down. I didn't know what to say.

"Do you want some coffee?"

"In a minute," she said. She stared at her feet. "I've made wet footprints everywhere. I'll clean them up in a minute."

"Don't worry."

"I don't quite know where to start."

"Well, don't look at me. My brain has exploded."

"I'm not surprised." She gave me a small, shy smile. "I heard what happened. What Mr Hibiki did to you."

"Oh."

"So I quit."

"You did what?" I said.

"Quit that very day. And told him to fuck off."

"Honestly?"

"Of course. If I'd known the Japanese for 'fuck off' I would have told him in Japanese. I mean, how dare he behave like that? That man is so *petty*." She looked at me. Her makeup had smudged a little in the rain, giving her an enticing raccoon look. "So you're broke now?"

"Just about. Stony broke. Yes."

"Well, you can share my money," she said. "Whatever I've got stashed away."

"I hope it's not stashed in any bank account Hibiki can get his hands on."

"Not anymore," she said, and put a fist to her mouth to stifle a yawn.

"Did you just fly in?"

"From Omura, yes."

"You must be knackered."

"I'm not too bad," she said. "Cold and damp, though. Can I have a bath?"

"Of course," I said.

"Lovely," she said, rising from her chair. "Lovely warm

bath. Maybe we can have some coffee afterwards."

"You bet," I said.

She went into the bathroom and started the bath running. I heard the water rumbling into the tub and Nevada humming. After a few minutes she opened the door and steam escaped and the cats zipped in to join her. The door closed again, trapping the steam and warmth and noise. It was an ideal opportunity to grind some coffee beans without upsetting anyone. I was about to do so when the telephone rang.

I picked up the receiver and heard music. A piano playing, jazz in cascading angular lines. Then a voice. "Hello, Chef?"

"Ree?"

"Yeah. How are you?"

"I'm okay... I'm fine."

"Good."

We both fell silent for a moment. The music continued, unfolding in endless fluency. Intricate but brisk, delicate but punchy. "That sounds great. Is it vinyl?"

She laughed. "It's not a recording, it's the real thing. Somebody playing the piano. Do you like it?"

"Yes. Where are you?"

"Hawaii. You'd love it here. Nice coffee."

"Are you on holiday?"

"Sort of."

I said, "How did the search go?"

"The search?" she said.

"For Easy Geary."

"Oh, that's over." The piano kept playing, primitive and raw yet urbane and modern.

"You found the grave."

"No," she said. "We were never going to find the grave."

"Why not?"

"To have a grave you have to have a dead body."

I suddenly realised why the music sounded familiar. I did the arithmetic in my head. It was possible. It was just possible. But it didn't feel just possible.

It felt inevitable.

"Are you still there?" she said.

"Yes."

"He plays pretty good for a guy his age, don't you think?"

"Yes."

"You've got to get over here," she said.

ACKNOWLEDGEMENTS

A big thank you to Ben Aaronovitch, who encouraged me to write this book in the first place (and for insisting I put the cats in); to the invaluable Guy Adams who made the crucial introduction; to the wonderful Miranda Jewess for reading it and getting it; to the excellent Ella Chappell for all her scrupulous work; to my agent John Berlyne; to Ann Karas for perusing—and enjoying—early drafts; to Peter Qvortrup for manufacturing and providing magnificent audio kit; to the other Andrew—the London Jazz Collector—for being so damned helpful; to Tom Evans for wondrous technical and electronic hi-fi wizardry; to Stephen Gallagher for loyalty, friendship and wisdom and to Ellen Gallagher, a chip off the old block if ever there was one; to Alan Ross for taking part in the story and for providing more records than I can count; to John Tygier for general hi-fi erudition and for loaning me his set of 300B thermionic valves when mine broke down. Greater love hath no man. And to all you crate diggers out there. Just remember, it might be in the next box…

ABOUT THE AUTHOR

Andrew Cartmel is a novelist and screenwriter. His work for television includes commissions for *Midsomer Murders* and *Torchwood*, and a legendary stint as script editor on *Doctor Who*. He has also written plays for the London Fringe, toured as a stand-up comedian, and is currently co-writing a series of comics with Ben Aaronovitch based on the bestselling *Rivers of London* books. He lives in London with too much vinyl and just enough cats.

THE RUN-OUT GROOVE

A VINYL DETECTIVE NOVEL

ANDREW CARTMEL

His first adventure consisted of the search for a rare record; his second begins with the *discovery* of one. When a mint copy of the final album by 'Valerian'—England's great lost rock band of the 1960s—surfaces in a charity shop, all hell breaks loose. Finding this record triggers a chain of events culminating in our hero learning the true fate of the singer Valerian, who died under equivocal circumstances just after—or was it just before?—the abduction of her two-year-old son.

Along the way, the Vinyl Detective finds himself marked for death, at the wrong end of a shotgun, and unknowingly dosed with LSD as a prelude to being burned alive. And then there's the grave robbing…

"Like an old 45rpm record, this book crackles with brilliance." **David Quantick**

"This tale of crime, cats and rock & roll unfolds with an authentic sense of the music scene then and now – and a mystery that will keep you guessing." **Stephen Gallagher**

TITANBOOKS.COM